Racing Through Darkness

G.K. Parks

Copyright © 2014 G.K. Parks

A Modus Operandi imprint

All rights reserved.

ISBN: 0989195856
ISBN-13: 978-0-9891958-5-0

For my mom and dad

ONE

After dropping my laptop on the kitchen table, I went to the fridge and filled a bowl with ice water before returning to my abandoned computer. It had been a long day, but the insurance fraud claims were resolved. Now I just needed to finish typing my report for the insurance agency, and I would be set to leave in the morning for the security conference and panel discussion. Spending the night at James Martin's, instead of at home, would cut an extra hour off the morning commute to the airport, and since I wasn't even remotely close to being a morning person, every extra minute of sleep counted.

I was in the process of revising the final draft, using only my left hand since my right was in the bowl, when Martin came up the steps. He tripped over my carry-on bag and cursed.

"Sorry," I called into the living room.

"Alexis?" Martin sounded confused. "I didn't know you were coming over tonight." He sauntered into the kitchen and kissed my cheek, brushing my long brown hair out of the way in the process. "Did you finish spying on the scam artist?"

"Yes, just finalizing the paperwork, and after I hit send,

I will be done for the day."

He took a seat and carefully lifted my hand out of the ice water. "Does this hurt?" He gingerly rubbed his thumb over each of my knuckles to assess if anything was broken.

"No," I responded distractedly.

He got up and scooped a few ice cubes into a kitchen towel and came around to the other side and pressed it against my swollen cheek. "All right, Slugger, what happened?" he asked but decided better on waiting for an answer, so he continued having dialogue all on his own. "Your exclusivity clause at Martin Technologies expired four days ago, and you already felt the need to find another job and knock someone around? What's the other guy look like?"

"He'll live," I replied nonchalantly. "It was a misunderstanding. Apparently, the man in question didn't care for my photographic proof that he was mobile and feigning injury. Maybe now he'll be able to fake it a little easier."

"And this couldn't wait until after the panel discussion? Aren't you scheduled to speak Saturday morning on the benefits of implementing uniform security protocols and the logistical superiority of having a pool of personnel who are interchangeable from one corporate branch to another?"

"You've spent way too much time talking to your VP, Luc Guillot."

"It is my company, so it helps when I know what the hell is going on," he remarked. "It would also help if my security consultant didn't look like she was competing in a MMA tournament."

"That's why I own concealer and foundation." I hit send and shut my laptop lid. "At least it's not a shiner." Martin pulled the towel away and ran his thumb across my cheekbone.

"Just to play it safe, keep the ice on it." Resisting the urge to say something snarky, I shut my mouth while he went upstairs to pack for tomorrow. He came back a half hour later with a garment bag, attaché bag, a carry-on, and a briefcase.

G.K. Parks

"There is something wrong with this picture," I commented, staring at my single carry-on and Martin's four different bags. "The conference is going to last a whole two days. We fly out tomorrow, have seminars and panels to listen to on Friday. Saturday, we're presenting our own," I cringed, hating public speaking, "and that's it. We'll be back by Sunday."

He frowned at my lonely travel bag and went into the guest bathroom to presumably pack even more items. I followed him and stood in the doorway, watching as he searched for something. He looked up, and his eyes met mine through the reflection in the mirror. Sometimes, I was stunned by how attractive he was with his stylish dark hair, bright green eyes, toned body, and impeccable taste.

"Alex," he caught my smile, "should I be afraid you're planning to jump me?"

"That wouldn't be fear so much as an open invitation," I teased, leaving him to pack whatever else he deemed appropriate. "However, I do have a question." I took a seat on the sofa in the living room. "Your company is paying for the hotel, which puts me in an awkward position."

He sighed and came out of the bathroom, carrying a tube of sunscreen. Maybe he had been a boy scout and wanted to be prepared for everything. "Is this the nice way of saying you don't want to share a suite?"

"This is the nice way of saying it'll look suspicious if I don't have a room reservation of my own, but since we're staying together, it's ridiculous to make your company shell out money for a room no one is using either."

"It's a conundrum." He was distracted, shoving the sunscreen into one of his bags that could only barely be unzipped. Maybe it was overstuffed from his excessive packing. "It's on the corporate card. Even if accounting bothers to read the bill, they're not going to pay close enough attention to see how many rooms we're getting. It will be fine." He came over and kissed me. "You're not even a full-time employee anymore. You're only on retainer, so why does it matter if people know we're dating?"

"It matters," I insisted.

*   *   *

The next morning, Martin woke me far too early for it to be considered a decent hour. I wasn't even sure if the sun was up yet since every chance I got, my eyes would close. We were in his town car, riding to the airport to catch the company jet.

James Martin was CEO and namesake of Martin Technologies which produced numerous items, the likes of which I couldn't even begin to comprehend. Originally, he hired me as his bodyguard, but once that job was concluded, he insisted I stay on as security consultant for his company. My background was in law enforcement, having started my career at the Office of International Operations before quitting for the private sector. While not always equipped to handle corporate matters, I was able to provide valuable input on security measures, practices, protocols, and had been instrumental in the complete security overhaul Luc Guillot wanted to conduct. Once Martin and I became romantically involved, he shifted the security aspect of business over to Guillot. This way, I wasn't sleeping with my direct boss, just the boss of my boss. It still wasn't a good idea. But we had been dating for nine months, and it was too late now.

"Luc and Vivi are flying out with us, along with Jeffrey Myers, Charles Roman, and Yuri Oskilov," Martin informed me as we neared the airstrip.

Vivi was Luc's wife. It had been a few months since I saw her and assumed she would chat my ear off as she often did. Jeffrey Myers was executive security guard, and Charles Roman and Yuri Oskilov served on the Board of Supervisors at Martin Technologies. The conference was meant for more than just security, and from the group assembled, the next two days would be insanely hectic for Martin. Thankfully, I wasn't the corporate type. After dealing with the security aspects, I was free to lounge around in the room. Rest and relaxation here I come.

"So much for a quiet, private plane ride."

Martin grinned lecherously. "Well, if it's a private ride you wanted," he cocked an eyebrow up, "that can be arranged, with or without the plane. Just think, in a couple of hours, we'll be settled in our room with no interruptions or distractions. We should have done this sooner. I can't believe this is the first vacation we've taken together."

"This isn't a vacation," I reminded him. "This is a business conference." He didn't seem deterred, but he was rarely deterred. It was too early in the morning for banter, so silently, we got out of the car with his personal bodyguard in tow and boarded the plane.

Three hours later, the plane landed. During the flight, Luc insisted on reviewing the presentation materials with me. Today was not the day to leave the thermos of coffee on the kitchen counter, but somehow, I survived. At least we were out of the cramped cabin and in the fresh air. Luc and Vivi disappeared into a car, heading straight for the hotel. Martin, being Martin, hired separate car service for the Guillots, one for Jeffrey, Charles, and Yuri, and a third for us. Normally, I would have complained about the look of impropriety, but I was ready for some peace and quiet.

Checking into the presidential suite, Martin tipped the valet and shut the door. There was a gift basket on the table, along with a bottle of pre-chilled champagne and a waiting room service order for brunch. So much for going back to bed.

Martin wrapped his arms around me. "This hotel has a full-service spa, but I wasn't sure what your opinion of massages and other luxuries were. Knowing you, I thought it best to ask before booking a couple's massage or hot stone treatment."

"Good thought," I murmured, staring out the window overlooking the pool and other scenery. Even though it was early October, it was unseasonably hot. "Having a stranger touch me and wonder or ask what caused all of my scars isn't on my to-do list."

"The only obvious one is on your thigh, and that wasn't from a knife or bullet. It was from some wire in a parking garage." Martin was being encouraging; although to anyone who didn't know us, it might not have sounded that way. "Your other actual battle wounds aren't noticeable for what they are to anyone who doesn't know to look for them."

I gave him a skeptical look. In the last two years, I had been shot, electrocuted, and sliced open. At least the rough patch had come to an end, coinciding perfectly with my refusal to consult for the OIO and local police department anymore. Maybe a researcher should investigate that correlation.

After brunch and too much champagne for this early in the day, Martin and I were on the couch in the central room of our suite, making out like teenagers. It had been a while since either of us had any free time without pressing issues to deal with, and it felt like we were playing hooky, which probably explained our adolescent-esque behavior.

There was a knock at the door. Immediately, he sat up, and I pulled my shirt down and wiped the smeared lipstick off his face. "James?" Luc called from the hallway.

"Dammit," Martin cursed quietly while I made sure my luggage was out of sight. He went to the door. "Luc, please come in." Martin could turn friendly on a dime. "I was just discussing the panel format with Alex."

"Please, don't let me disturb you," Guillot began, "I just wanted to let you know Vivi and I will be out most of the day, but I'll be back in time for the working dinner you planned, unless there was something else to deal with in the meantime."

"Nothing pressing, Luc. Go and enjoy your day." Martin glanced at me, confused by Guillot's appearance.

"Since you're here, Alexis, what room are you staying in?" Hopefully, I wasn't turning crimson. "The lobby couldn't find your reservation."

"There was a booking error," I lied. "They should have it rectified soon. In the meantime, Mr. Martin has been kind enough to treat me to brunch to make up for the inconvenience."

"D'accord." Guillot was a native French speaker, and sometimes, he forgot himself. "I e-mailed the presentation files to your account. If you believe changes need to be made, we can discuss them at dinner."

"Of course, sir," I responded. Martin walked Guillot to the door and bid him a good day. "We're so busted," I said once the door was shut. "He knows."

"He does not know," Martin insisted, "and so what if he does? Worse things could happen. It's my company. It's not like he can fire me."

"Speak for yourself."

"There's no rule on interoffice romance," he continued. "Let's not jump to conclusions in the meantime." He sat on the couch. "Now, where were we?"

TWO

The six of us were seated at a long rectangular table in the hotel's dining room. There were more tablets and laptops on the table than dinner plates as we attempted to streamline our presentation and ensure everyone was up to speed on what was being said and when it was being said. Guillot fathered the idea of revamping the security procedures, and his plan paid off since it was featured predominantly in business magazines. This, in turn, led to being asked to speak at this particular conference. Martin and the other board members were agreeable since they were already scheduled to be here for other reasons. They wanted to research and network on some new R&D project, but Jeffrey and I were solely here for the security aspect.

"Ms. Parker," Jeffrey whispered, "are we supposed to hear the rest of this discussion?" I chuckled and glanced at Martin. He was in a heated debate with Yuri over some new data chip.

"Pass the bread," I murmured back. He handed me the basket of rolls, and I picked one up and took a bite. "Be thankful we're through for the evening."

"Should we leave?" Jeffrey always did his job well, but he was timid, too timid most of the time. But he knew the office and protocols better than anyone. However, I would hate to see him in a firefight.

"Have a roll. We're here for the duration, although ten bucks says if we left, they wouldn't notice." Jeffrey selected a roll and slowly buttered it. I opened the chess game application on my laptop, and we killed some time as the night went on. Two games in, my cell phone began vibrating. "Excuse me," I said to the table, although Jeffrey was the only one listening. Getting up, I went to the lobby and hit answer.

"Parker, I need a favor," Detective Nick O'Connell said as soon as I answered.

"What's going on?" It had been several weeks since we spoke. Ever since my exclusivity clause prohibited moonlighting, I had fallen off the grid. Nick and his wife, Jen, met Martin and me for dinner a few times over the last six months, but we hadn't been in close contact for a while.

"Are you home? I don't want to discuss this on the phone."

"Actually, I'm out of town. There's a conference going on, but I'll be back Sunday. Can it wait?"

He hesitated, generating an uneasy feeling in the pit of my stomach. If he needed a favor, something was wrong. "Sunday's fine," he finally responded.

"Is everything okay?" Every time I needed a favor, he was there, and the one time he needed something, I was hundreds of miles away.

"It'll be fine." His speech was clipped, and he disconnected before I could say anything else.

Returning to the table, the men concluded whatever discussion they were having, and the electronics were powered down as after dinner drinks were served. Jeffrey handed over a folded ten dollar bill. "They didn't notice you were gone." I chuckled, but the feeling of unease was still present.

"Gentlemen," I spoke before Charles could suck them into a long-winded story, "it's been a long day. If there's nothing else, I'm going to call it a night." The men stood, which further irritated me, but at least they were gentlemen.

Escaping, I went to the room and ran through the mental checklist of people I could call. O'Connell's partners in major crimes, Detectives Thompson and Heathcliff, ought to have his back. Hell, even my former mentor at the OIO, Agent Mark Jablonsky, would lend a hand in a pinch. O'Connell should be fine. I was in the process of convincing myself of this when Martin let himself into the suite.

"Ducking out early to avoid the awkward elevator ride with the other board members?" he asked. "Or you figured the Dom in the room was better than the mid-priced liquor we were drinking downstairs?"

"Nick called." I bit my top lip, trying to figure out what he possibly wanted to talk about.

"Detective O'Connell?"

"What other Nicks do I know?" My anger has a habit of rearing its ugly head when I'm busy working through theories.

"How would I know? I'm sure you have friends I've never met." Martin realized arguing was not the way to go and switched tactics. "What did he want?"

"A favor, but he wouldn't tell me what it is. He said it could wait and hung up."

"Well, if it can wait, then I'm sure it's nothing." He flipped through the closet and pulled out the suit he was planning to wear tomorrow, making sure it was wrinkle-free. "Here's the thing," he continued, "my surprise is ruined, but it happens." Raising an eyebrow, I waited for some elaboration. "Saturday, after the panel concludes, I was hoping to whisk you away to my beach house. It's just a couple of hours from here. Think about it. Sun, sand, you, me, a string bikini."

I smiled. "But what am I going to wear?"

"Tease," he grinned, "unless you really want to see me in the string bikini, I figured that's what you would wear. Or nothing at all." His eyes adopted a devilish glint.

"I need to go home." I sighed. "O'Connell needs help on something, and last time I checked, we both owe him. The beach will have to wait. Honestly, who goes to the beach in October?"

"Alex, you said you were done working for the police

department."

"If it was a consulting gig at the precinct, Captain Moretti would call. This is something else. You know O'Connell wouldn't ask me to go back."

"True." He looked torn. "Why don't you call him Saturday and see if he still needs a favor. If he does, we'll go home. But if he doesn't," he waggled an eyebrow, "string bikini."

* * *

The next day was full of tediously boring speeches, panel discussions, and presentations. Thankfully, I managed to avoid most of them since anything not security related wasn't in my job description. I picked up my phone half a dozen times to call O'Connell, but I resisted. Finally, I gave Det. Derek Heathcliff a call. We were partnered together during one of my consulting gigs, and if he knew something was up, he'd tell me. Unfortunately, Heathcliff was completely puzzled by my phone call, and not wanting to say anything about O'Connell, I asked a few random questions about an old case and disconnected. Whatever was going on, Nick didn't tell anyone else. Parker, you're probably just paranoid, my internal voice scolded.

Maybe I was looking for trouble where there wasn't any. Perhaps O'Connell just wanted my input on a birthday present for Jen. Being away from the game for the last six months made me see problems where there weren't any. By nature, I was a trained federal agent. Forcing myself to fit into the corporate world where bullets and criminals weren't rushing past at every corner was supposed to protect me and Martin; instead, the last six months had been a slow torture. Martin didn't know this, but I'm sure he suspected it when he came home Wednesday and found me in his kitchen with ice water, bruised knuckles, and a swollen cheek.

Rubbing my eyes, I plopped down on the couch. My excuse to stay away from that world ended the moment my contract with MT expired. Now what would I do? Before I could continue further down the rabbit hole, Martin returned from a day's worth of conferences. He was on the phone with someone from the home office, and he was giving a concise breakdown of what he heard and what he wanted the company to acquire. Giving him space, I went into the bedroom and shut the door. Sleep wasn't likely, but focusing on the stillness might lead to a new perspective.

The next day, Luc, Jeffrey, and I delivered our presentation, followed by a Q&A segment. Amazingly, I played my corporate consultant role well and didn't fumble through my prepared speech as I imagined I would. For some reason, the prospect of armed conflict was a more welcome idea than public speaking. A few screws must be loose in my brain. After our segment, there were a few corporate security firms who attempted to derail MT's new protocols by trying to sell the finer points of having a separate agency provide security protection. They droned on, and I excused myself to call O'Connell. He didn't answer, so I was forced to go back into the meeting room. By the end of the day, everyone was mingling in the hotel's banquet hall.

Martin was schmoozing and networking while I sat alone at the bar. "Another lemon drop martini," I ordered. Swiveling on the stool, I caught sight of Vivi and Luc talking to a group who represented Lancer Securities. Although they attempted to undermine our presentation, Luc was in the midst of a civil, if not friendly, conversation. Let bygones be bygones, I suppose.

"Miss Parker?" a voice asked from behind. I turned in my chair to find a man around my age, in his early thirties, dressed in an expensive suit.

"Yes?"

"Maddock Howell," he introduced himself, handing me his business card. "I would offer to buy you a drink, but it's an open bar."

"And I already have a drink." Whatever this guy was selling, I wasn't buying.

"You can never have too many drinks," he responded. The guy was either a snake or car salesman; although, there wasn't much to differentiate the two.

"You shouldn't say that too loudly," I whispered. "People might start to think you have a problem."

"Maybe you can solve it." He tried to be suave. "I represent Wallace-Klineman Industries. They're looking for someone to overhaul their security." The light bulb clicked on; this guy was a corporate headhunter.

"Sorry, I'm comfortable where I am."

"Think about it, Miss Parker. If you have any questions, please don't hesitate to call." He got up from the barstool. "By the way, the number on the back is my personal line. Call anytime. Day or night." He smiled roguishly and disappeared into the throng assembled.

Sighing, I left the bar, intent on escaping to my room. As I passed Martin, he roped me into a conversation with Charles over computer encryption. We were discussing the need for a seasoned computer specialist when a tall, leggy, blonde let out a high-pitched squeal and launched herself at Martin.

"Oh my god, Jamie," she exclaimed, wrapping her arms around him and kissing him on the mouth.

Bruiser, Martin's bodyguard, appeared out of the blue, but his attempt to intercede was too little, too late. There would be a discussion on the finer points of bodyguarding at a later date. Right now, it was hard not to appear to be the jealous girlfriend.

"Francesca," Martin politely disentangled himself from her grasp, "wow. It's been a long time." Charles and I stopped speaking as we stared at Martin. "Charles Roman, Alexis Parker, this is Francesca Pirelli. We attended Harvard together," Martin said, even though it was an attempt to explain the situation to me. "We're old friends."

"That's what you're calling it now?" she responded in a challenging and sultry tone. "We were engaged for two seconds like twelve years ago." Oh, things get better and better. "Until you went on that trip through South America." She looked pointedly at him. "Now, I'm COO of," she continued to speak, but I tuned her out on account of my vibrating cell phone. It was Nick.

Walking off in the direction of the lobby, I answered. "Hey." A distraction was exactly what I needed. "I tried calling you earlier."

"Alexis?" Jen's voice took me by surprise. "Nick asked that I call you." She sounded off. "He's...he's going to be okay."

Of course, he's going to be okay. Why wouldn't he be okay? "Jen, where's Nick?"

Silence filled the void, and I ducked into the ladies room to hear better. "Nick was shot. He has a few broken ribs and a punctured lung, but he's going to be okay." Nothing about what she said was okay. Although, Jen was a nurse, so that would explain why she was handling things better than most.

"Did they catch the guy? Was Thompson with him?"

"It didn't happen on the job," she added in a whisper. "Thompson, Heathcliff, and half the department are here. You know how the guys are. They're all family, but whatever's going on, he hasn't told them. I'm not sure what it is, but he asked specifically for you."

"Of course. Anything." God, why didn't I fly home immediately when he called Thursday night? "I'm away at a conference, but I'll catch the earliest flight and get home as soon as possible. I should be there in a few hours." She rattled off the hospital information and room number.

THREE

"What do you mean all flights are cancelled until further notice?" I screamed into the phone. "It's not even raining." The woman on the other end of the line was explaining how strong, hurricane force winds grounded all the planes at the airport in preparation for the impending storm. Why didn't I consider the weather before making this stupid trip to this god-awful conference? Hanging up, I did a quick search on my phone for nearby airports within a fifty mile radius, assuming one of those might still have outgoing flights scheduled. Dialing another number, I barely noticed Vivi enter the ladies room. She washed her hands in the sink and assessed me as I paced back and forth in front of the stalls.

"Alexis, is everything okay?" She was concerned.

"No, not at all. I need to get home." Growling in frustration, I searched for charter companies, hoping to find someone willing to get me out of this hellhole tonight.

Vivi left while I continued to make call after call to every airline, airport, and private company I could find. Luckily, the room remained empty, allowing for curses to be uttered as loudly as necessary. There was a knock on the door, which I ignored as I waited for an airport a hundred miles away to answer their phone.

"Alex," Martin stuck his head into the ladies room, "is anyone in here?"

"Me." The on-hold music pissed me off, just like everything else this evening. He entered and flipped the lock on the door. "Vivi said you were trying to get home. Is this because of Francesca? Because I swear–"

"Shut up," I barked more at the music than at him. "O'Connell got himself shot. Jen called, and I can't get a goddamn flight out of this horrible place because there's a fucking storm moving in. It's the twenty-first century. Why do we not possess the technology to deal with some shitty weather?"

"Is he okay?" He approached cautiously.

"Jen said he'll be fine. But it doesn't sound fine. Nothing is fine. Ugh." I hung up and rubbed the bridge of my nose.

"Go back to the room and pack. I will find a way for us to get home."

"Martin," I began, but he shushed me.

"He's my friend too. Now go. I'll be up as soon as travel arrangements are made."

Taking my phone, I went straight to the elevator and up to the suite. If anyone had enough clout to make things happen, it was Martin. Although, even he couldn't stop a storm from closing the airports. Twenty minutes later, the door to the suite opened, and he entered. I looked at him expectantly as he went to the closet and threw all his belongings into one of his many bags.

"I told you I'd find a way." He zipped one bag and went into the bathroom to repeat the process. "Even the company jet and its pilot aren't willing to fly tonight, but I found a car service to drive the distance. They are on their way to pick us up, and by tomorrow morning, we should be home. It's a ten hour drive, but it's the best I could do."

"Thank you." Ten hours wasn't ideal, but it was better than nothing. "You don't have to come with me. There might be things you still need to do here. Plus, how will it look if you disappear at the same time I do?"

"I don't care." At the moment, I didn't either. "This is my fault. I shouldn't have dismissed his call so easily the other day. You were right, as usual." He offered a smirk.

"It's annoying how frequently that happens."

"Tell me about it." While he packed the rest of his belongings, I ran through the limited details I knew. O'Connell wasn't shot on the job. He didn't have any back-up when it happened, and whatever was going on, he didn't tell his partner or anyone from the precinct. "I hope to god he hasn't taken a page out of my playbook," I spoke aloud to myself.

The last case I worked in an official capacity landed me in hot water with a mafia boss and caused me to shy away from work. The lesson I took away from all of it was not to supersede the system, which appeared to be exactly what O'Connell was doing. The only question was why.

* * *

Martin and I were seated across from one another in the back of a stretch limo, almost two hours into the drive home, and Bruiser was up front with the driver. Martin spent most of the time on the phone with the board members he left at the conference, explaining his absence on account of an emergency. He didn't give any details, but no one would question him. He gave Luc, Charles, and Yuri separate instructions on what to do with the remaining time and contacts at the banquet. Even being away from work, he was still working. I, on the other hand, stared at my phone, trying to decide if I wanted it to ring. A call could be Thompson or Heathcliff filling me in on what was going on, or it could be the worst news imaginable, in which case no call was better than a call.

"Vivi told me you were upset," Martin said out of the blue. I looked at him, wondering when he hung up the phone or even how long he was off the phone. "She saw you duck into the ladies, and when you didn't come out, she went in. Maybe Luc's wife should be a security analyst too." He attempted to joke, but I wasn't in the mood.

"The more, the merrier, right?"

"Honestly, I was afraid you were pissed about Francesca."

"Why would I be pissed about some woman kissing you,

Jamie?" My words were biting. "Wait, no, maybe I'm supposed to be pissed to find out you were engaged." Running my hand through my hair, it didn't matter right now. There were more important things to worry about. "It's okay. At the moment, I don't particularly care."

The problem with not caring was we had another eight hours alone in the back of the limo. Without knowing any details about O'Connell's condition or the circumstances, there wasn't much to say on that topic. Shoptalk was the equivalent of beating a dead horse, so either we could continue to sit in the deafening silence, or we could talk about things that weren't pressing.

"When we started dating," changing my mind, I broached the subject, "you said you had been in two real relationships. Is it a pipe dream to hope Francesca counts as one of those relationships and not just another in your string of dalliances?"

He chuckled. "Like she said, it was twelve years ago. I was a dumb kid in my twenties, getting ready to graduate from business school. What the hell did I know about anything? It was a mistake, and after we called off the engagement, we lost touch."

"Happens. So your other real relationship? Let me guess. Ex-wife and kids?"

"No, it was before Francesca." He laughed. "High school sweetheart. We lasted through the first two years of undergrad."

"Damn, you're more dysfunctional than I thought. I'm the first real relationship you've had since school."

"What can I say? I know how to pick 'em." He stared across the small expanse. "Am I reading into things, or are you blaming me for the reason you aren't home right now?"

"It's not your fault." My words sounded hollow. It was someone's fault, mainly mine.

"It's not yours either."

"What if I hadn't," I began but stopped and shut my mouth. Playing the what if game wasn't practical. "Funny thing happened when I was sitting at the bar." I changed topics. "A corporate headhunter offered me a job at

Wallace-Klineman Industries."

"Bastards are always swooping in and stealing my people," he complained, and I gave him a cynical smile.

"You know I'm not meant for this corporate bullshit." I met his eyes.

"Sweetheart, I knew that from the moment I met you. Frankly, the paperwork to nullify your contract has been sitting in my desk drawer for the last six months. I'm surprised it took you this long to admit it."

We fell into a peaceful silence as the car continued racing through the darkness. It started raining, and every so often, there was a flash of lightning. It was the middle of the night, and I curled up on the seat. Martin leaned against the window with his legs stretched out, but sleeping in the back of a limo wasn't ideal.

At some point, I dozed because when I opened my eyes the sky had turned a pale gray, and Martin was on the phone with his personal driver and valet, Marcal. I stretched in the seat and looked out the window. We were close; another hour and we'd be arriving at the hospital.

"Do you want Marcal to deliver your bags to your apartment or just take everything back to my place?" he asked.

"One trip is fine. I don't expect him to run a million pointless errands." Falling into silence, I wanted time to grab a cup of coffee, a change of clothes, and for O'Connell to be playing a very elaborate joke, but none of those things were likely to happen.

When the limo pulled up to the hospital, Martin jerked his chin toward the door, and I was out of the car and flying across the parking lot to find someone who had some answers. The information desk sent me to the third floor. When I exited the elevator, Thompson and Heathcliff were seated in the hallway.

"Alexis," Heathcliff said, getting up and hugging me, "how'd you know?"

"Jen called." Everything was a jumble. Thompson embraced me as well, which was uncharacteristic, and his actions made my worry reach new heights. "Where's O'Connell? Do we know anything? How's he doing?"

"He's not saying much. They did a procedure on him last night. One of his ribs broke, and it punctured his lung." Thompson made a face. "They did something to fix it. I don't know. He's been sedated and resting mostly."

"Jenny's been with him since it happened. She drove him here," Heathcliff offered. Martin emerged from the elevator and joined the three of us. Even though he had spent some time with these guys, he seemed out of place. "If you find out what happened, we'd love to know. Shootings have to be investigated, but we're not allowed near this one."

"He's your partner," I insisted, "that's why you're here for moral support only."

"Who the hell is stupid enough to shoot a cop?" Thompson posed the question, but no one had an answer.

"Alexis, James," Jen called from a doorway down the hall, "you're here." It was time to find out what the hell was going on. Nodding to the boys, Martin and I went to meet Jen.

FOUR

"Formal attire wasn't necessary. The hospital doesn't enforce a strict dress code," O'Connell commented as we entered the room. Thank goodness he was speaking.

"Well, since you're here, I thought the place could use some classing up," I retorted. Jen and I exchanged a brief smile. Then I went to the chair next to O'Connell's bedside. "What the hell, Nick?" He cast his eyes toward his wife, and I got the unspoken message. "It's been a long night. Martin," I turned around, hoping he'd catch on, "would you mind finding us some coffee?"

"Sure, no problem." He caught my eye, and I saw the comprehension. "Jenny can lead the way to the cafeteria." She knew what was going on but shrugged and headed toward the door.

"Nick, you better be breathing when I get back," she warned.

"I promise I won't kill him," I replied before she and Martin left the room. Glancing into the hallway, Heathcliff and Thompson were still lingering outside, but they were giving us space.

"I take it Martin was thrilled that I dragged you away from work," O'Connell replied sarcastically. He tried to sit up and winced. Giving up, he pushed the controls on the bed and let the mattress contort into an upright position.

"You called Thursday and told me it was fine. Whatever the hell *it* is, and then yesterday, your wife tells me you were shot. Stop commenting and start talking."

"This is off the books." He shifted his gaze around the room. "It's a personal matter, and one that you're in a unique position to handle." Whatever it was, it wasn't good. "Alex, I know you said you're done chasing down these scumbags, but I trust you."

"Whatever you need."

"Not a word to Thompson or Heathcliff. Hell, you can't tell Jablonsky either, understand?"

"Nick, just tell me."

"Five days ago, my niece, Catherine, was kidnapped."

"Goddamn." I slumped back in the chair. His words caught me completely by surprise. "Does Jen know? Why haven't you turned this over to the FBI? You've personally worked with a few agents. I'm sure one of them could–"

"Parker, stop." He grabbed my arm more forcefully than I thought possible in his current state. "They said no cops. No agents. You know the statistics, just like I do. Sure, the Bureau says it has a thirty percent better chance of a positive recovery, but it's just a numbers game." I blew out a breath and paced the room.

"They shot you?"

"Yes." He was staring holes through me. "It was a warning to follow instructions or else. Remember, no cops. I thought I could get the slip on them. Get around and find out where they were keeping the girls."

"Girls?" Too much information, too little sleep.

"My niece and two of her friends were abducted while on a school field trip. She's seven." He swallowed and tried to get out of bed.

"Stay put." I sat down next to him. "Is anyone looking for her now? For them, I mean. Has there been proof of life? Ransom demands?"

Even though he was a cop, he was also a victim. That screws with perspective; I knew this firsthand. Running both hands through my hair, I waited for him to start at the beginning.

His sister, Evelyn, married Peter Cale, an administrative coordinator to one of the American ambassadors. The family lived and traveled abroad extensively from the time Catherine was an infant. Even though Cale was a glorified personal assistant, he was often seen on the outskirts of powerful political and economic circles. Thus, Catherine went to the right schools, was friends and classmates with the right people, and for all the grandeur, she was kidnapped along with her more influential compatriots.

"She's a nobody," O'Connell insisted. "Wrong place, wrong time."

"You said two other girls were taken. Why haven't their parents turned this over to the authorities?"

"What authorities?" he scoffed. "Foreign diplomats and influential moguls don't deal with authorities. They have their own system which circumvents ours. But my sister can't afford the two million dollars they want, so I thought I could handle it."

"Have you learned nothing from my fuckups?"

"One of the other girls has been released. Her family paid the ransom and got her back safely. But they took off for home first thing, so there's no information on how things went down." I nodded and bit my lip, trying to figure out what I could possibly do. "The other family is obscenely rich. Their wealth probably makes Martin's bank account look like chump change. They own a gold mining company in Peru." He adjusted into a more comfortable position. "They've hired a third party negotiator, a kidnapping and ransom specialist, who brokers deals like this professionally. His card is in my wallet, along with a picture of Catherine."

Nick's wallet was in his jacket pocket, and I retrieved it from the hook and pulled out the card. Julian Mercer – Personal K&R Negotiator. "Is Mercer on the level?"

"As far as I can tell. He told me not to go in. We were supposed to be there for recon only, but I saw a shot and took it."

"You're supposed to duck." My attempt at a joke was lame, but I'd been up all night. And O'Connell was on pain medication, so he should find it funny. He didn't. Probably since his current predicament made nothing funny. "Does Jen know what's going on?"

"No. She doesn't need to. The shooter contacted Mercer, warning him to listen to their demands and follow their rules. He found me, dropped me off at home, and Jen drove me to the hospital. She knows it's a family matter, but the less she knows, the better."

"What do Evelyn and Peter want to do?"

"They've put all their faith in Mercer to get their little girl back. He's trying to broker her into the deal he's making on behalf of the Estes family to get Adalina back. And I'm putting my faith in you to help him do it."

"Thompson and Heathcliff would bend over backward to work this." I tried to reason with him. "Maybe you should read them in."

"They're cops. I'm not risking Catherine's well-being or theirs."

"But you're okay with risking mine?" It wasn't a fair question, but the words still left my mouth.

"No." He let out a groan, shifting positions. "So for once in your life, don't go running into a situation like you're invincible. You're not. I'm not." He shut his eyes in thought. When they opened, there was a newfound level of conviction. "But you're not a cop or a federal agent. Not anymore. Therefore, you can assist Mercer, and it should be acceptable to the kidnappers' demands." He was determined. "Truthfully, I hoped to take care of it on my own, but Mercer needed a team. I was the only one around and thought we'd be able to handle it."

Before I could say anything else, Martin and Jen came into the room. Martin was in the midst of a story about something, and Jen was caught up in the theatrics, allowing a brief reprieve from the current situation. Heathcliff and Thompson entered the room a few seconds after they did.

"I don't understand." Speaking freely was out of the question, but if a deal was being cut, then why did Mercer need a team to move in? "Why take something when you're planning to pay for it?"

"Free and clear would be preferable," Nick muttered under his breath. We couldn't continue this conversation any longer. Time was of the essence, and I needed to find Mercer and figure out what the hell was actually going on.

"It was one hell of a drive," I said to the room. "Nick, stay in bed and get some rest. After I get cleaned up and check into some things," he knew I was talking about contacting Mercer, "I'll come back to see how you're doing." Martin wished O'Connell a full recovery, gave Jen a hug, and we were out of the room before Thompson or Heathcliff could stop us.

"Alex?" Martin questioned as I repeatedly hit the door close button on the elevator, hoping to escape before one of the detectives decided to pursue. "How bad is it? Will he be okay?"

"He'll live, but depending on how things turn out, he might not want to. The good thing about rock bottom is there's only one direction left to go." It wasn't true; this could simply be digging the hole that much deeper.

Outside the hospital, we waited for Marcal to pull the car around. My mind was racing as I formulated a plan. Going into any situation blind was a bad idea, so first thing would be to run reconnaissance on Julian Mercer and Catherine Cale. The fastest way of doing this would be to head to the OIO offices and grab a hold of an analyst, but that would raise too many red flags. Background checks, law enforcement database searches, and internet searches were all I had time for.

"I need my laptop," I muttered, "and my gun." Unfortunately, they were in separate locations. "Time needs to slow down, so I can catch up." Waiting a couple of beats, I came to a decision and fished out my phone.

"Hey," Mark Jablonsky answered on the second ring, "are you enjoying the beach?" Martin must have told him the plan.

"Yeah, it's wonderful." No reason to raise suspicion. "Do me a favor and see what you can dig up on a Julian Mercer. His name came up in the course of a conversation with one of these private security firms, and it sounds familiar."

"Parker, you're supposed to be on vacation with Marty

right now. Not burning the midnight oil."

"It's morning, and it's bugging me. Best to get it resolved or else it'll drive me crazy. E-mail me what you find."

"Fine. But when you get home, we're having a conversation about exchanging favors when you're no longer returning them."

"Sounds like fun." I hung up and got into the waiting car. Martin stared at me, shocked. "As far as Mark knows, we're at the beach. Don't you dare tell him otherwise."

"What's going on?"

"My place first and then to your house. Why didn't Marcal just keep the bags in the car?" I wasn't answering his question, but he was used to this type of behavior. After all, we had been dating for close to a year.

* * *

Two hours later, I was showered, changed, and reading through the information Mark sent on Julian Mercer. Mercer was former British Special Air Service. Now he worked exclusively in private security as a hostage negotiator or K&R specialist, if he wanted to sound fancy. Just another lost soul who left a government career for the private sector. Most of his military career was classified, and few facts were provided about his private sector work. All I had to go on was a dated photo, and Mercer's stats: 5'11, 180 pounds, forty-two years old.

A search on the Cale family turned up inconclusive, but like O'Connell said, they were nobodies. Peter was an assistant to an ambassador, but he was just a pencil pusher, not some spy, dictator, or millionaire. I picked up the photo of Catherine. She was seven, big blue eyes, strawberry blonde hair, and tons of freckles. I had to get her back alive. Sighing, I checked the magazine in my gun and stuck it into my shoulder holster. Turning around, I found Martin standing in the doorway with a steaming mug of coffee.

"I take it you don't have time for a catnap." He handed me the mug. "Do you need some back-up?"

"Are you offering?" I quipped. He provided a bittersweet smile. "I'm just about to call for some." I picked up my car keys, relieved my car had been at Martin's since Wednesday afternoon. "If Mark calls, we're at the beach. I'll see you soon. There's a very small window to get things fixed. In the meantime, keep an eye on Jen and Nick. When Heathcliff and Thompson ask where I am, tell them anything but the truth."

"Alexis, I don't know the truth. You haven't told me what's going on."

Making a split second decision, I opened my mouth and the words flew out. "Nick's niece has been kidnapped. I'm trying to get her back."

"Go." Without another word, I was out the door.

FIVE

"Julian Mercer," I said as the door opened, and I was confronted with the muzzle of a Sig Sauer P226, "mind putting down the gun? I have issues talking to someone through a steel barrel." The man had salt and pepper hair and some premature wrinkles from too much time outdoors, but other than that, there wasn't any indication of his age. There was a quiet stillness about him as if all movement was carefully contained and controlled because, if let loose, the force would be unstoppable and lethal. He had yet to lower his gun and instead roughly confiscated mine. "O'Connell sent me."

"Convenient." His accent was posh British. He took one step back, allowing me into the room, gun still poised.

"You want convenient, call a nine hundred number. You want help, then get your goddamn gun out of my face."

"Identification." Maybe he was only capable of one word sentences.

"I'm going to reach into my purse. If you blow my brains out, I'll be pissed." He didn't comment or react as I produced my wallet and held it out for his inspection. He flipped it open, glanced at it, then at me, and tossed it onto the coffee table.

"He called, announcing your arrival." Mercer lowered his gun and set it on the table next to mine. "Like I told him, I don't need any help."

"Quite frankly, I don't care." We were getting along swimmingly. "Here's the thing. You represent the Estes family. I'm here to represent O'Connell's niece. We can either work together in order to ensure we stay out of each other's way, or I'll take care of things the way I see fit."

Mercer assessed my appearance. He didn't strike me as the women's lib type. To him, I was inferior and unable to provide any type of actual assistance. "O'Connell failed to listen, and he was shot. If I allow you to stay, you will follow my lead and remain in the background." Obviously, he was slow getting the memo on my inability to follow orders. Oh well, he'd learn eventually.

"Fine. Catch me up to speed."

A group of four men was responsible for the kidnapping of the three girls, but their actual identities remained unknown. They simply referred to one another by the seasons: Winter, Summer, Spring, and Autumn. Thus, the Four Seasons. All communication, phone and video, utilized voice changing software and pixel distortion. Proof of life was provided for both Adalina and Catherine.

Along with the photographic proof, the Estes family was given a nonnegotiable demand. They had forty-eight hours to procure the funds to pay the ransom. The demand came in on Saturday at four p.m. which means tomorrow another call would provide further instructions. No demand was made to the Cale family yet.

"We believe Catherine will be the final negotiation," Mercer stated. "The demands for the first girl's release came immediately when the abduction occurred, and she was relinquished yesterday. Following this, the second demand was issued for the Estes girl, along with a warning."

"We?" Everything about the situation was infuriating, including Mercer.

"Correction, me. Miss Parker, unless my team arrives, I work alone."

"So do I." My eyes narrowed. "You were hired solely to negotiate the safe return of Adalina Estes. O'Connell

indicated you had a plan and needed help to get the girls out safely before the payoff was to be made. Is the Estes family unwilling to pay the ransom?"

"That is not your concern."

"Are you making a trade, or whatever it is you do, and riding off into the sunset a hero while Catherine ends up dead because her family can't afford to pay?"

"Madam," he despised me, "I am a man of my word. As I told the detective, with a proper team, there is a chance the location can be breached and the hostages freed." His terminology made it sound like he was President Carter dealing with Iran. "Unfortunately, as of now, my team hasn't arrived."

"More of your SAS pals?" He squinted at my question, the first sign of surprise on his controlled exterior. "I do my homework."

"Who comprises my team is also none of your concern."

Resisting the urge to growl, I took a seat on the sofa in this pre-furnished weekly apartment rental and put my feet on the coffee table. We were going to be here awhile. "This isn't your normal work environment. You typically work abroad doing things like this for the wealthy. The thing is," I plastered a phony smile on my face, "this is my territory. If you get a location, we'll get it mapped, figure out how big of a team we need, the firepower it will require, how much finesse, and we'll get this shit done."

He let out a faint laugh or rather the sound of a laugh since he was too controlled to actually laugh. "Little girl, you have no idea how things work."

"You'd be surprised." I stood up. "Last chance, are you going to help or am I doing this on my own?"

"Stay out of my way."

"No, stay out of mine." I picked up my confiscated gun and wallet and strode to the door. O'Connell would know a location. He must have been somewhere when he was shot. "If an opportunity presents itself, I'm not waiting to make sure your hostage is clear before I free mine. Hopefully, she won't get stuck in the crossfire." I was bluffing, but Mercer didn't know me or what I was capable of.

"Stay." He was back to one word sentences.

"Then we're collaborating on this particular endeavor." Jeez, I spent too much of my time in business meetings with Guillot.

Mercer escorted me into a back room where maps, photos, and blueprints were plastered to the wall. "The intel we've gathered," he was back to using the royal we, "indicates the girls are being kept inside a modified storage container. The actual location has yet to be determined. The detective was shot here." He pointed to the wharf where thousands of containers were stacked, awaiting shipping.

"What about the kidnappers?"

"Hard to say. They have surveillance to monitor their captives, but there is no way to determine if they are on scene or at a remote location."

"Are you sure nothing concrete can be deciphered from any of the communications?"

He turned with an angry glare, and a chill traveled down my spine. There was no doubt in my mind this man was a trained killer. Even though his résumé claimed private sector negotiations, the distinct impression he was a mercenary was unshakeable.

Replacing the angry glare with the controlled façade, he responded, "Yes. I am certain." Soaking up as much information as possible, I needed to get a more thorough retelling from O'Connell.

"Here's my card." I handed him my business card. "If anything changes, call me. If not, I will be back tomorrow morning."

"Fine."

Inside the confines of my car and speeding away from the rental, I wasn't sure which was more terrifying, Julian Mercer or the kidnappers.

*　　*　　*

Entering O'Connell's hospital room, I was surprised to find Martin and Thompson keeping Jen company. The three men were in a debate over a restaurant or a strip joint. It was hard to say for certain, but Jen wasn't amused.

The conversation came to a crashing halt as I took a seat on the arm of Martin's chair.

"Don't stop on my account," I said, staring at O'Connell and hoping he'd do something to clear the room. Thompson was giving me his best annoyed look.

"Oh, please," Jen rolled her eyes and stood up, "a break from the nonstop frivolity is exactly what I need."

I nudged Martin with my arm. "Stop being frivolous. You're driving everyone crazy." Jen laughed, and a snort escaped. My gaze was on O'Connell, determined to convey the need for privacy, but she took the lead.

"Would you mind coming out to the car and lugging in some of Nick's crap?" she asked Thompson. "I meant to grab it earlier, and then with the three of you going on like hyenas, I was afraid to leave you guys alone." Thompson couldn't refuse his partner's wife, but he was irritated. He begrudgingly followed her out of the room.

Martin glanced at the two of us and said, "I'll just step outside and keep a lookout."

"You told him." Nick didn't sound surprised.

"Nothing detailed." As soon as Martin shut the door, I began telling Nick what happened with Mercer. "He's a scary son of a bitch," I concluded. "Are you sure everything's on the level."

"He's not that bad. He probably just doesn't like you. What are you thinking of doing?"

"If your sister can't pay, then locate, infiltrate, retrieve, and hope to get out before they realize something's amiss. What were you and Mercer planning to achieve?"

"Same game plan, well, almost." I watched him closely. "There's no way to be positive, but letting the Four Seasons continue to breathe didn't seem to be on Mercer's to-do list."

"My guess, he's a merc." O'Connell shrugged but didn't disagree with my assessment. "Maybe the Estes family figured they'd pay the money, then Mercer goes in and cleans house. They get their savings back, and he gets a finder's fee."

"Hate to tell you, but I have no problem with putting these fuckers in the ground."

"Hey, I'm not your enemy," I reminded him. "And I didn't say I had a problem with that scenario either, but Mercer's dangerous. Going into the unknown without any intel and one crazy bastard won't end well. I need back-up. He said his team is on their way, but more like him isn't tipping the odds in favor of Catherine's safe recovery."

"No federal agents," O'Connell barked. He was on edge, and I couldn't blame him.

"What about Thompson or Heathcliff then? They're your friends. Your partners. Heathcliff can play a very convincing non-cop. I've seen him do it."

"It's Catherine's life we're gambling." He was livid. "And it's their livelihoods. You promised not to say a word. Don't make me regret this, Parker."

"What the hell do you want me to do? You tie my hands, but you still expect me to be a fucking miracle worker. I'm doing everything I can think of, but I am not enough."

"You have to be, or I'll get out of this goddamn bed and help you myself."

"Dammit," I slapped the wall, "stay put." Resting my head in my hands, I tried to think things through, but I was coming up blank. "Give me your sister's information and let her know I'm on my way. Maybe she has some information or theories on who the hostage takers might be. I need to start at the beginning to find another solution." He rattled off her address and phone number.

"Don't make this harder on Evelyn," he warned, "but I'll let her know you're coming. Kid gloves, okay?"

"All right." My hand rested on the doorknob. "I promise I'll do everything humanly possible to get Catherine back, but it might require a judgment call."

"Just make sure you think through the consequences before taking a leap."

SIX

Evelyn and Peter Cale were distraught. Their only child was taken from them, and they were stuck in limbo. It was the perfect exemplification of Schrödinger's cat. Until Catherine was returned, both hope and grief simultaneously existed. Unlike the cat in the scenario, I hoped to find Catherine alive and well, but there was no way of knowing until someone opened the box.

"Nicky's talked about you before," Evelyn sniffled. "He would hate for me to tell you this, but he said he's never seen anyone do this job better." She burst into tears, and Peter held her against his chest.

"Get our baby back, please," he begged.

After getting as much information on the last known whereabouts of Catherine Cale, the other two girls she was with at the time of the abduction, the school's address, field trip information, and anything else I could think of, I promised to do my best and went to my car. If Catherine wasn't recovered alive, Nick would never forgive me, which was fair since I wouldn't forgive myself, but I needed proper credentials to get the surveillance footage, access to question some witnesses, and financials on the other two victims' families. My OIO badge had been relinquished during my resignation, and if I couldn't ask for official help, then the rules would just have to be bent.

"Martin," I had him on speaker while I meandered through the streets, trying to find my way to Catherine's school, "get O'Connell's badge and bring it to me."

"Why?"

"Figure out a way to ask for it, and once you have it, call me back." I disconnected before he could ask any more questions. Impersonating a police officer was a crime but a victimless one in this situation.

Ten minutes later, my phone rang. "I have it."

"Good." I gave him the address of a café a block from the school and waited for him to arrive. The familiar town car pulled up, and before Martin could get out, I got in.

"Want me to come with you? We could pretend to be Cagney and Hutch or Starsky and Lacey." His attempt at being helpful brought a small smile to my face.

"Thanks, but I'll take it from here." Grabbing O'Connell's badge, I hung it from my belt. "Do you think I can pass for a first grade detective?"

"Cops are rarely as sexy as you, unless they're on television or strippers, so probably not."

"Thanks for the vote of confidence. If I get arrested, my one phone call won't be to you."

"What a shame. I would orchestrate a brilliant jailbreak."

"You're just being this annoying because we're not at the beach, right?" I teased.

"String bikini." He smirked, and I got out of his car and headed toward mine.

It was Sunday, but a few of the janitorial staff were hard at work. After flashing my borrowed badge and insisting on speaking with someone from the administration immediately, they phoned the headmaster. The school fell for my cover story hook, line, and sinker. After copying all the digital security cam footage from the two weeks prior to the abduction, I printed out a roster of faculty personnel. I lost track of how many laws I was breaking, or rather the school was for giving out personal information to some schlub off the street, but the fear of culpability or negligence in a criminal investigation was too much for the weak-stomached administrator to bear. Of course, embellishment was a useful tool, and without ever saying what the precise situation was, mortal peril and million dollar lawsuits were implied.

Gathering as much information as possible, I detoured to the science museum. It was the alleged scene of the abduction. There was one glaringly obvious blip on my radar. Why didn't anyone from the school notice three seven-year-old girls missing? From what I remembered of my formative years, field trips involved being ushered around in groups by teachers or parents and headcounts were taken constantly. Maybe years of seeing the worst made me a pessimist, but gut instinct said someone on the inside was involved, if not responsible.

My questioning of museum personnel led to the office of the museum director. He was giving a lecture to a tour group, so I was asked to wait. In the interim, I snooped through his desk. There were dozens of brochures for upcoming exhibits, some order forms, a calendar, a ring of keys, and random knickknacks.

"Can I help you?" a man asked, and I jumped away from the desk. Smooth, Parker. Real smooth. "Miss?"

"Detective," I corrected, "Heathcliff." It was my best bet since he was working a case, and if anyone wanted to call the precinct, they could verify a Detective Heathcliff was on the job.

"Detective." The man cocked his head to the side. "Don't you need a warrant to conduct a search?"

"Sorry," I mumbled, but his tone wasn't berating. "I get antsy when I wait."

"My apologies, then." He walked around the room and took a seat behind the desk. "Did your partner forget something earlier?"

"Partner?" What the hell was he talking about?

"The detective who was here earlier today. He said he was looking into a burglary ring. Isn't that why you're here?" Acting as if I was in the know, I let out a good-natured laugh.

"Actually, there was an emergency he was called away

on, so they sent me to go over everything he got, again. It's clearly an inconvenience, but your help would be most beneficial." I offered a conciliatory smile. The gnawing in my brain suspected Mercer had been here to gather as much intel as possible. The sneaky bastard.

"Not a problem. Have a seat. It should just take a moment while I pull up the files. Is a digital copy okay? Or do you need printouts?" He smiled.

Reading the nameplate on the desk, I tried to look demure. "Digital is fine, Mr. Tolbert."

"You can call me Jeremy."

Plying Jeremy for further details on the 'detective' from earlier led nowhere. He gave the man access to surveillance cameras due to the strongly held belief that it was to safeguard his museum from being the target of a crime. I didn't have the heart to tell him it was already the scene of a triple child abduction; plus, publicizing this fact wouldn't turn out well for anyone. It was a deep dark secret that only a small group of people were privy to, and I hated to be one of them.

Escaping Director Tolbert's office with the digital files and my clothes still on, I wanted nothing more than to go to the precinct, grab a hold of the real Detective Heathcliff, and get him to run through all the surveillance footage from the last two weeks from both the school and the museum, but O'Connell made me promise. The thought of using OIO resources was equally appealing, but Mark thought I was at the beach. If I showed up now, he'd be even more suspicious.

"Do you still want to play a cop?" I asked Martin, once he answered the phone.

There was never a situation where I wanted him involved in my line of work. He was a corporate bigwig. He paid people to handle problems. Hell, he paid me to handle this type of problem for him, but the grunt work wasn't dangerous. Unless we were somehow transported to a fictitious world where seeing a videotape could result in death in seven days, asking him to stare at surveillance footage wouldn't implicate him in anything or lead to gunmen chasing him down.

"Mmm," his voice was throaty, "does that include a sexy uniform and handcuffs?" His imagination was heading straight for the gutter, so I was surprised when his tone shifted. "Wait," he was giddy, "can you repeat that after I hit voice record?"

"It's not for me. It's for O'Connell, and I blame him." Pausing, I was struck by a brilliant thought. "Actually, how long do you think it would take to get a few monitors and DVD players set up in his hospital room?"

"I just got benched, didn't I?" He sounded dejected. "The man was shot and is busy recovering. Maybe you should let him rest."

Typically, I would agree, but O'Connell was going stir crazy. This was his case and his niece, and he needed to be involved, even if it was just by calling plays from the sidelines. Stopping to pick up my spare laptop, I went back to the hospital and brought O'Connell the museum feed. Thompson was still there while Jen ran an errand.

"Since you're laid up, I thought I'd bring you something to work on." If Thompson was ever going to have a blond moment, now would be the time. "I have two weeks' worth of surveillance footage, and I can't determine if anyone out of the ordinary pops up. Maybe someone's casing the joint. It's a museum thing."

"Thanks." The mattress flexed into the shape of a chair, and I pushed the bedside table over and put my laptop in front of Nick. "I'm bored out of my mind."

Thompson continued glaring at this exchange from his seat. "Parker, outside," he barked, heading for the door. "I'll be right back, man."

"Someone's in trouble," Nick mocked. "And he hasn't said more than a handful of words to me all day."

"Well, if your partner won't let you watch his back, then what kind of relationship do you really have?" My response was pointed as I went after Thompson.

In the hallway, he leaned against the opposite wall, waiting. Thompson and I had a somewhat tenuous relationship. He was a good cop, but we never worked extensively together. I'd worked with O'Connell and Heathcliff, and both adored me. But Thompson had always been more on the outside looking in. Maybe I'd stepped on his toes, invaded his territory, or just been like a bratty little sister who stole his toys and wouldn't give them back.

"What the hell happened?" he asked.

"O'Connell still won't tell you?" I pretended to be shocked.

"Parker," my name sounded like a hiss, "the official word is it was a random shooting, but I don't buy it. O'Connell swears he was just out for a jog, and the next thing he knows, he's on the ground. But why would he be jogging in a vest?"

"He was wearing a vest?"

"Damn Teflon casing." He sighed. "They call them cop killers for a reason. It was from a distance, and the bullet perforated but didn't penetrate completely. So don't you dare tell me this was a random event." He stared daggers, hoping I'd cave. "He has you working on this, doesn't he?"

"It's his call."

"I'm his partner."

"No shit. That's what I keep telling him, but he doesn't want this on the books." Thompson looked at me like I was stupid. "You have a badge and ethical guidelines to follow."

"Fuck ethics, this is Nick we're talking about."

"Fine, you want to help," I checked the hallway before continuing, "get everything you can on the bullet. If it's unique or can be traced to a gun, I'd love to hear about it."

"Tell me what this is about."

"Look, when the time comes, if an arrest is to be made, it's yours."

He let out a derisive scoff. "You think this is about a collar?"

"No, but do what you can. You have my number. In the meantime, go easy on him. Whether you realize it or not, he needs your support, even if it doesn't seem like it." I strode down the hall without another word.

In another life, I must have been a marriage counselor. O'Connell had surveillance from the museum to work on, and I would run backgrounds on every school employee and analyze the security footage. The clock was ticking, and Mercer was five steps ahead.

SEVEN

"Alex?" It was after midnight. I was exhausted from reviewing the school footage and personnel files for the past nine hours. "Come to bed." Instead of going home, I went to Martin's. His computer software and monitors were much more impressive than mine. It helped delay the fatigue to stare at a thirty-six inch screen rather than a thirteen inch screen.

"Can't." I hit pause and flipped through some information. Martin tried to help earlier, but after getting frustrated and throwing him out of the room, he found other things to occupy his time.

"Do you want to hurl another coffee cup at my head? It might make you feel better," he teased, taking a seat next to me.

"It wasn't a coffee cup. It was a paperweight, and I would have intentionally missed." Justifying destructive behavior was an innate talent. "Sorry about that." He chuckled. There hadn't been any actual flying objects, just the threat if he didn't leave me alone. "The only thing that will make me feel better is seeing whatever it is I'm missing."

"Maybe you aren't missing anything."

"Has O'Connell called?"

"He called four hours ago, remember? There was nothing from the museum. He even let Thompson go over it again, but neither of them found anything. Alex, there's nothing to find." The words were disheartening.

"Three girls go missing, and it all happens without any prior planning or at least none that can be tracked through school or museum footage. That can't be right."

"Didn't you say they were pros? Wouldn't they know better than to stake out the scene of the crime?" He had a point, but it didn't help us get any closer to the Four Seasons. Leaning my elbows against the desk, I put my face in my hands. This was getting me nowhere. "Clearly, I'm not making this any easier. Maybe you should have stayed at your place in the peace and quiet."

"Your equipment's better," I said through my hands.

"That goes without saying." His lips brushed my ear. "The only potential argument could come from individuals with a different sexual preference, but still, I'm sure they would recognize perfection." He was being lecherous and juvenile as usual.

"You really think you're something, don't you?"

"Hey, you're the one complimenting my equipment." Laughing, I rolled my eyes at his argument. "Consider getting some sleep. Last night in the car didn't count for much."

"Good night," I called as he left me with my work.

* * *

Opening my eyes, it was still dark out, but Martin flipped on the light and sat on the edge of the bed, holding out a cup of coffee. Sitting up, I tried to remember all the reasons why it was necessary to get out of bed. I took a sip from the offered mug.

"Are you sure you're up for this?" he asked. "When did you even come to bed? I looked at the clock. It was after three, and you weren't here."

"I don't know. Last night was a waste. There was

nothing to be found. All the background checks came up spotless. I don't have access to financials because that would require help, and I can't ask for any. Whatever Mercer has, he'll have to share." Getting out of bed, I rummaged through my luggage for a change of clothes.

"Do you want breakfast?"

"No. I don't have time. I'll just shower and head out, but I'll take some coffee for the road."

"You got it."

Forty-five minutes later, I was prepared to leave Martin's and meet with Mercer. The call should be coming in sometime this afternoon, but if he wanted to move in beforehand, we'd have to do it soon. Slipping my back-up into my ankle holster, Martin watched from the kitchen table.

"Yesterday was insane. It's an awful situation with O'Connell's niece being abducted, so I get that you can't steer clear. But he's in the hospital, recovering from a gunshot. Do your best not to follow suit." He caught my eye. "I've gotten that phone call before. Once was more than enough."

"I'll be careful," I promised before kissing him goodbye.

*　　*　　*

The ride to Mercer's apartment gave me time to focus. The provided proof of life was what tipped him off on the girls' location. But what if it wasn't a modified storage container? Honestly, they could be in an abandoned warehouse, an old building, a shitty apartment, the back of a truck, anywhere. Knocking on the door, Mercer opened it, looking as if he'd slept like a baby the night before. The desire to punch his lights in wasn't easy to quell.

"Parker." Back to one word sentences, he gestured inside.

"Did your friends arrive yet?"

"No." Clearly, asking yes and no questions wasn't the way to go with Julian Mercer.

"When is the call supposed to come in, and what are you planning to do between now and then?" He opened his mouth to speak, but predicting the outcome, I interjected, "Don't say it's none of my concern."

"It's not, but if you're all I have at my disposal, then you might as well serve some purpose."

The plan was infantile. He wanted to scout the cargo area near the wharf for signs of suspicious movement or activity. If the location could be positively ascertained and there was a decent chance of freeing the hostages, we would take it. If not, then he would go to the Estes' estate and wait for the call. At that point, the game would be determined based on the retrieval instructions.

"What solid proof do you have they are near the wharf?" I asked.

"The shooting."

"That's not proof. In fact, that's reason to assume the girls have been moved to a different location." My argument was sound, even if he didn't agree.

"It's the only lead we have." Unfortunately, he had a point.

Following him in my car, I instinctually knew our outing would be a bust. If these guys weren't on any of the surveillance footage, then they wouldn't leave their operation in a compromised location. No, they moved elsewhere. They were too smart not to.

Mercer instructed that I wait in my car while he looped the area, looking for activity. As my car idled, I dialed O'Connell's cell. Jen answered on the second ring and said he was asleep. At least someone was.

"I hope it's okay I brought him a laptop yesterday," I mumbled in lieu of an apology.

"Alexis, it was the only thing that calmed him down. He's been a basket case, and he won't talk to any of his police buddies. Should I be worried?"

"No," my voice was firm, "it'll be okay. I'll stop by sometime tonight if it isn't too late. If not, tell Nick I'll call when I know something."

Disconnecting, I stared out the windshield at the hundreds of cargo containers. We were looking for a needle in a haystack, the wrong haystack. Instead of destroying the environment any more than necessary, I shut off my engine and tried to figure out where to go from here.

"Parker," I answered; a blocked number was calling my phone.

"They aren't here." Mercer was up to three word sentences. Amazing. "The Estes family is expecting us. Follow me." He disconnected, leaving no choice but to trail him out of the city to a large country estate over an hour away. Thank goodness GPS navigation could get me back to the city without being dependent on Mercer, the merry mercenary.

We were positioned outside a gated fence, complete with guard post. Martin should consider investing in one of these. Hell, a moat and drawbridge might be even better. Mercer showed some credentials and made a few gestures in my general direction before the guard opened the gate and waved us through. The driveway looped to the front of the house.

"Don't speak," Mercer ordered as we walked to the front door where a man dressed like a Secret Service agent, complete with earpiece, wanded us, confiscated our weapons, and then passed us off to another man. The second man led us down a corridor to the veranda where a middle-aged couple was seated. "Senor Estes," Mercer gave a curt nod, "has there been any communications?"

"No." The man glanced in my direction. "Who have you brought?"

"She is representing the third kidnapped girl," Mercer said. "She does not matter."

She can hear you, I thought bitterly, but I kept my mouth shut. Estes didn't seem thrilled by my presence, and the rest of his conversation with Mercer was in Spanish. Besides catching the word muerta, dead, being thrown around, I wasn't sure what was going on. Eventually, the Secret Service poser escorted me from the room and into the foyer.

"Nice place. I must say this is the classiest joint I've ever been detained, and let me tell you, I have quite a list to compare it to." The man didn't seem amused by my monologue. "I've been meaning to ask, did you steal the suit and earpiece from the Secret Service?" He offered a dead-eye stare. "Oh come on, at least tell me you speak English. I'm wasting my best material over here."

"I'd hate to see your worst." Although it was a response and probably a joke, his facial expression never changed.

"Can I get some cold water to throw on that burn?" I smirked, but he wasn't willing to play along. "Sir," maybe respectful would work better, "have you always been employed by the Estes family? Or were you hired after Adalina was taken?" His eyes reflected something akin to disbelief, but he didn't respond. My sparkling personality and interrogation skills were both going to crap.

"Parker," Mercer barked from down the hallway, "quiet." Now wasn't the time for a confrontation, even though I would have loved to have it out. He jerked his chin toward the room, expecting my obedience. When this was finished, there were a few things we'd be discussing.

Inside, electronic monitoring equipment was hooked to the phone line. Computers were waiting to run traces, and there were enough computer geeks to make me wonder if anyone was left in Silicon Valley. Mercer was walking the interior, passing along instructions and making sure everyone knew what to do. Picking a spot on the wall, I leaned against it.

Less than an hour later, the call came in. The room went alight in activity, and once everything was turned on, the call was answered. Like Mercer said, the voice was indecipherable.

"Since you failed to comply with our rules, the ransom has been doubled. You have another twenty-four hours to procure the funds. In twelve hours, a location will be delivered for the exchange. Failure to obey will result in Adalina's demise." The call ended without further preamble. It didn't last long enough for a location to be determined.

"We've pinned it to somewhere in the United States," one of the techs provided. "North of Kentucky, east of the Mississippi River, and south of Maine." Great, we had it down to a three hundred mile radius, maybe.

"Bollocks," Mercer mumbled and strode from the room. That was as close to out-of-control as he was willing to go.

If it were me, there would have been a nonstop string of expletives and something smashing into a wall. Maybe I had self-control issues. "Parker, come." Maybe it would be Mercer I'd smash through a wall.

"Should I roll over and play dead too?"

"Senor Estes," he ignored my comment, "get the remainder of the funds together. No action will be taken until the drop. A plan will be devised and executed on your command. Adalina is still a valuable commodity. We believe she will not be harmed."

"Gracias," Estes said.

I caught sight of his wife still sitting on the veranda. She didn't say a word or acknowledge any of what was going on. The familiar twitch was set off in my brain, but being kept on such a short leash wasn't helping matters. Parker, Adalina is not your concern, only Catherine is. My internal voice reminded me. Mercer led us from the estate, collecting our weapons on the way out.

"Mercer," I wasn't backing down now that we were on even ground again, "what the hell are you planning to do?" He didn't respond. "Are you still planning to take down these sons of bitches at the exchange?"

"Perhaps." He got into his car and shut the door, driving away before I even started my engine.

EIGHT

Tagging along after Mercer wasn't a priority. There was a twelve hour window before instructions would be given, so I had until tonight to get my ducks in a row. But was I on a collision course with disaster and unable to locate the emergency brake? Heading back to Martin's, I collected all of my belongings, my surveillance disks, and then went straight to the hospital. The police presence was gone. It was Monday, and everyone was back at work. Checking in with Jenny, O'Connell was still asleep, and I was running out of ducks.

Surrendering to fate, I let myself into my apartment. Starting at my computer, I conducted a thorough search on the Estes family while the museum surveillance played in the background. Multitasking could be counterproductive sometimes, but since the surveillance was useless, it didn't hurt to keep it going, just in case. The Estes' gold mining operation was thought to be worth millions, and with smart investments, the family practically controlled the entire country. It made sense why Adalina was taken, but if she was the intended target, how did Catherine get caught in this?

The identity of the third abductee was still unknown. Giving in, I dialed the number O'Connell provided for

Mercer, but the disconnect message played through. Of course, he ditched the phone when Nick was no longer a viable asset. Paranoid freak. Leaning back in my chair, I shut my eyes. It would be a long day and an even longer night. Perhaps an endless night if Mercer decided on a tactical retrieval.

Setting the alarm for four p.m., I went to bed. This wasn't my operation, and the puzzle was missing more than half the pieces. Honestly, there was nothing else I could do, and if things went south, I needed to be functioning at one hundred percent. It was before four when the pounding against my front door began.

"Nick?" Opening the door, I reached out and grabbed his arm, helping him inside. "What the hell are you doing here?"

"Goddamn, Parker. Why can't you live on the first floor? Those six flights almost put me in the ground." He was winded and didn't look so good.

"They released you from the hospital?"

"Not exactly." He took a seat on my couch and propped himself against the pillow. "I have to get back before they realize I left. I convinced Jen to work her regular shift, and then I snuck out. Catherine needs me. You need help, and I dumped this in your lap."

"And it wouldn't have been simpler to read Heathcliff or Thompson in?" He shot an intense look my way, and sighing, I told him what happened so far today.

"There was nothing on the surveillance you brought, and you didn't find anything on your own. You have to get in Mercer's good graces. He knows more than you do, and if he's planning an assault," O'Connell looked glum, "Catherine doesn't need to be in the crosshairs."

"What do you know about the first girl who was taken and released? Anything on the Estes family or their business? Whatever Mercer's told you, it's time to share."

O'Connell didn't know much. The intel led to the wharf, but it didn't include any details on the other hostages besides number and gender. It was all a blur. I wondered if that was because he wasn't focused on the other things, being so caught up in saving Catherine, or if being shot impacted his recollection. During his rendition, he coughed a couple of times and clutched his side.

"You should get back to the hospital."

"I'd rather be in a body bag, knowing Catherine is safe, than back there not doing a damn thing." His conviction was startling. He was always more practical than this.

"We'll all end up in body bags if Jen finds out you left. What good will that do?"

He was stubborn and managed to pull himself off my couch and over to my computer. Running through the police databases for anything useful, he was looking for references to kidnappings, any mention of a team with aliases involving the seasons, Mercer, the Estes family, Jeremy Tolbert, the school's administrator, and anyone else he could think of. During his continued searching, there was another knock at my door. When you're popular, you're popular.

Thompson stood in my doorway, annoyed. "Is he here?"

"Great deductive skills, Detective." I stepped aside and let him in.

He cast a dark glare at O'Connell. "What the fuck, man. What the fuck?" Thompson was outraged. "I stop by to see how you were doing, and you're gone. I asked some CNA where you were, and she said you were still checked in, but here you are." Thompson turned his anger on me. "Did she spring you?" I was getting tired of being referred to as if I wasn't present.

"C'mon," Nick got up unsteadily, "I'm fine. See?" He wasn't fine, and Thompson steadied him. "Maybe my walk to stretch my legs should come to an end right about now." O'Connell glanced at me. "Parker?" I nodded. It was up to me now. After helping Thompson get Nick down the six flights of stairs and into the unmarked cruiser, I went back upstairs and checked the computer.

The searches turned up some interesting facts on the Estes' financial front. Most of their assets were tied to the business. How did they get the two million liquid so fast? And now they were expected to have another two million in twenty-four hours. It didn't seem humanly possible. Loans would require time, as would selling stocks or moving funds around. Since I couldn't call the forensic accountants at the OIO, I dialed Martin Technologies.

The accounting department was perplexed by my line of questioning. Trying to play it off as part of the new protocols in place and the need for the company to be prepared for all types of situations, I was bounced around from person to person. As I waited for someone to take me off hold, I unpacked my luggage. Might as well make the most out of my limited time.

"James Martin," Martin answered, sounding oddly personable for a CEO.

"I called accounting, and they sent me to you. Let Wallace-Klineman have all your employees and start over."

"Alexis?"

"I have a question about how easily and quickly company funds can be liquidated. We're talking millions."

He blew out a breath. "Off the top of my head, I'd say minimum a week." He paused to determine the reason for my question. "Are you planning to sell my company out from under me?"

"Dammit." Maybe the Estes family had inaccessible bank records, a secret account, or buried treasure. Either that or they didn't bother to get the money and had no intention of paying, meaning the play to rescue Catherine was going down a lot sooner than I expected.

Hanging up, I called Mark at the OIO. O'Connell might hate this, but I was out of options. Continuing to be vague and knowing damn well if Mark decided to track the location of my phone, he'd know I wasn't at the beach, I asked if he could pull every bit of information on the blocked call I received earlier today, including locations and a full list of phone records. He was even more confused than usual but said he'd do it.

In the meantime, I equipped myself as best I could for the unknown. There was a possibility I'd be part of a tactical assault, or I'd be on the front lines of a hostage negotiation. Either way, it was best to be prepared for anything. Decked out to the nines in an outfit I would have worn as a federal agent, complete with nine millimeter, a back-up, handcuffs, pepper spray, a few zipties, and a Flak jacket in the trunk, I detoured to Martin Technologies to ask a few more questions before resigning myself to being Mercer's wench.

Mark had yet to call with the information, and since I couldn't explain the urgency for needing it, I had to wait patiently. Taking the elevator to the seventeenth floor, I knocked on Martin's glass door, and he buzzed me in.

He frowned and pressed his lips into a hard line. "I hate that look on you."

"Unfortunately, it's the most practical because I don't know what's going on." Taking a seat on one of the couches in his office, I sighed. He wasn't supposed to be working, but since we were back from our trip early, he had nothing better to do. "Do you have a few minutes? I need help." Help was something I rarely asked for. I was out of practice and out of options, and Martin was perplexed by my request. Immediately, he dropped whatever he was doing and sat next to me.

"Whatever you need. You know that, right?"

"Hypothetically, you need two million dollars in forty-eight hours. How do you get it?"

"I don't know that I could. Does O'Connell need the money?"

"No, and he wouldn't ask. Neither would I. Not for that much. It's just, there are these people who have a gold mine, literally, but their liquid assets can't possibly be two million in such a short amount of time."

"Do they only mine the ore? Or is it stored for a duration before being melted or exported?" He was business savvy and had the habit of pointing out my flawed thought processes without realizing it.

"They wouldn't need to liquidate funds because they have access to gold." The realization hit hard, but two million dollars in gold ore was heavy. And it had to come all the way from Peru.

He smiled. "I'm glad my brilliance is contagious." I barely heard him because my mind was on the storage containers at the wharf.

Maybe they originally planned to ship the gold over on a boat, but with an earlier deadline, the only other option would be a cargo plane. Could the Four Seasons have moved their base of operation to a location closer to the drop off point for the money? At both, the wharf and an airfield, escape would be easy. Make the exchange and get the hell out of Dodge. But where would that leave Catherine?

"Any clue where a cargo plane might deliver a large lump sum of gold?" He shrugged, but he had done enough. "I have to go. Things are about to get crazy, so it might be a while before you hear from me again. Don't jump to any morbid conclusions," I warned, and he hugged me.

"Then make sure I have no reason to jump to those conclusions."

* * *

Mercer wasn't at his rented apartment, so I sat in my parked car, awaiting his return. This was a waste of valuable time, but all other avenues had been exhausted. The time crunch was fast approaching. A little before six, he pulled up. He parked and shot a cursory glance in my direction.

"Looks like the bird found her way back."

"Any word on the exchange?" I asked, ignoring him.

"Too early. Patience."

I followed him inside. I didn't trust him. There was no loyalty or love between the two of us, and it made it difficult to share the information I possessed. Luckily, before I said anything, he took a seat at the computer and clicked on aerial footage of private airstrips. At least we were on the same page.

"Are they shipping the ransom over on a cargo plane?" Playing a little slow couldn't hurt, especially since he already underestimated me.

"They must have a way to get it here." It wasn't an answer, but then again, that was true of most things he said. "My mates haven't arrived." It was the beginning of a joke, and I didn't think the punch line would be amusing. Stopping his reconnaissance, he reached over and lifted a folder off the edge of the desk. "No military training," he mused, "but advanced marksmanship, tactical training, preliminary hostage negotiation." He dropped the folder. "You'll do in a pinch."

"How the hell did you get my file?"

He cocked his head to the side but didn't answer. "You're here, so make yourself useful." Silently counting to ten, I needed to get in his good graces. This was about the safe recovery of Catherine Cale. When everything was said and done, then I could tell him exactly what I thought.

"I'd love to make myself useful." It sounded like a snarl. "Maybe I could if you read me in on what the hell is going on."

Glancing back, almost like a taunt, he clicked through a few more airstrip images. Settling on one in particular, he scribbled an address on a sheet of paper and handed it to me. "Go check this out. If you have anything to report," he scrawled a phone number, "call it in."

"What are you doing in the meantime? Enjoying some fine dining? Maybe catch a show?" Playing nice was not in my repertoire.

"Scouting other locations." He checked the time. "If nothing surfaces, be back here at twenty-thirty."

NINE

Sitting in my car, alongside some storage units almost a hundred yards from the edge of the fence that separated the airstrip from the rest of the area, something about the location felt right. Maybe it was the storage units lining the adjacent lot or the seclusion of the airstrip, but something made the hairs on the back of my neck stand at attention as I tried to determine what was going on.

The ringing of my phone served as a distraction from staring aimlessly into the empty airfield, and I answered. "Parker," Mark was all business, "what's going on?"

"What do you mean?" My innocent act wasn't convincing, at least not to him. That was the problem when dealing with the one person who taught you everything you knew.

"I don't know who called you today. The number was an unregistered burner, but since the three other numbers dialed besides yours belonged to ex-SAS, a gold mogul, and an Interpol agent, I'm going out on a limb and assuming you aren't working some corporate angle for Marty."

"It doesn't matter what I'm doing. What matters is who I'm dealing with."

"I can't tell. From the calls listed, it could be anyone

from a spy to a black ops security specialist. Maybe someone put a team together to orchestrate a hit or perform a recovery. So why the hell did you get a call?"

"Who knows? Damn telemarketers probably sold my name to Spies R Us."

He wasn't deterred. "Do you need back-up?"

"No."

"Are you even at the beach?"

"String bikini."

"What?" he asked, confused.

Letting out a chuckle, I replied, "Ask Martin. I have to go. Vacation time is a-wasting." It wasn't an answer, but it was better than an outright lie. "Do me another favor, see what you can get on private cargo planes leaving Peru and landing somewhere in the vicinity, presumably at a private airstrip."

"Parker," he growled, "be careful."

"People always say that. How come no one ever says, 'have another piece of cheesecake' or 'take it easy'?"

"The cheesecake, you'd eat without the insistence, and the take it easy part, you'd need a dictionary to determine the meaning." He hung up.

Obviously, Mercer received my records from whoever he called at Interpol since the OIO and Interpol often worked joint ventures, and maybe he was on the level when he said his pals were en route. Although, it didn't look promising that they'd arrive in time. None of it meant he could be trusted, but at least based on appearances alone, he was doing what he said. However, if push came to shove, Mercer was still a gun for hire, and I wasn't comfortable working with him. My limited experience with mercenaries involved putting a bullet in two of them and taking a third captive. The encounter left a bad taste in my mouth and nearly cost Martin his life. Mercer might not be my enemy, but he wasn't my friend.

"You're doing this for O'Connell." I reminded myself. "Catherine is an innocent little girl with a long life ahead of her." Sometimes, speaking aloud helped put things in perspective, or it simply reaffirmed that I was batshit crazy.

Getting out of my car, the only way to ensure the Four

Seasons weren't using this airstrip, hangar bay, and self-storage unit to keep the girls captive was to physically check it out. Starting at one end of the storage units, I walked up and down the rows of the two hundred individual lots, checking for signs of surveillance, something amiss, or the sounds of girls being held captive. Nothing seemed out of the ordinary.

The hangar bay would be perfect. It was secluded, protected from nosy outsiders by a chain-link fence on three sides and an airstrip separating it from passersby. With no other choice, I jumped the fence and scurried to the building. Tactically, I was in the open, and if surveillance was present, I was screwed. However, no shots were fired, and no one scolded me for trespassing on a private airfield. Pressing myself against the exterior of the hangar, I circled around in search of a door or window.

On the other side were a couple of windows, too high to peer through. Continuing further, I located a door. It creaked loudly as it opened, and listening for sounds, I crept inside. The room was dim. The only light came from the two windows I passed. The rest of the area was empty, except for some office furniture, a few filing cabinets, some equipment for plane maintenance, and a parked Cessna. There was no one in sight, and I rummaged through the desk and cabinets for any sign that this could be the place.

As I shut the drawer, voices approached. With no other alternative, I drew my weapon, holding it down at my side and ducking against the filing cabinet. The voices stopped outside the door, and angry words were exchanged. Two men were arguing over a delivery time.

"I'll show you the records," one of them huffed.

"Don't bother. It won't change what happened," the other responded. "You can't move up the pre-existing timetable."

"When are the girls coming?" Girls? I strained to hear. Could these be two of the Seasons, blundering away at their carefully laid plans?

"Not for another day. It'll give us time to get everything flown in and set up." Trying to determine the best course of action, I waited to see if they might reveal more. Giving away my location or confronting them wasn't a good idea, especially if they were responsible for Catherine and Adalina's well-being.

Crouching against the filing cabinet, I cautiously peered around the edge. The men were still outside, and I rolled to a position behind the desk. I wanted a visual to use for identification if necessary. Creeping along the desk, I pressed myself into an almost horizontal position against its metal frame. From here, I could only make out a sliver of one of their profiles. As I scanned the area for a better vantage point, my phone rang, shrill in the empty hangar.

"Who's there?" one of the men called.

Tucking my gun at the small of my back and making sure my jacket covered it, I carefully stood up.

"Sorry," I called out, hoping not to get shot or abducted, "I was cleaning out my ex-husband's storage locker. That lying sack of shit hid everything from the divorce attorneys. No good scumbag. Anyway, I was looking for the ladies room."

The two men entered the hangar, dressed like they belonged in jumpsuits and worker gear. They didn't look like kidnappers or criminal geniuses in their coveralls, but then again, I wasn't up on the latest in abductor fashion. "We don't have a bathroom," one of them supplied. "But if you go down the road about a mile, there's a twenty-four hour diner with facilities."

"Thanks. I'm sorry to barge in like this. I just saw the building and thought it was worth a try."

"No problem, missy," the second man said. "You have yourself a good day."

Strolling past the two men, I memorized the plate number on their pickup truck and figured I could run the plates. They were talking about girls arriving and missing flights. It was a long shot, but my time shouldn't be a complete waste. Maybe they weren't as wholesome as they appeared. Once back in my car, I checked for a tail or signs of tampering and started the engine. The missed phone call that had blown my cover was from Mercer.

"Are you trying to get me killed?" Melodrama was my friend.

"I've located their base of operations." He rattled off an address, and entering it into my GPS, I headed for his location. I wouldn't be surprised if the location I scouted was part of a wild goose chase to keep me out of his hair.

On the way, I dialed Thompson. He was still annoyed about O'Connell fleeing the hospital and taking refuge in my apartment, but since I was sworn to secrecy, tossing a few scraps here and there was the best I could do. "This is probably fruitless, but if you want to help, you can run these plates," I gave him the tag number, "and let me know what you find on the owner. By the way, how's Nick doing?"

Thompson let out an audible, exasperated groan. "I'm sure you'd know better than I would. He shouldn't be mobile yet, and Jen tore him a new one for leaving. Not that I blame her." He must have ratted on his partner.

"Did you get anything useful on the ballistics?"

"Teflon coated like I said. Medium caliber. The slug was too badly damaged from impacting the vest to be of much use. Tech says it was probably fired from a Glock." There was an uncomfortable silence before he spoke again. "Listen to me, Alexis, he's my partner and usually a by the book cop. Whatever's going down, I want in."

"Talk to him."

"I'm talking to you." This game couldn't go on much longer.

"I'm on my way to a meeting. When things begin to unravel, we might need some flashing lights and sirens to ride in and save the day. Keep your phone on." Depending on Mercer's plan, the boys in blue would either be responding to a multiple homicide or tracking escaped kidnappers. It was just a matter of time.

Finally, I pulled up next to Mercer's vehicle and cut the engine. He was sitting in his car, binoculars resting against the dashboard. He nodded, and I got out of my car and went around and sat in his passenger's seat.

"These blokes," he gestured toward a hangar bay much larger and more substantial in size than the one I just left, "must have serious surveillance. The electrical output is off the charts. Two guys were walking the perimeter twenty minutes ago. I've been timing the patrol."

"How can you be sure it's them?"

His anger flashed briefly in my direction before being silenced. My question wasn't pertinent enough to warrant a response. "We need eyes inside the building before a tactical breach can be made."

"You're not waiting for delivery instructions?" Although posed as a question, it was the assumption I initially reached after meeting Mercer.

"No reason to wait." He finally looked at me. "The objective is to recover the girl." Following my harsh stare, he corrected, "Girls. The authorities worry about evidence and making a case. The only thing you and I should worry about is retrieval."

"What about the kidnappers? Any specific resolution you have in mind?"

"That's discretionary."

"What if they're not inside?"

"Bloody hell." He let out a few harsh breaths. Poking a caged lion with a stick wasn't wise. "Are you such an incompetent sow that you can't figure out how to get a look inside without me holding your bloody hand every step of the goddamn way?"

"Well, since you asked so fucking nicely."

Getting out of the car, I slammed the door and got back into mine. Starting the engine and backing out, I headed away from the hangar. Walking up to the hangar bay was ridiculous. The foot patrol would see me coming, and red flags would be raised. No, quiet and stealthy wouldn't work. Distraction tactics were necessary. As I meandered around the property, staying on the main roads and noting weaknesses in the fence, Mercer called.

"Where are you going?" he asked.

"To find another way inside. And in five minutes, create a distraction. Tick tock." I hung up.

TEN

Five minutes later, the sound of metal crashing and the endless blare of a car horn interrupted the quiet. Hidden from sight, I waited for one of the doors to open at the warehouse. This time, I was smart enough to put my phone on silent. One man, dressed entirely in black, opened the back door cautiously and peered outside. This was the only door not covered by a surveillance camera, and he stepped out. The door shut behind him, and he stared into the dusk. There was nothing to be gained from his venture, but cautiously, he headed toward the far end of the hangar, closest to where the sound was originating.

Slipping out of cover, I held my breath and turned the doorknob. It silently opened, and I spun around the corner and entered the hangar bay. There were no planes or equipment. Instead, it was headquarters for some smoothly run operation. There was an individual seated in front of a cluster of monitors, watching surveillance footage as two sentries patrolled and the third man investigated the car crash less than a hundred yards away. At least Mercer wasn't skimping on his distraction tactics.

Stealthily, I crept behind the man, checking for cameras or other surveillance equipment as I went. The goal was to positively locate the girls. Hell, now that I was inside, if I found them, Mercer could delay the three sentries outside, and I could deal with Mr. Computer. Unfortunately, each individual room needed to be searched separately, and there wasn't enough time.

The man was still watching the screens, but I remained in the shadows, hoping to avoid being seen. There were six small rooms, three on each side of the hangar bay. Starting in the far corner, as far from Mr. Computer as possible, I carefully twisted the doorknob of the first room. It was a lavatory. Next, I tried the second door, but it was locked.

"Catherine? Adalina?" My voice was barely even a whisper. Just because there were four seasons didn't mean there were only four guys, and calling out could be a death sentence. No response.

I reached for the next doorknob, and Mr. Computer's chair scooted across the floor. Freezing in place, I pulled my gun. Not moving or even breathing, I waited. The guy stretched. There was a Glock on the desk next to him, and I wasn't sure if it was there before. Glancing at the monitor, one of the sentries was approaching the hangar door. Shit. Time was running out.

Quickly, I turned the other knob. It appeared to be a makeshift bedroom, but there was no sign of the girls. With no time left, I needed a way out. The back door opened, and I ducked into the bedroom and shut the door. Now what? Scanning the room for alternative exits, the only thing I found was an air vent. It wasn't very large and didn't look particularly sturdy. Heavy footsteps were outside the room.

"What was it?" a voice asked.

"Some drunk drove his car into the pole. He saw the runway lights and thought they were calling to him. Guy was a complete whack. He got out of his car and wandered off."

"Do you think the cops will roll in?"

"Nah," the footsteps stopped outside the door, and I swallowed, "who's out here to report it besides us?"

"I don't like it." Neither did I. "Get Spring and Summer and we'll make the call. No reason to take unnecessary risks." The footsteps walked away from the room, and I was torn between opening the door and hiding under the bed. If I planned to move, now was the time to do it. Listening, I couldn't be sure, but there was a good chance the back door opened, and the second man was gone.

Cracking the door, I peered out. Mr. Computer was busy setting up his anti-identity protocols, so I crawled out of the room and scurried in a crouch to the other end of the hangar. The other three rooms were empty. The girls weren't here. A chorus of expletives screamed through my subconscious as I went to the back door, took a breath, opened it as soundlessly as possible, and ran swiftly away from the hangar and back to my abandoned vehicle.

The last thing I wanted to do was leave, but I couldn't take down the kidnappers alone. I needed help. Mercer's help. Managing to open my car door, I slid behind the wheel and tried to calm my racing heart so a plan could be formulated. My escapade left me jittery as adrenaline coursed through my veins. My hands were shaking, and I gulped down air. I was out of practice. Taking a final deep breath, I started the engine and hit the highway.

Holding the phone with my shoulder, I looped the hangar. "Mercer, there's no sign of the hostages. Two of the bastards are inside. Maybe we should phone it in and let the police get a location for the girls."

"Negative. Estes just called. Instructions have been given. My car's been wiped and totaled. Pick me up."

Slowing to a stop on the shoulder, Julian climbed inside my car without another word. I turned and stared at him, waiting for an elaboration on the incident and an attack strategy. Instead, he jerked his chin at the windshield.

"We have to go back in. Even if the girls aren't there, at least two of the kidnappers are. We can question them for answers. We have to find the location," I protested.

"No."

"No?" I screeched, flabbergasted by his single word response. "They have Catherine somewhere. I have to get her back. This is a lead. A fucking lead."

"Drive. Now." He glowered at me. "Unless you've done this before and know precisely what you're getting yourself into, I suggest you drive this bloody car far away from here.

I have a scheduled meet, and if there is any chance of a positive recovery, I can't miss it."

"But—"

"If you go back in now, it's a guarantee they'll kill the hostages and scatter. Make a choice." I inhaled, unsure what to do. "We don't have time for this. Go. Now."

Shifting into drive, I sped away from the hangar, hoping I made the right call.

* * *

Julian Mercer liked to do everything in triplicate. He had a few burner phones and a few rental cars at his disposal. Although no obvious indication was ever provided, I suspected he had a few safe houses set up in addition to his weekly rental. Mercer went to meet with the Estes family to have a face-to-face concerning what would happen at the exchange. This time, I wasn't invited.

Whatever caused the change in Mercer's disposition between the insults and me picking him up, he decided I was trustworthy and competent enough to be left alone in his apartment. There was a good chance the place was under surveillance, but it didn't stop me from rummaging through everything, looking for some undivulged secret. Unfortunately, besides dozens of aerial maps of different locations, blueprints of hangars, warehouses, and docking bays, and a few photos of Adalina and Catherine, he didn't have any clue what was going on either.

"Parker," I answered the buzzing in my pocket.

"The plates belong to an aviation company out of Tulsa. They have branches all across the country. Small time stuff. Crop dusting, tourist attractions, small charter companies. Nothing seems sinister, but," Thompson was still annoyed, "it might be easier to find something out of the ordinary if I knew what to look for."

"Deadline's approaching." It was all I could say. "I'll keep you apprised of new developments."

"Ha. Yeah, right." He hung up, and I wished there was something more to tell him.

Mercer wanted to go in hot, and I had been in enough

firefights to know this was a suicide mission. There would be at least four guys and two hostages. Maybe the money would be delivered, and we could have a nice civil exchange. If not, I would prefer having ESU outside or a tactical team from the OIO or FBI busting down the door.

It was a little after two a.m. when Mercer returned. The two Secret Service wannabes accompanied him. Four of us did help to even the playing field. Mercer barely acknowledged my presence as he hefted a large duffel bag over his shoulder. Gold didn't travel well in duffel bags. Maybe he stopped at one of those gold for cash exchange places on his way here, unless the Estes family has more accessible money than I was aware of. The possibility of an insurance policy crossed my mind, but I filed it away. Now wasn't the time to dwell on such things.

"Barr and Keener, you're transporting the money to the exchange. Follow my lead and stay on my six." Mercer glanced my way. "Parker represents the Cale girl. She's a non-player tonight." Non-player, my ass. "Think you can follow us without getting lost?" he asked me.

"I'll find some way to manage. Maybe we should chain the vehicles together, just to be on the safe side." If I ever saw him again after this, it'd be too soon.

Driving in a convoy, we were instructed to wait under an overpass a half a mile away from the hangar I infiltrated earlier. It was late, and the moving shadows created by the headlights from cars overhead put me on edge. As I waited, my phone rang.

"Are you prepared to return fire if things go sideways?" Mercer asked.

"Yes." My response was curt. The silence filled the air space, and finally, I added, "try not to step in front of me. It'd be a shame if you took friendly fire."

"Cheeky sod." He chuckled. It was an unexpected sound. Something about the prospect of an impending standoff put him at ease and in a better mood. Sick fucker. "If there's an opening to get the girls and get out, do it."

"Okay." We disconnected, and I went back to waiting in the darkness.

The sky turned a pale blue, but the sun didn't break over

the horizon yet. We'd been waiting all night. Finally, a black, windowless van pulled to a stop on the other side of the underpass. I sat up straight and did an automatic check on my clip. Mercer was out of his vehicle, and the rest of us waited.

A man dressed all in black, complete with face paint, exited the passenger's side of the vehicle. Some words were exchanged, and then Mercer signaled to Barr and Keener, the Secret Service impersonators. One of them carried the duffel to Mercer.

As I watched, a second cloaked figure emerged from the van and opened the side door. Slowly, I opened my car door. There was no reason to spook them, but half a second could be the difference between life and death. Mercer walked the duffel to the man, who unzipped the bag, checked the contents, and re-zipped the bag. He nodded to the second guy, who pulled a hooded individual from the back. My assumption was it must be Adalina. But where was Catherine?

The first figure climbed into the driver's side, securing the duffel. The second man yelled something to Mercer, which I couldn't hear, and opened fire. Mercer scrambled behind his car as Barr and Keener returned fire. I was on the ground, crouching behind my door and taking aim.

"Hold your fire," Mercer yelled.

Whichever hostage was in front of us could easily be hit by a stray bullet, so Barr and Keener stopped shooting. The man dragged the hooded girl back into the side door of the van as the wheels spun gravel into the air. Aiming for the driver, I fired, but the glass was bulletproof. Emptying my clip at the fleeing van, it was apparent we lost them.

"Goddammit," I cursed.

Mercer said something to the two men who got back into their vehicle and took off. "I told you not to fire," he berated.

"Fuck you." It came out a snarl. "You let them get away. If Catherine dies, there isn't a goddamn place you can go where I won't find you and kill you."

"Now, now." He looked mildly amused. "Is that any way to talk to the man who put a tracking device in the money bag? They wouldn't take Catherine to this drop. So say thank you for the help in getting a location to rescue your abductee."

My blood boiled, and I bit my tongue. It was bad when your enemy double-crossed you; it was worse when your ally stabbed you in the back. "This better work because you might have just signed her death warrant and yours too."

"Hollow threats, bird. Hollow threats."

ELEVEN

My eyes didn't leave the single red blip on the monitor. After the failed exchange, we went back to Mercer's to ascertain the location. The money bag was still in motion and heading for the docks. Maybe the girls weren't moved from the original location. If they ended up where Nick had been shot, I'd feel particularly stupid for not realizing the base of operations didn't change. Instead, the blip careened off toward the warehouse district.

"How do you know we'll get to them in time?" It made no sense why we were waiting in Mercer's apartment for the kidnappers to get such a blatant head start.

"Barr and Keener are in pursuit. Mobile version of the tracker is connected to their GPS." As soon as the blip slowed, I grabbed my keys. It was time to end this.

Violating every traffic law, I made it to the warehouse in record time. If *Guinness World Records* has an entry for cross city driving, I was sure to be named champ. Barr and Keener were already inside, and drawing my gun, I went in silently. There was no reason to wait for permission. My singular goal was to get Catherine and get out. Instead, I found two bewildered Secret Service impersonators.

"Where are they?"

"When we arrived, the place was empty," Keener offered. The duffel was tossed on the floor with its contents still inside.

"They knew," I mumbled. Dialing Evelyn and Peter Cale, I knew it was time they made a decision. Nick was my friend, but it wasn't his kid.

"What's happened?" Peter answered, sounding frenzied and resigned at the same time.

"Catherine hasn't been located. We made an attempt earlier to find her, but they discovered the tracker. The girls have been moved. There could be an incoming ransom demand made, or," my voice dropped, "I don't know."

"What should we do?" Evelyn picked up the extension, and they were both on the line, looking for answers. For hope.

"O'Connell won't agree with this, but honestly, I'd like to call it in. Maybe the police or FBI can find some evidence or a lead. Anything. They are trained in these matters, but if you believe your chances are better without involving them..." The unstated implication hung in the air.

"Make the call. We want our daughter back," Peter said firmly. I waited for Evelyn to agree before disconnecting and calling Thompson.

"Here's the location." I gave him the address and told him everything I knew of the situation and my encounter at the hangar with two of the alleged kidnappers. "They're gone. The girls are gone, and this moron K&R specialist is a piece of work."

Just as I hung up, Mercer arrived. What took him so long? Didn't he care about completing his mission, collecting his paycheck, and moving on to whatever clandestine, illegal crap he did on a daily basis?

"Where are they?" he asked.

"You need to find a new line of work." I got in my car, noting the flashing lights and sirens fast approaching. Thompson was a miracle worker. That and everyone on the job was out for blood when it came to protecting one of their own.

"You rang the coppers?" The surprise was evident on his face.

"It's a cop's niece. You do the math."

I spotted Officer Taylor pulling up in a cruiser, and I nodded to her, putting my car in reverse. Mercer would be occupied for the foreseeable future, so at least he wouldn't be able to do anyone else any harm. I had to get to the hospital and tell O'Connell the new plan. I owed him that much.

* * *

"You promised," Nick bellowed. "How could you do this?"

"It wasn't your call. Evelyn and Peter made the decision, and I passed the message along to Thompson. You know they will work around the clock to find her."

"Get out." He was livid, but I didn't move. "Get out!" The monitors on the back wall went crazy, and a nurse came in to make sure he wasn't going into cardiac arrest. He was irate, but the only one in danger of dying was me.

"I'm sorry," I mumbled, escaping the room and bumping into Jen.

"Alexis?" She judged my appearance.

"Tell Nick it's for the best. Thompson will do all he can. The entire force will do all they can. He has to know that." Leaving Jen standing there stunned, I left the hospital and went home.

My mind was a jumble. Did I fail? Did Mercer? Was Catherine still alive? Why didn't the exchange go down seamlessly? At least then, Adalina could have been rescued. Maybe she would know where Catherine was. Glancing up, Heathcliff was leaning against my front door.

"Hey," he greeted, holding up a bottle of bourbon, "I thought you could use this."

"It's ten a.m."

"My shift just ended, so time of day loses its relevance." I unlocked the door, and he came inside. "Thompson caught me up. Then he called again with O'Connell's version. I stopped by the warehouse on my way here. It doesn't look promising. Captain Moretti's called over to the Bureau and asked if they are willing to work this as a joint venture. We're not turning over jurisdiction, but it's O'Connell. All the help we can get, right?"

"He should have said something sooner." Busying myself with taking off my holster, I screwed my eyes shut. "Maybe I should have said something sooner. Done something more." Opening my eyes, Heathcliff grabbed two coffee mugs from the drain board and started pouring. "I don't know."

"Drink." He held the mug out, and I took it. "You did all you could." It wasn't a question. It was his firmly held belief.

"How would you know? I might have been sitting here, catching up on my soaps and fucking everything else up."

"It's you. You did all you could." He swallowed the contents of his mug and poured another shot's worth into both our cups.

"O'Connell doesn't think so."

"Yes, he does, but right now, he's scared shitless. He's not thinking, so ease up on him." He poured another. "Ease up on yourself."

Half a bottle later, I was lying in my bed as the room continued to spin out of control. Heathcliff was passed out on my couch, and as far as I was concerned, there was no reason to surface from this misery unless someone decided they needed me to screw something else up. Obviously, I wasn't equipped to deal with hostage negotiations or rescue kidnapped girls. Self-pity and loathing were difficult to shake, especially when the depressant effects of alcohol only exacerbated the situation. Eventually, the spinning blurred into nothingness.

When I awoke, Heathcliff was gone. The remainder of the bottle was on my kitchen counter, and I had the worst hangover imaginable. Somehow, it was fitting to experience physical wretchedness to accompany the psychological torment. Taking a few aspirins and drinking a glass of water, I got in the shower. As I was getting out, the ringing phone threatened to make my brain rupture.

"Parker," I whispered, carefully considering how rude it would be to vomit while on the phone.

"Ms. Parker," Guillot sounded surprised that I

answered, "Mr. Martin has informed me of your friend's condition. Please take as much time away from work as you need."

"Thanks." My alcohol-addled brain couldn't determine the reason for the call. "Is that it?"

He hedged. "We need to schedule a final check of the new protocols to make sure everything runs smoothly," he added after a time.

"I'll be by later to work on details." Hanging up without another word, I found comfort in the cold porcelain. Later was a vague term, and after managing to get off the bathroom floor and back to some semblance of human dignity, I noted the time. It was after working hours. Tomorrow, I'd stop by MT and do whatever my corporate job required. The police would be calling or knocking soon enough for official statements, whereabouts, and alibis.

Attempting another glass of water and a few more aspirin, I searched inside my purse for my MT identification card. Unfortunately, it was nowhere to be found. The last time I saw it was Wednesday afternoon in Martin's kitchen. Unable to stay home any longer and currently too frayed to work on a feasible lead to find Catherine, I drove to Martin's.

"Hey, do you mind if I stop by?" I asked while parking outside his garage door.

"Of course not." He sounded distracted. Maybe he was at work or having a business dinner. "What time?"

"Now."

There was a moment of silence, and then the door in front of me opened. I pulled into the garage to find Marcal polishing the town car. He shut the door and offered a smile. Why he was here if Martin was in for the night barely registered as I trudged up the steps.

Opening the door, Martin was sitting sideways on the sofa with his arm outstretched across the back. Seated next to him was Francesca. She let out a soft laugh and ran her hand up his forearm. Wow, as if today couldn't get any worse. After losing the possibility of recovering Catherine and dealing with this god-awful hangover, the scene playing out in front of me shouldn't have registered, but it did.

"Clearly, you need a warning before I show up." Being utterly impolite, I stalked into the kitchen and searched the drawers.

"Alexis," he acknowledged, sounding friendly, but there was a hint of worry in his voice, "can I help you with something?"

"No, Mr. Martin," my voice bled disdain, "I believe I left my company I.D. card in your possession." He politely excused himself from Francesca's perfectly adorable grasp and came into the kitchen.

"I didn't expect to hear from you so soon." His voice was gentle. "Oh god, is she?"

"I don't know." I slammed a drawer shut and headed for the guest bathroom. There was no reason to think it was there, but I didn't want to be in such close proximity to him. Unfortunately, he followed, uttering some polite lie to Francesca on the way. "Look, Luc needs me to go over some shit at the office tomorrow, so if you find my goddamn MT clearance card, can you bring it with you to work and tell the yokels in the security office to let me upstairs?"

"Where are you going? You just got here." He wasn't stupid, so the fact he was asking completely idiotic questions did nothing but acerbate the situation.

"I'd hate to ruin your date, sir." Again my words were biting. He shut the door and blocked my escape.

"I don't know what you think you walked in on, but you should know me better than this, Alex." I snorted and looked away. "Francesca is in town to make a business deal, and since we ran into one another at the conference, she looked me up."

"Yeah, fine. Are we done? There are more important things I could be doing right now."

He squinted, assessing my appearance. "I doubt it. You wouldn't have stopped by if that was true." He reached out to touch my cheek, but I pulled away. "You've either been crying or you have one hell of a hangover."

"Screw you. Oh wait, either that's what happened twenty minutes ago or what's happening twenty minutes from now. Like I said, I should go."

"Fine." He was annoyed, and his own voice adopted an edge. There was no reason why I had to be the only one to bask in the misery. "Your I.D. is in the bedroom. You can either go get it or stay put while I get it." Not wanting to go upstairs for fear that my accusation, although entirely ridiculous and unsubstantiated, would be proven correct, I crossed my arms and leaned against the bathroom cabinet. "Give me a minute." He was angry.

Great way to piss off all the men in your life. Maybe while I was waiting I should call Heathcliff and bitch him out for inflicting bourbon on my battered soul. Clearly, he had to pour the liquor down my throat to get me to drink it. It had nothing to do with the desire to self-medicate the pity and helplessness away.

Five minutes later, Martin returned. He didn't have my I.D., but he apologized to Francesca for the commotion and politely concluded their evening together on account of his raging bitch of a girlfriend; although, he probably put a slightly more positive spin on it than that.

"What the hell is wrong with you?" he yelled. It'd been quite some time since we had a fight, and I was in no condition for the decibel levels we were capable of achieving.

"I'm gonna go, but I'll make you a list. Check your e-mail." I brushed past him, but he grabbed my arm. "Y'know, I would say it's not you, it's me, but the problem is, I tend to follow one basic principle. People don't change."

"What the hell is that supposed to mean? You've had a shitty day, so you're taking it out on me. Yeah, I know. I'm used to it."

Letting out a horrible sounding laugh, I yanked my arm from his grasp. "Oh come on, when I first met you, you were this womanizing playboy who liked to pull out the charm and flash the money around. Why the hell did I ever let myself think you weren't that guy anymore?"

He looked genuinely hurt. "I'm not that guy. Maybe I was that guy before but not with you." I turned and continued toward the door. The last thing I wanted was to have this fight. The reason I came here, besides the stupid I.D., was because when things went south, he was my port in the storm. Instead, I set the place ablaze and added insult to injury. "Don't go. Not like this."

"O'Connell threw me out of the hospital. I betrayed his trust and turned the situation over to Thompson. If I could do that to him, then there's no reason in this world why you wouldn't have at least entertained doing something similar to me. Betrayal isn't something planned. It just happens."

TWELVE

I sat alone in my car in Martin's garage. Marcal was gone, probably to drive the Harvard alumna back to her hotel or another suitor's house. My head was against the steering wheel. There was too much to process. After an unknown amount of time passed, Martin tapped on my window.

"Come upstairs." He looked defeated.

"Why?" Fighting with myself was tiring enough. I didn't have it in me to keep up the fight with him too.

"Because you need someone to talk to, even if it's just someone you want to vilify as a philandering, womanizing son of a bitch." He opened my car door. "I'm not going to apologize. I've done nothing to hurt you or jeopardize us. Whatever issues you have are yours. You sought me out tonight, so there must have been a reason."

I shut my eyes, dreading the question that played endlessly through my mind since entering the warehouse. When I opened them, I locked onto the green orbs in front of me. "What if Catherine's dead?"

"You didn't kill her."

"Maybe I signed her death warrant. Maybe by recommending Evelyn and Peter turn it over to the authorities, the kidnappers will just dump the body and start over with an easier mark. Maybe by firing at them, I pissed off the wrong person, and they have grown tired of the game."

"Maybe you need to stop with all the maybes." He knelt down to my level. "You were in a shootout?"

"Not much of one. Everyone walked away still breathing. Rather pointless if you think about it."

"Were you trying to make a joke? Because it's not funny."

"No. It's not." I sighed. "O'Connell is so upset. He'll never forgive me. I can't forgive me." Something dawned on Martin, but he didn't share his epiphany. Instead, he pulled me out of the car and dragged me up the steps.

"Thompson and Heathcliff must be relieved to be doing something," he added, continuing up another flight of stairs. Wherever we were going, I was done contesting his actions. If he wanted to throw me off his fourth story balcony, it would at least be a remedy to my infernal headache.

"They're working on it. The FBI is getting involved, but all this extra help could be a faster death sentence." A horrific thought dawned on me. "What if they never find her? Not knowing, never knowing might be worse than–"

"Sweetheart, stop." He led us to his bedroom.

"I've been away from this life for too long. What am I doing? Two of the kidnappers were a few feet away from me. I should have stopped them. Arrested them. Called the cops to arrest them. Something. I should have done something. Instead, we left and let them go. Stupid mistake. God. And right now, I should be out there doing something, not here picking fights with you."

"Tomorrow." He nudged me toward the bed. "Sleep on it. You're spinning yourself into the ground and trying to take everyone else with you." He flipped on the light in the attached bathroom, knowing I wouldn't be able to handle the dark in my current state. "Do you want a drink or some tea? Warm milk? I don't know what I'm supposed to do here."

"No alcohol. I'm hungover enough as it is." Meeting his

eyes, I wondered why he would be so patient after all the horrible things I just said to him. "Even if it rarely seems like it, I do love you."

"I know. Now get some rest. Tomorrow, things will be more manageable, and tonight, the cops will do everything they can."

* * *

"The van was torched. Ballistics pulled a bullet out of the hood, but everything else is useless. I'd say they dumped it first thing. We're pulling traffic cams now to see if we can get some idea of what they might be driving," Thompson relayed over the phone.

"The bullet in the hood is probably mine."

"Are you gonna come down to the station later to give us a statement, or do we have to track you down?"

"I'll be there in a couple of hours. Is Mercer in a cage?"

"It's a three-ring circus, but he's not going anywhere anytime soon," he assured me before hanging up.

Putting the phone down on the nightstand, I looked at Martin. It was six thirty. He had turned off his alarm and foregone his ritual early morning workout. Although he was pretending to be asleep, he'd need more acting lessons before I'd be convinced.

"I'm sorry about last night. If I could take back the entire day, I would." He opened one eye, and his lip curled up at the corner.

"You've never struck me as the jealous type." He rolled onto his side and watched as I fidgeted with the hem of the sheet. "If you were less defeatist and more crazed sex kitten, I could accept the jealousy thing a little easier."

"Meow." I rolled my eyes, knowing my outburst had very little to do with Francesca and everything to do with all the ways I screwed up yesterday. "One of these days, maybe we'll have a talk about our past relationships like your former fiancée and my ex-husband."

"Ex-husband?" He cocked a confused eyebrow up, and I snorted. "Evil." He watched me closely. "That was a joke, right?"

"Of course. No one's that crazy. But it smarts to have the unknown flaunted in your face. Hell, she was sitting on the couch, and you know how much I love that couch."

"It's the only reason you ever come over."

"Exactly." I got out of bed, fully dressed in my clothes from yesterday. It might save time, getting a jump on the day, if I didn't look too wrinkled, and my clothes were passable too. "Just so you know, my outburst wasn't really about Francesca." He nodded. Sadly, he understood me better than even I understood myself. "I have to get going on this. Whatever's going to happen is already in motion."

"Stop with the conflagration. When you blame yourself, you try to burn down every good thing you have. Sure, I'm this amazing godlike being with incredible abilities like empathy, phenomenal listening skills, and unparalleled sexual prowess, but," he smirked, "don't confuse that with a doormat."

"Doormat's typically say *welcome* while you tend to spout out smartass remarks and perverted jokes."

"See, you obviously know the difference." He wished me a good day, and I left as soon as he got in the shower. At least my temporary insanity didn't cause any permanent damage. I only hoped the same could be said concerning my relationship with Nick and the unknown status of Catherine's well-being.

By the time I made it to the precinct, there was a fleet of government issued vans taking up all of the visitor parking spots. Three-ring circus was too kind of a comment. My first step into the police station felt strange. It was akin to walking into a church after years of not practicing any faith. At least I didn't burst into flames. Heading up the back staircase to the major crimes unit, I was hoping to spot a friendly face.

In the roll call room, the current acting captain, Dominic Moretti, assembled a group of uniformed officers, some plainclothes detectives, and a group of suited federal agents. I took a seat at O'Connell's desk and shuffled inconspicuously through his belongings. There was a decent chance he might have been looking into some leads before he was shot that no one uncovered.

"Already did that," Thompson said, sitting across from me. "You're not the only one who took the investigation skills 101 class."

"Yeah, but I did it while wearing heels, so don't even try to top that."

He scoffed and pulled out a blank form from his desk. "Are you going to cooperate and stop being a pain in my ass, or do you want to do this in an interview room instead?"

"Here works." I gave him my biggest smile. After divulging everything I knew, which wasn't much, he added it to the three-inch thick file currently on his desk. "Are you charging Mercer with anything?"

"Like what? Interfering in a police investigation? If you want to push the issue, I can toss the two of you into holding for the next forty-eight hours."

"Be nice, Thompson," Heathcliff said from behind. "This reads O'Connell all over it in bold letters." He came around the desk and leaned in front of me. "Parker, let's take a walk." Checking Thompson for approval, he frowned and went back to entering things into his computer.

We wandered down the hallway, and Heathcliff ducked into the archive room. It was the closest thing to privacy we could find in a busy police station. The reason for our meeting was still unknown, but at least it was an improvement over Thompson's angry looks.

"How you doing?" he asked.

"Better today. Next time, let's try a five mile run, instead of downing half a bottle of bourbon." He remained silent. "Did you find a body?"

"No." He shook his head for emphasis. "They're in the wind. As far as we can tell, Catherine and the other girl are still being held somewhere. If they end up dead, the kidnappers get nothing. It'd be bad business to kill your cash cow."

"They left the money. It was in the warehouse." I inhaled slowly. "If it's not the money they want, then what's left?"

"Maybe they figured it was sequential bills, or they were paranoid because of the tracker. There's gotta be an explanation, but the guy with the accent isn't being cooperative."

"Julian Mercer not cooperating, there's a shocker. Are you sure you can't book him? The guy's a ghost. My guess, he's a goddamn mercenary."

"His business card reads professional negotiator. I suggested he add wet work specialist next to the K&R, but I didn't get a response. Maybe it's a dialect issue."

"Obviously. Toss in a couple pip, pip, cheerios, and maybe you'll get a better reaction." I was back to being flippant.

"What do you know about him? About the Estes family? Anything O'Connell might have told you that you haven't shared? We're in the freaking archive room. So it speaks for itself, this is off the record."

I gave him every shred of information I possessed from the hangar bays to the school administrator to the museum. The only thing I left out was my impersonation of a police detective. Some things were fluff and not necessary to divulge. "Jablonsky pulled some phone records, but since I'm supposed to be vacationing at the beach, he's been slow getting anything usable back."

"Does that mean you're hanging up your holster and calling it a day?" He was busting my chops. "What are you doing, Parker? Heading back to the shiny MT building, sitting behind a desk, maybe answering some phones, sending a few e-mails, and drinking coffee?"

"Sounds just like your job."

"Then why aren't you begging to get put on this case?" My silence was met with an odd look. "Nick put you in the doghouse, so you're trying to behave."

"If something happens to her, I don't want it to be on me."

"And if you aren't doing everything you possibly can and something still happens, then who's that going to be on?" I swallowed. Heathcliff made a hell of a point.

THIRTEEN

Seated behind my desk at the MT building, I reviewed the reports and signed off on finalizing the protocols. By the end of the week, everything would be set in stone, and by the beginning of next month, the entirety of the overhaul of MT's security would be completed. Why anyone would choose to do this job was beyond me. It was tedious, soul-sucking, and monotonous. My heart wasn't in it.

Taking a break, I dialed Jen's number. O'Connell and I weren't on speaking terms, but I wanted to make sure he was okay. After too many unanswered rings, it went to voicemail, and I hung up. Alex Parker, pariah. Heathcliff was right, I should be begging to work the case, but I was afraid of failure with the stakes this high.

"Ms. Parker," Jeffrey called from outside my open door, "here's your temporary I.D. card. We've removed all the access from your previous card, but it'll take the system twenty-four hours to reset before we can put you back in with a new permanent I.D."

"Thanks." He placed the card on my desk. "I'll try not to lose this one." I wasn't one to lose things, and it was irksome that I couldn't find my card. Maybe it fell behind something or was lost in the packing.

"Not a problem." He stared at the stack of paperwork on my desk. "Do you want some help?"

"That's okay. If I finish early, what will I do? Stare at the walls?"

By four that afternoon, I had gone over everything and brought the paperwork to Guillot. He was amazed it was completed and shocked that I spent an entire day at work, instead of agonizing over my personal situation. The only crisis I was having was what I was supposed to do. At least it was nice to know some people weren't completely heartless. On my way out, I spotted Martin in his office in deep conversation with Francesca. At least my volatile personality didn't harm Martin's personal or professional life.

Before I made it out of the building, my phone rang. "Evelyn and Peter want you on this. They will only work with you," Heathcliff relayed the message. "They received a delivery today via courier. We have proof of life and a ransom demand."

"I'm on my way."

* * *

The Cales' house was full of FBI negotiators, technicians, police detectives, and some other armed men whose actual jobs I couldn't decipher. Heathcliff was seated at the kitchen table across from Evelyn and Peter. The rest of the investigators were setting up in the living room. Being escorted into the house by an armed guard, Evelyn glanced up with red, puffy eyes.

"I told you we're not talking to anyone else or cooperating. Not until we talk to Alexis," she sounded resolute, and Heathcliff stood and nodded encouragingly.

"I'll see how the equipment's getting set up," he offered.

"Evelyn," as usual, I was confused, "what's going on?"

"When you phoned, you asked if you could tell the authorities that our daughter was missing, and that's fine." She sniffled loudly, and Peter pushed the tissue box closer to her. "But Nicky said to trust you. Not them. You."

"I'm not a negotiator."

"I don't care what you are." She was agitated. "Can you help get my baby back?"

"I'll do everything I can but don't shut out the guys with the suits and badges. They know how this goes better than anyone. Detectives Thompson and Heathcliff have worked with your brother for years. There is absolutely no reason not to trust them. They're his family, and that makes Catherine theirs too." She fell silent, and Peter nodded. "What did you receive?"

"Photograph," he swallowed and pushed it across the table, "and this note." The items were sealed in an evidence bag but still on the table. The techs hadn't collected them for fingerprinting or other evidence yet. Taking out my phone, I snapped a quick picture of each, just in case I needed access for some reason.

"Rudimentary demand. Simple instructions. Basic photo with today's paper from a Polaroid film camera. Old school technology which means less chance of evidence being doctored," I said, summing up the basics. In the photo, Catherine held up the paper. There were no obvious signs of abuse or injury. The instructions requested two million dollars, and a follow-up communication would provide a location within the next forty-eight hours. No cops.

"What if they find out everyone is here?" She sounded on the verge of hysterics.

"Don't worry about that right now. They're more interested in keeping their eye on the prize." It might not be true, but it sounded good. "I'm sorry to pry, but realistically, how much money can you compile if you liquidated everything?"

Peter had apparently given this some thought because his answer was quick. "Three hundred thousand, maybe. We'd have to mortgage the house, clear out all our savings, sell the cars, jewelry, everything. Borrow from everyone we know, but maybe three hundred thousand. Still, there's no way we could do all of that in two days."

"What would it matter?" She started to cry. "It's not two million. It's not even close."

"It doesn't matter. You're not in a position to pay which means either they have no idea who they've taken, or they actually want something else. This is a scare tactic. They want you frenzied and willing to give up or do anything. The point is to cause a panic. So whatever you do," I tried to put a positive spin on things, "don't panic. Everything is negotiable, and some of the best people are working on this."

"Parker, do you have a minute?" Heathcliff called from the next room.

"I'll be right back. Take a breath. This is a marathon, not a sprint. Okay?"

Going into the next room, Heathcliff opened the back door, and we went outside. Whatever was about to be said didn't need to be overheard. "Good job calming them down. Hopefully, your little cheering session will get them to work with us, instead of against us. But for my own curiosity, how much of it do you actually believe?" he asked.

"Can't hurt to put it out there, right?"

"We have the phones, internet, everything wired. There are a few teams outside, keeping watch. Whenever another message comes in, we'll know about it, and we'll trace it. With any luck, it'll lead right to these assholes and Catherine."

"It won't." My words confused him. "The Four Seasons, the men responsible, they know what they're doing. They know how to do it. If we want to find them, then we have to figure out who the hell they are first."

"All right, you stay here. I'm going back to the precinct, and Thompson and I will start digging."

"See if you can figure out who else they abducted. There was a third girl taken, but she was released. Oh, and speak to the Estes family. They might have received another message from the kidnappers. And Derek," I sighed, "spring Mercer. Call Jablonsky first and have him send his best guy to tail the douchebag. Whatever Mercer knows, it's a whole hell of a lot more than he's bothered to share."

"Okay. Hey, I'll swing by Moretti's office and warn him you're back to causing trouble in his house."

"Face it, you've missed me."

With Heathcliff gone, there were no friendly faces in the house. The government employed investigators viewed me the same way I viewed Mercer, and there wasn't a damn thing I could do about it. If the Cales weren't willing to fully cooperate with anyone but me, then we were all stuck in this very uncomfortable boat for the duration.

Once again, I asked Evelyn and Peter to go over the entire situation from the beginning. The cops pretended not to listen, but the point of this rendition was for their benefit. A few scribbled notes; others ran background checks and placed requests for DOT cameras around the school and museum. Afterward, Evelyn went upstairs, and Peter remained at the kitchen table.

"She's not handling this situation well," he commented.

"What do you mean?"

"Catherine's my daughter too, but everything has been *my brother this* and *my brother that*." He was annoyed. "Nick's a good man. Hell, he would have died to save our baby, but she still thinks he'll ride in on a white horse and save the day. She doesn't get that the people in this house are our last chance."

"Mr. Cale," I tried to be encouraging, "we will all do everything in our power to get Catherine back. The more you can convince Evelyn to cooperate, the greater the probability of a positive resolution."

"Be honest with me." He stared at the surface of the table, steeling his nerves before meeting my eyes. "Realistically, what's the chance we'll see our baby girl alive again?"

I hesitated. There was no way to answer his question, but he needed to hear something. "If we can identify the kidnappers, there's no reason to think we won't be able to bring her home safely." Rule one, never make a promise you can't keep. I promised O'Connell, and now I was promising Peter. Hopefully, the Four Seasons wouldn't make me into a liar.

FOURTEEN

The day was shot to hell. I arrived at the Cale residence late in the afternoon, but there wasn't much I could do at their house. Unfortunately, every time I tried to leave, Evelyn or Peter had another concern to quell or a question that no one else would answer. Hand-holding might be part of the job, but it wasn't bringing any of us closer to tracking down Catherine's abductors.

It was after midnight when I made it to the precinct. Thompson and Heathcliff were buried under a pile of paperwork as surveillance footage played on every available screen in the bullpen.

"Coffee, thank god." Thompson was relieved when I placed an extra large cappuccino on his desk. It was my peace offering. We were on the same team and needed to act like it.

"I thought you guys could use it." I handed Heathcliff a cup and sat at O'Connell's desk with my own coffee. "Any leads?"

"We sent a few unis to gather information from the school, the museum, the chaperones on the field trip, but we haven't heard anything back yet. It was too late in the day to track down a lot of people, so we're starting fresh in the morning," Heathcliff offered.

Thompson pulled a folder free from the pile on his desk and tossed it in front of me. "That's the third victim, Sonia Casanov. She's a diplomat's kid, but we've had no luck opening lines of communication. She and her parents checked out of the country immediately after the recovery." He sighed. "On the bright side, at least we know one of the girls is safe."

"Did anyone contact the Estes family?" I asked. "Has there been any news on recovering Adalina?"

"We sent officers to their house. I swear the legal team they have could get known terrorists freed from Gitmo," Heathcliff growled. "You know kidnappings have their own set of rules, and since they don't want us there, we're out. Jablonsky put a guy on Mercer, but there's been no word on that front either. Did you discover anything new from Peter or Evelyn?"

"They're scared. Evelyn's in denial, and Peter is trying not to give up the last remaining ounce of hope. This is complete bullshit." I sighed. "Have either of you talked to O'Connell?"

Heathcliff shook his head, but Thompson shrugged. "He was released from the hospital today, and Jen's put him under house arrest. I wouldn't be surprised if she handcuffed him to the furnace to keep him from doing something stupid. Well, something else stupid."

"Apparently, there's plenty of stupid to go around," a voice said from behind. Turning, Mark walked in, carrying a stack of files. "This sure as hell doesn't look like the beach."

"The guys swept away the sand because people kept falling in it," I responded. "And don't even get me started on all the issues due to the standing water."

"Julian Mercer," Mark said, ignoring my quips, "has been a professional negotiator for the better part of the last decade. He knows his shit, and without getting too bogged down with the logistics, he's had more positive outcomes than not. Last I heard, he's still at the Estes' country estate. We pulled some phone records, and immediately after the girls were taken, Miguel Estes phoned his business advisor who put him into direct contact with Mercer. Like clockwork, the guy shows up within the next eight hours to handle the situation."

"Are you saying he's involved in the kidnapping?" Thompson asked, bewildered by the possibility.

"No," I interjected. I knew how things like this worked. "But Mercer had days to work out the details."

"Bingo," Mark focused on me, "so why are you drinking coffee when you should be crawling into bed with Julian, metaphorically speaking."

"We didn't exactly hit it off, and when I turned over his negotiation to the authorities, well, you can imagine how many brownie points I earned."

"Demerits," Heathcliff corrected. Glaring at him, I picked up my half-full coffee cup.

"Wish me luck," I said to the room, "I'm off to woo Mr. Mercer."

"Parker," Mark's voice held a commanding quality, "keep your phone on. It'd be nice to know where you are in case something goes sideways."

"Remember, I'm at the beach."

* * *

"Now I find you waiting outside my flat," Mercer said, approaching his front door. He arrived home a few seconds ago, and I wondered if his tail was still somewhere nearby. "It's two a.m. If you're looking for a shag, you've come to the wrong place."

"I hate to break it to you, but you're not my type." Without waiting for an invitation, I followed him inside since he was in a talkative mood. "What's your next move?"

"Parker," he sat on the couch and stared at me, his gun still holstered, "what the bloody hell do you want?"

"Catherine. By any means necessary." The slightest sign of dark pleasure crossed his eyes before vanishing away.

"And you think I can help you?" It was a challenge.

"Name your price." He cocked his head to the side as if listening to something before getting up and moving toward me. Before I had time to react, he backed me against the wall, placing his forearm along my clavicle. His gun was in his other hand, against the wall near my head.

"Quiet," he commanded.

Shutting my eyes, I swallowed and took a deep breath, weighing my options. The pressure eased off my neck, and I turned to look at him. His back was against the wall. What the hell just happened? Meeting my eyes, he silently signaled, and I pulled my nine millimeter and crept to the other side of the front door and glanced out the window.

"What?" I mouthed. Two seconds ago, I was convinced he wanted to paint the walls with my grey matter.

"Cover me," he whispered and opened the door, going out high, so I could cover him from a crouched position at the front door.

"Bastian, Donovan," he lowered his gun, and I followed suit, "where's Hans?"

"You know Hans," one of the two men said. They exited an SUV with rental stickers on the windshield. One of the two hefted a sniper rifle over his shoulder and offered a grin. "We didn't realize you were entertaining. Shall we come back?"

"I'm not," Mercer practically snarled. Apparently, I wasn't his type either.

"Who's the bird?" the second man asked. "And if you're not entertaining, someone really should." He walked over and extended his hand. "I'm Bastian. It's a pleasure to make your acquaintance," he said in a thick Cockney accent.

"Just because I holstered my gun two seconds ago doesn't mean I won't still shoot you," I responded. My guess was these two blokes were part of Mercer's team.

"Ooh, sassy." Bastian raised an eyebrow. "I like a girl with spice and an excellent shooting record. Agent Parker, isn't it?"

"Let's take this off the streets," Mercer commanded and stalked inside without another word.

"He's rather curmudgeonly, but you'll get used to it. We have." Bastian winked and followed Mercer. Donovan, the man carrying the sniper rifle, kept his eyes on the ground as he went past. Two strong silent types and a class clown, it was going to be a long night.

Mercer must have silently conveyed to his fellow ex-SAS members to keep their mouths shut because no one said a word about recovering Adalina or the plan they were setting in motion. Since Mercer was still our best bet for making a positive I.D. on the Four Seasons, I took an unobtrusive seat on the sofa and crossed my legs. Donovan, the tactical support, was in the other room, skimming through all the blueprints and photos pinned to the wall. Bastian, whose role I had yet to decipher, was sifting through the contents of the fridge, and Mercer was seated across from me, staring at nothing. Not moving or speaking, it was hard to be certain if he was even breathing.

"I believe you were about to name your price," my voice cut through the silence like nails on a chalkboard.

"Was I?" He tilted his head ever so slightly. The crack in his hard exterior vanished as soon as his cohorts arrived.

"It's obvious you're waiting for me to leave, so you can discuss matters with your mates." Ridiculing his vernacular probably wasn't the smartest idea. But it was almost three a.m., and I was too tired to care. "Why don't you save us both some time and tell me what you want. I'll tell you what I want, and maybe we can reach some kind of agreement."

"Trust me, you don't want to know what this one wants. He's into too much kinky shit for the likes of a lady like yourself," Bastian interrupted, taking a seat on the edge of the coffee table directly between the two of us. "I, on the other hand, have only the most honorable intentions. No kinky shit, scout's honor." Mercer and I simultaneously glared at Bastian.

"Bas," Mercer dismissed him with a look, and silently, Bastian went back into the kitchen.

"Nice trick. You think you could teach me that?"

"You will not get in the way. The authorities will not interfere with my methodology, and when the time comes, you will do what I say, when I say it."

"I want everything you have on the kidnappers. If the cops get there and resolve the situation before you do, that's just how it is. If you're in the midst of a negotiation, with or without heavy artillery, it's your show. First on scene gets to call the play. Deal?"

"Whose side are you on? Mine or theirs?"

"There are no sides. We're all on the same team. But I'm getting Catherine out one way or the other. If the cops get there first, I'll be there. If you get there first, I'll be there."

"Isn't that cheating?" Bastian asked from the kitchen, but Mercer ignored him and continued to study me.

"You pull another cheap shot like you did today and I'll have no problem putting a bullet through you." His threat didn't sound hollow.

"Do we have a deal?" I asked, and he nodded, retrieved a USB drive, and handed it to me.

"This is everything concerning the Four Seasons, their suspected locations, and a copy of all the ransom demands up until this point. Stay away from the Estes family, or we will have a problem."

"Fine. You get a location, give me a call. You need support, give me a call. If not, let's stop running into one another like this."

"I wouldn't be certain of that." His tone was somewhere between a threat and utter resolve, but he had bigger problems than me. Although, the information could be completely bogus and just an excuse to get me to leave, but there was no way to tell.

At the doorway, Bastian reappeared, leaning against the jamb as I let myself out. "See you around, love," he called.

FIFTEEN

After spending the rest of the night reviewing the data stored on the USB drive at the precinct with Thompson, I changed clothes and went back to the Cales' house. No other communications were received. The only familiar face was the lead FBI hostage negotiator. Everyone else went home at shift change and was replaced by a crack team of fresh-faced law enforcement officers. Evelyn and Peter were in a zombified state, staring at the remnants of breakfast on their plates.

"Alexis Parker?" the negotiator asked.

"Yes," I sighed, "did you want to verify my credentials?"

"Not particularly." He smiled. "You were here yesterday. I'm SAC Brian Palmer. Jablonsky from the OIO called and vouched for you last night, as did Director Kendall. You have the run of my team if you need it."

"Trust me, nobody wants that," I warned. "But do what you have to, and if you need me to coax out some cooperation, I'll see what I can do for you. In the meantime, the police are looking into some potential leads." Stifling a yawn, I added, "If it's all right, I'd like to get some shut-eye while I can." The negotiator nodded, and I took a seat in the living room.

It was imperative I remain close, especially with the increasing chance of further demands, but until the call came in, there wasn't anything I could do. Sleep when you can; it was the cardinal rule we were supposed to live by.

After catnapping most of the day, the call came late that afternoon, another nondescript message that utilized the best in identification and location deflection technology. The techs moved at light speed to triangulate a location, and the negotiator gave Peter cues on what to say in an attempt to prolong the conversation as much as possible. Leaning against the desk, I knew they were seconds away from losing the caller. Catching the negotiator's eye, I raised a questioning eyebrow, and he nodded.

Grabbing the extension, I cut in on the call. "The Cales have employed me to negotiate the safe recovery of their daughter. I'm not a cop. I'm a private, third party K&R consultant. How shall I address you, sir?" Peter gaped at me, and the FBI negotiator wrestled the phone from his hand and placed it on the cradle. It was the only way any of us could see to buy time for the technicians.

"You may refer to me as Winter." The eerie computer-modulated voice responded. "To whom am I speaking?"

"We'll keep this simple. You can call me Parker. I'm authorized to speak on the family's behalf."

"The two million will be placed in a black briefcase and left next to the bus stop on Seventeenth. Deliver it at exactly 8:13 tomorrow evening. Come alone. Leave it and walk away. Do not look around. Do not stop. Further instructions will follow." Without further preamble, the call ended.

"Did we get it?" I held my breath, waiting for the response.

"They're somewhere on the southside, but we needed another three seconds for a more accurate triangulation."

"Goddammit."

"You tried," Palmer offered, but Peter continued to stare in horror.

"What have you done?" I wasn't entirely sure he wouldn't start swinging.

"Everything I possibly can to save your daughter." His

chin quivered, and he fixed me with a hard stare before abandoning the room.

"I thought you didn't want the run of my team," Palmer commented.

"I still don't, but we needed time. It just wasn't enough."

Unlike other crimes, kidnappings differ in one fundamental respect; the family always has final say. The FBI and PD were running themselves ragged to narrow the possible locations, and Thompson and Heathcliff were analyzing the data Mercer collected. The last I heard, they were tracking the kidnappers' country of origin. While this wasn't ideal, it might lead to similar case files or Interpol records which could lead to a possible identification. The problem was time. We were running out, and since the Cales couldn't pay the two million and Winter didn't give the option to negotiate, the drop would require some creativity.

After giving the Cales some time to cool down, I sought them out. We needed to work out the logistics for the money drop. Peter and Evelyn were ready for a fight, and I was the only enemy in sight. "You heard him," Peter's voice was forceful, demanding. "You have to go alone. There can be no cops."

"And what? You want me to pull the two million out of my ass?" Arguing with a grieving, frantic father was not the way to handle this situation. "Nothing about the drop will be the way Winter expects it to be. Demands are negotiable. He can't honestly believe you have access to that much money that quickly."

"What do we do?" he screamed. "We can't pay, so we just let him kill Catherine?" He sniffed and looked away, swallowing. Evelyn made a pitiful mewling noise at his side and buried her face against his shoulder.

Exchanging a look with the FBI negotiator, I had to walk away. I needed a moment to regroup. I can't do this. The words kept replaying through my brain. Taking a seat on the patio steps, I inhaled a deep breath. From inside, Peter's voice traveled as he berated Palmer, and Evelyn's strangled sobs reached new levels. Dialing the precinct, I prayed for some good news.

"Please," I practically begged, "tell me you have something."

"Parker?" Heathcliff sounded tense. "Is everything all right?"

"Tell me you've got something."

"Thompson went to the OIO. He and Jablonsky are working with an Interpol liaison. There have been three similar abductions in the EU, and we're hoping to run through the files and get a solid lead."

"Great, more agencies are involved." My tone was jaded.

"Jablonsky's helping because it's O'Connell." He waited a couple of beats, but when I remained silent, he asked, "Do you want some company at the Cales' place?"

"No. I'm capable of being a fucking idiot all on my own." I let out a sigh. "Derek, see if you can get in touch with Nick. Someone needs to make these people understand why we can't follow the ransom instructions to the letter."

"I'll try. But Parker, I'll have to explain that principle to O'Connell first."

Swallowing my insecurities, my anger, and my fear, I strode into the house with my head held high. No more outbursts, just pure, logical reasoning. This was a business transaction. There was no reason to view it with any emotional attachment whatsoever. Winter and the other three didn't see it emotionally. Mercer damn sure didn't, so neither would I.

In the kitchen, the FBI negotiator was being assaulted by the barrage of blame Peter was hurling at him. As any good professional would, Palmer stood quietly, waiting for the insults to cease.

"Mr. Cale," I interrupted, "your anger is justifiable. I apologize for my earlier outburst, but may we continue this at another time when the clock is no longer ticking." Palmer looked relieved and disappeared into the background. "As always, you and your wife will make the final decisions, but it is imperative you keep in mind the flaws in following Winter's instructions."

"We don't have that much money," Evelyn whispered. Her voice was on the brink of betraying her, and a whisper was all she was capable of.

"What you're suggesting won't get our daughter back," Peter choked out the words.

"Tracing the briefcase, keeping eyes on the drop site, and having back-up on standby are the best ways to locate your daughter," I insisted. "This is what the FBI team has trained for. They've done this countless times. They know what to do and how to do it without being compromised."

"Nicky said not to involve any authorities," Evelyn said meekly.

I bit my lip, resisting the need to mention that no authorities is what got O'Connell shot in the first place. "When I asked for permission to turn this over, you said it was okay." Pointing out the obvious might not hurt the situation.

"Why don't we come up with some alternative solutions to minimize your concerns," Palmer offered, appearing with a couple of his teammates.

"It can't hurt to have some options," I urged. Evelyn and Peter didn't seem pleased. Instead, they acted like they were being railroaded. But eventually, they acquiesced, and Palmer took charge of the train before we faced a total derailment.

SIXTEEN

I was two blocks from the drop site. It was 8:05, and with the remaining eight minutes, anything could happen. The Cales agreed to place a tracker in the outer lining of the briefcase, but they wouldn't let us have eyes on the drop. Since I was impersonating a K&R specialist, I was stuck delivering the bag.

"Parker, do you copy?" Thompson asked in my ear.

A Bluetooth was hidden underneath my long brown hair, and we were speaking over the phone. Radio signals could be intercepted, and the Cales were too skittish to allow unauthorized communications. Technically, I wasn't supposed to be talking to Thompson.

"Loud and clear." I checked the time and watched as the second hand hit the twelve. Seven minutes. "I'm starting my approach now."

"Okay. Heathcliff boarded the bus two stops back. He'll be on it when it makes the 8:15 pass. If anyone gets on the bus with the package, we'll have eyes on them."

"All right. Keep me apprised. I'm going dark until after I clear the area."

"Affirmative." Although we didn't disconnect, neither of us spoke a word as I continued toward the bus stop. It was the typical, clear Plexiglas structure with a wooden bench inside. A teenager sat on the far edge, listening to music on his mp3 player. An elderly woman was in the middle of the bench with a few brown paper bags from the local grocery store, and the rest of the area was deserted.

I walked toward the structure, resisting the urge to turn my head and glance at the other side of the street. One of the instructions was not to look around. So I faced forward, but my eyes continued to scan the area directly in front of me. There was nothing. Reaching the bus stop, I stepped under the makeshift roof and pretended to read the bus schedule while I placed the briefcase in the designated location. Checking the time, it was 8:12. Inhaling a steady breath, I continued down the street.

"8:13," Thompson's voice rang in my ear, but I continued walking.

Once I was half a block away, I wanted nothing more than to look back to see if the briefcase had been taken, but I was a professional. Two blocks later, I turned and checked for a tail. As far as I could tell, no one was watching or following me.

"It's done," I said. "Now we wait."

I hailed a cab and took it to my parked car. Thompson and Heathcliff were working off the books since no one was officially authorized to be part of the exchange except me. During the cab ride, Thompson informed me that no one suspicious got onboard the bus, but as far as Heathcliff could tell, the briefcase was gone. Thompson was pulling traffic cam footage. The DOT had cameras everywhere, but the Seventeenth Street bus stop was one of the few blind spots left in the city. The Four Seasons had done their research.

"I'm scanning nearby camera footage to see if I can get eyes on our guy via the briefcase tracker," he muttered as keys were clicked in the background. If Capt. Moretti knew what was going on, he'd nail two of his top detectives to his office wall. But none of us could worry about the consequences right now. Nick was our friend, our brother, and we couldn't sit idly by. Whether he thought I betrayed him or not, the sobering fact was we were all doing this for him.

On the drive to the Cales' residence, I wondered how long it would be before Winter called with further demands. The briefcase contained a tenth of the requested amount. Twenty thousand dollars was still a hefty sum, but the Cales were willing to part with it as a good faith gesture. My guess was it would piss off the kidnapper, and we'd get a call shortly. I had spoken extensively with Agent Palmer on the do's and don'ts of the situation, but I was still unprepared to interact with Winter for an extended period of time.

"The signal went dead five minutes ago," Palmer said as I entered the house. "Either it's out of range, or they found it." Before any further speculation could be provided, the phone rang. "Easy. Use neutral language. Remain calm. This is business. If you have to make him think you're walking away without buying the car, then do it." Nodding, I took a seat at the table and exhaled before lifting the phone from its cradle.

"This is not the agreed upon amount." It was hard to tell if Winter's voice was mechanical and cold or if that was due to the computer modulation.

"The money is a good faith gesture. We did not negotiate a sum. Two million is beyond my client's financial capability." Palmer sat next to me and began making notes on the conversation.

"This is not a negotiation. Two million is the price. Not a penny less."

"I am authorized to make a trade for one hundred thousand."

"If you only want one-twentieth of the girl back, then a hundred thousand dollars it is." Palmer scribbled the word 'humanize' on the piece of paper and slid it to me.

"Winter, you are not dealing with rich people. The head of this household is an assistant. These are working class people. The girl you've taken, Catherine, is seven years old. They want her back alive, but two million is well beyond a reasonable asking price."

"Two million," the mechanical voice repeated.

"There is no insurance to pay out. No company to incur

the loss. This is a family," I argued. "They aren't CEOs, moguls, or royalty. Just your average Joe."

"We shall send her to you in pieces." The line went dead.

It's only scare tactics, I reminded myself. Although, I had no way of knowing what would happen. Palmer insisted Catherine was a rare commodity; thus, it was in their best interest to keep her healthy.

"What did they say?" Evelyn asked, coming into the room. Thankfully, the FBI agents kept her away during the exchange since she didn't need to know what transpired.

"We're still negotiating. They'll call back," I replied. Palmer gave her an encouraging look, and satisfied with the answer, she left the room.

"When they call back," he whispered, "give them a higher number, and before they can respond, find a way to disconnect. It's important they feel they have some control, but we can't let them think they have all the power."

"And if they don't call back?" He didn't have an answer, and he left me alone in the room, waiting for a call that might never come. My heart raced. There was a part of me that wanted nothing more than to hyperventilate until I lost consciousness, but unfortunately, I was doing a wonderful impression of appearing cool, calm, and collected.

Ten minutes later, Winter called back. Power. This was about shifting the balance of power ever so slightly on its axis. Going in too strong wasn't recommended. Unfortunately, it was the way I handled most situations. This required finesse. Waiting until almost the fourth ring, I answered the phone with a very chipper sounding, "Hello."

"Parker, one hundred thousand is unacceptable."

"I can get you another fifty thousand. It will take some time. Consider the offer." I immediately hung up. What the hell was I doing? Less than a minute later, the phone rang again.

"The offer is still unacceptable."

"Then let's discuss a realistic figure we are both comfortable with."

"Two million," the computer voice bellowed.

"You're not getting two million. You won't even get a million. We do not have those kinds of assets."

"Do not take us for fools." Winter was pissed. "We know exactly who we have. You have the money, and you will pay or else the girl is dead. Seven a.m., pier nineteen on the wharf, come alone with the cash in non-sequential hundreds. If you defy us again, there will be no other chances."

"Sir," I tried professional, "defying you is not my intention, but that amount is not an option." Palmer was standing in the doorway, listening but providing no helpful tips. He didn't have any. "I can't make something appear out of thin air when it doesn't exist. What else would you be willing to take in trade?"

Palmer shook his head. Winter was taking the power back, but there wasn't anything else to be done. Negotiation required give and take by both parties.

"Two million, seven a.m., pier nineteen. You will bring the money."

"There is no money."

"Then there is no girl."

Palmer gestured wildly, and I pulled a page out of my own playbook. Whoever we were dealing with was well-versed on ransom negotiations, FBI tactics, and hostage negotiation. They weren't well-versed in Parkerology.

"Listen to me, you sick son of a bitch, if anything happens to that little girl, you won't see a dime. You will get nothing. Your only consolation will be running for the rest of your fucking miserable life because there will be no safe place for you to go. The good thing about leaving the authorities out of this is that I can hunt you to the ends of the goddamn earth. The feel of the wind on your skin will be my breath. The sunlight will be my eyes burning into you, and the dark," I let out a threatening, maniacal laugh, "well, you'll see what happens in the dark."

"Do not threaten me."

"It's not a threat. Last chance to take my offer. Hell, two hundred thousand in exchange for the girl and all of this goes away. Think about it. You have until seven a.m. to make a decision." I slammed the phone down. Palmer was moving like a bobblehead who just got flicked.

"Okay. Okay. We can handle this. They don't hold all the power, and they know we're serious about getting the girl back. They should take the offer." Nothing out of his mouth sounded sincere. I pushed too hard.

"Goddammit." I brushed past the few agents, past Evelyn and Peter, and went straight to the front door. I had to get outside. The walls were closing in, and I needed open spaces. Staring up at the starless sky, I wondered what would happen in the next nine hours.

SEVENTEEN

Why didn't we find a way to keep eyes on the warehouse or the goons inside the warehouse? Mercer and I had been in their vicinity. These assholes should be dead or locked up, not making demands. But at the time, Mercer was calling the shots, and I trusted the bastard with Catherine's life. Dumbass move, Parker. I dialed Mercer while Palmer ran damage control with Peter and Evelyn.

"Funny hearing from you again," Mercer drawled.

"Why the hell didn't we do more at the warehouse?"

"No visual on the cargo," he said matter-of-factly. "I was authorized to make a move only if recovery was feasible."

"Fuck you."

"Good evening, Agent Parker." He hung up. Dammit, this was how a proper negotiator dealt with a hard to handle situation. I called back and waited for Mercer to answer.

"Point taken. Have you been in contact with any of the Seasons?"

"Not your concern." My free hand opened and closed into a clenched fist.

"The Cales don't have the funds to pay, but we're supposed to make a trade in the morning. Professionally speaking, what would you do?"

"Interesting." In the background, I could hear Mercer calling to Bastian and the sound of markers squeaking against a whiteboard. My guess, Mercer was making a drop in the morning too. "Renegotiate. If that fails, follow the bloody bastards until they lead to something concrete. Don't you have official negotiators to confer with?"

Ignoring his question, I asked the only thing which might provide an answer, "Are you going in hot?"

"Too soon to tell." He disconnected.

Kicking a stray rock as hard as possible, I took a deep breath. Whatever Mercer and his team of ex-SAS mercenaries were planning, I wasn't privy to. Their operation was separate from mine, but I might need their help. My attempt at negotiating was pitiful.

"Parker," Palmer called from inside, "we need to talk."

Inside the house, the FBI was narrowing the location from the call. Optimistically, Winter remained on the phone long enough to allow for triangulation, and an extraction team could go in, procure Catherine, and take down the kidnappers. Unfortunately, all roads led to nowhere. The technicians were stumped as to how the signal continuously bounced from tower to tower. The final conclusion reached was the kidnappers must be using an encrypted SAT phone.

"Mr. Cale," Palmer spoke deliberately, "I would like to position a team here." He pointed to a spot on the aerial image of the wharf. "It would be helpful to have this exit and this exit monitored. In the event the kidnappers do not bring Catherine to the exchange, we shall follow them and ascertain her location."

"What if they see you?" Evelyn asked.

"They won't," Palmer tried to sound reassuring, but Peter hedged.

"I don't think we should take any additional risks," he said.

"Sir," it was about time I added my two cents, "it's the best chance we have to get Catherine back, unless you have some hidden accounts with the full two million dollars."

"We don't have that kind of money," Peter screeched,

and no one said a word as he and Evelyn exchanged a few meaningful glances. "Send your agents, but don't screw this up."

A couple hours later, Palmer and I were at FBI HQ with a tactical unit. He reviewed the plan and made sure the UCs knew where to stand and how to appear inconspicuous. The tactical team was leaving now to station themselves on the roof of a nearby building. Hopefully, the snipers were excellent shots. Since the exchange was to occur at a pier, there weren't many vantage points, and while the road could be covered, if the kidnappers traveled by boat, our chances to stop them were slim, just like the ground cover.

"We're pushing too hard," I sighed. The room had grown silent as logistics were worked out, and at the sound of my words, every face turned to me. "Peter and Evelyn don't want us to do this."

"It needs to be done," Palmer insisted. "You used to be on the job. You know how this goes."

"I've never done this job." My tone was heated. "O'Connell was afraid of this. God, what have I caused?" The agents went back to business as Palmer stared wide-eyed.

"I would say *there's the door* but the family requested you. So we're all stuck following your lead."

"Fine. Do what you do best, and to paraphrase Peter, don't fuck it up. I'll be at the rendezvous point in plenty of time." I left the office, dialing Thompson as I ran down the steps to avoid the elevator's dead zone.

After giving him every last detail, he let out a sigh. "Jablonsky gave us everything he had, but he's been called away. Heathcliff and I have been sorting through Interpol records and databases. We're waiting for the Polizei to fax over some files on a similar situation. We have a possible suspect, but without their files, it's too soon to tell."

"Do you have a translator if everything comes over the wire in German?" I turned the key in the ignition and backed out of the garage, heading for the precinct.

"Ja," Thompson attempted to joke. "Are you on your way?"

"Yes. See you in ten."

The day's events and my words to Winter kept replaying through my mind as I made the short drive from HQ to the precinct. Parking out back, I rubbed my hands over my face and prayed the cops received something useful from Interpol and their due diligence. Palmer was a pro, and he'd been working negotiations for years, but until I sat in the conference room while he went over the plan, I didn't understand O'Connell's reticence. There was a reason he didn't want the authorities involved. Too many risks. Too many guns. And statistically speaking, too low a percentage for a possible positive outcome.

Before I opened the door to the major crimes unit, angry, frustrated words traveled to the stairwell. "Who the hell would think a fucking vegetable could be a viable suspect?" Heathcliff growled, throwing the folder across the room as paper scattered everywhere. I opened the door and glanced down at the pieces of the Polizei's report, strewn across the floor.

"Goddammit," I swore.

"Our solid lead attempted to blow his brains out. He's been in a mental institution in Prague for the last two years." Thompson was the only calm one among us. How he was calm, I didn't know.

Heathcliff fumed silently, pacing the bullpen and shoving every single chair under the desks, even if they were already pushed in. "We're back to square one." He took a seat and banged away at the keyboard. "Unless one of you can pull a miracle out of your ass, we won't make the seven a.m. time crunch."

"Let's regroup." Thompson leaned back in his chair and considered our options. "They were in that warehouse. No one can be that meticulous. They must have left something behind. A print. A hair. A piece of paper or a friggin' napkin from a fast food joint. Something." He scooted the chair back and stood. "I'm going downstairs to forensics. Something's gotta track. It has to." Without waiting for any acknowledgement, he was out the door, leaving Heathcliff and me alone in the empty bullpen.

Sitting down, I supplied a rundown of the FBI plan. He

listened as he continued searching every criminal database known to man. When I was done, he shot a look in my direction.

"Parker, when I implied this was on you, it's not. This is on these sick motherfuckers who messed with the wrong cops. No matter what happens tomorrow, this is not your fault." He witnessed firsthand what a guilty conscious and failed rescue attempt could lead to after his previous partner killed herself when an abduction case went south.

"Derek," I swallowed, "I threatened to kill him, Winter, the ringleader or whatever you want to call him. I lost my cool. He wants two million, and they don't have it. He wouldn't negotiate."

"So you did what you always do." He chuckled. "It's about damn time someone put these assholes in their place."

"What if," my voice caught in my throat, and I blinked my insecurities away.

"No reason to play the what if game now. If," he met my eyes, "it happens, then I will help you bury them."

I nodded, unable to speak. The possibility was unimaginable which was mind-blowing in and of itself. I didn't know Catherine. Until a few days ago, I didn't know Evelyn or Peter, but it didn't matter. The thought of that little girl in the picture not coming back was beyond my comprehension.

Thompson spent the rest of the night downstairs, driving the forensic techs crazy. There were a few fibers, some partial prints, and a bag of garbage that contained a couple takeout containers. They were being tested for DNA, but that type of analysis took weeks to complete. The partial prints were being run through IAFIS, but so far, not a single hit had come through. Maybe they were too damaged, or the son of a bitch was never fingerprinted before.

"It's time to go." An FBI agent entered and handed me the two hundred thousand dollars that the Cales compiled during the course of the night. After signing the proper documentation, he left without a word. I looked at the clock on the wall. In an hour and a half, I might be confronting Winter and bringing Catherine home. "Whatever happens," I searched Heathcliff's face, "I'm not sure what else I should have done."

"You've done everything you can. The rest isn't up to you."

I bit my lip and looked away. "Just remember that when O'Connell asks."

"Alexis," he adopted a soothing tone, "call me when it's over."

I drove to the pier. The sun had just emerged over the horizon, and it bathed everything in a harsh glare. Parking my car, I dialed Palmer and made sure all the teams were out of sight and in place. As I waited a few minutes, I noticed some people unloading cargo and a few fishermen heading toward the marina. This didn't look like a place where a kidnapping exchange would occur.

Inhaling, I reached for the briefcase and strolled to pier nineteen. The area was abandoned, except for some seagulls circling overhead. I continued across the unsteady wooden planks. The slip was empty. No boats were docked nearby, and there was no foot traffic. At the end of the pier, the wooden boards were covered in a wet, sticky substance. Blood. The pool of blood stretched the width of the boards and ran down the sides. The water below was tinged red. Nailed to the dock was a piece of paper with my name.

Unfolding the paper, I read: *You were willing to pay a tenth of the ransom, so here's a tenth of the girl.*

EIGHTEEN .

"There's no body," Palmer pointed out. "You cannot jump to the conclusion she's dead."

"Look at the blood," I screamed. "All that blood." I screwed my eyes shut. "No one survives that amount of blood loss. The body's probably at the bottom of the ocean by now."

Sirens were approaching from the distance. The pier had been roped off, and the FBI and PD were sending in units to scour the area. No one had any idea when the blood was left. The tactical team on the roof didn't notice anything suspicious or see anyone near the pier.

"From the coagulation, I'd say it was still fresh when you got here. Maybe an hour before you arrived," one of the blood specialists offered. "Looks to be about three and a half, maybe four, pints. Hard to say how much of it went into the drink."

"Parker," Heathcliff said my name and grabbed my arm, spinning me away from the pool of red, "are you okay?"

"She's dead. She must be dead."

"We don't know if it's hers. We don't even know if it's human. It could be an elaborate joke or something," he offered. "Go home. Go anywhere. Just get out of here. You don't need to stay any longer. You've been staring at that for hours."

"Has anyone told Evelyn?" I asked, ignoring his suggestion. "What about O'Connell?"

"Don't you dare go near them. There's no reason to freak anyone else out when we don't know anything yet."

I let out an incredulous sound. "We know more than we want to."

"Get the hell out of here, Parker," he ordered. "I'll check on you later. Stay safe."

"Fine." I performed a final three-sixty of the area and went to my car. Standing around wasn't helping anyone. I couldn't go home. I couldn't go to the Cales or O'Connell. The authorities were investigating everything they could think of, so I dialed Mercer as I maneuvered through the streets, searching for nonexistent leads. There was no answer and no option to leave a voicemail.

I felt numb. My mind was fragmented in so many directions it was a wonder I managed to get to my office in one piece. Rational thought didn't hit until I was unlocking my office door. On autopilot, I checked the messages, discarded the junk mail, and stared at the walls. I needed to search for the bastards responsible. But right now, I couldn't focus. I was hollow and tired from being up longer than I could recall. Locking up, I headed for home but somehow ended up at the MT building.

"Miss Parker?" Jeffrey was stupefied by my appearance. "Is everything okay?" I didn't acknowledge him; instead, I ended up knocking on Guillot's door.

"Alexis?" His expression read alarm.

"Sorry, I must have my days confused and thought it was casual Friday." I noticed my jeans, my gun still in its holster at my side, and my leather jacket barely concealing this fact. "I need to do something. I have to focus on work." My eyes searched his face imploringly. "Anything. I don't care what it is. I just need to do something."

He pressed his lips together in thought. What felt like a century later, he went to the filing cabinet, pulled out a dozen folders, and handed them to me. "We're considering hiring a computer specialist to safeguard against electronic threats. Figure out the kinds of qualifications our applicant pool should have and send it over to HR."

"Yes, sir." Turning on my heel, I went to my office in an attempt to drown myself in this new project. Anything to keep my mind off the blood. Off the broken promises. Off Catherine. Off my guilt and the role I played in all of it.

A few hours later, there was nothing left to do. I even went so far as to break down the potential qualifications into required, recommended, and preferential. Everything was typed, rewritten, printed, modified, and retyped. After passing the report off to HR and a copy to Guillot, who looked surprised and still somewhat frightened, I sat behind my desk, staring at my cell phone. Someone would have called if they knew anything definitive. I should be tracking these motherfuckers at this very moment, but I knew I was compromised. Lack of sleep, lack of emotional detachment, and my one-sighted focus would hurt any real progress. It was too close.

After sleeping on it, things would be better. I would gain perspective, insight, and calm. But right now, the possibility for sleep didn't exist. I was frenzied. Frantic. Glancing down, I noticed my leg jittering up and down and my hand drumming against the desk. What time was it? It was a little after three, and sitting in this room a second longer would drive me out of my mind. I was halfway to the elevator when Martin came down the hallway.

"Alex," his tone came close to reducing me to a puddle on the floor, "my god." He put an arm around my shoulders and ushered me into his office, changing the clear glass to opaque for privacy.

"I can't do this right now." I pulled away from him. "I need something to do. I need to get out of my head. I didn't come here to see you. I was working. Trying to work. Guillot had a project, but I finished it. Now there's nothing left." The pool of blood on the pier resurfaced. "Nothing left," I repeated quietly. I feared I might be insane. What about Nick, Evelyn, and Peter?

Martin searched my face. He knew he was five steps behind, but he could let it go. "You need to burn off the nervous energy. Something to occupy your time for the immediate future," he surmised.

"Yes," I pleaded. "Something that will keep my mind engaged."

He frowned and took a seat at his desk, rummaging through the top drawer. "This is such a bad idea," he mumbled, pulling out a business card. "Francesca was here the other day, at the office, not my house. She's COO at Hover Designs. They've recently employed a management consulting team to review the company practices, and now they have a leak. She was hoping, since we've just streamlined our security protocols, that I'd have some helpful hints or a few names she could consider. I was going to ask Mark for suggestions, but if you want it, it's yours." I lunged for her business card.

"I'm not sure, but if she'll take a meeting now, at least it's something to consider. It'll give me something to do in the interim." I was halfway to the door when Martin stopped me.

"Don't sell out all of my company secrets or our bedroom antics." It was a joke, but I hesitated.

"Martin, the other night, I'm sorry. I was angry with myself, and I lashed out at you. It wasn't right. Are you sure it's okay if I start bumbling around in your past?" This was uncharacteristic, especially under the circumstances, but I felt I needed to rectify every negative situation I created, even this one. Karma might be a bitch, but I needed her on my side.

"Hopefully, it'll be business and not pleasure you discuss," he offered a grin, "but, at this moment, I'll do anything to get that morose look off your face." He hesitated, and in the silence, I knew he understood what led to my erratic behavior. "Give Francesca a call. It's late enough to assume she's finished with her meetings today."

"Thank you." Before I made it to the lobby, I dialed her number, and she gave me her room number. Anything to avoid reality for a while longer.

*   *   *

The meeting with Martin's ex-fiancée was brief. We

both managed to remain professional and courteous. Francesca provided a preliminary breakdown of the situation, a few names to consider, and the management consultant team they hired. Her hope was the leak was from the outsiders and not from someone on the inside. At least I had the sense to apologize for my rude behavior the other night. Graciously, she accepted my apology and held her tongue as far as asking what led to the outburst or my relationship with her no longer intended.

An hour later, I found my equilibrium and was no longer in attack mode. Stepping foot inside my apartment, I locked the doors, took off my shoulder holster, and went to bed. Fighting away the initial waves of indelible images of the bloody pier and the conversation I had the night before with Winter, I managed to have a few hours of dreamless sleep.

The incessant pounding at my door roused me, and I climbed out of bed to answer. Thompson met my eyes and, without waiting for an invitation, briskly walked to my table, dropped a thick tome of file folders on top, and pulled out a chair.

"You're not supposed to be on this. Word leaked, no thanks to the fucking numbnut agents at the Cales' place. They've thrown all of us out, especially you. O'Connell got word. He went there to salvage whatever's left of the situation. I've never seen him so fucking pissed before. Jen wants to shoot him up with elephant tranquilizers." He opened a large manila folder and spread the paperwork over my table. "None of this came from me. Moretti'd be so far down my throat that he'd pop out my ass."

I continued to stand at my front door, frozen as the words swam around in my brain. "Has it become official?" I squeaked.

"Nothing yet. They're testing the evidence now. Blood type matches," he kept talking as if it were just another case and not his partner's niece, "but the blood specialist thinks there might be something off. They're running tests now, and you know how long DNA takes to verify. Without a body, the department's not considering it a homicide."

"But you are."

"So are you," he snapped. My jaw clenched, and I remained silent. "Look, Parker, we don't always see eye to eye on things. O'Connell doesn't want you anywhere near this, and normally, I'd defer to my partner. But these are special circumstances. The feds are looking into whatever they can, but you've been blacklisted everywhere. We want to run this off the books and out of your apartment." He met my eyes. "Do you have a problem with that?"

"We?"

"Heathcliff and I." He still had the same defiant look. "Between the three of us, there's no chance these assholes are getting away with it. So are you in or not?"

"Tell me where to start."

NINETEEN

I sat with my head in my hand, staring at the pages in front of me. We had exploited all of our resources and still had little to show for our hard work. Interpol files and police reports were translated from half a dozen different languages and three different continents, but we still weren't any closer to determining who the kidnappers were. Heathcliff showed up after midnight, and the three of us went over everything with a fine tooth comb. Julian Mercer had yet to return or acknowledge any of the dozen phone calls I placed to him. The USB drive he provided did little except cast doubts on the Seasons' current whereabouts, all of which proved to be dead ends.

"The two of you got this?" Thompson asked, standing and stretching. None of us had moved in hours. "I have to be back at work in four hours, and maybe I can fit in a couple hours of sleep before then."

"Go," Heathcliff told him, still clicking through the files on the USB drive. "If you hear the investigation is moving, give us a call."

"Night, Thompson," I called as he let himself out. Leaning back in my chair, I stared at the ceiling and blew out a breath.

"We're chasing ghosts," Heathcliff announced. He was fed up with the search, and so was I. "Whoever took the briefcase at the bus stop was invisible. He must be Harry fucking Houdini. The surveillance from the school and the museum fail to show anyone suspicious. How did they dodge all the cameras?"

"They cased the place."

"We have footage from two weeks before the abduction, and there isn't any indication of that either."

"Inside job?"

"Okay," he picked up a pen and scribbled some notes, "who?"

"Don't you think we'd be kicking in some doors right now if I knew?" Bitchy and surly were vying for top position in my vocal cords.

"Just take a minute, regroup, and think." This was not the time for him to be at peace with the universe. It further irritated me, and I got up from the kitchen table and stomped across the expanse to my living room and flopped onto the couch. "Gut instincts, Parker. Let's hear 'em."

"Field trips have chaperones. How'd they not notice losing three of their charges?" This fact frustrated me since the beginning. "The museum curator or director or whoever the hell he is, Jeremy something, was very accommodating. Too accommodating?"

"Tolbert, Jeremy, museum director," he read from the compiled information.

"When I questioned him, he said a detective had been there earlier."

"Who?"

"Stop impersonating a freakin' owl," I snapped.

"Who? Who?" I glared, getting up from the couch to pace, but he let out a chuckle and defused the tension.

"My guess is it was Mercer. Do you want to take a ride to his apartment and see if we can get the bastard to talk to us in person?"

"We have eyes on the rental. He's not there. Taylor said she'd let me know as soon as there are signs of movement." Heathcliff paused and dropped his pen. "Could it be Mercer? Maybe he could conduct a perfect kidnapping.

What do we actually know about him?"

"I don't know. He responded to the hostage calls the Estes family received, but that doesn't mean he's not one of the men responsible. The two men I saw at the hangar might be part of his team." I slammed my palm against the countertop. "Why the hell didn't I do something when I had the chance?"

"You couldn't risk Catherine's safety. Compromising the situation is the first major no-no in hostage negotiation."

"Because losing your cool and threatening the abductor is perfectly acceptable." I kicked the base of the island in my kitchen. "Dammit." I pinched the bridge of my nose and shut my eyes.

"Mercer," he spoke forcefully to make me focus, "do we have a file on him?"

"It's a bunch of redacted bullshit." I picked it out of the Interpol files and handed it to him. "Ex-military. Private kidnapping and negotiation specialist, meaning a professional cleaner."

"Probably. Why would a resolution specialist get involved in kidnapping schemes? He's already getting enough work, negotiating problems away or sweeping the remnants of the problems under the rug."

"You're right. He's too controlled to get involved in such an uncertain business venture."

Picking up my phone, I dialed my contact at Interpol, Agent Farrell, and requested all information pertaining to Bastian, Donovan, and Hans be sent over to my apartment. Farrell would have preferred to have a first and last name, instead of just three names which could theoretically be either or nothing more than nicknames, but he promised to do his best. Why he was still at work in the middle of the night was beyond me, but I wasn't complaining.

"Four Seasons. Four team members." Heathcliff tapped his pointer fingers against the table to a slow drumming rhythm. "Think they could be the B-team. Maybe another ex-SAS group who didn't find the K&R industry as lucrative as Mercer?"

"Maybe. Or they're the Four Horsemen or the Four Tenors. Somehow, I don't think the number is worthy of speculation in and of itself. We need a break. The speculation is getting the best of us."

"You're right. I've been going nonstop for more than twenty-four hours."

"Derek, if word comes in, give me a call. If not, come back whenever you're rested and refreshed." I dug the spare key out of my kitchen drawer and handed it to him. "In case I'm not here, let yourself in."

"Where else would you be?"

"Who knows? Maybe trying to get out of my head by working some corporate espionage thing."

"Only you would find work a valid means to calm your panic." He shook his head. "Damn workaholics. Is it something for Martin?"

"No," I snorted cynically, "his ex-fiancée."

"Ouch." I walked Heathcliff to the door. "That can't be good."

"I've already made a complete ass of myself, so at this point, I doubt I could do much more harm."

"That's the spirit. I'll be back in a few hours. If you need anything between now and then, I'll keep my phone on."

Tossing a disgusted look at the paperwork littering my kitchen table, I went into the bedroom and planned to sleep until the sun came up. Instead, I stared at the ceiling and ran through every detail since the initial phone call O'Connell made while I was at the conference. No matter how I looked at it, it read like an inside job. Either someone from the school or someone from the museum must have orchestrated the abductions. We needed financial records and phone records in order to narrow our suspect list, but obviously, this would be a fishing expedition. No judge would grant such a sweeping warrant. When Thompson said we were operating off the books, he wasn't kidding.

Giving up on sleep, I played the security cam footage from the school and re-watched the museum feed to see who surfaced on both tapes. Faces without names weren't helping matters either. Everything was overwhelmingly daunting. Resisting the urge to hide under the bed, I froze the feed, enhanced the image, and printed out everyone's face. With my pile of photos, I searched through all the illegally obtained school information I had and eventually ended up on the school's website. Every employee had a photo on the website, and I began adding names to faces.

It was noon by the time I finished. Utilizing the largest empty wall in my living room, I pinned everything up. It would be more easily accessible, spread out and organized, instead of sitting in uncategorized piles on my table. Whenever we located these rat bastards, I'd have to spackle and repaint my wall, but that was a small price to pay for getting retribution for Catherine. Maybe it was revenge or justice. Words like this were in the eye of the beholder. The realization that I wasn't sure what I would do or what Thompson or Heathcliff would do once we found them sent chills down my spine. We weren't murderers. I had taken lives in the line of duty, but to kill someone in cold-blood was always unimaginable. But was it really cold-blooded when these kidnappers killed an innocent little girl, maybe two?

"Knock, knock," Heathcliff called from my front door, shaking the moral issues from my brain. "I brought breakfast." Looking at the time, I lost over six hours on my project and still felt as if I wasn't any closer to a real lead.

"It's about damn time," I teased, grabbing the bag of donuts from his hand. "Wow, real cop food. What more could I ask for?"

"Goddamn, Parker, have you been at this since I left?" He gestured to the wall. "Make any headway?"

"No." I poured two cups of coffee and stood next to him as he scanned the material. "All I've done is match some names with faces, and they're probably all squeaky clean, upstanding members of the community."

"Let's hope not." He dug into the donut bag and pulled out a jelly, biting into it as thoughts worked their way through his mind. "We're doing this wrong."

"No shit, but what's right?"

"We need O'Connell. He's bound to know more than any of us. He was around from the beginning. His sis would have told him a lot more than she told any of us."

"Except he's in no condition to work, and he isn't

speaking to me."

"It's worth a try, isn't it?" Heathcliff picked up his phone and dialed O'Connell. I made an excuse that I needed a break and pulled out some clean clothes and locked myself in the bathroom.

Thirty minutes later, I emerged with my hair still wet and makeup covering the dark circles under my eyes. Heathcliff added additional information to my wall and pulled down a few people he didn't believe could be involved. How he made those judgment calls, I didn't know. But it didn't matter. He was good at his job, and whatever sound reasoning he had was good enough for me.

"Did you talk to Nick?" I asked.

"He's on his way." He was at my kitchen table, sifting through all the possible links to the Four Seasons. "He wants to talk to you." The way Heathcliff said it made me consider leaving and not coming back. Ten minutes later, my doorbell rang.

"Here goes nothing," I said, opening the door.

TWENTY

"What the hell were you thinking?" O'Connell screamed as soon as the door opened. "What the hell was *I* thinking?"

"Good morning to you too." Flippant wasn't the way to go, but then again, most of the things that came out of my mouth didn't need to be said.

"I never should have trusted you. I must have hit my head on the fucking concrete or had a goddamn aneurysm to think asking for your help was a good idea." He continued to yell as he stormed into my apartment and forced me back against the far wall.

"Hey, man, take it easy," Heathcliff was standing close by, prepared to intercede if O'Connell tried to physically harm me.

"Take it easy?" He spun toward Heathcliff. "Did you hear the recording?" He turned back to me, slamming his fist into the wall for emphasis. "Why the hell didn't you just tell the bastard to go fuck himself while you were at it?"

"I'm sorry," I said quietly, resisting the urge to argue. This was my fault, and Nick was justifiably angry. There was no reason to add fuel to the fire. "But I'm not a negotiator. I never was a negotiator. I tried," my voice shook with fury and sorrow, "but he wouldn't budge. There was no two million. What did you want me to do?"

"Anything else," he snarled. "How could you do this? How could you let this happen?"

"C'mon, O'Connell, you know this isn't on Parker." Heathcliff must have decided someone needed to defend me since I was letting the endless barrage continue.

"Stay away. Stay away from me. Stay away from my family. We're done. You got that?" he growled before taking a step back. He stalked toward my door before turning the confrontation to Heathcliff. "Don't worry. Parker's far too fond of herself to become suicidal like your last partner. It's a perk of being a heartless bitch. It doesn't matter to her if a child gets killed or not. My suggestion, stay the hell away. Everyone close to her gets hurt or worse." My front door slammed shut, and I locked my jaw. I was torn between two obvious courses of action, property destruction and crying. Instead, I inhaled and counted to ten.

"Are you okay?" Heathcliff asked. I nodded but remained silent. "The things he said, this isn't your fault."

"Eh," I shrugged my shoulders, having put my game face on, "no skin off my nose. All perks of being a heartless bitch. Sticks and stones, my friend. Sticks and stones." I smirked, but he wasn't convinced by my bravado. "Y'know, considering how helpful that little encounter was, Nick could have just called and left an ugly voicemail, instead of wasting gas on the drive here. Someone should teach him to have more respect for the planet and carbon emissions." Cracking jokes was my go-to response, but every word he uttered cut deeper than I thought imaginable. He was right, maybe about everything.

"Well, that lead turned into a complete bust," Heathcliff muttered. He held up the half empty bottle of bourbon that was still on my counter. "Do you want to drink to another dead end?"

"No, I'm okay."

He turned his attention to the digital clock on my stove. "Weren't you supposed to be digging yourself into a hole on a corporate gig?"

"But that would mean I'd have to dig myself out of this one first." My eyes narrowed. "Are you kicking me out of my own apartment, Detective?"

"Yes." He held my gaze. "I know you well enough to know you'll let all that bullshit O'Connell was spewing get into your head, and it will impair your deductive skills. Get out of here for an hour or two and do something else."

"Fine." I picked up my jacket, wanting to be away from the reverberating accusations that were bouncing off my skull. "I'll just take out some of this pent-up anguish on Francesca."

"Hell of a name."

"With a personality to match. When I get locked up, you might as well leave me there to rot. It'd be the best thing for everyone concerned."

"Alexis," he looked apologetic, "when Nick cools down, he's going to regret everything he said. Hell, I'm sorry for him."

"Yeah, yeah. If you hear something between now and the time I get back, call me."

Grabbing the bare minimum, I left my apartment. I really didn't want to meet with Francesca again, but everything I wanted to do led straight back to O'Connell. Unfortunately, Heathcliff was right. I needed to distance myself from the accusations.

*   *   *

"Ms. Pirelli," I knocked on the door to her suite. Thirty seconds later, the door opened.

"Ms. Parker, do come in," she stepped into the room, and I shut the door behind me. "I wasn't sure if you would be willing to look into the matter for Hover Designs or if you were simply going to let my issues fall to the wayside."

"To be honest, ma'am," calling her ma'am was business appropriate, but in my mind, it was a total insult, "I'm spread a little thin right now. If you want this resolved imminently, it would be best for you to go elsewhere."

Francesca stretched out on the couch and tapped her perfectly manicured fingernails on the end table. "Jamie's only had the nicest things to say about you." Her eyes narrowed, and the statement seemed like a challenge or possibly a threat. "Clearly, his business sense and professional opinions should not be ignored. He has an empire after all." Her expression betrayed her, and I could see the regret she felt for letting him get away. It seemed best to remain silent unless an actual question was posed. "How old are you?"

"Excuse me?"

"Fine, I'll ask it another way. How much experience do you have as a security consultant?"

"I've been employed by Martin Technologies for a year and a half. Prior to that, I was a federal agent for close to five." She gestured to the chair across from her. Apparently, my responses warranted the privilege of sitting in the same room as the amazing Francesca Pirelli, COO of Hover Designs.

"I don't want anyone at the company to know what's going on. If there is a leak, gossip will spread like wildfire and the culprit could cover their tracks or point the finger at someone else. Do you think with access to the files, the leaked information, and the internal computer systems you could locate the individual responsible quickly and quietly?"

"There is no guarantee, but honestly, I won't know until I have a chance to look into it. I thought you were under the impression the management consulting firm was responsible for the leaks."

She tilted her chin up and stared down at me. "Ah, it seems Jamie has let on more than I thought he would."

"Mr. Martin prefers to clue his employees in on the whole picture. Bits and pieces result in incorrect conclusions or miscommunications."

She laughed and shook her head. "Sorry, it's just the way you characterize him. He's not the same man I once knew. In B-school, he studied hard and played hard, but to get a straight answer out of him about anything was like pulling teeth." She stared off into the distance, remembering some long-forgotten detail. "C'est la vie, right? Back then, he was so conflicted. I always imagined he'd be that guy, the statistic, the one that graduates top of his class and everyone thinks he'll become something, but ten years later, he's living out of a cardboard box. If only I had been psychic."

I remained silent. The reason I was in her hotel suite wasn't to listen to her go on about how she wished she was still with Martin. "Shall I look into the management team first? Or would you prefer I start with an internal review of your personnel, system, and files?"

"Alexis," she paused, "you don't mind if I call you Alexis, do you?"

"It's my name." Bitch.

"Alexis," she smiled, "I'll give you whatever you need, but you can start anywhere you like. If Jamie trusts that you know what you're doing, then so will I."

"Very good, ma'am. If you could have the information on the management consultants forwarded to me, I would like to begin there. They seem the most likely cause of the breach. In the event that is a dead end, then I will require access to more sensitive internal information." I gave her my card. "Is there anything else?"

"Not at the moment." She showed me to the door. "The files will be sent to you tonight. I will be in town for the next week and a half. Hopefully, this will all be fixed before I fly home." Don't forget your broom.

*   *   *

On my way home, I detoured to the OIO. Being persona non grata with the PD and FBI likely meant I would also be shunned by my former brethren, but to my surprise, I was greeted amicably by the Interpol liaison, Patrick Farrell.

"What can I do for you?" he asked.

"I was in the neighborhood and thought I'd see if you found anything on those names I gave you." He scooted a few photocopies across the desk. "Also, I have one last favor."

"Shoot."

"Someone at Interpol pulled my file a couple of days ago. Any way of finding out who it was?"

"I can do some digging, but our offices are worldwide. Maybe I can call some of the IT security personnel and have them check, but if it was the physical dossier, there's no way of knowing." He scrutinized my expression. "Are you afraid there's been a breach?"

"No. Nothing like that." I shook my head and told him everything I knew about Mercer. "If I can figure out who he contacted, maybe I can get some more information on the jackass."

"I'll do what I can but don't hold your breath."

Checking the time, I needed to get back to work. Heathcliff was alone in my apartment, possibly raiding my panty drawer. I just parked my car when my phone rang.

"Parker, the blood report came back." Thompson was practically giddy. "It was leukoreduced."

"Thompson, speak English."

"It was donor blood." I leaned my head back and took a deep breath. "Catherine might still be alive." When his proclamation was met with silence, he asked, "Parker, are you still there?"

"Yes." I couldn't think to put a sentence together. She might be alive, and if she was, then we had to find her. "O'Connell?" Luckily, my one word question was understood.

"He knows. He's staying at his sister's in case the kidnappers call back with a new demand."

"It doesn't mean," I couldn't bring myself to say the rest of the sentence. "Um...now what?"

"Now we work that much harder to find these assholes."

TWENTY-ONE

Inside my apartment, Heathcliff and I restarted the investigation. With the possibility that Catherine was alive, anything or anyone could lead to her location. Although, my subconscious was being a pessimist. Just because the blood wasn't Catherine's, it didn't mean she wasn't dead. Why would the Four Seasons leave a note basically solidifying that fact if they were still planning on cashing in on their third hostage? Maybe it was just to dramatize her death. Perhaps they couldn't risk us finding the body when they still had the Estes family on the hook for four million, possibly in unrefined gold ore.

I felt Heathcliff's hand on my shoulder, and I looked up. My eyes were closed, and my face was in my hands as I tried to force myself to be positive. Clearly, I was failing miserably. "I thought you were going to clear your head. Is this self-pity, or are you actually thinking about something useful?"

"Why did they leave the note? The blood was scary enough. Was it supposed to conceal the actual location of the body?" My stomach flip-flopped, and I was suddenly nauseous.

"Don't make me kick you out of your own apartment

again," he warned. "Let's not focus on the why. We have two more important and pressing questions to answer. Who and where."

"You and the damn owls," I bitched. "All this 'who' crap. Sheesh. But our who is some douchebag who refers to himself as Winter and the rest of his team, affectionately dubbed the Four Seasons. Maybe he thinks the name is apropos since he tends to send a chill through my veins."

"Funny. Okay, so we have a pseudonym for the who. Any clue as to where?"

"We've been through this a hundred times. A warehouse, the wharf, an airstrip, some storage units. Who the hell knows?"

"We're still going about this wrong." He went to the wall and rearranged some of the notes we pinned up. He was muttering to himself as he reworked half our notations. "Three children are missing from a school field trip." He was facing the wall but speaking out loud. I wasn't sure if it was to me or himself. "Normally, we'd try to find the connection. Why these three? Why then? But we can see the connection. They were all from the same school and all together on a field trip. The kidnapping could have been convenience or opportunity. Maybe it would have been a different group of kids or one or two, instead of three. Who knows? Who the fuck cares?"

Maybe I wasn't the only one losing it. He continued to ramble as I skimmed through the paperwork Farrell provided on Bastian, Hans, and Donovan. Nothing important was listed. They may or may not have been on the same SAS team as Mercer. It was merely more redactions and a brief physical description of each man. The Brits really knew how to protect the identities of their assets.

"Someone at the school is responsible," his determination drew my attention. "No one was staking out the museum, waiting for an opportunity. We don't even see the girls on the security cam footage. They weren't taken because they were at the museum. They were taken because someone knew where they would be."

"Holy shit." I put the disk containing the museum

footage into my computer and let it play through. "They weren't taken from the museum."

"No?" His eyes brightened as understanding dawned on him. "They were taken from the school, but how did we miss this?"

"Mercer said it. The Estes family told him the girls were taken from the museum. I ran through the school footage and didn't see anything. We watched the museum footage and still nothing. But the school makes more sense since the chaperones didn't realize the headcount was off."

"It wasn't off since they were never there. We need to talk to the teacher," he surmised.

As Heathcliff made a few phone calls, I let the wheels turn inside my brain. The girls were supposed to be going on a field trip. It required them to arrive at school, turn in permission slips, and then board the bus which would take them to the museum. Whoever grabbed them had to time it just right, so the school officials wouldn't notice when they went missing and not be suspicious when they didn't go on the field trip.

"I have a meeting with the principal and their primary teacher set for 3:30. Do you want to come?" Heathcliff asked, jolting me from my thought process. I had already been to the school once and didn't need to risk getting myself or Heathcliff into any more trouble.

"No," I met his eyes, "but I think I know how they were taken without anyone noticing. Someone must have discarded the permission slips and then abducted the girls after they arrived at school but before getting on the bus."

"Do you realize what that might mean?" I nodded. "Great, so a parent or teacher is responsible for this whole mess."

"I'd say the Seasons are pros, but an insider would be a useful accomplice. Maybe someone took a bribe to look the other way. I don't know, but teacher salaries are probably as shitty as cop salaries." I shrugged. "We need financials on everyone, and I can't get them. Hell, you can't either since Moretti is prohibiting you and Thompson from working this."

"It's for O'Connell. I'll pass it on to Thompson, and he'll

tell the detective in charge of the investigation to run with it."

"What are we doing in the meantime?" I hated being on the outside looking in. I hadn't worked any cases in months because I wanted distance from this life and this job, and at this particular moment, I would have given anything to be an official police consultant or even have my badge and job at the OIO back.

"Look," he stood up and put his jacket on, "I'm going to the precinct to see what I can find out. Then I'll head to the school for my appointment." He attempted a sly grin, but neither of us was in a pleasant enough mood for it to be convincing. "And whatever I discover I'll pass along to Thompson, and he'll run it by when his shift ends. I'm supposed to be back at work by six tonight, so I'll see you when I see you. Maybe you should call up some of your buddies and see if anyone is monitoring Mercer. Officer Taylor said they lost track of him, but wasn't there a federal agent tailing him?"

"I'll check." This was what we needed, a plan of attack. "If anything urgent surfaces," there was still the very likely possibility Catherine's body would be discovered, "call. If not, I'll try to find Mercer. I wish the Cales didn't cut our access. Hell, even the Estes family could be helpful if they were willing to cooperate."

"Maybe Thompson can smooth the waters and with a bit of coaxing get us back in the Cales' good graces. Meanwhile, you and I are both on Nick's shit list, so we'll give him plenty of space until he cools down. Got it?" His suggestion sounded a little like a threat.

"You don't have to lump yourself in with me. You could easily go see O'Connell, complain about what a conniving, self-righteous bitch I am, and I'm sure you'd be his best friend."

"Well, then maybe I don't want to deal with him right now." I saw the anger in his eyes, and I knew it was because of what Nick said about Derek's old partner. Some wounds never heal; they just stop bleeding until someone rips into them again.

After Derek left, I studied the wall for another couple of

minutes. I knew we were right. The girls were abducted before they went on their field trip, and the person responsible was either a parent or school official. Neither of these possibilities restored any faith I lost in the human race. Calling this the civilized world was a joke.

Dialing the OIO, I waited as the call was shuffled around from person to person until I got a final negative response. Mercer eluded his tail. We were blind. Sighing, I picked up my car keys, locked my apartment, and drove to Mercer's rental. I had no qualms about breaking in to determine if he changed locations. Luckily, I didn't have to go through all that trouble for an answer. As I pulled up, I spotted the rental car that Bastian and Donovan drove.

Knocking loudly on the door, I waited, but no one answered. I felt the hood of the SUV, but it was cold. Wherever they were, they hadn't been here in a while. "What the hell," I muttered, pulling out my lock picks. There was no reason why I couldn't make myself at home in the meantime.

I shut the door, turned on the lights, and physically checked for surveillance equipment and booby-traps. Mercer seemed to be just delusional enough to believe that someone would break in to his apartment to spy on him. I wondered if it was paranoia or pragmatism since I broke in for that particular reason but decided not to worry about it. All's fair in love and war, and while this probably wasn't either, this was a life or death situation. I just hoped the correct answer was life and not death. Catherine was so young. I shook the thoughts from my brain and perused the surveillance footage and documentation Mercer compiled.

The hours flew by, but I wasn't any closer to actual answers. The photos were all of similar looking locations. The maps marked hangar bays, warehouses, shipping yards, and the docks. It meant nothing. As I was getting ready to give up, I came across a file folder concerning the Estes family and Adalina.

"Did you want to test my conviction for putting a bullet through you?" Mercer asked. His Sig was out and pointed at me.

"Where have you been?" I didn't react to the firearm as I continued to read as much of the file as I could, knowing Mercer would confiscate it as soon as possible.

"Get out."

"Aww, let her stay." I heard Bastian yell from the next room. "She makes you so much more fun to be around."

"I went to the drop. Before I even had a chance to leave the money," I put the folder down and stared at him, searching for an ounce of compassion, "the pier was painted red in blood. The police don't believe it's hers, but there's been no communication since. She's dead, isn't she?" I felt my chin tremble, and I locked my jaw in place to hide any signs of weakness. He was not a person to show weakness to.

"Perhaps." Everything about him remained unyielding.

"What do I do?"

"Leave."

I stood up, not sure if my aggression would remain contained long enough to walk past him without laying a hand on him. "Did you get the Estes girl back?" My voice remained low, cold, and detached.

"Not yet. Negotiations are still being made." He jerked his gun toward the door. "Out."

"Funny," I sounded cynical, "for someone so set on being a huge pain in my ass, you're doing an awful lot of talking."

"He's a pain in everyone's arse," Bastian offered as I went into the next room. "Here's the thing, love. We have proof of life but nothing else. After your blunder, the Estes family changed the play."

"Bastian," Mercer snarled, "silence."

"Pish," Bastian was either ballsy or stupid, "you don't know where they are or what they want either. Why not work with the Yanks to figure this out, especially the leggy ones."

Mercer opened the front door. His gun was still unholstered and pointed in my general direction. "You need to learn to listen. Next time, I won't be so nice."

"You still have my number. Just remember, we're on the same side. If you hear anything about Catherine, please," my voice betrayed my begging, and Mercer slammed the door in my face. Asshole.

TWENTY-TWO

By the time I got back to my apartment, Thompson was already there. I wasn't used to coming home to company, and he watched as I attempted to conceal my drawn weapon. Giving up, I put it on the counter.

"I went to see Mercer. He needs to work on sharing, but from what I gather, Adalina is still alive."

"Does he have any idea where the girls might be," Thompson asked. He said girls, which meant at least one of us was still holding out hope for a positive outcome. The only problem with being positive was the disappointment in being wrong.

"I don't think so. Although, he's not forthcoming. Did anything turn up for you or Heathcliff?"

"Moretti got wind of what we were doing." He rolled his eyes. "Needless to say, the Chief of Detectives had a nice chat with our department."

"Oh no."

"Yep," he gritted his teeth and jerked his head to the side as if he wanted to throw off an invisible shackle, "Jacobs is in charge of the investigation. Under no circumstances are we to investigate, snoop, or otherwise insinuate ourselves into the missing person's case."

"Missing person?" My mouth dropped. "Catherine Cale was kidnapped."

"No shit. But the PR is a nightmare, so until further notice, she's a missing person. The Cales want us out of their business. Nick's on sick leave. So we're painting a lovely, flowery, version of events." Before I could say anything else, Thompson pulled a pile of folded papers from his breast pocket and put them on my counter. "I'm going to see Jen. If anyone can talk some sense into my partner, it'd be her."

"Did Heathcliff tell you about this morning?"

He nodded as he continued toward my door. "Thanks for keeping your cool." He turned in the doorway. "Parker, you didn't deserve it." I nodded, even though I wasn't sure I agreed. "I'll stay as close to O'Connell as I can get. Maybe he'll divulge something or pave the way for me to talk to his sister. You and Derek fly under the radar and figure out who's on the inside."

After he left, I leaned against my front door and stared at the ceiling. No matter how much progress we were making, it wasn't enough. The clock was ticking or maybe time already ran out. Catherine had been gone for ten days. How much longer could she remain missing?

The paperwork Thompson provided was the financial information for faculty personnel. I was sure it had been illegally obtained, which meant in court proceedings it'd be fruit of the poisonous tree and the guilty party might get off scot-free. Fortunately, finding Catherine was a higher priority.

I was wrong to think the teachers' salaries were miniscule. It was a private school with private funding and large endowments. It seemed most of the faculty was well compensated. There were no suspicious bumps in anyone's personal accounts. Unless the money was in an offshore account, it didn't appear anyone took a payoff. However, money wasn't necessarily the only motivation for child abductions.

The majority of child abductions were committed by family members. Typically, it was a custody issue that would lead one spouse to take a child from the other.

Depending on how nasty the divorce or separation might be, sometimes outside family members would join in. But three girls were taken. This wasn't a normal abduction. This was a kidnapping and ransom. Professionals choreographed the demands, the money drops, the locations, everything. I was in the hangar. One of the Seasons had been a hundred feet away from me. Why didn't I do something?

This was on me. I slammed my palm on the counter hard enough to hurt. Perhaps I could have stopped it from getting to this point. The blood on the dock might never have happened. If I had done something different, Catherine might be at home now, instead of classified as missing. But I did nothing to stop the kidnappers when I had the chance. I pissed them off on the phone. I didn't negotiate properly. I didn't listen to what the Cales wanted, and now there was the strong possibility Catherine was dead. O'Connell was right.

Refusing to let the self-loathing completely derail me, I spent the entire night reading through the financial records and pulling up every public record I could find that might explain why someone would be willing to sell out three girls to a team of kidnappers. All roads led to nowhere. After going through the fifty-three school employees, I surmised financial incentive was not the reason for the abduction.

It was four a.m. when the flaw in my logic crashed through the forefront of my thoughts. I was analyzing the situation in reverse. The kidnappers didn't need to incentivize the insider. The insider had to get the kidnappers on board. Luckily, the hours of hard work weren't a complete waste of time since the financial records didn't show any large withdrawals either.

I needed sleep. I was making sloppy mistakes. I shut my lights, checked the lock on my door, leaving the security bar off so Heathcliff could get in whenever his shift was over, picked up my handgun which was next to me at the counter, stripped down to a t-shirt and shorts, and went to sleep.

As I lay tossing and turning and trying to silence my

thoughts, I realized the one glaring defect in all of it. Mercer fucked up worse than I did. He met the kidnappers, and the situation escalated into a firefight. Instead of sending him remnants of Adalina, the ransom was doubled. Why wouldn't they have tried a similar tactic with me and Catherine? Something was off. As I tried to unravel the mystery, I fell into unconsciousness.

Without opening my eyes, I could feel a presence hovering above. In one fluid motion, I flipped the uninvited guest onto the mattress, pinning him to the bed with one of my hands against his chest and the other holding my gun to his temple.

"You might want to reconsider," Mercer said, seemingly unfazed as he glanced down to the space between our bodies, and I noticed the muzzle of his Sig pressed against my ribs, "unless you think you can flip your safety and pull the trigger before I can fire. It's your call." He looked smug.

"What the hell are you doing here?" I growled. I wasn't lowering my weapon, and neither was he. I heard rustling come from the other room, followed by the sound of another gun being cocked behind me.

"Whoa," Bastian burst into my bedroom, insinuating himself between Donovan and my bed. "This isn't Mexico. Let's try to avoid a standoff."

"Too late," I muttered, releasing the pressure from Mercer's chest. Immediately, he flipped me onto my back and stared down at me. I wasn't entirely sure what he was thinking or if I wanted to know. Eventually, Bastian hauled him away, and without my view being impeded, I noticed Donovan had gone into my living room. Mercer tucked the Sig behind his back, and I lowered my gun, but it didn't leave my hand.

"Turnabout is fair play," Mercer muttered and went into the living room. "Get dressed. It's time we talk."

Bastian lingered behind, looking at me with something akin to an apology. "Ah, love, this might have been more fun if you were the negligee type, but at least it wasn't quite as embarrassing." He turned and followed Mercer into my living room.

For the brief amount of privacy I was afforded, I sent

Heathcliff an urgent text to get to my place. Then I went into the living room to see what the hell led to the early morning break-in.

"I told you to get dressed," Mercer commented. He was sitting on my couch, looking completely at ease. Donovan was studying the wall, and Bastian was familiarizing himself with my kitchen.

"What do you want?"

"Working with amateurs is not a high priority for me, but the Four Seasons are not behaving in a manner I am accustomed."

I snorted. "Are you asking for my help?" Mercer remained silent as he considered his options.

"Bloody hell," Bastian murmured, peeling an orange he had taken from my fridge, "we want to work together." Mercer turned an icy stare on him, but Bastian overlooked it as he came around the counter and sat on one of the stools. "Winter and the lot still have the Estes girl. Our boss is getting annoyed that things are taking so long, and we figured you might be able to shake things up."

"Will you tell me everything you know?" I looked at Mercer who was silently seething at Bastian.

"I'll tell you what you need to know," Mercer acquiesced.

"No." I was adamant. "You will tell me what I want to know. If I ask a question, I want the truth." Our staring match went on for what felt like minutes before he gave a curt nod. "Fine." I buried my resentment and anger as best I could. "Make yourselves at home while I get dressed."

My words were anything but cordial, but Bastian grinned and held up the remainder of the orange. "Cheers."

Quickly throwing on a pair of jeans and a different t-shirt, I went back out to my living room. Bastian was sniffing a carton of leftover Chinese in my fridge, and as far as I could tell, Mercer and Donovan hadn't moved.

"Do you mind, love?" Bastian asked, holding up the carton. I looked at him, bewildered, and shrugged. He found a fork and began eating.

"Is Catherine alive?" I leaned against the counter, my gun was in my shoulder holster, but the snap was opened for easier access just in case Mercer and I felt the need to engage in any more gunplay.

"I don't know." Mercer was the only one speaking, and I was sure that's the way he liked it.

"Do you think they would kill her? You defied them much more obviously than I did, but Adalina's alive. Right?"

"I don't know what they'd do."

"Then what do you want from me?"

"Throw them off balance," he said simply. "The next communication I receive, I'd like for you to answer."

"Not a good idea." I flashed back to my heated threat. "Do you want to get another girl killed?"

"If they believe we're working together, they'll be caught off guard."

"What the hell did the Estes family hire you to do?"

"None of your business."

"Wrong answer," I snarled.

Donovan cleared his throat, and Mercer turned to him. "Seems she's narrowing in on the insider," Donovan surmised. Bastian went to the wall and examined the school records that were pinned up.

"It's time you start at the beginning," I commanded, taking a seat on the couch and folding my arms across my chest. "I'm waiting." Before any of the ex-SAS could respond, I heard Heathcliff at my door.

"Parker," he yelled, knocking loudly. I heard the key in the lock, and then the door opened. Heathcliff burst in, gun in hand, and looked at me. "Is everything okay?"

"For now," I sighed. It was nice to know he took the word urgent to mean imminent danger. "Derek Heathcliff meet Julian Mercer." Heathcliff holstered his gun and looked questioningly at me. I shrugged.

"Bollocks," Bastian cursed, "looks like the bird's got herself a copper boyfriend."

"We've met briefly," Mercer commented, glowering at Heathcliff, "you were kind enough to release me from lock-up."

"Is that something I should regret?" Heathcliff asked, coming and standing next to me. Normally, I didn't deal well with protective attitudes, but on this particular morning, I appreciated the support.

Mercer narrowed his eyes but didn't respond. "We'd like some privacy."

"The hell you would," Heathcliff retorted, and I interceded before things turned into a pissing match or worse.

"Mercer thought he should break-in to my apartment this morning to ask for assistance. He was just about to start at the beginning." I looked pointedly at him. "Right?"

TWENTY-THREE

Despite the fact speaking in front of Heathcliff was never part of the arrangement, I left Mercer with little choice. He reverted to his inscrutable, stone-faced exterior and began to divulge a good deal of the story. All of it was off the record, of course.

Miguel Estes, the gold mogul, planted a tracking device on his daughter. Two years ago, he had taken out a ransom policy for his family members at the insistence of his business manager, Estobar Santino. In order to get a decrease in the insurance rates, a tracking device was placed inside Adalina's necklace. The morning the girls went missing, the necklace was delivered to the Estes' estate with a note. The family was immediately made aware of Adalina's capture and was instructed to wait for further demands.

Miguel contacted his lawyer, the insurance company, and his business manager for advice on what to do. The insurance company worked with Mercer and his crew before and made the relevant phone calls. Within twenty-four hours, Mercer was on scene to handle the situation.

However, the situation was not the ordinary demand negotiation. The Four Seasons insisted on delaying the initial ransom request until the first girl was released. During that timeframe, Mercer did all he could to track the Seasons and narrow in on their position. This was also when Nick got in touch with Mercer, and the two attempted to locate the girls.

"Why were you certain they were established at the wharf?" I asked. It was where Nick had been shot, but Mercer had yet to explain how his random hunches turned out to not be so random.

"In-depth analysis," Mercer supplied. "We analyzed everything from the paper stock to environmental elements on Adalina's necklace to background noise and reflections in the video and audio feeds."

"We tried that too," Heathcliff added, "but we never got such an obvious hit on a location."

"You lack proper access to the equipment needed," Mercer commented with a level of superiority. Sure, he had friends in high places, but if he was so great and powerful, he wouldn't be asking for my help. "Needless to say, the detective was spotted. It almost blew the entire operation, and if he didn't call for help, he'd be dead right now." Without looking, I felt Heathcliff tense. Thankfully, he held his tongue, so Mercer could continue.

After O'Connell's initial blunder, Mercer informed Senor Estes of the updated situation. Estes was not pleased and believed that the kidnappers might not be willing to deal, even if the money was delivered. It was at this point Estes hired Barr and Keener to assist Mercer at the drop. It was also around this time that I entered the picture.

"So the Secret Service rejects are the newest additions to the Estes' estate?" I asked.

"Yes." Mercer still preferred his one word responses.

"Do you know who was in charge of the Estes' security at the time Adalina was taken?"

"The normal three team bodyguard unit was supplied by an outside agency. The agency's contract expired two days before the abduction, and the Estes family was in re-negotiation at the time."

"What company?" Heathcliff asked, jotting down a note. Mercer frowned. Off the record apparently meant different things to different people. Heathcliff glanced up. "C'mon, it's very possible they're involved."

"They are not. I checked." Before any more barbs could be exchanged, I decided it best to defer to Mercer's expertise and get him to continue the story.

"Okay," I put my hand on Heathcliff's knee, "who knew of the gap in the Estes' security?"

"Only the immediate family, Estobar Santino, and the personal security agency."

Heathcliff scribbled Santino's name down and excused himself to run background on my computer. The rest of the information Mercer provided was already things I knew from my involvement in the case. He didn't know where the Four Seasons currently were, and all of the communications he received since the time I lost Catherine were delay tactics. Unfortunately, we didn't know why.

"Donovan," I turned my attention to one of Mercer's minions, "you said something about closing in on the insider. Any leads?"

Donovan looked to Mercer who continued to speak for the group. "We believe someone close to the girl must be responsible for the abduction. The amount of money requested, the timeframe for the funds to be brought here, and the necklace being delivered to their home is all information someone close to the family would know. We ran through friends, business associates, and the security team, but they were all clean."

"Squeaky," Bastian added, finishing off the Chinese and tossing the carton into the trash. "How'd the school officials look?"

"Squeaky," Heathcliff piped up from behind my desk.

All the information was a jumble, but I felt certain there was something to be gained from the mess. I just needed a bit of time to process through all of it.

"You have what you want." Mercer's tone drew my attention. "You will assist." It wasn't a question.

"Fine," I sighed, "but recovering Adalina is still primarily your responsibility."

"I wouldn't have it any other way."

"Good."

Mercer took a burner phone out of his jacket pocket and placed it on my coffee table, along with my MT identification card. "Keep the phone on at all times. If a communication comes in, I will be able to reroute the call to you if I believe it is in the best interest of my client." He narrowed his eyes. "In the meantime, I'd suggest you and the copper keep this quiet. Off the record means just that."

"Since when is pick-pocketing in the military's repertoire?" I snarled.

"It's imperative I have a complete picture of the people I deal with. Perhaps you should pay more attention when some bloke takes your wallet," he chided and tossed a glance to Donovan and Bastian. "I'll be in touch. I strongly urge you to answer when the phone rings." He stood and approached, close enough that we were practically touching. "Don't be fooled. I know more about you than you'd ever imagine. Consider it insurance in case you sabotage my mission." He lingered for a moment.

"I've told you, we're on the same side."

"Indeed." He let himself out of my house, followed by Donovan and Bastian.

"It's been a pleasure," Bastian smirked, shutting the door.

Heathcliff sat, jaw tight, waiting for my reaction.

"That was Julian Mercer and his merry band of mercs," I supplied while visually sweeping my apartment. I didn't put it past Mercer to bug the place. Although, since he had taken my MT security card and had a full dossier, courtesy of Interpol, surveilling me might be considered overkill.

"The text you sent seemed more indicative of a full-scale assault."

"What can I say? Waking up to three men in my bedroom, two of them armed, tends to have that effect on me." He studied my expression to determine if I was embellishing. "Anyway, did you get anything useful yesterday from the school or at the precinct before the Chief thwarted our brilliant plans?"

"Like I told your pals, the school's squeaky clean." He rubbed his eyes and leaned back in the chair. "Do you have any coffee?"

"Derek, I appreciate the rescue but go home and get some sleep. I'll see what I can find on Santino and the Estes' security faux pas."

His gaze shifted toward the door and then my bedroom. "Maybe we shouldn't be alone right now," he suggested.

"What happens if you get that urgent phone call?"

"Is my paranoia contagious?"

"Maybe I don't want to have to rush out of the shower because of another 9-1-1 text from you."

"Fine. You have two options. You can sleep here, or I'll pull out the espresso maker."

"I wouldn't turn down a nap."

He jotted a few notes while I converted my bedroom into a guestroom. This wasn't ideal, but he had a point. And since Thompson was busy coaxing information out of O'Connell, there was no one left to keep me company. After Heathcliff was settled into my bedroom, I shut the door and began reconstructing everything Mercer divulged.

The more I thought about things, the more the abduction seemed to hinge entirely around Adalina Estes. The flaw in her security was perfectly timed, and she seemed to be the hostage the Four Seasons were intent on keeping. More importantly, they supplied the numerous proofs of life for her and continued to negotiate, despite Mercer's antics. Why would they do this, instead of just making the trade, unless Adalina escaped or was killed? Then again, Catherine Cale was still missing, presumably dead.

I read through the notes Heathcliff made on Estobar Santino, the insurance company providing the ransom policy, and the defunct security providers. Dialing the OIO, I was calling in a few favors. Kate, my forensic accountant friend, agreed to look into the financials for the security firm, the insurance agency, and the Estes' business and personal funds. All of this was on the down low. Then I spoke with a few analysts to ask if they could run a thorough check on the security firm and Estobar Santino. Someone had to be dirty.

After I ran out of owed favors, I pulled all of the school personnel off the wall and started over with our new prime suspects. As I stared at the scribbled names, my mind wondered what the connection was between the three girls. Maybe Catherine and the third girl were taken to throw us off the scent of what was really going on. But why Catherine?

Catherine Cale was the odd-shaped piece in this puzzle. Her family wasn't rich. They were middle class, upper-middle class, but still middle-class. Hell, she might have qualified for financial aid at that private school with the types of bank accounts the other families possessed. I ran a complete workup on her father and mother, but Peter and Evelyn were nobodies. Peter was a pencil pusher with little actual power and not much perceived power either. He was only on the outskirts looking in. Evelyn was a stay-at-home mom. She started out as a school teacher, but after marrying Peter and having Catherine, she wasn't even a blip on the radar. The only possible reason I could imagine someone would take Catherine would be as payback because of Nick.

O'Connell and I weren't on good terms and rooting around in his past wouldn't mend our friendship, but I didn't see any other motive for Catherine's abduction. I dialed Jen's cell phone, hoping she'd speak to me.

"Alexis?" she whispered. "Has anything changed?" Apparently, O'Connell finally told her the situation.

"I don't have news." I felt guilty for getting her hopes up. "Heathcliff and I have been trying our damnedest to get something solid, and the only thing I could think was it's someone out to get Nick." He was shot, but they didn't kill him. Did they mean to, or was it just a warning, like he insisted?

"Thompson thought that might be a possibility. The department's analyzing all of his old cases, checking into recent parolees, known associates, but Nick doesn't think that's it. If someone wanted to make an impact, he figures they would have taken me or killed him when they had the chance."

"I'm sorry to have bothered you. I'm sure he wouldn't be happy to know I called."

"I married him. I know what a hothead he can be

sometimes. There's no reason he needs to know you called, but if you need me to ask him something, I can do that."

"No," my mind decided on a new possibility, "is Thompson there?"

"Yes," I could hear Jen smile, "I have faith the two of them will figure this thing out." I suspected Thompson must have shared the leukoreduced blood factoid with the O'Connells. I just prayed that his positive attitude wouldn't make all of them hit rock bottom that much harder. "By the way, tell James thanks for sending over that care package. I don't think I've ever seen such an elaborate gift basket before."

"I will. If you need anything, I'm here."

I went back to my notes. The first girl, Sonia Casanov, was released within forty-eight hours of the abduction. There had been no glitches in the demand, exchange, and recovery. She was uninjured and no longer in any danger. Hypothetically, the Four Seasons were currently in possession of Adalina and Catherine. Adalina was supposed to have been released, but after Nick's blunder and the shootout under the overpass, Winter delayed her release. This led to the Seasons issuing ransom demands for Catherine.

I failed royally, and as punishment, they painted the pier in blood. How they managed to pull that off without being seen was still a mystery. As far as I knew, negotiation for Catherine's release ended, and according to Mercer, they were hedging on a timetable for Adalina. Obviously, something must have gone wrong.

"I was thinking," Heathcliff said from the doorway, rubbing his face and trying to appear awake, even though he only slept a few hours, "the Seasons can't release Catherine because they're afraid of what Mercer would do if he was left unimpeded."

"Wow, sleep turned you into a genius."

He ignored my remark. "That would mean they must be aware of who he is and what he does."

"How would they know?" I asked. "Unless you think O'Connell's actions tipped them off."

He frowned and went into the kitchen to pour a cup of

coffee from the pot I made while he was asleep. "What if the insider is still on the inside? The Estes have staff, advisors, et cetera. We have no access to them. We can't touch them. But what if someone inside their house is choreographing Winter's movements?"

It made sense. Actually, it made a scary amount of sense. I filled him in on what I processed out of the information, and the two of us sat in the quiet of my apartment, trying to determine the best way to force the inside man to expose himself.

TWENTY-FOUR

"We've cleared the members of the insurance agency and the security personnel the Estes employed," I announced, hanging up the phone.

"It has to be Santino," Heathcliff muttered. "He suggested the ransom insurance and knew of the cracks in the family's security. He possesses knowledge of where the girl was, where the tracking device would be, and who his boss hired to deal with the situation. Hell, he probably knows more about Julian Mercer than we do.

"Can you prove it?" I asked.

Proof was the thing I hated the most about the job. From a legal standpoint, it made sense. We were all human and prone to make mistakes, but sometimes, a gut instinct could never be corroborated through official means and guilty parties got away. It's probably why cops always tended to vote Republican. Right now, I didn't care if all the guilty parties walked away, just as long as we got the two little girls back safe.

"Shit, Parker, you want to push papers for the DA's office?" He was irritable, and I understood why.

"You can't arrest him. You can't detain him. We can't encroach upon the family's property, given the current crisis, so what the hell do we do?"

"Doesn't Mercer take care of things like this?"

I blew out a breath. "Do you think he's in on it?"

"Mercer?" He considered the possibility. "I asked you that before."

"I just don't understand how he wouldn't realize the party responsible was standing next to him in a room," I growled. We were only theorizing, and it was getting us nowhere, but despite this, he laughed. "Did I say something funny?"

"Mercer negotiates and shoots people for a living. He isn't in the business of determining who's responsible. He's just there to talk and shoot."

"Then it's about time we get him on board to do something more than that. If Mercer can get us access to the Estes' estate or something solid to use against Santino, then you can bring the bastard in and shake something out of him."

"Do you want me to tag along?"

"No. Mercer and I have an understanding, and if he reneges on our verbal agreement, then just make sure to make his life short and miserable." It was sort of a joke.

"Okay, watch your back. I'll drop by the precinct and then head home, unless I hear from you."

"I'll see you tomorrow." He collected his notes and a few items he wanted to further analyze and left my apartment.

My head pounded, and I wanted all of this to have a simple and positive resolution. Clearly, that wouldn't be the case. I changed the sheets on my bed, took a shower, and dressed in more work appropriate attire. Dialing Mercer, I waited for an answer. But he was preoccupied at the moment, whatever that meant, and we could meet at his rental in two hours.

Glancing at the time, I went to the MT building. It was almost six p.m., but there was a good chance with the conference last week and the new security implementations that the building might still be busy. Swiping my new card at the door, I found Jeffrey in the security office.

"Do me a favor," I held out my old card that Mercer had

taken, "make sure no one tried to access the building or any of MT's records. If my card was used for anything since Sunday onward, find out what it was and send copies to my office."

"But you found your card," Jeffrey protested.

"No. Someone delivered it." He didn't understand my cautious attitude, but if Mercer was snooping around, I wanted to know what he was looking for. "And flag the old access strip and number. I know it's deactivated, but if anyone tries to use it, I want to know." There was also a possibility Mercer could have duplicated my card.

"Will do, Ms. Parker." Jeffrey smiled warmly. "Anything else I can do for you this evening?"

"Has Mr. Martin left for the day?"

"I don't believe so."

"Okay, thanks." I took the elevator to the seventeenth floor and knocked on Martin's door.

"Hey." He smiled up at me from under a sea of paperwork. "Are you okay?"

"I think so. I was here to talk to Jeffrey and thought I'd stop by. Thanks for the distraction the other day and for putting up with me, and Jen said thanks for the gift basket. You didn't have to do that." Martin looked confused by my rambling. "O'Connell and I aren't speaking at the moment, so I hope you don't end up being in the doghouse by association."

"I'm not too worried about it."

"Okay, well, I have a meeting to get to. I'll give you a call when life returns to normal." I headed for the door.

"Alex," he hesitated, "did they find her?"

"No. Thompson thinks she's still alive. Heathcliff and I are working leads, and the PD is calling this a missing person. No one knows what the fuck is going on."

"You'll figure it out. You always do."

I let out a cynical laugh and rolled my eyes. "Not always. And not always in time." Leaving the MT building, I went to Mercer's apartment, hoping he'd have something concrete we could use against Estobar Santino.

* * *

"Lovely to see you again," Bastian said, holding the door open so I could enter. "Pity you're still not in a lacy, little see-through number."

I narrowed my eyes at him. "Where's Mercer?"

"Julian stepped out for a moment. He'll be back soon." No one else was in the apartment. "Care for some tea?"

I took a seat on the couch and tried to determine a practical use for Bastian. "Let me guess, you're Mercer's houseboy?" It sounded a bit more scathing than I intended, but he laughed it off.

"Not quite, although I'm sure Jules would love that." I raised an eyebrow and waited. "Tit for tat. Are you game?"

"Of course. Can't you tell, I'm an open book."

"Anything but, love." He sat across from me. "How'd you get roped into this mess?"

"One of the girls taken was my friend's niece." He leaned back and nodded. "My turn. Explain the dynamics of your team."

"Boxers or briefs would have been more insightful," Bastian smirked. His commentary was meant to make me uneasy, but it seemed harmless. Maybe I was accustomed to infantile comments and jokes from spending too much time with Martin. "Donovan is our long-distance resolution expert. Hans deals with reconnaissance. Julian," he looked toward the door, probably afraid his commander was about to walk in, "coordinates, and I do a little bit of everything."

"Jack of all trades," I surmised.

"Why are you assisting if you think the girl's dead?"

I paled. "Is she?"

"You think she is. Is this penance for screwing up?"

"You don't do a little of everything. You're the goddamn analyst." He grinned at the comment. "How do you read this situation?"

"I don't think you have the proper clearance."

"This isn't the fucking SAS," I retorted.

He cocked his head to one side. "True." He scrutinized me for a moment. "Ah, bird," he smiled, "you're not letting this go, are you?" I remained silent. It was one of the few talents I possessed, thanks to my days interviewing suspects at the OIO. "This reads like an inside job. The third girl, Sonia Casanov, was released practically the moment she was taken. Whoever grabbed the girls didn't want the Russians involved. She wasn't the intended target or the main motivation. That means we're left with two, Estes and Cale. Miguel has a gold mine and unofficially controls the entire country. Money, power, politics, there are a million reasons to nab Adalina, but the kidnappers are barely scratching at the surface."

"Four million is scratching at the surface?"

"Four million is an asking price. Don't tell me you buy a car off the lot without haggling," he looked pointedly at me. "Reasonably speaking, we could negotiate down to a million and a half, maybe two. But that doesn't explain why the kidnappers aren't asking for something more substantial, like power, protection, or an insurance policy to make sure we don't shoot the blokes in the back once we get the girl."

"Is that why they keep delaying?"

He laughed. "They're delaying because they don't know what the fuck to do with your hostage."

"You know Catherine's alive?" I leaned forward, practically jumping off the couch.

"Not the point." He was being unreasonable, and I resisted the urge to leap across the coffee table and strangle him. "They took Cale for show. She wasn't the main target either." Everything he said went along with at least one of the theories Heathcliff and I were considering.

"But she's nobody."

"Aw, how darling. You remind me of a kitten playing with a ball of yarn, full of wonder and amazement."

"Careful, I have the claws and fangs to match."

"I don't doubt that," he smiled roguishly, "but Cale has something that no one else at that school does." He leaned back like the cat that swallowed the canary, which made all the names he'd called me even more confusing. I ran through my knowledge of the other students and Catherine.

"Her uncle's a cop." The truth hit like a ton of bricks. "They had to ensure the police would get involved."

"Bloody brilliant, isn't it? They can specify no cops, but they have a cop's niece. There will definitely be some coppers, and just in case your buddy wanted to follow directions, they shoot him in order to turn it into an official police investigation."

"Holy shit." I eyed Bastian as the pieces tumbled together.

The cops would add to the legitimacy and ensure the insurance company issued the ransom payout. Maybe the amount was doubled or even tripled to get as much as possible, but there must be a cap on the policy. The only problem with Bastian's theory was after the police became involved, Catherine was no longer a sought after commodity. She was expendable.

"If you'd like to snog now, I wouldn't mind," he spoke, breaking my thoughts into a million fragmented pieces.

"I'll pass."

"Suit yourself." He fished his phone from his pocket and sent a text. Within three minutes, Mercer entered the apartment.

"Up-to-date?" Mercer asked.

"Were you afraid to give me the details yourself, or do you really like to delegate?"

"You seem more amicable with Bastian." It wasn't an answer, but apparently, Mercer realized we would butt heads, instead of exchange valuable information. Although, it was another illustration of how he was manipulating the situation and me. I didn't like it.

Having limited options, I filled in Bastian and Mercer on our suspicions concerning Estobar Santino and the insider still being a valuable asset or member of the Estes family. When I was finished with my rendition of the facts, they exchanged a meaningful look.

"Santino is under a microscope, but nothing has surfaced," Mercer offered. Our give and take seemed taxing for him, probably because it required he hide his loathing long enough to converse civilly.

"Can you get me inside? This is what I do," I retorted.

He frowned. "No." I swallowed the urge to slap more than a one word answer out of him, and Bastian gave him a hard glare. Finally, Mercer spoke again. "But I will try to sway Senor Estes to permit you on the premises."

"In the meantime," Bastian decided it best to break the tension in the room, "we've been using satellite imaging to locate the Four Seasons' base of operations."

"We were at their base of operations, and we didn't do a damn thing," I argued.

"That was one of their mobile locations," Bastian interjected. "We thought it was the location for the girls and planned a recovery. It wasn't. They've been moving around every six to twelve hours to avoid permanent detection. Actually, only two of the four kidnappers were present. The two patrolmen were rent-a-cops with no idea what was going on."

"How do you know any of this?"

"We know," Mercer replied, and from his voice, I knew the way he obtained the information involved torture. The bile rose in my throat, and I forced it back down.

"What do we do in the meantime?"

"You stay by the phone and answer it when it rings. Other than that, stay out of my way." He was back to being his warm and cuddly self. There was no use in arguing, so I stood.

"Fine. Call as soon as you know anything." Glancing over my shoulder, I added, "And if you hold me at gunpoint one more time, I'd suggest you pull the trigger."

TWENTY-FIVE

Instead of going home, I went to the OIO. After meeting with Kate and a few government sanctioned hackers, who preferred to be known as internet specialists, I had a clear picture of what the Estes' gold-mining business and ransom insurance policies looked like. The gold-mining industry was lucrative and stable. Thousands of dollars were mined daily. And the ore was stockpiled in a warehouse before being shipped to another facility for purification and melting, or maybe it was smelting. The actual procedure didn't warrant my full attention.

The more helpful tidbit was the cap on the ransom insurance policy was set at two million. That's how the money was so swiftly and efficiently placed into the duffel bag and taken to the exchange. It's also probably why the sum was doubled after the shootout at the exchange. The Estes had assets, but another two million liquid was beyond their capabilities.

"They could liquidate enough stocks and sell more shares of their company," Kate Hartley, forensic accountant, was discussing some possible options. "They could conceivably have the additional two million in a couple or three weeks."

"So who is benefitting by the kidnappers' delay strategy?" I asked, but Kate shrugged. And I sighed loudly. "Which is easier to trace, big blocks of gold or cash?"

"Depends on a number of factors," she wanted to be helpful, but her answers led me in circles, "if it's cash, there's a possibility of marked bills, but it's easy enough to distribute them around. Then again, maybe they want bearer bonds or wire transfers or..." I put my hand up, and she stopped midsentence.

"I got it. Keep those accounts flagged. If anything major disappears, let me know."

"You got it, Parker." She smiled as I retreated from her office. Before I made it out of the building, I bumped into Mark, who was on his way in.

"Any luck on finding O'Connell's niece?" he asked.

"No, but I think I'm finally in bed with Mercer."

"I'm so proud," he replied sardonically. "I wish I could be more help, but," he lowered his voice, "middle of an op."

"I understand. Heathcliff, Thompson, and I are working off the books anyway. The PD's put a PR spin on things so the public doesn't panic, and everyone who didn't work directly with O'Connell is busting their ass to figure this thing out." Mark pressed his lips together in thought.

"The Bureau's backing them. It was Director Kendall's call, but we're assisting in the evidence analysis and collection. The family still doesn't want any federal agents within a couple hundred feet of their house because they're scared."

"Scared, not grieving?" Winter must have made contact, or Mark's information was wrong.

"Scared." He nodded almost imperceptibly and continued down the corridor. I took a deep breath and leaned against the wall, saying a silent prayer of thanks to whoever might be listening. I wasn't sure how Mark came upon his information, but if Peter and Evelyn were scared, then Catherine was definitely alive. Time wasn't up, yet.

On my drive home, I analyzed everything Kate and Mark said. At home, I updated our wall of information, checked the answering machine, and even though it was after midnight, I called Thompson. He answered right before it switched over to voicemail.

"Parker," he said in a hushed tone, "is everything okay?"

"Jablonsky hinted Catherine's alive. I was hoping you could verify."

He chuckled. "Yes." His response was barely audible. "There was a new POL sent this morning. Polaroid photo. O'Connell got a call from Evelyn a couple of hours ago. I can't talk now," he said quickly, "I'm with Nick."

"Okay. We'll exchange information later."

And he hung up without so much as a good-bye. At least he had an excuse for not calling with the information; he was still babysitting his partner. On the plus side, Catherine was alive. I didn't kill her.

An unknown amount of time passed while I sat at my kitchen counter with my face buried in my hands, completely overcome by this fact. When I looked up, the weight was no longer bearing down on my chest. I earned some breathing room.

The guilt-induced fog cleared out of my brain, and I dug through the paperwork, looking for the forensic report on the leukoreduced blood. If the Four Seasons used donor blood, then it had to come from a hospital, clinic, or blood bank. Find the source, and we'd find the thieves.

Scanning the databases, news reports, and any other possible source I could think of, I was determined to come up with a solid, irrefutable lead. The sun was up before I found anything useful. Apparently, a free health clinic reported a break-in four days ago. Basic medical supplies, blankets, and towels were stolen. It wasn't considered a priority by the police since it was in the ghetto and no narcotics or other control substances were lifted.

A key scraped in my lock, and I jumped and lifted my nine millimeter, waiting. Thompson and Heathcliff came in, and I immediately laid my gun on the table. "Morning," Heathcliff offered. He looked the most rested out of the three of us, but that didn't mean his eyes didn't possess their own little bags to carry their fatigue around in. "You're up early."

"You mean I'm up late," I countered. "Thompson, an update would be most beneficial." I gave him my winning smile, and he grunted on the way to the coffeemaker.

"Coffee would be beneficial," he glared at the empty pot. "What I have counts as a miracle."

"Even better."

"The Cales worked themselves into a tizzy. The Four Seasons are no longer demanding two million." He dug through my cabinets for coffee. "Apparently, the bull-headed negotiator emphasized the point they didn't have that kind of money."

"At least I'm good for something." I watched as he searched the cabinet. "Second shelf and the water comes out of the faucet."

"Thanks, smartass." He dumped some coffee into the filter without measuring and filled the pot. "They have yet to make an actual demand, but no cops, no agents, and no outsiders involved or else."

"But they told O'Connell," Heathcliff piped up from his spot in front of my wall. "Or was he granted special clearance since he's such a great guy?" The sarcasm wasn't lost on me, but Thompson ignored it.

"Either Nick isn't telling me what they want, or they haven't decided what they want yet," Thompson concluded as the coffee began to drip, and he pulled a mug from the drain board.

"What's your read on the situation?" I asked.

"O'Connell told me and only me." He threw warning glances at Heathcliff and me. "It doesn't leave this room. Whatever his sis wants to do, I'm sure he's helping in any way possible, but I'd bet they're jumping through hoops to satisfy all the stipulations these sons of bitches are throwing around. All three of them, Nick included."

"Then what the hell are we doing?" Heathcliff asked. He hadn't forgiven Nick's outburst, and I rolled my eyes at how juvenile men could be.

"We will figure out who these people are, what they want, and bring them down," I responded. With Catherine alive, Mercer playing ball, and my former OIO brethren sharing information, I was ready to blow this mother out of the water.

"It's about damn time," Heathcliff grinned, and I told

the two detectives everything I learned in the last twenty-four hours.

"Let's divide and conquer." Thompson was taking charge, and I had no desire to argue. "Heathcliff and I can investigate the clinic. It is official police business, and Moretti has everyone so wrapped up in the kidnapping, I doubt they've given this much thought. You," he pressed his lips together, trying to come up with something productive, "have to wait for Mercer's call. If you can get inside the Estes' house and close to Santino, then do it. In the meantime, you're stuck waiting for more information or something to follow-up."

"Maybe you should get some sleep," Heathcliff suggested, but I stared at my empty mug. That no longer seemed like a possibility, at least until the caffeine wore off.

"I'll go back over everything. Maybe we missed something." Waiting was always the hard part. Heathcliff and Thompson left for another fun-filled day at the office, and I worked my way through the reports, our suspect list, the financial records, and the few phone records that my hacker friends 'accidentally' ran across.

From my perusal, I felt reassured that Adalina Estes was the intended target. Whoever was responsible for her abduction had to be close to the Estes family and know the goings and comings of the household. Estobar Santino had the access, the knowledge, and probably a decent enough alibi to keep official suspicion off of him. Good thing nothing I did was ever official. Assuming Bastian's analysis of the situation was accurate, Catherine was taken to ensure police involvement and squelch any official concerns the insurance firm might have. Through my reasoning, it was also the best way to keep the police at bay. Sure, abducting O'Connell's niece would lead to a full-scale investigation, but it also meant the police would be even more cautious because they couldn't risk Catherine becoming a casualty. It was almost the perfect scenario.

I shut the last folder and paced my apartment. We knew why Catherine was one of the victims, why the third abductee, Sonia Casanov, was released so swiftly, and we knew where the girls were taken from. It was a start.

Maybe a late start but still a start. At least we had some strong indications of who was involved, and if Mercer could get me into the house, I was sure I could find something to stick to Santino.

Slumping down in front of the computer, I wasn't sure what to do. As Thompson determined, there wasn't anything for me to do until someone called with a lead or more information. I considered sleeping, but too many cups of strong coffee and facts turning over and over in my mind weren't conducive to sleep. I considered going for a run because that was the best way to clear my head, but I didn't want to add to my own fatigue with everything hanging so precariously in the balance. Instead, I opened the folder I received from Francesca Pirelli and decided to find a more civil topic to focus on.

TWENTY-SIX

Hover Designs created the schematics used in designing household fixtures, everything from toilet bowls to cabinets. They were a well-established home décor and hardware corporation which was surprising since Francesca didn't strike me as the hardhat type. Then again, corporate bigwigs were about as far removed from the real work as one could get, and although she was the chief operating officer, I was sure she spent her days behind a nice big mahogany desk, signing paperwork and attending meetings. At some point, COOs and CEOs were all interchangeable; I'd just have to remember not to share that insight with Martin.

The management consulting firm, Insight International, was hired to evaluate the cost-efficiency of Hover Designs and the best ways to allocate resources. In other words, they were hired to cut the fat. It was a shitty job, but one many large corporations valued. It was nice to pass the blame for why a hard worker was getting fired on to an outsider. Excuses such as *we value your work but your department is no longer necessary* seem much nicer than *we're cheap assholes who don't want to pay you.* Corporate America, I cringed at the prospect. The lovely four-man team from Insight International had total access to all of HD's financial information and upcoming projects. This was standard operating procedure, but a week after Insight International was dismissed, the new designs for HD's upcoming countertop revolution were leaked.

Timing has a habit of being everything, and I sifted through the information concerning the new countertop construction, materials, and specifications. A countertop was a countertop to me, but apparently, these were light-weight, cost-effective, constructed from recycled materials that could mimic the look of either granite or ivory, and were meant to be more durable, eco-friendly, and supplied at a fraction of the cost, making them the envy of both high-end builders and numerous government contractors. Who knew countertops could be so lucrative?

I ran background on Insight International. The management consulting firm had been in business for over a decade, and there were no complaints about the firm or its workers. Blowing out a breath, I ran criminal records on the four-man team. What the hell was up with everyone functioning in four-man teams? Craig Robinson was the leader and had no discernible criminal record. The other three members, Paige Augusta, Cynthia Dowes, and Jeremiah Little, were equally clean.

Dialing MT, I asked HR if they had any dealings with Insight International, but they did not. I didn't want to risk confusing the OIO with any more requests when it was imperative they track Catherine's kidnappers. Instead, I considered my limited options and found Maddock Howell's business card in my wallet. "What the hell," I muttered, dialing.

"Howell speaking," he answered, sounding just as sleazy as he did the night we met.

"Mr. Howell, this is Alexis Parker. We met at a conference a week and a half ago."

"Ah, yes, Ms. Parker, lovely to hear from you. Have you reconsidered my offer?

"Perhaps," playing along might be the only way to get the information I needed, "I was concerned about a potential conflict of interest. In the event I seriously consider the possibility of a job at Wallace-Klineman Industries, I need to know if your company has ever employed a management consulting firm?"

"I'm not sure how that would impact you in any manner." Howell wasn't as pliable as I hoped.

"Let me put it this way, Mr. Howell."

"Maddock, please."

"Maddock, I'd be willing to meet for drinks or take an interview or whatever it is you want to do to try to woo me, but I'd like an immediate quid pro quo."

"I'd love to woo you, but we'll see." He sounded skeptical. "What were you hoping for in exchange?"

"Have you ever worked with Insight International?" I could hear him clicking away at the keyboard.

"We haven't used them. Not much for a quid pro quo," he commented.

"Come on, Maddock, you're a well-connected man. I'm sure your ear's to the ground. Have you ever heard anything less than stellar about the firm?"

"Let's meet for drinks. I assume you're back at the flagship MT building, and I'll be in your neck of the woods next weekend. It must be kismet." Agreeing didn't guarantee I'd show up. "As a sign of good faith," he stopped typing, "I've just e-mailed you all the corporate information Wallace-Klineman has compiled on Insight International. Although we've never used them, we did consider hiring them at one point. I hope you will find this beneficial."

"Thank you. Drinks next weekend. E-mail me the details."

"I just did." And he hung up. As I tried to determine how he had access to my e-mail address, I realized he e-mailed my corporate MT account. Just what I needed, a job offer at my current place of employment. Thankfully, I was the security consultant and dating the boss; it really didn't matter.

Skimming through the data Howell sent, I found a mug shot of Craig Robinson. Although official charges were never filed, he had been arrested for drunken disorderly and possession. The charges were dropped, and I suspected he paid off some unsavory official to look the other way. Maybe there was more than meets the eye when it came to Insight International.

Insight International had a stellar reputation for getting companies out of the red and into the black. The tactics they employed were cutthroat but cost-effective. They were a small organization with an estimated ten to twenty evaluation teams. These teams each consisted of four to six individuals who were trained to evaluate PR proposals, marketing, worker/department efficiency, and the overall health of a company. It was amazing the types of things this firm could do.

When Hover Designs hired them, they signed the boilerplate nondisclosure clauses and were given access to any information they requested. While Hover Designs was one of the few companies not in the red, their profit margin stagnated. The new countertop design was meant to make their stocks soar. The new production line would open up hundreds of new employee positions, a few new factories, and earn the one-percenters another zero on their bonus checks.

Craig Robinson's team was sent by Insight International because of their expertise in marketing strategies. These four individuals specialized in maximizing exposure and advertising while minimizing cost and preventing overspending for a project that had yet to produce any viable profits. On the surface, it all looked cogent.

Although I signed the same nondisclosures, I was only seeing what was meant to happen. This was based solely on the proposals drawn up by Insight International. I lacked the files and resources to evaluate what the management consulting firm sifted through. Placing a call to Ms. Pirelli, I asked for a log of the files Robinson's team accessed during the course of their evaluation. Since getting this information would take some time and finesse on Francesca's part, I decided to analyze Insight International's findings concerning the countertops and their profitability.

By the third page of the one hundred and seventeen page evaluation, my eyelids began to droop. Soldiering on, by the eleventh page, I ran across the name of Hover Designs' marketing executive, Liam Naysley. Insight International cautioned that the numbers Naysley produced on the profitability of the proposed marketing campaign were substantially off. After comparing the Insight International prediction to Naysley's, I decided to run a full background on him. After entering in a few key search terms, I leaned back in the chair, waiting for the criminal and financial records to pop up.

The phone rang, and I jumped. Grabbing for it, I noticed it was almost six p.m. I had fallen asleep while my computer ran the search. At least corporate files were good for something, namely putting me to sleep.

"Parker," my voice came out hoarse.

"Heathcliff and I have the surveillance tapes from the clinic. Get this, along with the other supplies, there were five pints of blood taken from the cooler. They assumed it was some teenagers vandalizing or a gang initiation since there was nothing of any real value taken. The drugs were all locked up and no signs of tampering on the lock. Just basic supplies."

"Pillows, blankets, general first-aid?" I asked.

"Yep. The kinds of things you might need if you're keeping a couple of kids hostage," Thompson added. "We're getting some IT guys and lab techs together to see if we can get an I.D."

"Do you think it's the Four Seasons?"

"It's worth checking. Maybe they hired some local to get supplies, but it could lead somewhere. Police work is ninety-nine percent legwork, one percent luck."

"Good luck, Detective." I was skimming through the information on Naysley as Thompson was talking. Before I could hang up, he asked the question that I would have been wondering had I not just woken up and been preoccupied with less important things.

"Did Mercer call?"

"No. When he does, I'll let you know." We disconnected, and I printed out the basic facts on Naysley. Not wanting to sit at my desk a minute longer, I stood up and stretched. My bones popped and creaked, and I had a hell of a kink in my neck. Sleeping at my desk was not one of my better ideas.

After giving Naysley's information the precursory read, I took a shower and changed clothes. While I was getting ready for the day, which was more accurately night at this point, I considered the dilemma Francesca Pirelli faced. If the leak was from the outsiders, then whoever hired them would be held at least unofficially accountable. Although, if the leak was on the inside, then someone who had possibly spent years at the company could be responsible for the corporate espionage, dating back months, years, or even decades.

Liam Naysley was facing foreclosure on his estate. The house was valued at two million, but he overextended himself with boats, cars, numerous vacation homes, and enough credit card debt to fund a small island. So far, I had only looked into one Hover Designs' employee and the outside consulting firm, but both provided the possibility of guilt. This wasn't as easy as I hoped.

I rummaged through my kitchen, drinking the last of the cold coffee left from the pot Thompson brewed this morning while trying to find dinner or breakfast. Time lost all meaning, and I honestly couldn't be sure if I was coming or going. The phone rang again, but this time, I wasn't startled and didn't nearly jump out of my skin.

"I have information," Mercer said without preamble or greeting. "There has been no contact, but we should meet in person."

"When?" I asked, shutting my fridge and hoping he wouldn't say now.

"Immediately at my flat." Without waiting for a response, he hung up.

Rolling my eyes, I put on my holster and grabbed an extra clip. With Mercer, there was no telling why we were meeting, so it was best to be prepared. My flak jacket was in the trunk, and on my way out, I grabbed a granola bar. Hopefully, this only counted as breakfast and not dinner, or I'd be pissed.

On the drive across town, I considered calling Thompson, but since I didn't know what Mercer wanted, it could wait. I finished the granola bar and regretted not bringing a bottle of water along for this journey. I suppose I could drink out of the tap at Mercer's place. He ought to be bound by the Geneva Convention, even though I suspected he probably considered the sanctions more a suggestion than actual rules.

"Took you long enough," he muttered, opening the door, and I entered the apartment.

"You wanted to talk, so talk." Not waiting for an invitation or standing on formality, I continued through the living room and into the kitchen. He followed, seemingly unfazed by my making myself at home. He had yet to speak as I opened a few cabinets, looking for a drinking glass. "Well," I turned to him after I located the glass and filled it with water from the sink, "what the hell is going on?"

"That couldn't wait?" he questioned.

"No. It couldn't." I glowered at him. I heard Bastian in the other room with two other voices, presumably Hans and Donovan.

He narrowed his eyes, and I glimpsed the controlled intensity or maybe rage just beneath his impenetrable exterior. "Senor Estes is considering my request to bring you on board for future negotiations. At the present, Senor Santino is encouraging him to take a guarded approach before allowing others to become involved in his daughter's recovery." No shit, I thought but remained silent. "However," Mercer turned and strode from the kitchen, leaving me no choice but to follow, "Hans spotted the Cale girl."

I practically spat the water out. "What? Where?"

"If you would like to be part of the extraction," his tone sounded condescending, "get your gear. We leave in twenty."

"What?" I repeated. Extraction? Weren't we negotiating? What was the probability of a safe recovery and not another blunder, tipping Catherine's fate closer to death instead of life? What would O'Connell think?

"Are you stupid?" he snapped. "Bastian will brief you in the car. Get your shit so we can head out." I noticed his fists clench as he left me alone in the living room while he went into the other room with the rest of his team. I wasn't the obedient type. Deciding it best to be properly accessorized in case Mercer wanted to shoot me, I went to the trunk and put on my vest. Back inside, I went into the room where the four men were.

"Welcome back, love," Bastian greeted. His tone was still friendly, but I could sense the pre-op jitters in his voice and posture. "Are you ready to rock and roll, like you Yanks say?"

"I'm not going anywhere until someone in this room explains the likelihood of a positive outcome." I wasn't backing down. Donovan continued to pull up schematics that he and the man I assumed was Hans were evaluating. Hans glanced in my direction, looking completely bewildered by my presence.

"Is she the pain in the arse you've been harping on?" Hans asked Mercer. Mercer let out a snort, the closest thing to a laugh that he was capable of.

Bastian stepped in front of me. "We'll get your girl back." There was nothing but conviction in his voice. "Step into the other room, and we'll have a go over the major points before we roll on this."

"Fine." I backtracked into the living room.

"Hans was scouting the Four Seasons prior location. The place was cleared out, but they left a cell phone behind. He pulled the SIM card, and using the GPS tracker, we determined a secondary and tertiary location. From our intel and recon, we have eyes on Catherine. She's being held in a modified storage unit."

"What the hell are we waiting for?" I asked. My mind was focused on one thing, calling Thompson.

"We don't know if Adalina is there." Bastian met my eyes. "It's part of a climate-controlled self-storage unit. The lots are connected to one another. The only way in and out is through a steel door we believe to be booby-trapped."

"How the hell are we getting in?"

"We accessed the schematics. We can breach through a different unit in order to get inside."

"I can call this in." It seemed more reasonable to have

the bomb squad and professionals dealing with this, instead of a crack team of ex-SAS and a washed-up former OIO agent.

"No," Mercer growled from the doorway. "It was just a courtesy I invited you to join us. If Catherine is the only girl there, we can't afford to have the police fuck up our recovery, or the Estes girl could become collateral damage." From his reaction, there was more to the story than what I was being told. "Either agree and get in the fucking van or go home." The location had not been divulged. Their plan hadn't been explained, and there was nothing solid to go on. Logically, going along with Mercer was the only way I could mitigate the possible danger Catherine faced if I left the mercenaries to their own devices.

"I might as well help you make someone else's day miserable," I retorted. Bastian let out a slightly nervous chuckle, and Mercer and I remained locked in a staring match.

"You follow my orders," he snarled. "Understand?"

"Aye, aye, sir." My words bled contempt, but the response was satisfactory enough for Mercer, who strapped on a vest and grabbed a few extra magazines for his Sig before meeting the rest of his equally equipped team in the hallway and opening the front door.

"Bastian, you're coordinating from inside the vehicle," he remarked, and the five of us were on our way.

TWENTY-SEVEN

The van, as Mercer referred to it, was modified to resemble the surveillance vehicles most law enforcement agencies used. However, I assumed the equipment was vastly superior. Hans and Donovan were up front. Hans drove while Donovan assembled a sniper rifle and added an infrared scope. The fact they thought we needed a sniper rifle did nothing to quell my unease. Mercer was seated as far away from me as physically possible in the back, and Bastian was across from me.

"When we arrive, Hans will scout the area. He's been here before. He knows what to look for." I nodded at Bastian's words. "If we have the all clear, we'll determine an entry point and breach."

"How many hostiles?" I asked. Thankfully, I had gone from zero to sixty on the situation and was poised to strike, along with the rest of Mercer's team.

"We don't know. We have a few toys that might give us a peek inside." He smiled encouragingly. I rolled my neck from side to side, checked the clip in my gun, and took a deep breath, shutting my eyes and concentrating on my breathing and heartbeat. When I opened them, I noticed Mercer, silent and still. "It's like looking in a mirror, isn't it?"

I shifted my focus to Bastian. "Excuse me?"

"Never mind," he stared at a monitor, hooked to the seat next to him, "if you don't see it, then don't worry about it." My brow furrowed.

"He believes we're cut from the same cloth," Mercer spoke. His tone was sedate. The only time I saw him at peace, perhaps even congenial, was when danger was imminent. "I fail to agree."

"Actually," I snorted, "that might be the only thing you and I agree on." Mercer's eyes betrayed amusement, but he didn't crack a smile. "As far as I can tell, we're on completely opposite sides of the spectrum."

"You just wish we were." Mercer's words were ominous. "You loathe my actions, but it's only because you've been forced to do the same." I looked to Bastian, but he removed himself from the conversation. "I can see it in your eyes." I wished Mercer would go back to being his monosyllabic, single word persona. "You've killed. Perhaps if you let yourself acknowledge it, you'd realize you even enjoyed it. Relished in it because you knew it had to be done, and so you did it to fix a problem or find a solution. But you're afraid to let the demons out to play. You hide them away. Pretend they don't exist. That they don't live inside of you. So they fester. You're probably plagued with nightmares. Which is worse? The one where you're killing someone or someone's killing you?" He lifted a questioning eyebrow. "You're afraid if you acknowledge what you're capable of, you'll turn into a monster or turn into someone like me." He actually grinned. It was a discomforting, vulgar sight.

"Wow, someone's been drinking the Kool-Aid." I looked away, focusing on anything but Mercer. I preferred him barking orders, instead of rambling nonsense in his adrenaline-induced euphoria.

"Suit yourself. Just because you don't want to believe it doesn't make it any less true." I ignored him, and he went back to the silent stillness.

A few minutes later, the van came to a stop. Mercer stood, and he, Hans, and Donovan exited to run reconnaissance. Bastian flipped through satellite imagery and blueprints of the facility. His radio chirped, and Mercer gave the all clear. Bastian flipped a few switches, and a lifeless monitor showed the heat signatures of the interior of a fairly large building.

"How the hell do you have military-grade technology?" I was astounded.

"Details." Bastian waved the question away, calibrating a few switches. The entire inside of the van was alive with flickering lights and sounds. There were real-time cameras monitoring the outside of what appeared to be a very narrow warehouse. It wasn't a warehouse at all, but many large, climate-controlled storage units all interconnected in a long rectangular row. There was a small heat signature in the center unit that resembled a human, which wasn't moving. The first unit was completely lit up, and no human forms could be deciphered. The other six units had areas of hot and cold, but not indiscernible shapes or forms. "It doesn't appear there are guards inside, unless their heat signatures are masked." He pointed to a few of the hotter areas on the screen. "Hard to say."

The van door opened, and Mercer climbed back inside. "Donovan is setting up across the way." He leaned over Bastian and pointed to an area on one of the maps. I wasn't sure if he was speaking to both of us or if I was considered invisible once more. "Hans is scouting the area. There's a vehicle here," again he pointed to the map, "but no outside patrol. We checked the area for surveillance, but it's too vast. It's possible we aren't seeing it."

"I'm monitoring electrical output," Bastian responded, "but nothing is spiking outside the storage units. Everything they are using is likely inside."

Mercer turned to me. "We believe the main door is covered by a trip wire. There's no way of knowing if it leads to an alarm or an explosion. We've found a possible entry point." He pulled up the building schematics and pointed something out; then he turned and narrowed his eyes at me. "How much do you weigh?"

"Excuse me?"

"Oh for fuck's sake," he sighed, "you're probably fifty-two kilos." My conversion to the metric system didn't go over so well, and I glanced at Bastian for help, but he was too busy to offer a number. "Do you think it'll hold?" Mercer asked Bastian.

"It's not the weight so much as the width." Bastian turned and gave me his full attention. "Lose the vest. It'll make your entry a bit easier, but it's still a tight squeeze. I hope you aren't claustrophobic, love."

"Come." Mercer jerked his head toward the van door and exited.

"Break a leg," Bastian replied as I followed Mercer. "Actually, don't."

Outside, we were fortunate enough to have some cover in the dusk. The sun set an hour ago, and the dim light shielded our approach to the back corner of the storage unit block. If Mercer didn't stop short, I might have run into Hans as I followed after him.

"The inside is still dark. Bastian, any movement?" Hans asked.

"Negative." I heard the squawk through Hans' earpiece.

"Donovan, any movement?" Mercer asked.

"Negatory," he replied.

"Parker," Mercer handed me an extra earpiece, "stay in contact, but maintain radio silence unless you have something to report. I don't need to hear your idle chitchat." I glared at him, but I wasn't sure he noticed in the growing dimness. He climbed on top of an air conditioning unit and reached up and ripped a metal grate off of an air duct shaft. "Ladies first."

Sighing, I tugged at the Velcro straps on my vest and wrestled it off, tossing it behind the air unit. Reattaching my shoulder holster and tightening it, I stowed my nine millimeter and climbed on top of the unit, next to Mercer. "This seems like a round peg in a square hole situation." He looked quizzical. "I don't see how you think I'm going to fit in there. In case you haven't noticed, I have shoulders and hips."

"Then scrunch together." He leaned down and grabbed my legs, hoisting me up to the opening. I grabbed the edge and tried to pull myself inside. If this was the job, I should have signed up for Cirque du Soleil instead. Finally, I maneuvered my shoulders inside and pulled the rest of my body in. Leaning against the vertical shaft, I put my right leg on one wall and my left on the other.

"Anyone got a light?" I called out the opening. Mercer reached up, and I barely managed to grab the flashlight. "How am I supposed to know when I get there?"

"Keep moving. Bastian will let you know when you've made it to the center room. There should be a few more grates between here and there. You'll have to remove one and lower yourself down, then evaluate the door, and provide feedback so we can get inside."

Sure, that sounds all well and good when you're not the one crawling through a very small enclosed space. I swallowed. I wasn't exactly claustrophobic, but I'd never been in such tight quarters either.

Moving vertically up the shaft, I tried to remember the basic premises of climbing. One leg on each wall, arms for balance, and back against the side. If nothing else, my quads were getting one hell of a workout. At the top, the air duct shifted from vertical to horizontal, and I had the arduous task of squeezing through again. Dragging myself in a military crawl through the horizontal duct was slow going. The problem was I couldn't move. The flashlight was stuck between my teeth, and there wasn't any room to do anything other than lay flat on my stomach and drag myself across the dirty and dusty duct. I tried not to imagine spiders or rats crawling through this same space.

"What the hell's taking so long?" Mercer growled in my ear.

"I just thought I'd stop and take a break," I muttered sarcastically through my teeth. "Maybe have a picnic."

"Cut the chitchat."

I rolled my eyes and pushed on. The metal creaked as I continued forward. Moving inch by inch was taking a lot longer than even I expected, and the metal would sporadically shift and groan under my weight. This wasn't a good idea. Then again, everything involving Mercer wasn't a good idea. I was letting him lead me around by the nose and following his orders. Why was I letting him call all the shots? I let out a sigh of frustration as my hips snagged again in the duct, and I shifted the left side of my body forward while keeping my right still in order to get unstuck. I was a size two trying to push my way through a double zero air duct. It just wasn't working.

"You're over the first unit," Bastian remarked. "Two more to go."

"Roger," I replied, passing a grate and glancing down, catching the smell of wet earth and cannabis. Whoever owned the first unit was growing some grade-A marijuana. Maybe for shits and giggles, I'd drop an anonymous tip to the narcotics division when this was all over with.

Continuing forward, I was internally debating the reason Mercer was in charge of everything, including me. It was simple. He was the K&R specialist with the information to boot. I didn't have the resources, the toys, or the wherewithal to develop these leads. Until the police had a positive I.D. on the clinic thieves and managed to connect them to the kidnappers, I was forced to obey Mercer. After all, he had satellite imagery, military-grade surveillance equipment, and a team of highly impressive operatives, even if I would never admit any of these things to myself if I wasn't stuck in a very tiny metal tube.

The metal squealed loudly as I passed the second grate, and I briefly thought it might pop open under my weight and send me tumbling to the ground. Luckily, it remained intact as I continued onward.

"Stop," Bastian urged, and I halted my progress. "I think the next three units have been modified to consist of a single, large unit. Can you get visual confirmation?"

"Hang on, I'm approaching the slatted grate now." I inched forward and looked down, but I couldn't see anything. "I'm not sure. I can attempt to remove the grate."

"Negative, continue on," Mercer ordered. "You've wasted enough time." Gritting my teeth around the flashlight, I dragged my body across the next grate, but this time, I was sure the air duct leaned to the right. Maybe I was hallucinating. I maneuvered further along the path when the metal let out a shrill shriek. Something popped from above, and the metal duct lowered.

"Love, you might want to hurry," Bastian interjected.

"Something's not—"

But I didn't hear what else he said because the part of the air duct I was in came unhinged from its place on the ceiling, and without warning, it crashed into the ground.

"Parker, do you copy?" I shook my head and tried to get up, but I was stuck inside a crushed tin can.

"Hang on," I muttered, bending one of the metal sides out of my way and crawling out of the dented and broken duct.

"Are you okay?" Bastian asked.

"My dignity might be irreparably damaged," I muttered. My hip took the brunt of the impact, and I already had a knot the size of a baseball over my pelvic bone. "Hostiles?" I asked, standing in the dim lighting and trying to make sure no one was about to jump me. The room was large, dark, and cavernous, or at least that's how it appeared after exiting a two by two rectangle.

"Get to the door. Now," Bastian insisted.

TWENTY-EIGHT

The flashlight was on the fritz, and I attempted to maneuver the interior using my other senses. There was a faint light coming from somewhere, but I wasn't sure where. I stuck to the wall, making my way across the back of the room. I found a ninety-degree angle where a movable metal wall had been placed to separate the storage units. Following it forward, I noticed light coming from underneath an opening at the end. Bastian was right; at least one other unit was opened to allow interconnectedness between the interior storage units.

"Bloody hell, get going," Mercer growled.

I decided to throw caution to the wind, seeing as how they were my eyes at the moment, and I double-timed it to the front wall. Giving the flashlight a good shake, a beam of light came out of the cracked contraption. "I'm at the door. There's a wire connected to some type of conduit," I relayed.

"Any sign of a det cord or incendiary device?" Bastian asked.

"I don't see one." I'm sure my answer was subpar by Mercer's standards, but I wasn't positive of anything.

"Explain what you see," Bastian ordered, and I gave him

the specifications on the number panel in front of me, the wire, and the colors of cord protruding from the conduit and around the door. "Do you see any type of pressure sensor?"

"No."

"Okay," he blew out a breath, "avoid the edges, Hans, when you take out the middle of the door."

"Light 'em up," Mercer gave the command. "Parker, scout the inside and check the connected units for signs of surveillance."

"Roger," I responded, hoping my flashlight wouldn't go dead. I moved back to the opening I found, and holding the flashlight in my left, under my poised gun, I slowly entered the next unit. In the center of a room was an old rusted row of lockers and attached to them, or perhaps behind them, was a metal cage. The cage itself was maybe six feet high, four feet wide, and eight feet in length. There was a single cot inside.

Something scraped across the expanse of the unit, and I ducked behind the lockers. "Parker, someone's approaching from the other end of the room," Bastian informed me. I didn't respond as I shimmied along the lockers, wondering if I should extinguish the light or use it to blind my incoming target. "Make that two." I held my breath, straining to identify the location. "Shit, do not engage. He has a child with him." I bit my lip to keep from responding. Fuck.

"Parker, we will provide a distraction and take out the hostile. Get to the kid," Mercer commanded. I extinguished the light and waited. What was happening on the other side of these blasted lockers? "Bastian, make sure you jam all frequencies so they can't radio for help. We're going silent until the threat is neutralized," Mercer commanded. Static filled my earpiece, and then a loud bang came from the other unit as the middle portion of the metal door clanged to the floor.

"What the fuck?" a man exclaimed. A metal gate latched closed, and then there was movement at the other end of the lockers. I barely glimpsed a figure going into the other room as I went around the other side.

"Catherine? Adalina?" I asked. I wasn't sure who might be imprisoned inside the steel cage. My gun was still at the ready, and I flipped the flashlight on. Sounds of a scuffle were growing louder from the next room. The flashlight came on, and I saw the big blue eyes of Catherine Cale staring back at me through the cage. "Catherine," I said relieved, "I'm Alexis. I work with your Uncle Nick. I'm going to get you out of here." She looked like a deer caught in headlights, ready to hide or possibly scream. "Is Adalina here? Have you seen her? Are you hurt?" I had a million questions and not much time. I shoved my nine millimeter into the holster and went to the door of the cage. A padlock kept it shut.

"Addy's not here. We were always together, but yesterday, they separated us." Catherine sniffled loudly on the brink of bursting into tears. "Where's Uncle Nick?" The kid was smart. She wasn't falling for anyone's line of bullshit. The only problem was I was speaking the truth.

"He got hurt, but he's been trying to find you. He asked me to help. I've talked to your mom and dad. They can't wait to get you back."

I scanned the area for something strong enough to break the padlock. Locating a fire extinguisher against the wall, I picked it up. Yelling came from the other room, and I could make out Mercer's threatening voice.

"Alexis," she said uncertainly. She sat on the cot and pulled her legs in front of her, making herself as small as possible.

"Are you hurt?" I asked, slamming the extinguisher down, but the lock didn't budge.

"No. The men let us have food and blankets and stuff." She flinched as I brought the extinguisher down again. "I want to go home."

I raised it again and brought it down as hard as I could. The padlock broke in two, and I was pulling the remaining metal piece free when I heard a gunshot. Shit.

Opening the door, I dove into the cage with Catherine, grabbed her from her perch on the bed, and shoved her underneath the cot, throwing myself into the space between the cot and the lockers to shield her from any bullets that might rip past.

"Bloody hell, do you have him or not?" Mercer squawked as the scuffle grew louder.

There was another loud bang, and the floor trembled in what felt like an earthquake. There was more crashing and metal scraping, and Catherine screamed beneath me. When everything settled, I shushed her with my best attempt at soothing. She was crying, but the screaming stopped.

"Clear," I heard through my earpiece. "Parker, are you still alive?"

"Yes." I tried to back out from underneath the cot but felt something hard against my back. "I have Catherine. Adalina's not here," I responded. Catherine quieted and listened to me, probably wondering who I was talking to.

I heard footsteps. "The metal wall tumbled when that bloke decided to resist detainment. It's crashed into the lockers, and they tipped over. It might take some effort to get you out," Mercer said. Great, I was pinned under part of the cage, some lockers, and the thin, movable wall.

"A little help," I retorted.

"I called the coppers. That Heathcliff fellow is on his way. But there are bigger fish to catch, and the clock's ticking on saving my girl." Mercer turned on his heel. "Thanks for the help."

"Wait," I called after him, but he left. "Bastian," I tried speaking through the earpiece, hoping for someone to stay behind and get me out of this mess.

"Sorry, love," he replied, and then he must have disconnected my earpiece because all I heard was static.

"Fu—dge," I had to remember I was in the presence of a seven-year-old, "sorry your rescue is taking longer than I anticipated. Are you okay?"

"Yes," she said timidly, "I don't like the dark, and I don't like it here."

"Detective Heathcliff is on his way. He'll get us out in no time."

As we remained under the cot, waiting for help to arrive, I had to remember I was dealing with a child who had been kidnapped and away from home for the last twelve days.

Asking a million interrogation questions about how she was taken and by who was not the way to go. Instead, I rambled on about how much I liked the couch in her living room and how long her uncle and I had known each other. She eventually relaxed, and her sniffling ebbed. Sirens were approaching, and I was glad we were getting out of here. After today's adventure, I was seriously considering becoming claustrophobic.

"Parker?" I recognized Thompson's voice, and I yelled a response. Within seconds, he was crouched on the floor with a flashlight in hand directly in front of us on the outside of the cage across from the cot. "Catherine?"

"Uncle Tommy," she squealed happily.

"Thompson, get us out of here." I resisted the urge to beg.

He looked at me uncertainly. "No problem." There was something he wasn't saying, and I figured there might be a few bodies in the other room. "You hanging in there, Cathy?"

"Uh-huh. Alexis has been telling me stories about Uncle Nick."

"Has she now?" Thompson motioned someone over and took a pair of bolt cutters from them. "She's really great at storytelling, isn't she? Did she tell you about the time she got stuck underneath the bed in her apartment, and the fire department had to come in because they were afraid the entire structure was unstable and would collapse on her."

"No." Catherine seemed puzzled.

"She's been here long enough, Thompson. No more stories. I can hold it up while you get her out."

"Parker, this isn't a good idea."

"It's been long enough. I'll be fine. It's not that heavy." He didn't like my idea, but he wanted to get her out of here just as quickly as I did. He cut through most of the steel cage, enough so he could pull it free so she could slide out. "On the count of three, I'll lift up, and Catherine you're going to slide over to Uncle Tommy."

"Okay," she said uncertainly. We counted down, and after two, I struggled to raise myself against the underside of the cot. I managed to get my arms underneath me and lifted up, pressing my back into the bottom of the cot as Thompson removed the piece of cage and helped Catherine get free.

"She's clear," he announced as my arms trembled under the weight of the combined wall and lockers. They collapsed without my permission, and I heard more metal clanking and slamming. The cot above me tipped on its side as the legs closest to the cage broke off further trapping me. "Parker?"

"I'm okay," I called. There was a small triangle directly in front of me where I could still see out, but on either side, I was trapped by the broken cot or the broken lockers. "Take her home. I'm not going anywhere."

"Rescue squad's on the way. There are a few uniformed officers positioned around, so if you need anything."

"I got it."

He lifted Catherine up, and I watched his footsteps disappear. I closed my eyes, assessing my situation. My hip was throbbing, my arms were sore, but I could move all of my appendages, and I didn't think I was bleeding or impaled by any of the metal. Honestly, I felt pretty damn fantastic. Catherine was safe. She was on her way home or to the hospital or whatever. Her mom and dad would be thrilled. O'Connell would be thrilled. Today, the score was good guys – one, Four Seasons – zip. Although, questions about who they were and what Mercer was going to do threatened to ruin my euphoria, so I decided to stick with happy as my main emotion for the time being.

"Jesus, Parker." There was a pair of shined shoes in front of me, and then Heathcliff got down on his stomach and stared at me from the other side of the cage. "How the hell do you get yourself into these tight situations?"

"Did you come up with that on the drive here?" I asked sarcastically.

"Are you okay?"

"I'm great." And that was my sincerest sentiment. Heathcliff matched my grin with one of his own.

"Well, while we wait for the rescue squad to show up, do you want to give me your statement?"

"Are you kidding?"

"No." He continued to smile. "She's safe, so guess who gets to go back to work."

"Lucky bastard." I told him what I knew, leaving out as much as I could when it came to the ex-SAS team.

"Damn, you really need to lay off the donuts," he remarked as I concluded the story. "Crashing through the metal, skeletal structure of a building," he shook his head and made a tsk, tsk sound, "I'm signing you up for Jenny Craig tomorrow."

"Only if you get me a cheeseburger first, I'm starving. My dinner was interrupted by Mercer's call, and I've only had a rotten granola bar all day."

"One made out of lead," he teased. It was easier to joke then it was to consider the possibility of the wall and lockers further collapsing on top of me. "As soon as they get you out of here, I'm taking you for that burger."

"You better."

The rescue squad arrived and finished evaluating the situation while Heathcliff and I chatted. He got off the floor at their request. He disappeared and came back a few seconds later.

"Ma'am," one of the firemen said, leaning down next to Heathcliff, "we'll try to saw through the metal and remove the rubble, layer by layer. If you feel anything shift, an increase in pressure, or the metal becomes too hot, signal to your friend here, and he'll have us stop immediately."

"Great plan, but let's drop the ma'am. It's Alex."

He nodded and stood up. Heathcliff kept an eye on me, but the sound of the electric saw cutting through steel made conversation impossible. At least the darkness was replaced by dozens of flood lights that lit the room up brighter than a discount store during the Christmas holiday shopping season.

Thirty minutes later, the lockers were lifted off of me, and the remnants of the cage were shredded. One of the firemen stepped in to help me up. I was unsteady and sore from my earlier fall, so he insisted I get the quick once-over by the paramedics parked outside. After checking my scrapes and bruises, I was free to go.

"Were you serious about the cheeseburger?" Heathcliff

asked as we drove toward the precinct.

"I've never been more serious about anything in my life, except for the fact that I want some fries to go with it." I laughed, and he stopped at a twenty-four hour fast food joint before continuing to the station. We had a lot to discuss.

TWENTY-NINE

"I thought you were starving." Heathcliff jerked his chin at the brown paper sack that contained my dinner. I nibbled on a couple of fries and took a bite out of the burger, but after everything that happened inside the storage unit, I was too keyed up to eat.

"Maybe I've been reconsidering the calories."

He glanced at the ice pack against my hip. His idea, not mine. We were in the bullpen at the precinct, and I made myself at home behind O'Connell's desk. Heathcliff was next to me, and Detective Jacobs was sitting at Thompson's desk across from us.

Jacobs skimmed through the report one last time and scrunched his face, his eyebrows knitting together in thought. "You have a few gaps in your story."

"Must have hit my head during the fall," I suggested, "might have impacted my memory."

Jacobs didn't look convinced as he narrowed his eyes. "Okay, I'm willing to accept that you received an anonymous tip that the girl was being kept in the storage unit. I'm even willing to go along with the fact that you somehow managed to climb up to that air vent by yourself and crawled along until you came to the middle unit."

"There's no somehow about it. She fell through the ceiling and took half the ductwork with her," Heathcliff interjected, and I gave him a warning look.

"And sure you managed to break into the cage and rescue Catherine Cale," Jacobs paused, "but that doesn't explain the hole blown through the metal door, the collapsed room divider and lockers, and the blood spatter inside the connected unit."

"Don't forget the bullet holes," Heathcliff offered, and I kicked him in the shin.

"I can charge you with interfering in a police investigation," Jacobs threatened. I shrugged and decided to give the fries another try. "Or are you going to tell me what really happened?"

"I told you what happened. Either I'm not aware of how the rest of it went, or I don't feel it's in the best interest of the remaining kidnapped girl to divulge this information to you at the moment." I was stubborn, but the last thing Mercer needed was flashing lights impeding his rescue attempt. If it was just Mercer's ass on the line, I would have drawn Jacobs a diagram of everything, but I was concerned with Adalina's safety. Someone had to be. "But here's a helpful hint, if you're arresting me, you have to read my Miranda's first, and yes, I would like a lawyer present before any questioning commences." Jacobs looked to Heathcliff for guidance, but Heathcliff reached into the bag and pulled out a handful of fries instead.

"I'm going to talk to the Captain. Don't go anywhere," Jacobs insisted.

Thirty seconds later, Capt. Moretti was standing in front of me. "Parker, great job." He extended his hand, and we shook. Jacobs sighed as he went to file some paperwork. "I know you haven't been on the payroll in a while, but hell, you got O'Connell's niece back. The bastards responsible are still in the wind, and you have more insight into this than most." He glanced at Heathcliff. "Since everyone's out of the doghouse, shall I dust off those consulting forms and get your help on this?"

"Sounds good."

Moretti went back into his office to print off some forms

or maybe get approval from his boss. Either way, it looked like I was employed by a law enforcement agency again. It was nice to be home, even if I originally tried to avoid it.

"What the hell did they put in those fries?" Heathcliff asked, interrupting my thoughts. "You look ecstatic, bordering on manic."

"It's good to be back."

After signing the paperwork and settling in more permanently at O'Connell's desk, I still wasn't ready to divulge any more information on the situation in the storage unit. If something surfaced and it became important, I would talk but not until then. Instead, I read through all of the official police paperwork concerning the kidnapping, surveillance, suspects, witnesses, financial records, and reports. Although most of this was new information, the majority led nowhere. The leads the three of us determined in my apartment were far more accurate than what the police department surmised. Politics and public relations had done a lot of harm. I was glad Mercer didn't play by the rules, or we'd still be looking for Catherine.

Thompson entered the bullpen and smiled brightly. "Are we sure it's a good thing they freed you from that cage?" he asked.

"Moretti thinks so." I held up my consultant credentials as he sat down. "How's Catherine?"

"They took her to the hospital for a check-up. She's fine. No signs of abuse or mistreatment. Evelyn, Peter, O'Connell, and Jen are with her now. A few officers and some social workers are talking to her about what happened. We don't want to re-traumatize her, but she has the answers."

"I'm glad she's okay. She's a tough kid."

"She must be if she was stuck under that cot with you for an extended amount of time." He winked and went to talk to Moretti.

I finished skimming through the case files and looked at the clock. It was almost five a.m. The adrenaline rush from earlier subsided hours ago, and the caffeine coursing through my veins ceased working an hour ago. I was ready to go home, get a few hours of sleep, and start fresh by early afternoon. I tossed Estobar Santino's name around to a few uniforms to do some legwork and run a full profile while I was gone. Heathcliff left, and I was logging off of Nick's computer when a voice interrupted.

"Parker," it came out a growl, "what the hell do you think you're doing?"

"Fulfilling a promise," I told O'Connell. "She's safe, isn't she?"

I saw the smile tug at the corners of his mouth. "First, you take my badge. Now you're taking my desk. Am I this easy to replace?" It was a joke. It wasn't exactly an apology, but it was better than nothing.

"That's what happens when you get hurt on the job; someone has to fill in until you learn to duck and cover." We studied one another for a moment. "Anyway, you can have your desk back. I'm going home to sleep." I stood up and remembered my car was at Mercer's. Maybe I could borrow one from impound since I was technically working for the police department. "Are you even supposed to be here?"

"No, I'm still on sick leave, but there were reports to file. Catherine's had a lot to say, and sooner is better than later."

"Take it easy, Nick."

"Alexis," he put up a hand to stop me from brushing past, "Evelyn and Peter wanted to say thanks."

"No need. I was just helping out a friend." He gave me a small smile, and I went in search of a ride home.

After a bit of conniving, a fresh-faced rookie dropped me off at Mercer's apartment. I got out of the car and waved the officer away. Once the cruiser was out of sight, I knocked on Mercer's door. There was no answer and no sign of the van. I gave the front door one last look, considering the pros and cons of breaking in. The sun was coming up, and I was starting to feel the stiffness creep into my muscles and joints. Settling into my soft mattress seemed like a much better idea than rummaging through Mercer's information. I dug my car key out of my pocket and drove home.

My apartment was a welcome sight, and I barely managed to change out of my clothes and brush the dust and debris out of my hair before collapsing on the bed. Setting the alarm seemed too tedious of a task, so I hoped I'd wake by my own volition by noon. Shutting my eyes, I managed a few dreamless hours of sleep before my subconscious began to weave facts and questions into my REM cycle.

I woke up horrified. Maybe I was just jumping to conclusions, but the man keeping guard over Catherine was taken by Mercer. The shots fired and the blood in the next room were indicative of someone being injured, and while there was the possibility one of the ex-SAS was grazed, I felt pretty sure that wasn't likely. My mouth tasted salty, and I swallowed. What my subconscious decided was Mercer took the injured man someplace secluded to torture him for answers. It wasn't that some sick kidnapper didn't deserve what he was getting, but this wasn't exactly how things should be done either. Maybe I was still suffering from memories of being tortured myself.

Getting up, I took a shower and dressed for a day at the precinct. My hip was a lovely blackish-purple and hurt to be touched, but it was of little consequence compared to the assessment I gave my once battered and bloody wrists. The scars left from the rope burns and cuts had long since healed and were barely visible, but I couldn't help but think what techniques Mercer might be inflicting upon the only current lead in finding Adalina and the Four Seasons. Maybe if I were in his shoes, I'd do whatever it took to find Catherine too.

I decided to splurge and pick up coffee on my way to the station as a way to distract myself from the morbidity of my morning. Getting a few coffees for whoever might be at work, I pulled into the parking lot and carried the four cups into the bullpen. Thompson and Heathcliff were both there, and they looked relieved to have a better beverage option than the mud that was brewing in the break room.

"Any news from our favorite K&R specialist?" Heathcliff asked as I found the folder on Estobar Santino atop O'Connell's desk.

"Not a word." I surveyed the bullpen, but no one was paying much attention. The kidnapping was old news after last night's recovery. "Any bodies turn up today?"

"Bodies always turn up," Thompson muttered from his seat across from me, "but no one of interest." I assumed Heathcliff must have connected some of the dots and shared them with Thompson.

After reading through the workup on Santino, I still didn't glean anything useful. I leaned back in the chair and propped my leg up on the opened bottom drawer, trying to figure out a way to circumvent rules, regulations, and Mercer and his mercenaries. There had to be a way to get close to Santino without jeopardizing Adalina's safety or the Estes' wishes. If I could get eyes on him, maybe he'd lead me somewhere solid.

Heathcliff interrupted my thoughts by slapping a stack of papers on the desk. "Do you think this is a vacation?" he teased. "You claim to have mad case-solving skills so get cracking." I could tell he was as frustrated as the rest of us. Our joviality over Catherine's recovery lasted through the night, but now the need to prevent the same group from doing this again in the future was overriding all the warm, fuzzy feelings.

Picking up the papers, I realized it was Catherine's file, containing everything from medical reports to preliminary evidence collection to her statement. This would lead somewhere. Only Catherine could tell us where she was, how many different abductors she encountered, and how long she and the other captives had been held and where. The problem was, unlike her uncle, she wasn't trained in police procedure and the finer art of noticing small nuances. She was also seven. Still, it was worth a shot.

She wasn't malnourished or dehydrated. Hell, she wasn't even exhausted. By all accounts, the Seasons kept her in excellent physical shape. There wasn't so much as a cut or bruise on her. From what she told her parents and the officers, the men gave her and her friends blankets, pillows, and access to all other necessities. It seemed the only thing the girls were missing were extra sets of clothing. They even had access to showers and bathrooms.

They were given privacy, or seemingly their privacy, so at the very least the kidnappers weren't perverts. They were told numerous times if they needed anything or wanted something to ask. What kind of kidnappers were we dealing with?

As I continued to peruse the reports, Catherine said they were moved four different times. The last place was the scariest because it was dark, and she was alone. Adalina had been with her when they were transported to the storage unit, but they didn't remain together. There was a guard keeping her there, and before I arrived, he just escorted her back to the cell from another room where she had been given dinner and allowed to watch cartoons. The contradictory nature of the abduction was making my head spin.

"Who the fuck are these people?" I mumbled.

"Minus the lack of free will, it sounds like a vacation," Heathcliff answered.

Some things were already pinging in my brain, but I decided to finish reading the file before chasing any particular theory through my psyche. Officers canvassed the entire lot of storage units but recovered nothing, except my discarded flak jacket which was in evidence for the time being. The other room that Catherine spoke of was another interconnected unit. It contained a television, a refrigerator, a makeshift bedroom, a sofa, and various toys and games to entertain a seven-year-old. Why did they want to keep the girls happy? To gain their trust and compliance, or to discourage any attempt at escape? How would they even know what a seven-year-old would be interested in? I had no clue, but from Evelyn and Peter's remarks, which were added to the file, I could tell the kidnappers were well-versed in current trends. I felt the gnawing in my brain. Something just wasn't sitting right.

"Hey," Thompson commanded my attention, and I looked up, "we're checking out a lead on the clinic break-in. Did you want to tag along?"

"No." I stood up. "I'll do some digging on my own."

He nodded, and the two detectives headed out. I collected my belongings and drove home. My apartment was a much better place for pacing and investigating matters that the police department was not officially privy to.

THIRTY

The large wall in my living room had more holes in it than a pincushion after all the reworking our theory underwent. The kidnappers had a familiarity with the girls and with the interests of seven-year-olds. They also kept them safe and reasonably happy, even if they had no problem leading me to believe they were ruthless killers. My eyes narrowed, scanning through the endless list of suspects. The only clear fact was someone intimately familiar with the Estes' household was involved.

I blew out a breath and fought the urge to throw something. Means, motive, and opportunity, my internal voice was working through the basics needed for warrants. Estobar Santino had the means. The motive I could assume was financial, but I would assume motive for any kidnapper was financial unless circumstances dictated otherwise. Opportunity, I scratched my head. We couldn't get close enough to him to even get an alibi. He might have an airtight alibi, or he might have grabbed the girls straight from school.

School. I stopped. There were no signs of physical trauma. Why would three seven-year-olds willing go with someone they didn't know without so much as a scream? I went back to the report based on Catherine's story. She said the girls were taken on the way into the building, but no other details were provided.

"Answer your phone, Nick," I urged, listening to the ringing through the earpiece.

"What?" I knew we didn't completely patch things up, but surely, I should have received a kinder response than that.

"O'Connell," I began but stopped, realizing he knew more than he was letting on, and for some reason, he still wanted to keep everyone in the dark. "Why did you go to the precinct to file the paperwork?" I blurted out. It wasn't the question I intended to ask, but there was something off.

"Despite what you may think, I'm still a cop."

"Yeah, but the responding officer should have made the report. Thompson brought Catherine in. Why isn't he the detective on record?"

"Did Moretti hire you to be the paperwork monitor?" O'Connell retorted.

"No."

"Then who the hell cares? Paperwork is paperwork. No one wants to do it." He was being defensive, and for no reason I could discern.

"Why'd your niece willingly go with her abductor?"

"Drop it, Parker," he warned. I heard a posh British accent in the background. "I have to go."

"Are you with Mercer?" My blood pressure spiked, and I wasn't sure if I was more appalled by the fact that a detective sworn to protect and uphold the law might be assisting in torturing someone or that he still didn't feel he could trust me to help deal with the situation.

"No." He hung up before I could ask anything else.

"Fuck you," I said to the dead air space.

Launching a pillow at the wall made me feel a little better, even though nothing crashed or broke into a million pieces. There were a few other options, but calling on the Cales and persuading them to let me speak to Catherine wasn't the way to go. The girl had been through enough. I tried dialing Mercer, but he didn't answer. With nothing better to do, I called Thompson and asked that he do his best to keep his partner out of trouble.

Eventually, I cooled down and went back to work. I was reviewing the surveillance feed from the school, watching as a chauffeured town car pulled up. It idled for a few minutes. The front of the vehicle was out of the camera's range, making identifying the driver or passengers impossible, and then it left. Initially, I believed it was a parent or driver, dropping a child off at school, but what if that was the vehicle used to pick up the kids? It'd be easy enough to convince the girls that one of their parents arranged for a separate ride to the museum. Stranger things had happened, and with the affluence of the school, it wouldn't be uncommon for town cars to arrive on a daily basis.

I managed to get a partial plate number from the grainy feed and called it into the precinct. They were running vehicle registries and would get back to me with any feasible matches. It wasn't much, but it felt like progress. I tried to review the rest of Catherine's file, but I was too annoyed with O'Connell and Mercer to concentrate. Maybe I needed a break.

I took a nice long jog to clear my mind. It was intended to be a run. But my hip was sore, so a slow jog had to suffice. The fresh air and freedom from the confines of my apartment eased the tension and hostility I was harboring, and my mind went back to ruminating on the questionable facts in Catherine's statement.

By the time I made it back to my apartment, I was positive the reason the girls were treated so well was because whoever took them cared deeply about their well-being. If this had been a single child abduction in a custody battle, I would have expected as much because the parent would want the child to feel safe and comfortable. But this wasn't a custody battle, and more than one girl was taken. Could we be looking at things all wrong?

I conducted a search for any public news stories or paparazzi articles concerning the Peruvian gold moguls. If Peru was anything like the U.S., the rich would be treated like quasi-royalty or at least celebrities. Could there be marital unrest? I flashed back to my brief encounter with

Senor Estes and his wife. She remained silent and on the outside. As far as I could recall, the two never interacted, and something seemed strange about the grieving mother.

After I set my computer to conduct its search and translate any non-English results into English, I took a quick shower as my mind continued to race through my new theory. Unlike all our other theories which didn't hold water or failed to produce results, I was beginning to think I might be getting closer to a plausible explanation for all of this. An explanation would lead to the kidnappers. It was too much to hope for, but I couldn't help myself. This had been going on far too long.

Tying up my wet hair, I stood in front of my computer, skimming through the results. The problem with tabloid news was it wasn't always reliable. There were a few stories which spoke of outlandish arguments and threats made by Senora Rosa Estes, promising to take Miguel for all he was worth. The only issue was these stories were dated a year or two back. The more recent tabloid articles spoke of reconciliation, a possible pregnancy, and the two together at various charity functions. It seemed the fighting stopped and was replaced by true love. I scoffed at the notion.

I wished there was a way to get in contact with Rosa Estes, but there was no way around the family's order preventing a police presence at their estate. The next best thing was to compile a complete workup on her. An hour later and there was still next to nothing on Rosa Estes. Hell, even her maiden name seemed to be top secret. With the way the day had gone, I was positive I was losing my touch.

"Parker," I answered the ringing phone.

"We identified the perp from the clinic break-in." Heathcliff got straight to the point. I hadn't seen his no-nonsense attitude much since he started coloring outside the lines, but now that he was back in Moretti's good graces, he was acting like his usual cop self again.

"Real cops don't call the suspects perps," I teased, but he ignored it.

"Anyway, he's a local kid from the neighborhood. We issued a BOLO, but Thompson and I think we might have eyes on him. One of the informants for narcotics said he saw the kid go home. We knocked, but there was no answer, and we're waiting for the ink to dry on the warrant."

"How old is this kid?" I asked. Another sign of getting older, we referred to everyone as kids, even if they were in their early twenties.

"Seventeen. He has some priors for drugs, petty theft, and distribution."

"Are you bringing him in?"

"Just as soon as the arrest warrant's signed. Weren't you listening?"

"You lost me after perp."

He grumbled, but I pushed on, filling him in on the possible kidnapping lead and the town car. As soon as he and Thompson returned to the station, he'd ask Moretti to call in some favors with the state department and get backgrounds on Rosa and Miguel Estes. The one for Estobar Santino was already in the works, so it was just a matter of time. I had exhausted my resources at the OIO and didn't want to have to call in any more favors unless circumstances turned dire. As it stood, under normal circumstances, Director Kendall and Mark hassled me enough with returning for a consulting stint here and there.

After hanging up, I felt progress was being made; although, Mercer was probably fifteen steps ahead. Thoughts of Mercer made my annoyance with O'Connell return. What was he doing any of this for? His niece was safe and sound. I tried to distract myself with tracking the Four Seasons, but all leads were being followed. It was just a matter of waiting for the results.

I made dinner and sifted through the files for Hover Designs. With nothing better to do, I took another stab at Insight International's hundred and seventeen page report. Any names, projects, or departments that seemed suspicious would be investigated, but after speed reading the bulk of the report, I concluded the only flawed individual Insight International discovered was Liam Naysley. I found the information I printed on him and read through all of it.

Naysley was drowning in debt, but he had no criminal record. By all accounts, he was a model citizen without so much as a jaywalking citation. His work was often lauded by business magazines and journalists. Although he was a pencil pusher, he made smart decisions and had a keen business sense. Why couldn't either of my cases be simple?

Maybe Naysley went over to the dark side, or he had an affinity for making questionable business practices seem legitimate. I needed a business savvy individual to review his work to see if their conclusions coincided with Naysley's results or Robinson's team. More than likely, either Naysley's report was fictitious, or Robinson's management consulting report was a false accusation. Checking the time, I dialed Pirelli with my current dilemma.

"I don't want to risk hiring a third party to review Mr. Naysley's work," she insisted. "This is how I got into this mess to begin with."

"Ma'am," again it was an insult, but she didn't catch on, "I don't have a business or accounting background. I also don't have the resources at my disposal to review this information, but it's imperative that we discover which figures are accurate. This alone could lead straight to HD's leak." She sighed heavily into the phone. I didn't understand why she couldn't review the information herself, but maybe she wasn't a numbers person either.

"Fine," she sounded irritated, "I will find an unbiased third party to review the project and provide his own feedback. Do you think you're capable of comparing the reports?"

"Yes." Today wasn't the day to be condescending. "Do you think you're capable of–" Before I could finish my statement, the doorbell rang. "Please inform me as soon as the task is completed. I will not be able to continue investigating this matter until it is provided." I hung up. She was lucky she was saved by the bell.

Glancing out the peephole, I wasn't sure if I should pretend I wasn't home or answer the door. Unfortunately, for whatever the reason, I decided to open the door.

"Hi." O'Connell stood before me, looking guilty as sin.

"Talk fast. I need one good reason why I shouldn't slam the door in your face."

"Can I come in?"

"Not a reason." I started to shut the door, but he put his palm against it.

"I wasn't with Mercer. He was with me."

"And there's a difference?" I raised an eyebrow. "Fine, come in."

"Mercer showed up at my sister's place this afternoon," O'Connell began without so much as an apology. "He asked if Catherine provided any definitive leads that would help him locate and recover Adalina Estes."

"Did she?"

"You read the report."

"That's not an answer," I snapped.

"No." He met my eyes. "It's been rough on all of us, and I don't want that man around Evelyn or her family."

I bit my lip, not sure if I should ask the next question. "What happened to the kidnapper who was guarding Catherine at the storage unit?" My insides clenched.

"It doesn't leave this room," he insisted, and I nodded. "Mercer's team has him."

"What are they doing with him?"

"Who cares," O'Connell sneered. "How the hell can you give a damn about the son-of-bitch who took my niece?"

"Do you have any idea what Mercer's capable of?"

"Do you have any idea the hell I've endured, that my family has endured? I thought you had my back, Parker."

"Where the hell is *Detective* Nick O'Connell? Because let me tell you something, he would not stand by and let some guns for hire torture the answers out of some slimeball."

O'Connell's features darkened. "Don't pretend you stand on a pedestal above the rest of us. If this was Martin or Jablonsky or someone you actually gave a shit about, you'd be there to beat the answers out yourself."

"But Catherine's back safe and sound."

"No thanks to that bastard." He fixed me with a hard stare as if to say *no thanks to you either.*

"Is this how it's going to be now? Vigilante justice? One

of these fuckers shoots you and kidnaps your niece, so now all bets are off. You're letting some mercenaries deal with the situation while you stand idly by as chaos erupts."

"That's not fair."

"Don't you dare talk to me about fair. I've had your back since the phone call whether you realize it or not. But you're coming unhinged. I can't blame you, but you need to step the fuck back," I warned. "You can barely stand," I jerked my chin toward his side which he had been holding since entering my apartment. "You haven't slept in days, and even though your personal family crisis has been resolved, you still haven't learned to take a breath."

"I can't until they're stopped."

"Nick." I understood. He knew I understood better than anyone, but some lines could never be crossed. And right now, he was teetering on the edge of one of those impenetrable lines. "You're going home. If Mercer contacts you, tell him to come see me. You're not involving yourself in any of this. Get some sleep. If you can't, pop a few extra painkillers to make sure you sleep, and stay home. Talk to your sister, play with your niece, whatever. But don't go to the precinct, don't help Mercer, and don't do anything else on your own."

"How can I let it go?"

"You're going to let it go, or I will make sure Thompson puts a fucking detail outside your house. You're still not thinking straight." He teetered slightly and leaned against the back of my couch. "For once in your life, Detective, trust someone else to get the job done."

"Alex," the need for vengeance was replaced with a pitiful, sorrowful, begging, "please."

I shut my eyes for a moment. Agreeing wasn't easy. But even now, I'd still crawl my way through hell for O'Connell, and he was asking for just that. It wasn't the easy choice, but he made a strong case. And it was the right thing to do. I grimaced. Things were always darkest before the dawn, and I'd be heading into the pitch black with Mercer.

"I'll handle it."

"Okay," he smiled wanly and collapsed.

THIRTY-ONE

"Dammit, Nick," Jen cursed loud enough that I heard her from the hallway. I was sitting in a chair outside Nick's hospital room. The EMTs arrived at my apartment quickly and rushed him to the ER. He had been readmitted. At the moment, I was throwing myself a pity party while Jen ripped into her moronic husband. "What did I tell you about getting rest? No, instead you go traipsing around town with that ex-military idiot and somehow end up at Alex's place. It's a good thing too because what would have happened if you were in the car driving?"

"Honey," he began.

"Don't honey me, Nick O'Connell. I'm a cop's wife. There isn't a day that goes by that I don't feel my stomach flip when I see a uniformed officer walking in my direction. I'm not willing to lose you, so sit down, shut up, and let the doctor do his job."

"Jenny," he tried again. I stared at the floor, not wanting to intrude any further into their personal matters.

Her voice dropped, and I couldn't make out any more words. When I looked up, I caught a glimpse of them kissing. O'Connell was practically killing himself to help Mercer track the Four Seasons and get his revenge, and I agreed to act as his proxy. Maybe I had a martyr complex. I was willing to further fragment my soul and risk my own well-being for a man who in the last week had done nothing but castigate me. A doctor entered the room, and Jen ducked outside. She took a seat next to me and stared at the doctor's back through the window.

"Here." I found a pack of tissues in my purse and handed them to her. "Is he going to be okay?"

"Yes," she swallowed and dabbed at her eyes, annoyed with her herself for being so worked up. "He's such an ass!"

"He's male." She snorted. "What's going on with him?"

"Alexis," she turned to face me, figuring O'Connell wasn't able to escape the room with the doctor in there, "I wish I knew. He's never been like this before. I know getting shot is a traumatic thing, and my god, we've all been so worried about poor, little Catherine." She looked guilty. "But it's beyond the scope of worry with him. He hasn't eaten. The only time he sleeps is when it's medically-induced." I raised an eyebrow. "The antibiotics and pain meds make him sleepy which probably explains why he stopped taking them. He said he needed a clear mind."

"He was worried about his niece."

"Then why is he still acting like she's in danger?" Only one thing came to mind, and I stood up.

"Jen, if you need anything, let me know, but keep an eye on him. If you have to go to work or go out or whatever, ask Thompson to look in on him. Making one 9-1-1 call is more than enough."

"I'm relieved he was with you when it happened. At least someone has a brain, and don't worry, he's not going anywhere. He's staying in the hospital, and if I have to ask Bud from security to sit outside his door, I'll do it." She looked confused by my retreat. "Where are you going?"

"I promised the knucklehead in there that I'd handle things for him. And at the moment, I have my suspicions what's been making him act like a lunatic."

* * *

"Mercer," I bellowed, pounding on the door, "open up."

I recognized the rental parked out front and figured someone must be home. I continued to bang against the door, but no one answered. "Either you let me in, or cops and federal agents will be storming the place in the next ten minutes." I stopped knocking and pulled out my cell phone. "Really, can you be any more childish?"

The door opened, and Hans stared at me, bleary-eyed. "Julian isn't here. Stop the racket."

"Where is he?"

Hans blinked a few times. Obviously, he had been asleep, and I woke him up. "He's with the others."

"Your insight is unparalleled."

He shrugged and stepped aside. "You can come in if you'll just stop talking."

"Fair enough." I followed him inside and shut the door.

By the time I turned around, he had disappeared into another room, presumably to go back to sleep. Considering our deal, I quietly walked through the living room and kitchen, looking for clues as to where Mercer might be. Eventually, I meandered into the room Mercer used as his op center.

All of the surveillance photos, blueprints, and maps had been taken off the walls. The stacks of files on the table were greatly diminished, and I wondered what became of everything. Were the ex-SAS in the process of relocating to another safe house or whatever he was referring to his weekly rental as?

Being here wasn't helpful, and with Hans either asleep or avoiding me, he wasn't of any use either. Hell, maybe that was the plan to get me to leave. I went back into the kitchen and searched the cabinets and fridge. The cabinets were empty, except for the furnished bowls, plates, cookware, and utensils. The refrigerator was also sparsely populated with a couple containers of takeout and a few cans of beer on the top shelf. The middle shelf was empty, and the bottom shelf had what appeared to be some spilled wine or maybe grape juice that hadn't been completely wiped away. I guess I must have missed the party.

I glanced down the narrow hallway. There were three doorways, all closed. I couldn't be sure which was the bedroom Hans ducked into and which might be Mercer's room or the bathroom. My snooping was being impeded by the sleeping ex-military man. Boredom was starting to reign supreme, and I settled onto the couch in the living room.

Thinking about O'Connell, there was a good chance Mercer manipulated the facts to make Nick believe the Seasons might make another run at Catherine or his sister. I dialed Heathcliff, and once he answered, I asked if a unit was stationed outside the Cales' house. After being on hold for a few minutes, I was told the PD and FBI both had people watching the house and family. Winner, winner, chicken dinner.

The front door opened, and Bastian, Donovan, and Mercer entered. Donovan disappeared into one of the rooms down the hallway, and I heard water running. I didn't get a good look at him, but I didn't believe the reason he immediately went to the bathroom was because he drank too much coffee today. I glanced at Mercer, who hadn't moved from the front door and was glowering at me.

"Glad to see you got out of that tin can, love," Bastian chimed in as he went into the kitchen. He looked exhausted. "Want a bite?" he asked, holding up a takeout container. I shifted my gaze away from Mercer momentarily to shake my head.

"What did you say to O'Connell?" I asked, my voice coming out hoarse.

"The detective needs to be aware of the situation."

"He's also back in the hospital because of you." My tone remained neutral, but my expression trembled slightly as I struggled to force it to maintain the same neutrality. "So until further notice, if you want something done, I'll do it." I bit off the last word.

"You'll get your hands dirty," he cautioned.

"My hands are already dirty," I hissed. He took a step away from the doorway. His eyes had that knowing quality from the van, but he didn't say another word. "Why did you go to Nick for help?" Every syllable was full of bitterness.

"He's a policeman." Mercer went to the kitchen sink and

washed his hands, taking his time to wash any trace of his victim's DNA or blood from under his fingernails or to avoid conversation with me a bit longer. It was hard to say for certain which was true.

"That's not an answer," I said, but he ignored it as the water continued to run. Bastian leaned over next to him, whispered something in his ear, and then plopped down on the sofa next to me. His leg brushed roughly against my hip. "Mother," I growled, sucking in air and scooting away.

He looked amused. "Appears you didn't make it out of that tin can so easily after all." There was no apology. "Are you sure you're up for whatever Julian throws at you?" He jerked his chin at Mercer.

"Don't test me." He smiled and chomped away happily on his lo mein.

Mercer shut the tap and methodically wiped his hands on a towel. "Let's take a ride. I'd like to see the level of your interrogational skills."

My eyes widened. "You didn't kill him?"

"Not yet." His eyes brightened, but it didn't seem genuine. The effect was phony, and I suspected it was to gauge my reaction. "Are you volunteering?"

Two could play at this game. "Depends on what he has to say."

He tipped his head ever so slightly. "Bas, we'll take another run at him. If Hans wants to join us, give him the address." Bastian nodded, slurping up the last of his dinner.

"Bring back a pizza," he called as Mercer led me to the door, holding it open as if he were a proper gentleman, but I wasn't fooled.

The ride across town was in complete silence. I couldn't imagine where the prisoner was being kept or what state he might be in when we arrived. The fact that he was left completely unattended didn't bode well. Mercer turned into an abandoned lot and headed for a dilapidated storefront. How he found a secluded, workable location on such short notice was beyond me. If I had to wager a guess, I'd say Julian or his team scoped out locations in the event any wet work became necessary.

"He's in the back," Mercer said, shutting the steel door behind us. "Room's soundproofed. He doesn't know we're here, how many of us there might be, or who we're working for. It's imperative we keep him blind, metaphorically speaking."

"What do you know about him?" I asked, scoping out the front room. All of the surveillance photos had been moved here, along with the missing files from the apartment. It seemed Mercer wanted to make this location workable in the event he needed to be mobile.

"Not enough. Bas ran his prints, but he's not in any system. Donovan's tried his persuasive techniques, but the bastard's a hard nut to crack."

"Did O'Connell take a stab at him?" His implacable exterior was back in place, and soon, he'd be back to one word sentences. The only thing different about him was the barely contained rage was no longer threatening to bubble to the surface. Apparently, taking out his aggression on one of the kidnappers had done wonders for his demeanor. "Metaphorically speaking."

"No. He supervised."

I stretched, trying to determine the best play under the circumstances. We were thinking outside the box on this one. All the interrogations I had seen or been a part of utilized the threat of imprisonment, implied violence, or the perception of having ratted out some scary SOB. While the tried and true good-cop, bad-cop routine might work, I wasn't sure how convincing it could be when the only two options were death or freedom. Pain and violence were a guarantee.

"What are you planning to do with him when this is over with?" I asked.

"Not your concern." He judged my expression. "Do you really want to know?"

"Depends on the answer." He let out a slight snort but remained immovable. "Is he restrained?"

"Yes." Some elaboration would have been nice, but I didn't expect it. I also didn't pretend to fathom that Mercer's sadistic streak and imaginative torture techniques would be lacking. I had an idea, but it was by far one of the worst ideas I ever came up with, and in my lifetime, there had been quite a few doozies.

"Hit me."

"What?" The pristine exterior was shattered by complete confusion.

"Are you deaf? You've wanted to take a pop at me since we met, just fucking do it." I screwed my eyes shut and tried not to flinch. "And try not to break my jaw because it'll be hard to talk to the kidnapper if I can't move my mouth."

"You're daft." I opened my eyes, and he studied my face as if seeing me for the first time. "Don't tense, it'll hurt worse." And then he threw a hard punch. It knocked me back, and I resisted the urge to spit blood. Instead, I wiped my mouth on my shirt for effect.

"You hit like a girl. Again." He didn't comment but shook out his shoulders and hit me again. Recovering, I proceeded to muss my hair and rip my shirt. It was important to look as if I had been put through the wringer too. My split lip was a nice effect as was my swollen cheek. I wasn't willing to go so far as a broken nose, and I was glad Mercer had been kind enough not to inflict that type of pain. Tearing and bleeding on my shirt would add to the illusion, and I made sure my bruised hip was partially visible over the waistband of my pants.

"You okay?"

I laughed. "Like you care." I dug through my purse for a compact to check my appearance. I looked worse before, but hopefully, this would be convincing enough. "Toss me inside, accuse me of not answering your questions or whatever. I don't give a shit. I'll see if I can get the asshole to give us something. He might be more apt to talk to a fellow captive."

"How long?"

"Thirty minutes. If he starts to open up, you can always throw me back inside later."

"We need a location."

I narrowed my eyes as if to say *no shit*, and he grabbed my arm and a fistful of my hair and dragged me to the door. "Let me go. I told you I don't know anything," I shrieked as he opened the door and shoved me into the room. I landed splayed on the ground in front of the man bound to a chair.

"Tick tock." He slammed the door closed. The latching of the lock was the last sound I heard from the outside world.

THIRTY-TWO

I pretended not to notice the man, beaten and bloodied, with his head drooping and tied to the chair. Judging by the bloodstain on his shirt, he had been shot in the arm in the vicinity of his shoulder, but it didn't appear to be life-threatening. Instead, I scrambled off the ground, playing up my injuries as I ran to the door and pounded on it. "Let me go. Please. Please," I screeched, doing my best to make my voice sound hysterical, and the stinging in my cheek made my eyes water, adding to the illusion. After a solid minute of begging to be released, I crumpled to the ground and pulled my legs to my chest and rocked with fake sobs.

The man tied to the chair cleared his throat, but I continued on, pretending not to have noticed. He tried again a little louder, and I stopped and looked up, appearing fearful.

"Oh my god," I exhaled, "are you okay?" I slowly approached him.

"Who are you? What do they want?" His voice was harsh, probably from his earlier screams.

"Lola," I said on the verge of tears. "I don't know who they are or what they want. Last night, I was on my way home, and this guy, he just," I sniffled loudly and made a show of taking in a breath, "he grabbed me and brought me here. He keeps asking where some girl is, but I don't know. I don't even know who he's talking about." I brushed the hair out of my face and winced as I pretended to try to find a way to untie the kidnapper. "He and his friends had me in another room, and," I swallowed as if the thought of whatever happened in there was too painful to recollect. I leaned over the guy to see around the side of the chair. "Do you know what they want? Why they took us?" Interrogation 101, find common ground.

All my screaming made him more alert, and I noticed his eyes on my bruised side as I maneuvered around him. "Can you get me free? Maybe the two of us can find a way out of here." He was attempting to be a knight in shining armor, but so far, he wouldn't answer any of my questions. "Those monsters did that to you?"

"You don't know the kinds of things they wanted to do," I cringed, hoping I wasn't overplaying the brutality. I wanted this man scared. He needed to be if I was going to convince him to trust me. "Do you know who they are? What they want?"

"They must have said the same thing to me that they said to you," he suggested. "They wanted to know where Adalina was."

"Adalina?" I looked puzzled. "That doesn't sound right." I shook my head and tugged at the duct tape covering the rope. "What's your name?" I asked. He fell silent as I continued to search the tape with my fingers for a place to begin peeling it away.

"Adam, sorry." His hesitation indicated he wasn't completely sure about me. "Where'd you say they grabbed you?"

"I was walking home from work at the diner. The damn bus was behind schedule, and I was hoping to catch a cab. But you know how that goes in the shady part of town." I sighed. "I just kept walking. I don't even remember where it was." I stopped and sat on the ground in front of him. "This guy pulls up in a van, the door opens, and someone jumps out and grabs me. They put a hood on my head, and then I wake up in this room." I scrunched up my face and wiped at my eyes. "We're going to die," I sobbed.

"Lola, hey, look at me," Adam said gently. This guy was way too calm for someone who was trapped and tortured. He knew the tricks of the trade when it came to abductions and interrogations. "We'll get out of here. It'll be okay. Just get me untied." I scooted back from him.

"No one knows where we are. These guys are trained killers. I saw military tats all over one of them. We're never going home. I'm never going to see my baby again." He paled, making the contrast between the caked blood on his face and his skin that much more dramatic.

"Listen," he hissed, growing annoyed with my constant theatrics, "if you can get me out of this rope and chains, I'll get you out of here."

"Who are you? Harry Houdini?"

"No, but I have friends who can help. Really."

"And what, you're going to make them appear out of thin air, Mr. Houdini? It's hopeless."

"If I can get a message to them, they'll rescue us."

"Are you a cop? Are they cops?"

"I'm not a cop, but it's something like that. They'll get us out just as soon as they realize I'm in trouble."

"How would they know where you are?" I crawled to the place behind the chair and tugged at the tape. Mercer bound Adam with handcuffs, a chain and padlock, some twine, and duct tape around his wrists. Talk about overkill. To make my attempt at progress more realistic, I pulled at the tape around his wrists and removed a few tiny thin strips as we spoke.

"GPS," he said simply, and I knew he must have a tracker on him. I was also certain Bastian worked his technological magic and jammed any and all frequencies.

"Then why aren't they here already? I'd love for some cops to bust down those doors and give those assholes what they deserve."

"They aren't cops," he repeated for emphasis, "but they'll make sure these bastards can't hurt anyone else." I pressed my lips together, wanting nothing more than to bash this bastard's head in. He was worried about letting Mercer hurt people when he was a goddamn kidnapper.

Talk about hypocrisy.

"Oh my god, are you with the mob?" I asked. "I don't want any more trouble. What was that name you said, Adalind? Is that your boss's wife or something. Oh my god. I didn't think things could get worse."

"No." His voice adopted an edge. "I work for well-connected people but not that type of connected."

"I don't understand. Who the hell are you? Why did these idiots take you?"

"Because," he hesitated, indicating maybe some progress was being made, "my friends and I stole something from them."

"So give it back," I screamed. "I don't even know how I got caught up in any of this, but just give back whatever you took and maybe they'll let us go. I want to go home." It's what Catherine said when I found her, and she must have said the same thing to him because he softened.

"We tried to, but," he paused again.

"But what?"

"The lady who hired us to steal it changed her mind." This was making no sense. Was every word out of his mouth a load of bullshit or did the person pulling the strings change the plan?

"Who cares? Just tell these guys where it is, and maybe they'll let us go."

"It's not that simple."

I was getting frustrated, and the longer I spent with this piece of shit, the more I wanted to beat him into a bloodier pulp myself. "I don't even know you, and they're going to kill me because you stole some stupid trinket and won't give it back," I shrieked.

"Get me free, and I'll make sure you're safe." He realized I was his last chance of escaping.

"I can't. Underneath the tape are handcuffs and a chain and padlock. There's nothing I can do." I went around and sat on the ground, wiping my eyes with the hem of my shirt.

"Miss," he tried to calm me. "Lola?" I glanced up. "Maybe you can get word to my friends."

"How am I supposed to do that? Do you have a cell

phone in your pocket?"

"No." I could still sense a degree of uncertainty, but time was running out.

I ran my tongue along my bottom lip where it was still bleeding as subconscious reinforcement that Mercer and his team hurt me too. "I don't either. We're trapped here with those sadists."

"Maybe not." He looked hopeful. "Do you think you can reach into my back pocket?" This sounded like the beginning of a bad joke.

"Why?"

"There's a tracking chip sewn into the lining. If we can activate it, someone can hone in on my location." I squinted at him.

"Why do you have a tracking chip? And how do we activate it?"

"You ever watch TV where they show people under house arrest?" He spoke quickly, getting more frantic as the minutes ticked by that Mercer would return to finish one or both of us off. "It's like that. If the circuit is broken, it'll alert my friends."

"The friends who stole the mystery item? They're the reason I'm here. We're here. And you think they can save us?"

"They will," he promised. "Hurry, please."

I moved behind the chair, not enjoying the idea of copping a feel of this guy's ass as I accessed his back pocket. "What did they steal? I'm pretty sure we won't make it, and I think I deserve to know why I was grabbed for being in the wrong place at the wrong time."

"It's not important," he said quietly, leaning as far forward in the chair as the bindings allowed.

"It damn well better have been a Ferrari or Rolls Royce or something pretty fucking awesome." I found a plastic card with a single wire molded to the plastic and a computer chip in the middle. If Bastian could trace where the location of the signal's transmission ended, we'd have the rest of the Seasons and Adalina, I hoped.

"No. It was nothing like that. Did you get it?"

I came around the chair and stood in front of him. "How

does this work?"

"You see the red strip melted to the card? Just unplug it from the center square, the one that looks like a little computer chip, and bingo."

"Okay," I moved as if I were about to do it but stopped, my hand hovering over the card. "But first you're telling me what you took. I'm not risking getting shot full of holes if you're smuggling guns or nuclear missiles or something." Hopefully, he'd think I was as much of an airhead as the name I gave him indicated.

"It was a kid," he bellowed. "Just a kid."

"Why'd you take a kid?"

"Someone told us to."

"Who?" He strained to see me more clearly through the dim light. "You stole a kid." I knew the small amount of trust I earned just went to shit, but I tried anyway. "No wonder these guys want to kill you. Can't you just give the kid back?" He went silent and glared daggers at me.

"Who are you, really?"

I straightened my shirt as best I could and ran my fingers through my hair. "Does the name Parker mean anything to you?" My tone was icy, and I saw the recognition dawn on his face.

"Fuck. You're working with Mercer? You were supposed to be concerned with nothing except recovering Catherine."

"Until you covered the pier with blood and made me believe she was dead." It wasn't a conscious thought, but I backhanded him hard, causing the chair to teeter. "Did you get your rocks off watching her parents squirm? Making me squirm? Shooting her uncle?" I wasn't aware that I was hitting him until someone grabbed me from behind and dragged me away. I kicked my legs out, hoping to get enough momentum to break free.

Mercer shoved the door shut, and only then did I realize I was pleading with him to let me go. He dropped his hold on me, and I swallowed, gasping down breath and refusing to think of what I just did and what I would have done.

Recovering, I put on my game face and held out the tracker. "This will signal his friends if the circuit's broken. Maybe Bastian can determine a way to reverse engineer the trace and then you can set it off and recover Adalina."

"Okay." He tucked it carefully into his shirt pocket.

"I need to get out of here. Can we go?"

"Yes."

THIRTY-THREE

The drive back to Mercer's safe house was in total silence. I leaned my cheek against the cold glass window and avoided looking at my hands. The encounter with Adam turned into something I wasn't prepared for. I heard people speak of rage blackouts before, but if Mercer hadn't gotten inside the room when he did, I was certain I would have beaten the man to death with my bare hands. I swallowed unsteadily, afraid I would be sick.

After what felt like an eternity, Mercer stopped the car and removed the key from the ignition. Something changed in him, and he nodded to me as he climbed out of the car. I was numb and exhausted. I followed him inside and heard Bastian ask where the pizza was. It seemed an absurd question, and I continued into the kitchen to wash Adam's blood off my hands.

"Bloody hell," Bastian swore as I came into view, "what happened to you?"

"Mercer." I didn't feel like elaborating. Either Julian could fill him in or not. It didn't matter, and I didn't care.

After watching the last remnants of the red water run down the drain, I dried my hands on a towel. My hand throbbed, and the pain radiated up my arm. I didn't want to think about how forcefully I must have been pummeling that man for the impact to have jarred the rest of my body. If I ached, I'd hate to think what he felt like. Again, there was the possibility I might be sick. There was also the possibility he deserved much worse than what I did to him.

"It'll take a while to engineer a program to trace a sent signal," Mercer said quietly. "It might be a couple of days even." He pressed his lips together, perhaps considering offering a smile but thought better of it. "Get yourself cleaned up."

"Try not to need me for anything else," I snarled. Bastian opened his mouth to say something but melted into the background as I went to the door.

I wasn't sure I had enough energy to make it home. By some miracle, I pulled up to my apartment building and went upstairs. Letting myself in, I locked the door and went straight to the bathroom. Stripping down, I stood in the shower, leaning against the tile wall. The emotional and psychological toll exhausted me, and I stared blankly at the faucet. There were no thoughts. My synapses were fried. I wasn't even sure if I had enough sense to use the shampoo and body wash, but when the water ran cold, I stepped out of the shower, wrapped myself in an extra large bath towel, walked into my bedroom, and curled up in bed, pulling the blankets over my still wet body and damp towel.

A couple hours later, I opened my eyes and stared at the digital blue glow from my clock. On autopilot, I got out of bed, dressed, and arrived at the hospital. It was dark out, and it was either early morning or late in the evening. Entering, I headed straight for O'Connell's room. Opening the door, he met my eyes.

"Parker," he whispered, and I noticed Jen asleep in a chair.

"Oh god, Nick," I exclaimed, just as quietly. I went around and sat on the edge of the bed. "I almost killed him." I felt a tremor travel through me, and O'Connell grasped my arm.

"It's all right." His words held nothing but conviction. "You did it for me." I looked away, and he squeezed my forearm to get my attention. "The asshole had it coming." I didn't like it. It didn't matter what Adam did; we weren't supposed to act like this. Whatever happened to the good guys wearing the white hats and acting within the confines of the law? "It's okay. Tell me what happened."

I gave him the short version, and he nodded. I noticed halfway through my rendition, Jen turned to face us. Her eyes were half open. So much for a peaceful night's rest. "Mercer will call with an update," I concluded. Just telling the story made me want to crawl back to bed. "What the hell am I supposed to do now?"

"What do you mean?" O'Connell seemed genuinely confused by the question. "Hopefully, your intel will lead to the other kidnappers and the still missing girl."

I glanced at Jen who shut her eyes again. Either she went back to sleep, or she was trying to give us privacy. "Am I supposed to help the mercenaries kill the kidnappers and dispose of the bodies? Or should I show up at the precinct in a few hours and fill in your partners on what's going on? Oh yeah, by the way, I'm working for Moretti again." I sounded cynical, and I rested my head in my hand.

"Well, that explains the outfit," he attempted to joke as he glanced at my blue button-up blouse over black dress pants and gun holster. "Alexis, I," he frowned, collecting his thoughts, "I shouldn't have put all of this on you."

"Too fucking late now," I said more loudly than I should have. Jen didn't move, and I knew she was awake and listening to everything. I sighed. "I don't know what they'll do with Adam." Saying his name made me feel both remorse for my actions and regret for not doing more. I was about as conflicted as one could be, and I had no idea which emotion would win out in the event I was confronted with a similar situation.

"Don't worry about it." He met my eyes. "Tell Thompson the situation in case anything turns up." I looked away, not wanting to admit anything to anyone else. "He would have done the same. Maybe worse. Alex, listen to me, you're not a monster."

"It sure as hell feels like it."

"I'm sorry." He released his grip on my arm. "But you got Catherine back safe, and there's no reason in this world why someone shouldn't beat the daylights out of that guy." I saw the rage flitter across O'Connell's eyes. "Yesterday, Mercer wouldn't let me near him." He lowered his voice to something barely audible, and I was positive Jen who was five feet away couldn't hear since I could barely make out the words. "There's not a doubt in my mind that I would have killed him and made it as painful as possible." The dark determination in Nick scared me, and in that instant, I realized the hell that the Four Seasons inflicted made crossing that line a very real possibility for Nick, for me, and probably for Heathcliff and Thompson too. They brought us to the point of no return, and the moral quandary was something we'd deal with only as an afterthought.

Jen must have sensed the shift in conversation because she stirred and stretched, yawning loudly. "Alexis, my god, do you want me to call down to x-ray?" I shook my head. She heard enough of our conversation to know not to ask what happened. She stood up from the chair, leaned over and kissed her husband, and then headed for the door. "I'll be right back. Make sure this one doesn't plan a jailbreak in the meantime."

I got off the bed and paced the enclosed space of Nick's hospital room. He watched but remained silent. It would be a while before the elephant cleared the room. "How are you feeling?" I asked. The silence was oppressive, and I couldn't take it.

"I'm all right." He pushed a button and sat up a little higher. "I'd be better if I wasn't stuck in this room but doctor's orders. Although, I think Jenny gave them to the doctor herself."

"This is what happens when you scare the shit out of all of us." The pacing was exhausting. Honestly, everything was exhausting. I sat in the chair Jen vacated and stared at the wall across the room. "When this is all over with, assuming I'm not locked up, we have to figure out a way to keep you out of trouble."

"Isn't that usually your schtick?"

"Until you called, I was staying out of trouble," I snapped. I had every right to be resentful.

"You were bored," he joked.

"I was supposed to be at the beach."

"What?" He had missed a lot. Being wrapped up in family drama and kidnappings could do that to a person. "It's October."

"Yeah, I made that same argument." I filled him in on my missed trip with Martin while we waited for Jen to return. Halfway through my pointless story about the corporate conference and meeting Francesca, which was my way of keeping my mind focused on other things, Jen returned with half of the stockroom.

"Are you sure you don't want to get an x-ray?" she asked, cleaning and bandaging my swollen hand. "I'm not a doctor, but I think a few of your knuckles are broken."

"It's fine."

"No, it's not." She met my eyes, and I saw the unsaid apology. "Ice and ibuprofen until you decide to get an actual medical opinion on this."

"You're a nurse. Your opinion is good enough for me."

"Shh," she glanced at the door, "this is off the books."

"Right, sorry."

"The lights suck in here." She escorted me into the small bathroom and closed the lid over the toilet to create a makeshift chair. "Sit," she instructed and set to work on my face. "I heard you two talking," she admitted, applying a liquid bandage to the cut across my cheek. I shook my head and cast my gaze at the ceiling. She took the hint and finished working on my cheek. "Hang on," she retrieved her purse and came back in, "let's see if I can work some miracles with foundation and concealer."

By the time she was finished, I no longer looked like I went a few rounds with a gorilla. My bottom lip was still swollen and red, but to someone who didn't know me, it looked like I just went a bit crazy with the lipstick. With the exception of the butterfly bandages, the cuts and bruises on my face were barely noticeable. Everything appeared good as new. Maybe that was half the battle.

"Want some breakfast?" O'Connell asked when Jen and

I emerged. "It tastes like dog shit, so I'm more than happy to share."

"I'm going to the precinct," I decided. "Thompson and I need to chat."

"Take care of yourself, Alex," Jen called. "If I can do anything, I'm just a phone call away."

I chuckled. "Didn't I say something like that to you yesterday?"

Seeing O'Connell and his wife helped me gain perspective. At least I didn't feel like I needed to be imprisoned or under a mandatory psych hold. The things the Four Seasons made us endure caused the situation, and I was on the cusp of allowing myself to drop the blame and the guilt. The only thing left to harbor was the darkness. The desire, buried so deep it would hopefully never see the light of day, to end Adam's life and exact revenge for the pain he and his friends caused. Mercer's words from the van played through my mind, and the truth they held terrified me. The possibility we weren't that different any longer scared me shitless.

*　　*　　*

"Parker," Thompson was behind his desk when I came into the bullpen, "I never heard from you. What happened with the K&R specialist?" I wondered if there was a reason he didn't refer to Mercer by name, but it wasn't a priority.

"Can we talk in private?"

"C'mon," he got up, and I followed him out of the building and to an unmarked cruiser, "we'll get some coffee." On the drive, I told him what happened, leaving out certain facts like the location of the storefront or the condition Adam was in when I arrived and when I left. "Okay." He gritted his teeth, not liking any of this. "The kid that broke into the clinic said he was hired by some guy with an accent to grab some stuff."

"What kind of accent?"

"Spanish, maybe Mexican, Portuguese, Italian," Thompson shrugged, "he wasn't sure, but we know it wasn't English or Australian."

"Well, hot damn, that only leaves everyone else in the world as a suspect." Snarky was back. I had missed it. It was a sign that the world was starting to turn in the proper direction on its axis once more. We picked up a tray of extra large coffees and went back to the stationhouse.

"Did you get a description of the guy?" I asked, taking the lid off my coffee and pouring a few sugar packets into it. Normally, I didn't like my coffee sweet, but I needed the extra boost.

"Kid's working with a sketch artist. They've been at it most of the night."

"You've been here all night?"

"Don't tell me I missed the time clock and the rules stating I have to punch in and out at a certain time." Apparently, sarcasm was contagious. He went to the filing cabinet, selected a folder, and dropped it in front of me. "Interview log from the kid. Get to reading. I'll see if we have a composite yet."

He disappeared down the hallway, and I skimmed through the folder. There wasn't anything important. I had been told all the juicy details, and the rest was filler and fluff. I closed the folder. It was time to revisit the information I gathered with as much emotional detachment as I could muster. I outlined the events that culminated in Catherine's freedom. Next, I connected the dots to what I knew about the Four Seasons and Adam, and finally, I wrote out the remaining questions and loose ends. While I was in the process, Heathcliff walked in.

"Who did that to you?" he asked, and I looked up, surprised.

"I walked into a wall."

"Does the wall have a name?" He glanced at my bandaged hand and smiled. "Did you and Mercer reach another understanding?"

I played it off as if his assumptions were completely accurate. What he didn't know wouldn't hurt him. "No wonder you're a detective." He continued to his desk and checked his e-mail and messages. Picking up the phone, he made a call. By the time he was done, Thompson had returned.

"Did you get the same lead I did?" Heathcliff asked. I looked from one to the other. They both looked like kids in a candy store who just located the biggest jawbreaker ever. Thompson held up a composite, and Heathcliff swiveled his computer monitor around to reveal the same image. "Do you feel up to tagging along, Parker?"

"Just as long as I don't have to hit anyone else."

THIRTY-FOUR

"Police, open up." Heathcliff pounded against the door. The two detectives exchanged a look. "Mr. Santino," he tried again, "open up." Faint murmuring came from the other side of the door, and Thompson stepped back, hand against the butt of his gun. Heathcliff was on one side of the door, and I hoped we wouldn't have to break down the door or run after our suspect.

"Coming, coming," a man responded, muttering more words in Spanish.

Thompson's shield was on a chain around his neck, and Heathcliff pulled his from where it was clipped on his pocket. I know they refer to their badges as shields, but the way I had seen many law enforcement officers lead with their badge often made me think they believed it could protect them from bullets. Inwardly, I sighed.

"Get dressed," Thompson ordered as the door opened and Estobar Santino stood before us in nothing but his birthday suit. Obviously, he wasn't armed, so I took the opportunity to turn away. Heathcliff stepped back, more than happy to let Thompson handle this matter.

"Is anyone else here?" I asked, focusing on the ruddy hallway carpet.

"No. I'm alone." Santino went into the bathroom to dress; apparently, we interrupted his shower.

Thompson entered the apartment. An invitation inside could be revealing as long as something damning was out in the open and in plain sight. Heathcliff edged into the apartment to assist his partner, and I stayed in the hallway. Sometimes being a consultant had its perks.

Heathcliff chuckled. "At least we know he was talking to us and not a prostitute."

"Maybe he was on the phone. Sex hotlines are making a comeback," I quipped. He looked disgusted, and I hid my laughter. Thompson turned to give us both a stern look. This wasn't a joking matter, but it was a better alternative than watching Santino put on a pair of pants.

There weren't any looted medical supplies lying about or evidence indicating he might be involved in a kidnapping plot. There weren't any weapons or drug paraphernalia either. It made things more difficult when the crooks didn't leave tools of their trade within plain sight, but we would find another way around if need be.

"The Estes family requested no involvement from law enforcement," Santino stated, returning to the main room in a business suit. I preferred him with his clothes on. "This may be construed as violating their privacy and endangering the life of their daughter. I wish to contact the family immediately so they may get in touch with their attorney."

"We're not here because of that," Thompson said, ignoring Santino's threat. "The matter at hand involves an unrelated crime. If you would be more comfortable answering our questions at the station, sir, I'd be happy to personally escort you there."

Estobar blanched. "I will cooperate, but please keep your questions brief. A child's life hangs in the balance, and anyone who works for the family has been instructed to avoid the authorities. Can you please shut the door? I can't risk the kidnappers having a spy watching me."

Stepping inside his apartment, I narrowed my eyes as I shut the door. Normal people weren't typically this paranoid. My back rested against the door, and I crossed my arms over my chest. Thompson and Heathcliff ran through the perfunctory questions about Santino's relationship with the clinic, the personnel who worked there, and with the kid who was paid to break-in. None of his responses were helpful, but as I stood waiting, I had the opportunity to examine the room.

As I scrutinized the furniture, décor, and knickknacks littering the table, the possibility that Santino lived alone diminished. When Thompson took a break from the questioning to consult his notes, I stepped away from the door and went to the window to look outside. Santino sat up a little straighter and edged toward the end of the couch. Heathcliff caught my eye, and I began to wander around the apartment.

"Please don't do that," Santino sputtered. I stopped, inches away from a curio, and cocked my head to the side.

"I'm not doing anything, sir." I continued onward, trying to determine what he didn't want me to find. "Is there a reason you're so nervous? I promise not to touch or break anything."

"Just be careful," he huffed and made a show of looking at his watch. "Detectives, I'm late for work, and under the circumstances, I need to get going."

Before he could say another word, I spotted the tiny Lenox picture frame among the other crystal and ceramic collectibles. Inside was a photo of Rosa Estes and a baby girl. I caught Thompson's eye and jerked my chin at the curio. As I stepped away, he went to the spot I vacated and looked down.

"Is this your family?" Thompson asked, ignoring Santino's attempt to get us to leave.

Santino glowered and looked away. "You should leave now."

"Estobar Santino," Thompson pulled the cuffs from his belt, "you're under arrest."

"I've done nothing," he squawked.

"The picture of Mrs. Estes and her daughter says otherwise," I remarked as Thompson read Santino his rights and escorted him from the apartment. His lawyers would have him released by lunch, but there was a chance it could be the break we were looking for.

* * *

I read Santino's file from my seat at O'Connell's desk. As our theory unfolded, he became our prime suspect. The framed photo in his apartment did nothing to alleviate the appearance of guilt. Heathcliff and Thompson were questioning him, but I declined the invitation to watch through the two-way mirror. Instead, I wondered why the lawyer Santino requested wasn't the same lawyer from the Estes' house.

It had been a long two weeks, and I couldn't remember the last time I slept through the night. This needed to pan out. Every step was bringing us closer to finding the kidnappers, maybe Adalina too. But it would be nice if Santino sang like a canary, and we could bust the Four Seasons before Mercer called with their location. I would go with him and his team if he asked, but I worried what the consequences would be.

"Get anything?" I asked Thompson.

"No." His response was gruff, and he picked up his jacket from his chair. "I'm going home."

Before I could say anything else, I saw Santino's lawyer emerge and shake hands with Moretti's boss before escorting his client down the hallway. Apparently, Santino had friends in high places.

"Son of a bitch," Heathcliff muttered, walking past me.

I waited for the brass to be out of earshot before getting up and leaning against Heathcliff's desk. "What now?"

"It's not a crime to have a photo of your boss's family in your living room."

"What about everything we've pieced together?" I argued.

"Circumstantial." His eyes burned fiercely. "We're fishing. We should investigate alternate avenues."

"Bullshit," I sighed, rubbing my sore hand. Other avenues weren't legally viable. "Where'd Thompson go?"

"He's been working too many doubles. Not enough rest in between shifts has impacted his professional perception and caused him to make errors in judgment."

"So he's suspended?"

He snorted. "Forced to take the next thirty-six hours off as mandated by union rules." He glanced up at me. "So yeah, and Santino walks."

"This is ridiculous."

We needed to keep eyes on Santino in case he was choreographing the Four Seasons, now Three Seasons. If he even sneezed wrong, someone needed to know, but once again, our hands were tied. Powerful people always pulled the strings.

Sitting back down, I dialed Mercer. For once, he answered. I told him what happened with Santino and figured if anything were to change it might be beneficial for him to pass it along. This was the only time we spoke without him arguing or controlling the conversation. It was strange.

"Parker," Moretti barked from his office door, "get in here." I stood up, expecting to get fired after being on the job for a day. At least fired would be better than being brought up on charges for assault and false imprisonment or maybe it was kidnapping. Had Mercer kidnapped the kidnapper? My head spun, and I couldn't be bothered to think about it. It was hard enough not thinking about the reason my hand ached.

"Sir?" I asked from the doorway.

"Close the door." I obeyed and took a seat in front of his desk. "I'm not telling you to keep tabs on anyone, especially someone who I've been ordered not to harass any further. I've instructed everyone under my command who possesses a badge to steer clear of the Estes' family, and this morning, I added Mr. Santino to that list, despite the fact he has a very odd fondness for his boss's wife and daughter. The same daughter who is currently missing. Do we understand one another?"

"The police can't interfere with the Estes family or Santino which is counterproductive since something doesn't sit right when it comes to Mr. Santino."

"Right," Moretti gave me a curt nod.

"I believe my consulting would be better applied outside

the walls of this precinct," I responded, standing. "If my expertise is needed here, please let me know."

"I'm glad we understand each other, Miss Parker. Have a good day."

Even Moretti wanted answers. Not having a badge could get me into trouble, but it could also keep the precinct out of trouble. Parker, you're getting yourself mixed up in too many things, my subconscious warned.

I left without a word to Heathcliff. I couldn't tell him what I was doing. He was back at work and required to uphold the law. Thompson was benched for the next thirty-six hours, and hopefully, he was smart enough to follow orders, instead of getting himself in deeper. He knew what transpired between me and Catherine's captor, and in the event I needed someone to cover for me, I'd like him to still be on the job.

I drove to Santino's apartment, but his car was no longer there. There was no way of knowing where he went or what he was doing. Mercer would have to keep his ear to the ground at the Estes' house to determine if anything changed. With no other options, I went to Mercer's flat.

Bastian was still figuring out a way to track the signal. Mercer was at the Estes' estate. I knew what I wanted to do and what I needed to do. I just wasn't sure I could pull it off.

"Can I have a few minutes with Adam?" I asked.

Bastian looked up from the computer, completely perplexed. "Love, are you sure about that?"

"Is he still breathing?" I inquired. "Because I need him to answer some questions."

"I'll go," Hans offered from his spot in the kitchen. He had just reassembled his handgun. "The waiting is making me loony." Bastian nodded. Apparently, he was in charge when Mercer was away.

The drive to the storefront was awkward. I said a handful of words to Hans, and I wasn't sure what his take was on interrogation procedures. He stopped the car, and we got out. After unlocking the door, he ushered me inside.

"I can handle it," I insisted. Now that Adam knew who I was, maybe things would go differently. At least I hoped they would.

"Sorry, Julian wants him kept alive. I'll observe." He unlocked the room that held our captive. "Do what you like, but I'll make sure you don't get out of control."

"I'm not a killer."

"Never said you were."

"Okay." The door opened, and I strode into the room. Adam looked as if someone shoved his face through a meat grinder. "Hello, Adam." My stomach lurched, but I swallowed and kept going. "We're going to have a nice chat. I'd suggest you answer swiftly and honestly."

"Bitch," he mumbled, but I didn't hit him. I just leaned against the wall in front of him and waited for him to pay attention.

"Which Season are you?" No response. Not that it mattered, but I continued anyway. It would be nice if I could get some answers out of him on something. "I'm guessing Autumn, maybe Spring. Definitely not Winter. Winter's in charge, and if the guy in charge was left to guard the least important captive of them all, well, that'd be downright pathetic."

"Whatever."

"Not whatever. You work for someone. A good and bad thing really. It means you have bargaining chips you can cash in. There are people you can turn on, and it'll get you out of this mess. The bad news, which you've probably figured out by now, is you got stuck holding the bag, and no one is coming for you."

"They'll come."

"No. They won't." I let out a resolute sigh and took a step toward him. "Do you have a life, Adam? Maybe a girlfriend, boyfriend, wife, mother, father, a child of your own? Is there anyone in this world that would give a damn if you never made it home?"

"Only me."

"Only you because you're afraid these lovely British chaps," I jerked my head toward Hans, "will track down and torture everyone you know and love? Or is it because there isn't a single person on this entire planet who can stomach being with a son of a bitch who kidnaps children and holds them for weeks at a time for ransom?" His eyes shone angry in the dim light. "You've done some terrible things," I surmised, "but it doesn't mean you can't turn it all around."

"Fuck you."

"Hmm," I cocked my head to the side and assessed him, "I don't think so." I stepped forward and tapped him on the shoulder, and he flinched. "Pussy," I chuckled. He was still afraid. It was advantageous, but I was afraid too, afraid of what could happen if I lost control again. As long as he didn't sense it, I could play the game.

"Parker," Hans cautioned, helping my act a little. I turned and playfully scrunched my nose at him, grinning, and Adam audibly swallowed.

"We can make this real simple," I continued. "We cut you loose and follow you. That means either we'd get the opportunity to take care of your seasonal friends and maybe find Adalina, or you'd lead us right into your real life. The one that doesn't involve kidnapping and ransom. It'd be worlds colliding."

"Why don't you try it and see what happens?"

"Might." I pretended to weigh the options. Mercer would never go for it, and I knew that. "Then again, maybe it'd be easier to turn you over to the police department."

"You'd be arrested."

"I've always enjoyed the concept of mutually assured destruction, but frankly, you kidnapped a cop's niece. Whoever turns in the bastard responsible would be worshipped. Hell, I think there might even be a ticker-tape parade." He looked green, but maybe it was the lighting. "Did you shoot the cop?" I asked, catching him off guard with such a direct question.

"No, Summer did."

"See, that wasn't so hard. Was it?" I paced in front of him. "I figured you were either Spring or Autumn. Why don't you just give up your handle, Adam? It doesn't make a bit of difference does it?"

He considered my point for a couple of seconds. "Autumn," he finally relented.

"Very good." I turned on my heel and walked out.

"What did that accomplish?" Hans asked, latching the door.

"Nothing." I snorted. "It's about cooperation. When was the last time he ate?" I asked, and Hans laughed. "Let's pick up a sandwich for this guy. He's getting a reward for answering the question."

"This will take forever," he pointed out as we went back to the car.

"It doesn't matter. Either he'll tell us what we want to know or not. In the meantime, Bastian's working on a location, and Mercer's scoping out the family. Something will lead somewhere." Hans didn't look convinced but did what I asked anyway.

THIRTY-FIVE

The way to a man's heart was through his stomach, or so I'd been told. After convincing our captive that the sandwich wasn't poisoned or drugged and it was simply a reward since he was being such a good boy, he warmed to our presence in the soundproof room. I convinced Hans to unshackle his left hand, and the two of us were keeping tabs on him in case he somehow managed to break out of the rest of his restraints.

"Things don't have to be difficult," I said. "You told me a woman hired you. Who is she?" Adam shook his head and stared at the floor.

Hans reattached the restraints, making our captive helpless once more. "Answer the lady's question," he urged. He was bored and probably wanted to be anywhere but in this cruddy room.

"Some lady," Adam retorted.

"That's right," my patience was wearing thin, "do we need to go another round before you decide to open your mouth with an answer?" His eyes showed great loathing, and I was positive if he wasn't bound, he would probably try to kill me. Oh well, I would add his name to the ever-growing list. "Or we can use this opportunity to brush up on hostage negotiation. You can be the hostage." I smiled menacingly. "I'm guessing you want to be released, which means you have to meet my set of demands. Isn't this fun?" Hans snorted in amusement, but I didn't want to risk losing my serious edge by looking at him.

"You're fucking insane."

"Damn straight." It wasn't every day I got to play the villain. I threaded my fingers together and slowly circled his chair. "Here are my demands, pay attention. I want the location of the girl, the identities of your accomplices, the name of the woman who hired you, and," I stopped and stood directly in front of him, "detailed information on how you managed to kidnap the girls without anyone noticing."

He shook his head as if a fly was buzzing around. "I'm not telling you a damn thing."

I leaned down, placing my hands over both of his forearms and staring into his eyes. "Talk fast. We have Estobar Santino in holding, and he is not as strong-willed as you are." The blood drained from his face, and I knew whatever I just said meant something to him.

"Shit. Holy shit," he muttered. His breath hitched, and I stepped back, gloating. "If you have him, why are you asking me these questions?"

"I like you. We got off on the wrong foot, but I'd like to make amends. I'm really just a softie at heart, so this is your last chance. It'd be nice to have someone corroborate the things he's been saying."

"I don't know much," Adam began, and I heard the voice in my head let out a gleeful cheer. "Winter hooked me up with this job. The entire thing was written line by line, where to go, what to do, how to do it. We were paid up front and told someone would contact us with further information on when to release the girls. Even the threats, drop-offs, and ransom requests were spelled out."

"By whom?"

"Some chick. I don't know, but I heard her talking to Winter before the job began. She said Santino would make sure it all went off without a hitch."

"Who the hell is she?" I screamed.

My temper was erratic, and Adam flinched but didn't

say anything else. I stepped back, thinking. Hans took over and asked for additional information, but I couldn't concentrate or focus on what he was saying. There was something here. I just needed to pinpoint it.

"Let's go," Hans commanded my attention, and I looked up, bewildered.

"You said you had well-connected friends. Winter hooks you up for jobs. Is he family?" I inquired, but Adam remained silent. "Not family," I narrowed my eyes, "but you run in the same crew. You probably have a record." I strode to the door at Hans' insistence. "Last chance," I tried over my shoulder, "want to give me a name for any of the other Seasons or your last name?" Adam spit in my direction, and Hans grabbed my wrist and pulled me from the room before I could retaliate for the disrespect.

"What the hell are you doing?" Mercer was in the storefront, staring horrified at me.

"Questioning our captive."

"On whose authority?"

"Mine," I growled, and he glanced at Hans, who shrugged. "I didn't kill him. He's perfectly fine. Hell, he's better than fine. We fed him. You know you have to give people food if you don't want them to die."

"He wasn't going to die of starvation," Mercer growled. "Do you think he's a pet you can keep because you've decided he's cute?" I ignored the comment. "No," his tone changed, "you couldn't stomach what you did earlier. You're trying to make peace with one of the men responsible for all of this."

"I need answers. You aren't getting them."

"And he gave them to you?" Running through my options, Hans already knew everything Adam divulged, so I might as well appear to be sharing. I filled in Mercer on the woman who hired the Four Seasons and Santino's alleged connection. "Very well." I wasn't sure what that meant, and he didn't elaborate. "Let's go back to the flat. Bastian may have a lead."

*   *   *

"It's not a tracker," Bastian admitted. "Honestly, I haven't got a bloody clue what it is. I've been trying to reverse engineer it, and I still don't know what it could be."

"And you want to believe the things that lying bastard says," Mercer retorted, looking pointedly at me. "Rubbish."

"Fine. He's a lying sack of shit. We'll add it to his résumé, right under kidnapper." I wasn't in the mood. "Did Santino show up for work at the Estes' estate?"

"Yes, but he didn't report any of the delays to Miguel." Mercer was being helpful, even though he looked to be in utter pain by the attempt.

"Can you get a list of all the female employees and staff who work for Miguel?" I asked. Mercer scoffed, but before he could respond, Bastian shoved a list at me. I looked at it. Everyone Miguel Estes employed in his private life covered the first page, and the next three sheets were all company employees.

"Now run along and play with your copper pals. We have actual work to do." Mercer nodded toward the door, and not wanting to be in his company any longer, I left without protest.

I went back to the precinct, copied the list, and passed it on to Heathcliff. Picking up Catherine Cale's account of the kidnapping, the only description she provided of her captor was a Caucasian male with brown hair. I was also sure those weren't her exact words. At least I could give a more thorough description. I found one of the sketch artists and explained how I might have caught a glimpse of a man leaving around the same time I snuck into the storage unit to rescue Catherine. It would have been easier to take a photo of Adam, but bruised and bloodied would be difficult to explain. When a decent facsimile was created, I went upstairs to Moretti's office.

"Find anything on that special project?" he asked as I handed him the sketch.

"Nothing out of the ordinary, but this guy might be involved. It's been a hectic few days, but I remember seeing him within the vicinity of the storage unit. He's probably a repeat offender, and maybe he has a crew. It might be good to check them out."

"I don't want to know," he picked up the paper, "but I'll get some guys to skim through mug shots and databases and see what we find. Any idea where this scumbag might be?"

"Not a clue."

"Okay." I didn't know if my lie was believable or if he decided the less he knew, the better. "I'll give you a call if something surfaces on this. If not, you might want to get an early start on that special project tomorrow morning."

"Yes, sir." I was being dismissed.

Stopping briefly at O'Connell's desk to conduct a few quick searches, I found an e-mail from Francesca. The information I requested was at her hotel, and I was instructed to pick it up at my earliest convenience. After ending up with all dead ends on my concise search history of a few of the female employees on the list, I decided to leave the detective work to the detectives. That meant a brief reprieve which could be filled with my unrelated corporate consulting work.

On my way home, I detoured to Francesca's hotel and rode the elevator up to her suite. Maybe whatever paperwork she had would help put me to sleep. Although, I probably didn't need the sleep aid after everything that occurred in the last forty-eight hours with Adam. I was still emotionally drained and being in that room with him for a couple hours today did nothing to rectify the situation, regardless of what Mercer may think. All of this was playing through my mind as I knocked on her door.

"What are you doing here?" I asked, stunned. Martin opened the door, and I was flummoxed.

"Waiting for room service." His eyes danced.

"I guess I deserved that one," I admitted.

He smiled. "Just a little." His grin quickly inverted as he assessed my face and hand. "But you didn't deserve that." I swallowed. "What happened?"

"It's nothing. Why are you here? Where's Ms. Pirelli?"

"Business and she's on a conference call." He held the door open, and I stepped inside to find the dinette table covered in opened manila folders and dozens of computer printouts of graphs and charts. "What did I tell you about hitting people?"

I looked away and took an unsteady breath. "Please don't do this now." I wasn't in the mood for his teasing.

He gently touched my cheek, instinctively knowing he said the wrong thing. "Will it hurt if I kiss you?"

"It'll hurt more if you don't." Martin put his arms around me, and normally, I would have preferred to remain professional. But this morning, I had been close to unraveling in Nick's hospital room, so I was allowing myself this brief moment of comfort.

"Ahem," Francesca cleared her throat from the bedroom doorway, and I made a move to pull away from Martin, but he kept an arm around my shoulders as I stepped back. "Jamie, what you do with your consultants is your business, but when you let me borrow one, I'd prefer if you didn't harass her in my hotel suite."

"Under normal circumstances, I wouldn't," he remarked, and I wondered what dumbass thing he was about to say since he was searching my eyes for permission. "But when your consultant is also my girlfriend, the lines blur."

"Girlfriend?" she sputtered. Now it made total sense why she went on and on about Martin. He didn't tell her. Why the hell was he telling her now? She snorted. "I'm not surprised." I had a feeling she was, but I didn't see any reason to say anything.

I stepped away from him, reestablishing professional boundaries. "Ma'am, I just stopped by to pick up the information I requested." Vague was important after all those nondisclosures I signed.

"Right." She opened a briefcase and removed a stack of files. "Here you are." I reached for them, barely managing to get a grip with limited use of my bandaged hand. She looked sheepish and annoyed, probably due to the feeling of embarrassment Martin caused by not telling her sooner. Then again, until now, we hadn't told anyone he knew. Maybe I shouldn't leave him alone in her hotel room. Was this a signal for help? Was the sexy COO attempting to seduce him? "Have you made any headway?"

"Some."

She turned to him, adding, "Whenever the numbers are finished being crunched, I'll pass along that information as well."

"Sounds good." I edged toward the door. "Was there anything else?"

"Not presently," she said, and I felt the temperature in the room start to drop.

"Alex," he opened the door before I could reach for it, "are you sure you're okay?" His volume was low, so she wouldn't hear from fifteen feet away.

"Are *you* going to be okay?" My eyes darted in her general direction, and I smirked. It was a joke, and he smiled pleasantly.

"I'll see you soon." I nodded and headed for the elevator.

THIRTY-SIX

I rubbed my eyes and looked at the clock. It was later than I realized, but at least I finished analyzing the information Insight International gleaned during their intensive study on the new countertops. I made some final notes on the matter and stretched in the chair. Rereading my notations, I needed to see the unbiased financial report on the estimated countertop profit margins before I would have solid ground for determining a prime suspect. At this moment, I was leaning toward a member of Insight International. They reviewed sensitive materials; the same materials that were leaked concerning the design, materials, and schematics for the coming countertop revolution. Jotting down a reminder to do a more thorough evaluation and background on each of the four members, led by the questionable Craig Robinson, I got up from my desk and changed for bed.

Staring at the ceiling, I tried every trick to make myself stop thinking and fall asleep. But it was one of those nights when nothing helped. My mind wandered, and I made a mental pro and con list. After tallying the results, I still had no idea why I couldn't resist the lure of detective work and insinuating myself into police matters. Even after all the shit that happened to me and all the things I did, it was simply who I was. Fighting to stay away from one of the fundamental aspects at the very core of my being was fruitless and exhausting. This was who I was. The good and the bad. Mercer's words came back, and I shuddered, burying myself under the covers.

Obviously, at some point, I fell asleep because my nightmares were of nothing but pools of blood and beaten and battered men. There was a sound, and I wasn't sure if it was the metal grate in my dream, dragging a path through the blood, or if it was something in the real world. But I jumped up, drenched in sweat and trembling. I reached for my gun and edged to my bedroom door, carefully leaning around the jamb. My gun was raised, and it took a moment longer than it should to determine the man in my apartment wasn't a threat.

"Alexis, take it easy. It's just me." Martin was near my counter. The metallic sound had been the empty soda can that he knocked over with his portfolio.

"What the hell are you doing here?" I swallowed, remembering to lower my nine millimeter. My hands were shaking. "Don't you know better than to show up uninvited? Especially when I'm working. How did you even get in here?"

"You keep a spare key at my place." He stared at me as I tried to calm my rattled nerves.

"That's in case I lock myself out. That's not for you to use." I gulped down some air and retreated to my bedroom.

"I was just dropping off the financial files to save you a trip to Francesca's hotel. I didn't even think you'd be home, so I brought the key and didn't plan to disturb you."

"You could have knocked first," I scolded. I was in my room, remaining out of his field of view while I calmed down. Every now and again, nightmares would lead to full-blown panic attacks, and waking up to the unexpected didn't help. Neither did the possibility that I could have shot him if I didn't realize the noise wasn't a threat.

"I did," he sounded indignant. He came into my room and found me on the floor, against the mattress. "You didn't answer, and I don't believe for a minute that you're okay." He knelt down and held me against his chest. "Relax, Alex. You're shaking like a leaf."

"I almost shot you," I squeaked, dislodging the last remnants of blood and bodies from my mind.

"No, you didn't." He awkwardly took his suit jacket off while keeping at least one arm around me at any given time. At least his suit wouldn't become a casualty of my hysterics. "What's going on? I thought this was over. Nick's niece is safe, isn't she?"

"We haven't found the kidnappers. The rest of them. I'm consulting at the precinct and working with a specialist, and fuck." I jumped up, frantic. "I'm supposed to keep tabs on this dirty bastard." The clock read a little after nine, and I missed my chance to follow Santino. I slumped down on the bed and rubbed my face, wincing because of my bruised cheek and swollen lip.

"Hey," he sat next to me, "it's okay." The remnants of my nightmare faded, and I felt steadier. The realization I needed to get to work kick-started my resolve, and the panic ebbed away. "How did this happen?" he asked gently, brushing against the elastic bandage Jen wrapped around my hand.

I didn't want to talk about it, but I didn't want to hide from it either. "I almost beat a man to death." I met his eyes, expecting to see fear or disgust. Instead, there was nothing but sorrow and compassion. He kissed my forehead and stood up.

"I've wanted to do that to the people who hurt you," he said quietly, slipping his jacket back on. "The only thing that matters is you did it for the right reason, and you didn't follow through. Are you okay?"

"Probably. I have to get to work."

"I know." He took a step toward my door. "That's why I brought the financials to you. I didn't think you had a lot of spare time to waste on traipsing across town."

Getting up, I followed him to the door. "Why were you at Francesca's hotel last night? Did the room service ever show up?"

He smirked. "No room service or champagne toasts," he clarified, a slight teasing quality to his voice. "Don't be offended, but there's a chance I'm moving in on your consulting gig. She asked me to assess the financial viability of her countertop project since I am a business genius."

"And modest too."

"Absolutely." He kissed me a second time. "I won't show up unannounced again, but I might call to check on you."

"I'm okay."

"I'll call anyway." He stepped into the hallway, and I spotted Bruiser. At least he brought his bodyguard with him. "Maybe I'll start the conversation by asking what you're wearing." I smiled and shut the door. Hell of a way to begin the day, I thought wryly.

After pulling myself together, I went back to Santino's apartment. I didn't see his car outside but figured it wouldn't hurt to make sure he wasn't at home. Knocking on his door, I hoped he wouldn't answer. If he did, Moretti would probably have to answer for his consultant's rash behavior, and that wouldn't go very well. Luckily, or maybe unluckily, Santino was gone for the day. I wanted nothing more than to let myself into his apartment and look for clues, but I wasn't sure how that would play out either. Erring on the side of caution, I sat in my car and sipped my coffee, deciding on my next course of action.

While I considered all the pieces that were still missing from the puzzle, Kate phoned. "Parker," she began, "there's been a large withdrawal from Miguel Estes' private account." Her volume was barely above a whisper, and I knew keeping tabs on his financials was illegal and could get her into a lot of trouble. "It was a wire transfer directly to a private security firm."

"Which firm?"

"That's the thing. The account says Security Associates, but until twelve hours ago, they didn't exist. And right now, they only exist on paper."

"Can you figure out their actual identity?" I inquired. "How much did he wire them?"

"I'll see what I can find." She sighed and didn't sound particularly positive. "This would be easier if you had a court order."

"Let's pretend they're terrorists then." The Patriot Act should come in handy for something.

"It was two hundred thousand. I doubt it's a ransom amount, but I don't know what it could mean."

"I do." I hung up and dialed Mercer.

"Psychic?" he asked as way of greeting.

"What the hell is going on over there?"

"Final instructions were delivered this morning. The kidnappers will trade the girl for three million. Estes has twenty-four hours to compile the additional funds. The money will be left at a drop site where Adalina's location will be revealed."

"And he hired a hit squad to take out the kidnappers?" I asked. It was the only thing that made sense.

"My job is retrieval. I don't ask questions."

"You should start asking questions." Since we have Adam, a.k.a. Autumn, I was surprised the kidnappers didn't request a prisoner trade as well. Obviously, the Seasons didn't have warm, touchy feelings for one another.

"Are you with Estes now?"

"I just left."

"Did you see Santino?"

"My job isn't to keep tabs for you." He was agitated, but it didn't matter. I waited for an answer. "I saw him briefly, but Barr and Keener escorted him away."

"What do you mean 'escorted'?"

"What do you think?" And he hung up. His friendly demeanor hadn't lasted past the initial half hour after I beat the shit out of Adam, and I thought we were making such progress too.

With nowhere else to go, I went to the precinct. There were too many questions, not enough answers, and a constant countdown. At least, this time, Catherine was no longer in any danger.

I ran criminal checks on every name from the list Bastian gave me. There was a smattering of misdemeanors, but no one had any felony convictions or ties to hardened criminals. At least none that I could discern. The woman who orchestrated the kidnapping still had a connection to the Estes family, perhaps even to the school, but I didn't know who she was or what her motivation was. Santino was involved. If I had any doubt, despite the photograph in his apartment, Estes had the same suspicion. I doubted we were both wrong. That meant at least two people affiliated with the Estes family orchestrated the kidnapping. Now all I needed was motivation, a solid lead, and a confession might be nice.

Sitting behind a blank computer screen, I couldn't pinpoint where to go or what to do. Our window of opportunity was closing, and I was stuck between a rock and a hard place. I really needed to start keeping cushy blankets with me at all times to help alleviate this problem in the future; my internal voice was being a smartass. No wonder so many people found this irritating. I was aggravating myself with these pointless jibes.

Heathcliff was responding to a call on an unrelated matter, and Thompson was still out on account of his mandated thirty-six hour break. Drumming my fingertips on the desk, I made a judgment call. I picked up my purse and left the precinct. O'Connell asked the authorities not to get involved, and even though the entire situation morphed into something completely out of his control and mine, there was no reason to get officials involved now. In all honesty, if Moretti knew of the situation concerning Adam, Santino, Adalina, and Miguel Estes' transferred funds, a shit storm would rain down on us all. The Captain needed plausible deniability, and my hands were too dirty to be washed clean until the situation was resolved.

Pulling into the parking garage of the OIO building, I planned to check in with Kate, talk to a few of the hackers, and see if Mark was around. Mark Jablonsky would give me hell, but he was one of the few people who could keep me grounded and ensure I didn't go completely off the rails. Unfortunately, Kate didn't make any headway, and her expertise was being called away on a large-scale fraud investigation. She handed over all the relevant banking information, so I could attempt to keep tabs on my own. My hacker buddies, who still wanted to be called internet specialists, were trying to find a correlation between Santino and one of the female employees or close family friends, but I had little faith they would find a solid connection in such a short amount of time. Eventually, I made it to Mark's office.

"Parker," he looked up from his desk, "what brings you inside a federal building?"

"Shut up." He liked to bust my chops every chance he got. "I need your input." He raised an eyebrow and gestured to the seat in front of his desk. I shut the door and sat down. "This is all hearsay and off the books, understand?"

"I heard you recovered Catherine Cale. How is she?"

"She's a tough kid. It might take some time, but I think she'll be fine." I bit my lip and wished I didn't. "That's why I need someone to bounce ideas off of."

"Consider me rubber." His eyes narrowed. "Kidnapper did that to you?" He jerked his chin toward my face, which I didn't bother to cover with makeup.

"How this happened is beside the point." I was tired of people asking the same dumb questions. I lowered my voice and glanced around the room to make sure no one appeared out of thin air. "Mercer has Cale's captor someplace secure. The guy's name is Adam. He went by Autumn. He says a woman hired his crew to grab the girls, and they were given instructions about everything."

"Is his information on the level?"

"I don't know." I intentionally lifted my bandaged hand and brushed my hair back. "He was properly incentivized to be forthcoming."

"Where is he now?" The question Mark really wanted to ask was *how is he.*

"He's secure. There's been movement in Miguel Estes' bank account, and his business manager is suspected of being involved."

"Do the cops have him?"

"No. His lawyer got him released yesterday. Estes might be conducting his own interrogation as we speak."

Mark leaned back in the chair. "What's the problem? The family wants all law enforcement uninvolved, and it sounds like he's handling the situation." I readjusted in the chair, frustrated and antsy. "Oh," he was smarter than he let on, "you tried to color outside the lines, but all those rules and regs I drilled into you must have stuck." He looked pleased. "'Bout damn time you listened to something."

"Anyway, you told me to get in bed with Mercer. So do I screw him over or let him finish what he started?" Mark blew out a breath and picked up his pen, absently chewing on the cap.

"You have to see this through to the end." He knew me well enough to know there was no other possibility. "I say let Mercer get his rocks off, and whatever pieces don't get swept under the rug, you drag them down to the precinct. You are working for Moretti, right?"

"Yep."

"Okay." He considered something for a moment. "That might insulate you from any fallout concerning abducting and beating a man."

"Assuming he's still alive by that point." I stood up, thankful that Mark helped me reach the only viable conclusion. This was Mercer's show, and I was just playing a supporting role.

"Damn mercs," he added, waving me away as I opened the door. "Watch yourself out there. If you need someone to save the day, you have my number."

"Careful, all that hero talk is likely to make me swoon."

THIRTY-SEVEN

I shook out my shoulders and neck. After my therapy session with Mark, I went home. Investigating the bogus security firm led to nothing, and only Kate could work magic with bank accounts to make this mindless drivel translate into usable information. I was a people person, not a mathematical genius. Slowly pacing the confines of my apartment, I started over at the beginning. The girls were taken from the school by someone familiar. I needed Catherine to talk to me. She possessed the missing pieces, even if she didn't know it. Hopefully, if I called the Cales, Nick and I wouldn't end up in another knockdown, drag-out fight.

"Mrs. Cale," I tried to sound professional, hoping Evelyn wouldn't hang up on me, "this is Alex Parker."

"Alex," her tone sounded cheerful. "I've been meaning to call. Thank you so much. I had my doubts, but Nicky was right about you." Her gushing was making my stomach hurt. It might also cause some cavities with all that sugary sweetness.

"Evelyn, there is still a child missing. Do you think it might be possible to ask Catherine a question?"

She hedged. It was her way of protecting her daughter.

"She's been through so much already."

"I know. Maybe you know the answer to this. I don't know exactly what was said or reported to the police department." O'Connell censored most of the report due to Mercer's insistence. "But your daughter was taken that morning from the school. Catherine, Sonia, and Adalina all left without so much as a peep. Do you know what they were told in order to gain that level of cooperation?" I almost said trust but thankfully changed my mind.

"Supposedly," her voice was full of hatred and disgust, making the family resemblance between her and Nick that much more obvious, "Adalina's mother sent the car for the girls. It was a birthday treat for her daughter. Can you fucking believe that those sickos would use a line like that?" She had gone from protective mother bear to vengeful parent in a heartbeat. But I barely noticed because I was blinded by the epiphany that just flipped the switch in my brain.

"I have to go. Thanks." I disconnected and read the names on the paper in front of me. The only one missing was the guilty party. "Holy shit," I breathed. Grabbing my keys, I was out the door without a moment's hesitation. Mercer was the only one with access, and hopefully, he would use his skills of persuasion to get me inside the Estes' house.

*   *   *

"It's bloody brilliant," Bastian remarked. The others sat silently as I instilled upon the ex-SAS crew my belief that Adalina's mother, Rosa Estes, was responsible for the triple kidnapping.

"You've lost your mind," Mercer added, shaking his head for added emphasis. "Why would she take her own daughter? I must have hit you harder than I thought. It knocked out the last bit of sense you possessed." Biting my tongue, I knew arguing with Mercer was completely pointless. "Can you substantiate any of these insane claims?"

"She knew everything. She had access. She," before I

could continue, he interjected.

"She's fucking grieving. The woman's barely even able to put a sentence together because she's so overcome, and you want me to get you access to the house to question her. This is rubbish."

"Julian," Bastian interjected while I ran a hand through my hair, fighting to keep my anger in check, "just stop and think about it for a minute."

"Rosa and Santino have something on the side. There's a photograph of her and Adalina in his apartment. The way the place is set up, I bet she spends most of her days there," I added.

"Not only is she a kidnapper but she's also an adulteress? Any other allegations you want to add?" I didn't understand Mercer's attitude. Why wasn't he on board? "Hans, check it out." Silently, Hans collected his gear and left the apartment. "You have something to say?" he barked at me, but I stared at the ceiling, afraid of what might come out of my mouth. "Well, speak."

I unclenched my jaw. "If I'm right, you're walking into crossfire."

He snorted. "And?"

"The Seasons were hired by Rosa Estes. Either they're still acting on her orders in which case you won't find the girl, or they've gone rogue."

"Jules," Bastian piped up, "the team Miguel hired will turn this into a spaghetti Western." I saw the fury radiate in Bastian's direction, but Mercer held it together. "You're not stupid, Commander." I watched the silent standoff between the two. "It won't hurt to let the bird do her job. Maybe we can save some lead on this one."

"Donovan, go speak to our friend," Mercer ordered. He was doing a lot of that today. "Bas, either figure out what the bloody hell that chip is or not, but sitting here wanking off isn't helping." He turned on me next. "You and I are going for a ride. Don't open your mouth unless you're told otherwise."

I didn't take kindly to orders or threats, and I glowered at him. "Someone woke up on the wrong side of the bed," I remarked, just to piss him off. He looked temporarily shocked that I said something, and I saw the briefest amused flicker before he replaced it with a glare and headed out the door. "And typically, I'm the bitchy and insane one. Hell, it's nice to be the calm and rational one for once."

Seated next to Mercer in his rental car, I was organizing the evidence against Rosa Estes and Estobar Santino in my mind. There was the possibility they weren't responsible for the kidnappings. There was also the chance that I'd hit it big playing the lottery. Mulling it over, I wondered if Miguel had any idea his wife was responsible. Was Adalina even his? Or was she Estobar's? Hell, I should have spent my days watching telenovelas to have a better handle on the intricacies of this case.

"Parker, you don't know what you're walking into. The Cale girl is safe. The detective was assisting, but even he wouldn't be this far out on a limb." I faced Mercer. He was focused on the road, and I didn't know why he was speaking to me.

"We had a quid pro quo. I don't renege on my agreements."

"I don't need help."

"I want these bastards behind bars." He squinted into the distance. "You've said it yourself. You're in this for retrieval only. I'll just pick up the shit left behind and turn them over to the police."

"There won't be loose ends." His tone was ominous. "Senor Estes hired an additional team to deal with any remaining mess."

"Well then, I guess I'll be making a call to the coroner after everything is said and done."

"You should back off." For once he didn't sound threatening. He sounded resigned to the fact that I wasn't going anywhere.

"I can't."

"Why?" He looked at me. "You have what you came for."

"I'm not a killer. I'm not heartless. And I'm not prepared to let these creeps get away with things. Despite what you may think, I mostly follow the rules, but every once in a while," I let out a breath, "the ends are enough to justify the means."

"Bastian's right. We aren't so different after all." This time the thought wasn't nearly as chilling. The rest of the car ride was in a peaceable silence, and I was willing to follow Mercer's lead inside the Estes' estate. It had taken us long enough, but we finally managed to achieve a truce.

Following the path leading to the estate, Mercer left the car parked near the front door. Obediently, I trailed him into the house, surrendering my nine millimeter without protest to Barr. He didn't seem surprised to see me again, but he might have been attempting to perfect his impersonation of a statue.

"Mr. Mercer," Estes greeted, pretending I was invisible, "is everything set for the exchange?"

"Sir," Mercer nodded, "we will be ready to go as soon as the location is verified. Are there any additional details or stipulations?"

Estes shifted his gaze to study me. He said something in Spanish which I didn't catch. I remained silent, and Mercer began what sounded like a long-winded explanation. Fighting the urge to interject or wander through the house, I took a page out of Barr's book. When the non-English portion of the meeting was over, Estes spoke again in English. "Miss Parker, you are part of Mercer's team, but do not think that means I have hired you, nor that I want anything you witness to be reported to the authorities."

"Understood." I don't know why I was being so agreeable, but it probably couldn't hurt. Estes turned and strode briskly from the room. Apparently, he had nothing else to say.

Mercer put his hand against the small of my back and leaned in. "Rosa is at your three o'clock. No accusations. Make the conversation brief. I'll meet you at the car in ten minutes." He stepped away, following Estes down the corridor. Now was my chance. Inhaling, I wasn't sure what to say or do.

"Senora," I began, standing on the threshold to the veranda, "I'm so sorry for all that you've endured. Is there anything I can get you?" A matching pair of metal bracelets perhaps?

"Gracias," she attempted a smile, but it didn't make it past the ends of her lips. "Has my husband hired you?"

"No, ma'am. I was originally hired to recover Catherine Cale." I watched for signs of guilt or some type of acknowledgement, but she stared at the floor. "Since I was familiar with the situation regarding the kidnappers, Julian asked for my assistance."

"I see." Although she spoke Spanish, she had no discernible accent. "Do you do work like this often?" She stared with a fierce intensity.

"Often enough."

"I can tell." She stared at my bandaged hand. "What type of work is this for a woman?"

"The same type of work it is for a man." Holding my tongue wasn't going over well. "What can I say? I fail to succumb to gender stereotypes."

"You have no husband to object?"

"I'm not married."

"What about a father or brother? How can any man in your life allow you to act this way?"

Wow, I felt like the sexual revolution never occurred. Granted, lack of equality was still something argued when it came to wages and sexual harassment in the workforce, but this was neither the time nor place for an ideological or political discussion. It was also possible this was a cultural difference, but my bet was that Miguel laid down the rules and didn't take no for an answer.

"I don't need permission." But I needed to find an in to get her to open up. Some common ground would be nice. "But my boyfriend is supportive." I saw the briefest flicker in her eyes. It was the first sign of life I'd seen since stepping outside to speak with her.

"It must be nice," there was a forlornness about Rosa that was almost heart-wrenching, "to do as you like without consequence."

"There are always consequences. Sometimes, the easiest thing to do is nothing at all. But when you reach a breaking point, it's hard to remember that a simpler solution might still exist. Maybe it's best to just walk away." I saw the alarm register in her eyes.

"It is too late for that."

I nodded, stepping back. "I hope your daughter is returned safely. There has been enough violence and bloodshed already." None of the other girls were hurt, but she pressed her lips together in acknowledgment of this fact. "I hope Mr. Santino was not greatly inconvenienced by the police visiting him yesterday morning." She turned away, facing outward toward the yard.

"Estobar determined his own fate." Before I could say anything else, heavy footsteps sounded from behind. Barr was approaching, and it was time to go. Rosa didn't confess, but her words removed the doubt from my mind. She was involved. Maybe she wasn't running the show or calling the shots, but she was partially responsible at the very least.

THIRTY-EIGHT

The five of us were back at the apartment. Everyone's outing had been a bust. Adam was still not cooperating, despite Donovan's insistence. Hans tossed Santino's apartment and discovered a few additional photos in the bedroom, but nothing blatantly screamed out affair. He photographed the pictures, and I skimmed through the images. But they were all of either Rosa or Adalina. Estobar wasn't in any of the frames with the women, and it would be a hard sell to say any type of unscrupulous activity occurred. I wondered if Keener had any luck interrogating Santino. As Rosa said, Estobar made his own fate.

"It's not a tracker," Bastian broke the silence. "It's more of an alarm. From what I can tell, it sends a brief transmission and then fries itself."

"Like in Chechnya?" Mercer inquired.

"Similar," Bastian cocked his head to the side, "but I'd say it's probably more of a trigger for an alarm. Something along the lines of *you've been discovered, haul ass.*"

"It means they operate independently without a required check-in." Mercer rubbed his chin. "Do you think they're aware we have one of theirs?"

"Probably not," Hans answered, looking completely

bored. "Given the layout and the locations, they were probably working in two-man teams. But with only one girl remaining, maybe Cale and Casanov's captors were free to go on holiday."

"They already have two million," I realized. Somehow, this fact had eluded me, but Casanov's family paid, and the money I dropped off at the bus stop was still missing. "They're probably someplace safe, sitting pretty."

"I'd say they split up to avoid detection," Bastian added. It was a new angle to work.

"Makes no difference," Mercer concluded and left the room. Hans left too, and I realized Donovan hadn't been with us. It was nice to know I wasn't the only one who suffered an emotional toll when torturing someone.

"What's your plan?" Bastian asked, disturbing my reverie.

"Do I look like the type who has a plan?" The room was devoid of everything, except the computer and electronic equipment he was using. "What's Mercer going to do at the exchange?"

"He'll bring them the money and hope to get the location for the girl. We're assuming she's being held somewhere else, but it won't matter. Either way, he's there for the recovery."

"How do these recoveries usually go?"

Bastian glanced toward the door. "As long as no one gets in the way, he retrieves the package and exits. Obstacles are often eradicated." I swallowed. It was fast and potentially justifiable, but it was also brash and a bloodbath waiting to happen. I thought about the blood on the pier and solidified my resolve. "You're going with him, aren't you?"

"Yes." I stepped out of the room, and wanting to stay close, I took a seat in the empty living room.

Sometime during the interim, I sprawled out on the couch, an arm thrown over my eyes to shield them from the light from the setting sun invading the room through the slats in the blinds. Regardless of how calm I appeared, I could feel the pre-op jitteriness permeating throughout the apartment. Mercer went to wait at the Estes' estate to field the final call, and Donovan and Hans were in a back room. From the constant metallic ratcheting, I was sure they were cleaning their weapons and making sure everything was assembled in proper working order. They weren't that different from the FBI tactical unit I worked with that horrible morning at the pier.

Without looking, I heard Bastian rummage through the kitchen. Less than a minute later, the rustling of a potato chip or maybe pretzel bag sounded close by, followed by a constant crunch. "Love?" He asked quietly as if he were afraid I was asleep. I shifted my arm and looked at him with one eye. "No one's ever this calm before a mission. I was afraid you might be dead."

"Normally, that's something to worry about if I'm not moving after a mission." I considered sitting up but decided against it. "How many packs did you smoke a day?"

He grinned. "Two. How'd you guess?" He looked down at his hand covered in cheese puff orange. "It's that obvious, isn't it?"

"It's not the cheese doodles." I sat up and snatched a handful. "You've practically been eating nonstop since we met. And unless you have the world's fastest metabolism, I'd say this is a recent development." Attempting trivial conversation was one way to avoid the urge to pace and check my gun a thousand times.

"How's your hip?" he asked around a mouthful of junk food. "And your hand?"

"The hip's okay. Still bruised, but it's fine." I unwrapped my hand, realizing the bandage would make it difficult to pull the trigger, and tentatively, I flexed my fingers.

"Sore?"

"Manageable. It's not an impediment." Dammit, now I couldn't avoid the nervous energy anymore. "What's the plan? You guys do this for a living, right?"

"Circumstances have never been quite like this. It's rather disconcerting." He wasn't in to sugarcoating. "Whenever we discover Adalina's location, Donovan will set up in the distance to provide cover support. Hans will ensure no other players present themselves. I'll be coordinating, unless additional firepower is required." He wiped his mouth and tried not to look grim. "Normally, Julian goes in and recovers the package. I suppose you will be assisting him."

"Now we wait." I got up and circled the living room. More than likely, Mercer would make the drop, get the location, and we'd recover the girl. Guns wouldn't be necessary, and everyone would walk away breathing. The problem was the second team Estes hired. If I was right in my assumption that Rosa and Santino were involved in the abduction, either they hired their own hit squad to pit against Estes' team, or the Four Seasons were operating off the rails which could mean anything. I blew out a breath. "Did you make any progress on the chip?"

Bastian's technological speak burned through the remaining daylight hours. It also kept me from turning into a complete basket case while we waited. After a few final tweaks, he declared the signal could be transmitted, but there was no way to trace it. However, if we already knew the location, it might be enough of a distraction to make the remaining Seasons scramble. It was just a thought, but it sounded better than most.

When Bastian went in search of another crunchy snack to fill his need for a cigarette, I fidgeted with my phone. I wanted to call Heathcliff, Thompson, and Mark. Flashing blue lights, an FBI tactical team, and snipers would have been a nice touch to have assisting on the recovery, but I was resigned to following Mercer's orders. Hopefully, no one would get killed. More importantly, I hoped not to get shot. Martin insisted that this not happen again, and I didn't want to break that promise. Furthermore, O'Connell was already in the hospital, and I didn't want to be his roomie.

"It's go time," Mercer announced, opening the door. Donovan and Hans were at the kitchen table, going over maps and satellite images. Apparently, Mercer texted them the location prior to his appearance. He looked at me. "I have a spare Flak jacket you can borrow for the duration. Don't put any holes in it."

"I'm not planning to."

We piled into the vehicles. Mercer and I rode together in one; the three ex-SAS in the other. I checked my gun and clip. On the drive to the drop, I took the extra magazines from my purse and put them in one of the vest pockets, then I put my cell phone in my jeans pocket, along with my identification. It might seem ridiculous or downright morbid, but worst case, I didn't want to be lying in a cooler for a week while they determined who I was and who to call.

The second van slowed and remained far behind us as Mercer pulled up to an out-of-service bus depot. It was in a shady neighborhood. The windows were broken, and graffiti covered every surface. My eyes darted around. There were a few unsavory individuals near the street corners, dealers and whores, but no sign of any kidnappers or children. Hopefully, Adalina wasn't being held someplace nearby. This wasn't a safe neighborhood for anyone.

"Stay here." Mercer opened the car door and stepped out. "I'll signal if I need you."

He opened the back door, took out a locked briefcase, and entered through the broken glass door. Hans was monitoring for any surrounding movement, so I focused on the dilapidated bus depot. Glancing at the clock, it had only been a little over a minute, and I wasn't sure if I should move in. I was reaching for the door handle when Mercer emerged. He got back into the car and started the engine. Picking up his phone, he hit a single key and spoke to the rest of his team. We were moving across town to a private airfield.

"What was inside?" I asked. I couldn't help myself. Information was my friend, but I could see the planning, the thoughts, and the meditation going through Mercer's mind as he drove through the darkness.

"This." He held up a sheet of paper with nothing but an address. "If she's not there, we've lost her." He was stoic, but despite the business tone to his voice, it was apparent he felt more than he would ever show.

"That's the same airfield you sent me to investigate."

"What did you find?" he asked bitterly.

I thought about the two men I encountered who spoke of girls and planes. There hadn't been enough time to process any of it because he called me away to meet him at the second hangar bay where we didn't apprehend either of the two Seasons who were present. Something was starting to stink, and I was afraid it might be Mercer.

"Nothing," I stammered. Thompson ran the plates on the truck. Nothing sinister about it. Maybe it was sheer coincidence. "Since you sent me to check it out, isn't it strange it's the same location the kidnappers left Adalina?"

"No." He tore his eyes from the road and looked at me. "All the locations we scouted were believed to be viable places to hold the girls based on the information we collected from the various forms of communication with the Seasons." Catherine said they were moved four different times. Maybe I had been a lot closer than I realized. Or he was involved. "Parker, don't you trust me?"

"Not in the least." I smiled cynically.

He let out a chuckle. "Bloody hell." He continued driving. At this point, it didn't matter. We were about to enter into a potentially hostile situation, and if it didn't go smoothly, there was no guarantee either of us would walk away in one piece.

THIRTY-NINE

Breaching required some finesse, and Donovan was positioned on the roof of the self-storage units, facing the hangar. It was a distance away, but he had a high-powered sniper rifle and was a great shot. Hans was scouting the rest of the area. If he encountered any issues, Bastian would provide back-up, and if things were clear, he would find a spot to establish crossfire in the event we encountered uninvited guests. Mercer and I crept to the hangar. From my previous adventure, I was aware of the windows, the layout inside, and the cover positions. The desk, filing cabinet, larger airplane equipment, and parked Cessna were the only obstacles within the otherwise open hangar.

"Parker," Mercer whispered, pressed against the side of the building, waiting for affirmation of an all-clear before moving in, "we'll begin in the hangar. If we encounter unfriendlies, you locate the girl while I deal with the situation."

"Fine."

"If she's not inside, we'll check all of the storage units."

"What about Estes' secondary team?"

"I'd like to find the girl before I call them. We're against a time crunch, and Miguel wants a response imminently. We must hurry."

"Okay."

After getting the all-clear, I stayed on Mercer's six as he went in the only door to the hangar. It was empty, except for the furniture. The Cessna was gone. On the desk was another note with additional instructions. It felt like we were on a scavenger hunt. Frankly, I hate scavenger hunts. Mercer and I performed a thorough search of the hangar before leaving. He radioed his team that we were on the move again; this time, we were going back to the original warehouse where I first encountered the Seasons.

"Delay tactics," he muttered under his breath as the odometer neared a hundred, and he swerved through traffic. "This is fucking bullshit." I braced myself against the seat as the truck in front of him slammed on his brakes, and we narrowly avoided getting hit by a car driving in the opposite direction.

"Why delay? They got the money." I swallowed, regretting asking questions and diverting any of his focus from the colorful streaks that we flew past.

"Maybe they're planning to abscond with the money and the girl." He jerked the wheel to the side, and we were on the sidewalk. I wasn't positive we weren't momentarily airborne. "Bollocks." He laid in the horn as a few late night pedestrians scattered out of the way. "Radio Bastian and tell him to get Estes' team in play."

"What?" The point was to avoid this situation.

"We'll give them the hangar we just left. It might buy us some time."

He launched the vehicle off the sidewalk and back onto the street, through a red light, and down the next block. We were getting close. Doing as he asked, I tried to sound calm, even though my heart was in my throat, and I thought Martin's driving was insane.

Instead of screeching to a stop, Mercer drove directly through the fence and used the SUV to block the front doors. There were only three ways remaining to get in or out of the building. He grabbed the radio from my hand and gave instructions to Hans and Donovan to cover both side exits. Until they caught up, we were on our own. "Parker, take the side. I'll go in through the back." He met my eyes for a moment. "This is it." As soon as he said the words, I felt it, the brief moment of serenity before the violence breaks. That eerie quiet predicting an uncertain future. Nodding, he ran to the back as I edged to the side.

Listening, I heard Mercer throw open the back door. The metal door clanged against the frame, and then there was silence. Holding my breath, I turned the knob, but the door was locked. Fuck. Remembering my lock picks, I found them in one of the many pockets of the bulletproof vest and quickly went to work. The lock popped a few seconds later, and I eased the door open. The room was dim. Across the expanse, there were a few monitors casting shadows as they flickered.

Squinting, I could make out a form, hands raised in the center of the room. There were two other figures, each holding a gun. Dammit, Julian. As stealthily as possible, I edged away from the door. There were words exchanged, but from this distance, I couldn't hear what they were saying. Taking cover behind one of the support poles near the edge of the large converted hangar, I spotted a third man edging forward from the other side.

Hans and Donovan hadn't signaled, so whoever was hiding in the shadows was not part of Mercer's team. The light glinted off the end of a rifle, and I reacted. "Mercer, down," I screamed, firing at the third man and launching myself forward.

Gunfire echoed off the walls, and I lost track of how many shots were fired or even the direction they were coming from. My back was against a desk, and other than a few support pillars, and some machinery, there was no cover in the open. The six rooms, three lining each side of the hangar, might provide some tactical coverage, or they'd be deathtraps.

The man with the rifle was down, and I wasn't sure who took him out. The other two, who had Mercer at gunpoint, sought cover on the opposite side of the hangar. They cowered behind a Cessna. Carefully, I approached Mercer's position. He made his way to one end of the hangar and threw open one of the doors to use as cover.

"Adalina," he hissed. In the firefight, I forgot our purpose.

"Who are they?" I asked.

"Not the time," he broke cover and checked the other two rooms.

The two men fired again, and I returned fire in their general direction to provide some cover for Julian. He finished the search of the third room and shook his head. We were close enough that I could make out even his slight movements. In a duck, he ran toward the center of the room, narrowly missing a shot that bounced off a support pillar four inches above his head. The other shooter fired at me, and I rolled behind the desk.

The other side door opened, and a large group of men poured inside. In the dim light, I lost count, but there were at least four. Maybe six. From the way they sprayed the room, it didn't matter if we were friend or foe, they wanted everyone out of the picture. Mercer didn't notice their entrance since he was focused solely on the hunt for Adalina.

A shooter took aim, and without thinking, I vaulted over the desk and across the expanse, knocking Mercer to the ground and landing on top of him. Without missing a beat, he rolled us over and underneath a table as the gunfire left pockmarks on the floor beside us. I wasn't sure I was breathing, afraid even the slightest sound would give away our position. He was above me, and as the gunshots hit into the top of the wood surface, threatening to splinter it at any moment, he acted as a shield from the incoming barrage.

The gunfire shifted away from us and back toward the other two gunmen. "Looks like we're even," I exhaled as Mercer slid off of me and cast his glance around for a vantage point.

"It won't matter if we both end up dead. Dammit, where the bloody hell is our support team?"

We didn't have time to wait. Cowering would mean death in no uncertain terms. He turned his gun and fired at one of the men. I heard a cry of pain and hoped we had one less hostile to deal with. But now our position was compromised. Mercer was on the move, back toward the remaining three rooms, and I shoved the table onto its side and fired.

Only when I pulled the trigger and heard the click did I duck completely below the table to reload. Mercer checked all three rooms and shook his head. Or at least I think he did. It was hard to tell in the dark. Another barrage hit the table, and the wood splintered, splitting the table into two separate, ineffectual pieces. I scurried to the back corner of the room. Two guys were down. Another two still with guns. And no sign of Adalina.

"Sorry for the delay," Bastian's voice sounded in my ear. It was about damn time. "Half a dozen unfriendlies are out here. Hans and Donovan are working on the situation."

"Don't let anyone leave," Mercer growled. Did that mean alive or did that mean at all? Shots erupted from behind the parked plane, and my gut instincts took over.

"Cover me," I shouted, sprinting across the expanse. Of the two men that had taken cover behind the plane, only one of them was still breathing. He turned, aghast that I was running toward him and fired. Thankfully, he wasn't adept at hitting a moving target, and I slid across the floor and straight into him. Wrestling for possession of his gun, random shots went off in all directions. The sound was deafening, and I focused on not letting the barrel of the gun point in my direction.

More gunfire continued, but after being so close to the discharging pistol, it sounded muffled. Finally, the man dropped the gun. I kneed him in the groin, and he doubled over. Following through with an uppercut, I knocked him back and out cold. God, my hand hurt. This would have been easier if I didn't run out of bullets.

Before I could even turn around, the barrel of a weapon pressed against the back of my skull. Shutting my eyes tightly, I didn't want to see what was about to happen next. They say you never hear the bullet that kills you. I hoped I wouldn't feel it either. Although, if you want to shoot someone, getting this close was asking to be taught a lesson.

Knowing any sudden movement might cause the trigger to be pulled that much faster, I didn't see any other choice but to spin. My forearm was up, and I knocked the unsuspecting weapon away. Hearing the impotent click signifying an empty magazine, the man holding it stared at me, stunned. Amateur, I thought, kicking him hard in the ribs. He made an oof sound and stepped back. Clearly, he was surprised to encounter a woman, and I used it to my advantage to grab his gun. I pulled the trigger, and nothing happened, ensuring it was empty and didn't just misfire.

"You goddamn son of a bitch," I snarled, cold-cocking him across the face. The echo of a shot from a high-powered sniper rifled filled the hangar, and like clockwork, the remaining men were taken down. With the crack of the rifle, another man hit the ground. Mercer rushed toward me, and he landed an elbow on my attacker. The guy hit the ground. He wouldn't be getting up for a while. "Bastard." I kicked him for good measure.

"Okay?" Mercer's voice held just a slight hint of amusement.

"Yep." I heard the all-clears via the radio, and at last, the threat was neutralized. "Adalina?" I called, knocking against the plane. "Sweetie, are you inside?" There was no answer, and I noticed a few holes where bullets pierced the exterior.

Mercer managed to get the door open and went inside, coming out with a terrified child. She had a few nicks and cuts from the broken windows and metal frame, but after performing an assessment, she appeared healthy.

"Package recovered," Mercer said into his earpiece. "Bastian, remain here with Parker. Hans, Donovan, let's go." He glanced at me as he hefted her into his arms and whispered something to her in Spanish. "Thanks."

As soon as he made it to the door, I collapsed against the plane. My eyes never left the unconscious man, and I knew I needed to check the other downed men to see who might wake up and pose a threat. The aftershocks were just starting, and my hands trembled as I found my phone and called Thompson. I gave him the location to pick up Adam. Then I called 911 dispatch and reported the incident at the hangar.

"Bloody hell," Bastian exclaimed, shuffling through the broken glass and fragments as he stepped around the downed gunmen. He found a light switch against the wall and illuminated the place. "Why didn't you turn the lights on?"

On wobbly legs, I worked my way through the bodies. Three were dead. The other four may or may not be, depending on how long it took for the authorities to arrive. Bastian was armed with a loaded handgun, and I gave him strict instructions to shoot anything that moves. In the meantime, I tried my best not to touch anything. It would be hard enough explaining why I was in this hangar bay in the first place.

"Just breathe, love," Bastian encouraged as I took a seat on top of a bullet-riddled desk. "My god, if you get this worked up shooting people, I'd hate to see what you're like post-orgasm." It was a tossup between laughing and glaring, and I went with laughing.

FORTY

It was a circus. Cops, FBI, and dozens of EMTs swarmed the hangar. All of the downed men were being bused away. We weren't in the business of killing, so whoever could be saved would be. My empty gun was confiscated, but as of yet, the cuffs weren't slapped on. Bastian was being questioned by Detective Jacobs and an FBI agent that I recognized but didn't remember his name.

"Ma'am, can you get off the desk?" a police officer asked. It had been twenty minutes since the shootout, but I was still shaking. Placing a foot on the ground, I stood, my knees knocking together uncertainly. "Are you okay?"

"I'm fine." The preliminary questions began immediately, and I answered. I was on autopilot. The officer watched me for a few moments before she stepped away to pass along some information over the radio.

"Jesus, Parker," Heathcliff exclaimed. He just arrived on scene and held me at arm's length, examining my appearance. "Why didn't you call?"

"I did. Didn't you notice everyone else hanging around, taking statements and collecting evidence? Sure, they're cops, but they aren't psychics." My smartass remarks were back in full swing.

"Did you get the girl?" he asked as his eyes focused on something.

"Mercer's taking her home." Bastian caught my eye, and I realized he just said the same thing to the group interrogating him. "You can send some uniforms over there now. I'm under the assumption half the men involved in the shooting were hired to be Estes' hit squad." Heathcliff radioed in the information, but he didn't let go of me.

"Let's get that vest off of you."

"Derek, I know we're friends, but what the hell? I'm not in the mood to perform a striptease."

"Humor me." He peeled off my jacket and helped as I unhooked the Velcro straps. His hands ran along my sides. "Does anything hurt?"

"No, but you might want to stop before I claim sexual harassment," I teased. He held up my jacket, and I saw the hole ripped through the side. "Shit." The room teetered. The adrenaline shock was enough. I didn't need him to point out near misses at this particular moment.

"Want to get checked out?"

"No. But I wouldn't mind sitting down." He smirked and led me out of the hangar and to his cruiser. "Whenever you're forced to arrest me, I won't resist, so if you keep the cuffs off, I promise not to tell anyone."

"We're not arresting you. Hell, I don't think we'll arrest the British chap either." More officers pulled up, and a dozen government vehicles followed suit. It was a mess.

By the time everything was sorted out, it was hours later. Thankfully, having friends with badges served a dual purpose. Not only were Bastian and I somehow managing to avoid being arrested, but we'd been brought coffees and sodas. After some conniving, an officer even went to pick up an extra large bag of potato chips for Bastian.

"Are you ready to go to the station and start on all the paperwork?" Heathcliff asked as I sipped my third latte.

The stress from the shootout finally faded, and the adrenaline left my system, only to be replaced with caffeine. At least that was one way to level out. I nodded. Bastian was taken in an hour before by an officer, and from the radio chatter, Mercer and the gang were being questioned in conjunction with the shooting and recovery. At the station, I gave my statement again before Moretti dragged me into his office. Everything that happened from our arrival at the bus depot to the shootout was divulged. He sent another team to scope out the other two locations we visited during our adventure. Mercer and his men were being interrogated as we spoke, and although I was curious to hear what they said or perhaps fabricated, the simple truth was Julian Mercer saved my life and I his. Moretti looked up when my story concluded. "You're still rattled."

"Sir?"

"It's okay. I've seen photos. The place was a bloodbath. It looked like shooting fish in a barrel. Lucky for you, you weren't a fish today." He stood and shut the shades. "Parker," his tone was hushed, "Thompson received a tip last night about one of the kidnappers being held captive." I shut my eyes, not sure what to say. There was no escaping what happened. Maybe I wouldn't look so bad in jumpsuit orange. "Like I said, you're rattled. So I don't need you discussing any of this right now. Also, stay clear of that part of the investigation. And stay away from the guy."

"Yes, sir."

"Are you okay to stay here a while longer? We're compiling information now. If I need anything clarified, I'll let you know." He jerked his chin toward the door, and I left.

Sitting at O'Connell's desk, I did as I was told. Typing my statement with one hand took time, but I listed all the facts I knew to be true and explained the kidnapping and ransom. Starting a new document, I listed all the facts and theories on Rosa Estes, Estobar Santino, and the nearly thwarted recovery of Adalina. This aspect was a huge mess, and I wasn't surprised when Keener, Barr, the Estes family, and Santino were dragged into the precinct. Santino looked comparable to Adam. Soon, lawyers were throwing fits and threats were made to contact consulates and embassies.

The phone at O'Connell's desk rang, and I was summoned downstairs to assist. Arriving downstairs, where they were cataloging evidence, I provided the crime scene techs an insider's view as they worked on bullet trajectories and flagging the proper casings with the proper weaponry. The markups on the photos and computer models resembled an overzealous child who discovered the joys of permanent markers. While down there, Agent Palmer arrived. He took one look at me and grinned.

"And you thought you fucked up." He chuckled.

"No thanks to you," I retorted.

He was here to take my statement in order to close the FBI file on the situation since it was technically a kidnapping. Almost two hours later, there was a write-up of all the details. Not even minor points went unnoticed. At least government bureaucracy didn't fail to instill upon him the necessity of dotting I's and crossing T's. After my vast knowledge was siphoned from my brain, I went upstairs with the hope of going home.

Thompson was at his desk with a poker face, and I wasn't sure if he was pissed about rescuing Adam or if he was pleased. Finishing his report, he shoved it inside a folder. "That tip you called in, I don't know how you heard about it, but we got the guy. He's a total nutjob though. Must have heard some cops talking about our consultant because he kept claiming police brutality against some chick who called herself Parker."

I swallowed the lump in my throat. "Thompson," I let out an unsteady breath, "should I call a lawyer?"

"Why?" he asked, the smile crinkling the corners of his eyes. "Hell, it turns out the guy seemed to have the timetable for his injuries down to the day, and it wasn't you. There's no way it could be you. Seems you've been alibied out without even having to provide an alibi." My heart skipped a beat at the words. We were all in enough trouble over this. There was no reason anyone else should stick their neck out. This was on me. "Word of advice, don't brag about it."

"Thank you."

"Not me. The O'Connells and Martin." He jerked his chin at Moretti's office. Jen and Martin were both inside. My guess, Bud must be guarding Nick at the hospital.

"Like I said, if you change your mind, I can probably get

the security feed from my house, complete with timestamp," Martin said, shaking hands with Moretti.

"That won't be necessary." Moretti smiled at me, and Martin turned.

"Hey," he grinned, and Moretti went back into his office to speak to Jen. Without giving heed to where I was, I launched myself into Martin's arms and kissed him in the middle of the precinct like a mindless idiot. "Are you feeling okay?" he asked as I hugged him.

"Now I am," I mumbled into his neck. It had been a long night.

"I was on my way to work, but," he looked uncertain, "I can move some things around." Releasing my grip, I shook my head, but Thompson caught my eye and jerked his head toward the door. Someone needed to tell me what was going on.

"Can I have five minutes?"

"Of course." Martin followed me out of the precinct and into the back of his waiting town car. After exchanging the briefest of pleasantries with his driver, he put up the privacy window. "Nick called. I don't need to know what happened. All I know is that after he collapsed in your apartment, you took him to the hospital, and when you left the hospital, you came straight to my place. And you didn't leave until the next morning. Apparently, at that point, you went back to the hospital and had breakfast with Jen."

"I don't want you lying for me. Moretti won't look into it, but what if someone else does? This isn't your responsibility. They could arrest you."

"Whatever you did, you had your reasons. I'm not here to pass judgment. Hell, you don't have to say another word. But I'm not sitting idly by when there's a chance I can get you out of trouble for once."

Trying to come up with something to say, I had nothing. I was speechless. Looking down, I noted my injured hand. At least now I had a legitimate reason for a few broken knuckles, and one that wasn't quite so suspicious.

"Tonight, I agreed to go over some numbers with Francesca, but," he brushed his thumb across my cheek, "maybe you'd like some company instead."

"Nothing would make me happier, but no. This will be resolved soon. Hopefully, I can go home, get some sleep, and help close the files tonight." Before either of us could say anything else, Heathcliff knocked on the tinted window.

"I hope I'm not interrupting a quickie, but if you could tear yourself away for a moment, we have some pressing matters still in play," he said as Martin rolled the window down.

"I'll see you soon," I insisted, getting out of the car.

"You better," he glanced behind me to make sure Heathcliff was gone, "especially after the way you kissed me earlier." Smiling, I leaned into the car and kissed him again. "Now you're just compounding the problem. I'll call you," he promised as the window rolled up, and the car pulled away.

"Did you tell him?" Heathcliff asked as soon as I stepped foot inside.

"Tell who what?"

He rolled his eyes and scoffed. "That the girl he's dating is bulletproof."

"And that's why you aren't in a relationship," I responded as we went upstairs to major crimes. "What was so urgent that you had to drag me back inside?"

"We just need you to sign off on a few things and verify some of the statements Julian Mercer made." He tossed a confused look in my direction. "Not everything he said makes sense."

"It's a complex situation."

"Right. Let's try to simplify it." That was the story of my life, wasn't it?

FORTY-ONE

As I waited for Mercer to be brought into interrogation, Jen reappeared with a first-aid kit. She bandaged my hand and made a show of asking how it happened. Maybe she was as paranoid as the rest of us, or Nick gave her explicit instructions on selling the story. After everything, it was nice to know, despite our disagreements, we still had one another's back. After tightening the bandage and insisting I show up later for an x-ray or else she would send Bud to fetch me, she left so we could get back to work.

After buying a cola from the vending machine, Thompson popped the top and handed it to me as the two of us stood inside the observation room. Heathcliff was reexamining Julian Mercer's story, and there were enough holes to make it look like a mouse devoured almost the entire block of Swiss cheese. The only accurate aspect of the story was our hunt across town to locate Adalina.

"He hasn't said a word about Adam Dowery a.k.a Autumn," Thompson whispered in my ear. There was no surveillance equipment in the room, but skittish came with the situation. "When they brought him in, I suggested it'd be in everyone's best interest if he kept it quiet."

"Mercer doesn't listen." I stared at him through the

glass. He wasn't nervous. He was just Julian. "But he won't say anything to incriminate himself or his team." Hopefully, after our partnership inside the hangar, that included me. "Frankly, there's no reason for you to hold him."

"We're not. He can go anytime he wants. We haven't brought charges against him. He was doing his job. It just doesn't make sense."

"How many bodies were pulled out of the hangar?"

Thompson glanced at me from the corner of his eye. "Seven dead. Three are in custody."

"Ten guys." The words rang hollow in my ears, and I still wondered who they were and whose side they were on. If they were the hit squad Estes hired to eliminate the kidnappers, then why did they open fire on us? Mercer knew who they were. He also knew he was free to go, but I couldn't figure out why he was staying. "And no one here wants to put the blame on someone for the body count?"

"DA's office flipped their shit. Three girls were abducted from an affluent private school. One of them was a cop's niece. The PR department put such a bullshit spin on it that we had to deny the kidnapping claims in the first place, and to add the cherry on top, Miguel Estes isn't even a fucking citizen. So, no. We aren't looking for an arrest or conviction."

I rubbed my forehead; my head ached from the recount of this circus. "Seven bodies." I swallowed. There was no way to determine if I was responsible for any of them, so my psyche was willing to deny my involvement for now. "Three hostiles, either hired guns or kidnappers, are in custody, and you're questioning a group of K&R specialists." I snorted. "Was there even a crime committed at this point?"

"Look, you're here to elaborate on the situation concerning whoever was responsible for Adalina's kidnapping. The Cales are satisfied that Catherine's back, and Nick's assured them that the guilty party has been dealt with in one way or another. The Casanovs are completely removed from the picture, so we just need to figure out the Estes' angle."

"This is such crap," I muttered under my breath. "And the FBI isn't investigating?"

"They are. You spoke to Agent Palmer, right?" Making a face, he continued, "But we're not working together. We just need to close this on our end."

"In that case, I'm on the wrong side of the glass." I sighed. "Put me in there with Mercer, and we'll come up with something feasible."

Thompson didn't look happy, but we left the observation room to start the entire process over inside interrogation. Everything said was on the record and highly censored. Twenty minutes later, an outline of Mercer's involvement was laid out. My own impact on the case was interjected whenever absolutely necessary, but there was nothing solid or new. All the suspicions we had about Rosa, Miguel, and Estobar were wholly unsubstantiated.

"I'm leaving," Mercer announced, standing. He checked his watch. "When will my property be returned from your holding facility?"

"We have more questions," Heathcliff insisted. My guess was Thompson didn't tell his partner the truth about Adam.

"Then I'd like to hear the charges." Mercer put his jacket on. "If not, my property?"

"It has to be processed. We'll call you," Thompson offered.

"I'm sure I'll be seeing you later, Parker." He left without another word.

I was sure Bastian, Hans, and Donovan left as soon as they could. It was Mercer's show, and he was the spokesman. At least I knew he'd take the heat for his men. Maybe there were a few redemptive qualities to the ex-SAS bastard.

"Y'know what," I glanced at the two detectives who seemed as far from their comfort zone as they could be while still within the confines of the precinct, "I can't do this right now. I've been up all night getting shot at and," I made sure the recording was shut off, "shooting. My hand hurts. And there's more caffeine circulating through my body than blood. So someone is taking me home or picking up my car, which is at Mercer's, and after I wind down and get some sleep, we will whatever." I gestured to the notepad on the table.

"Okay. I'll take you home, and Heathcliff will deliver your car," Thompson offered. We went back into the squad room, I gave my keys to Heathcliff, who might take the opportunity to speak to Julian and his pals in a less formal setting, and Thompson grabbed the keys to his car.

We didn't speak during the drive. Instead, I shut my eyes and felt the tension leave my body. The girls were safe. There were still so many unanswered questions, all a jumble inside my brain, but right now, it was simply a swirl of nonsense. The hangar left me physically and mentally exhausted, and I earned the right to sleep.

Thompson waited for Heathcliff to arrive, and after the keys were dropped off, they left with the promise I'd call them later tonight or tomorrow. Only after they were gone did I realize they worked all night too. We all deserved some R & R, even if it was only for the next few hours.

I took a shower, microwaved a bowl of soup, and tried some meditation techniques to clear my mind. As usual, the deep breathing exercises did nothing except remind me what it felt like to have fractured ribs and not be able to breathe deeply. Refusing to think, I brought my pillow and blanket into the living room, turned on the TV, and fell asleep in front of some family-friendly programming.

The phone rang, and I glanced at the clock. The television was airing a paid-advertisement, and it was dark out. "What are you wearing?" Martin asked as soon as I answered.

"A string bikini."

He laughed. "I just finished going over the numbers with Francesca. She was wondering when you can assist."

"Soon," I sighed. "Tell her a couple of days." It was too late to consider going to the precinct, especially when I was committed to going to bed and sleeping for the rest of the night.

"I will." The silence filled the void as I turned off the TV and took my pillow into the bedroom. "What are you doing?"

"Going to bed," I mumbled, nestling into the covers.

"Tease."

"Not a joke. Not even close." I shut my eyes. "I owe you an explanation and a thank you but not tonight."

"Good night, Alexis." Hanging up, I instantly fell asleep only to wake four hours later with nothing better to do than work on the Estes case.

Most of the world was asleep at three a.m. This meant there was plenty of time to think without interruption or distraction. As always, being a consultant meant hard evidence wasn't a requirement. Sure, it helped to demonstrate whatever conclusion I reached, but it wasn't a necessity.

Diagramming the kidnapping and everything else that had to be true, I finally had the twenty-twenty hindsight necessary to see the situation for what it was. Mostly for what it was. The few strands of knowledge I lacked, Mercer possessed.

Not bothering to consider the time, I dialed his number. When he answered, neither of us seemed particularly surprised. "Mr. Estes apologized for the intrusion. He was relieved to get his daughter back from the clutches of his conniving, soon-to-be-ex-wife," Mercer volunteered.

"Tell me what you know."

"My clients expect the utmost level of confidentiality," he replied, reminding me that speaking to him was like slamming my head into the wall, "but I don't enjoy taking friendly fire or having my work reassessed by a secondary team." The anger mostly reserved for me bled over onto Miguel. Pity. "With the exception of the three men who dubbed themselves the Seasons, the rest of the men in that hangar bay were hired by Estes. They should have practiced a higher level of discrimination before firing on us."

"Is Adalina okay?" I asked. If Senor Estes was as ruthless as it sounded, returning her might not have been in anyone's best interest.

"She is unharmed." There was hesitation in his voice. "This job may not be completed yet." There was a pregnant pause, but I didn't offer to fill the void. "Bastian will deliver documents later. Do with them as you see fit."

"Mercer?"

"I'll be in touch. Right now, I have arrangements to make." The line went dead. He needed to work on being more helpful and transparent. All this cryptic crap was infuriating.

By the time the rest of the world was awake and preparing for their day, I had a skeletal outline of the kidnapping based solely on my gut instincts and a few hints that the ex-SAS dropped along the way. My phone rang, and I grabbed it, hoping it'd be Bastian.

"I know it's early," Martin said, already in apology mode, "but if you're home, I'd like to drop by with breakfast before I go to work." Without knowing what else to say, I agreed. Sometimes, the sweetness factor bordered on making the cynic in me physically ill, but it could also melt the hopeless romantic to a blubbering pile of goop, thereby making the cynic even more nauseated.

Glancing over the outline, I feared what Mercer's next move was. My personal inclination was the abduction had been orchestrated by Rosa. Either Estobar assisted in the scheme because he was her lover or because he was Adalina's biological father. My stomach twisted at the thought of a mother putting her seven-year-old child through the horrors of such a situation for weeks on end, unless she told Adalina what would happen ahead of time. Did Adalina say anything about it to Catherine?

Mid-dial, there was a knock on my door. Opening it, Bastian surprised me, coming inside with a sealed envelope. I hung up the phone and met his eyes.

"Hi ya, love." He smiled and placed the envelope in the center of my counter.

"What is it?" Eyeing the parcel, I wasn't sure I wanted to know.

"Confidential information. It could make the case for your copper mates. Jules said it's up to you to decide."

"Bastian, I need to know who hired the Four Seasons to kidnap the girls."

"Read this first."

"Tell me." He was heading for the door, and I blocked his path. "Was it Rosa? Did she do this to her daughter?"

"Love," he wouldn't budge, "in due time." Taking a breath to calm my nerves and resist hitting something or someone, I remained between him and my still open front door. "I have to get back."

"How long have you known? How much do you know?" The accusations were starting, despite the prematurity.

"Read the documents." His eyes betrayed him, and I saw actual remorse. "Whatever remaining questions you have, they will be answered." He kissed my cheek. "You saved your girl. You might have to help us save ours. Just remember, lives might still be on the line."

"Bas," I was tired of all the cloak-and-dagger, "why can't you explain?"

"Oh, look," his gaze shifted behind me, "you have company." He escaped without another word, brushing past Martin.

"Bad timing?" Martin asked.

Shrugging, I shut and locked the door as soon as he stepped inside. "Did you happen to bring some sodium pentothal? My questions haven't been getting answers recently, and I'm not sure how else to up my game."

"So now wouldn't be a good time to ask why the British gentlemen kissed you on the cheek and left your apartment at seven a.m. after you apparently went to bed early in a string bikini?"

"What do you think?"

"I think I forgot to put truth serum on my shopping list."

FORTY-TWO

Martin didn't have any early morning meetings planned for the day. So as he stood in my kitchen, cooking breakfast, I opened the envelope and spread the contents out on my kitchen table. It became apparent why Bastian left so quickly. There were dozens of communications between Estobar Santino and the Four Seasons. Locations, maps, times, negotiating tactics, the entire scheme was expressly laid out, even hiring the kid to steal the supplies, pouring the blood on the pier, and leading me to believe Catherine was dead. I was livid. Slamming my palm down, I screamed in pain and cursed.

"Alex," Martin dragged me away from the table, "relax." Without releasing me, he grabbed a bag of peas from my freezer and laid it against my hand. "What the hell's going on?"

"I'm going to fucking kill him." The desperation resurfaced. The entire time, Julian knew she was alive and who was responsible, and he did nothing to help. "How could he? That sick bastard." With my free hand, I rubbed the bridge of my nose.

"In that case, it's a good thing I can alibi you out. But let's eat breakfast first, that way when they ask how the eggs were, you'll at least have an honest answer to give to one of their questions." Regaining my composure with the sobering reality that acting like a time bomb would end badly for everyone, I took a few steady breaths and tried to detach myself from the circumstances. It was damn near impossible. "Just for my own clarification, are you planning to kill the guy who was here earlier?" It was a sad attempt at a joke.

"He's only guilty by association."

Burying my face against his shoulder, I had to get through the information and determine what was pertinent and what to bury. Honestly, if O'Connell knew the information I possessed, I was afraid to think what he'd do. At the moment, I was still afraid of what I might do. Thoughts of Adam's bloodied face emerged in the forefront of my thoughts, followed closely by the seven lifeless men from the hangar. Someone would make restitution through proper channels. My days of vigilantism were over.

"What is this?" he asked, sifting through the documentation.

"Did you say you had a free morning?"

"Absolutely. I just need to make one call."

* * *

One thing was painfully obvious; there was zero possibility that I could be unbiased. My emotions had been put through the wringer since the first phone call O'Connell made. There was no amount of distance or perspective that would permit rational thought to make a decision. Instead, I gave that responsibility to the man I loved.

Never in a million years would I have dreamt of a day where I would lay all of the cards on the table and tell James Martin everything about a case. Yet, somehow, here we were. He listened intently as I detailed everything, including my involvement with Adam and the previous night's rescue. The only thing I failed to mention was my personal reaction. Being stuck in my own head was clouding rational thought, and he tended to crawl inside on numerous occasions without permission. This was not the time for him to react simply because I was. When I finished, he read through the communications and documents Bastian delivered. I sat patiently, picking at the forgotten eggs and resisting the need to lash out.

He pressed his lips together, putting down the final sheet of paper. His eyes met mine, and I looked away. "What do you want me to say?" he asked.

"I don't know. I have to come up with a solution, and since you can consult for Francesca, you can consult for me too." I forced my eyes closed and shook my head. Asking for help didn't mold well to my personality. "You know what happened. You know everything that's happened. And you know what's just been unearthed. Mercer dropped the bomb in my lap, and either I defuse it, or I let it take everyone out." The rage was back, and I tried to push it aside.

"You don't do either." He put the pages in a pile and slid them into the envelope as if their presence alone was the cause of my aggression. "First, you determine the outcome you want. Next, assess the ramifications and collateral damage. Then make sure it's something you can live with, turn over those facts to the police department, and wash your hands of the rest." It sounded so simple when he said it, but it wasn't that easy.

"He let Nick get shot. He led me to believe Catherine was dead, and it was my fault. I practically beat a guy to death because of it. We faced off against ten armed men who were all just pawns in this sick game. Seven of them were killed, and you stuck your neck out to cover for me." I bit my lip and got up to wash the dishes. "What do I do with that?"

"I'm not a factor," he argued. "That's something between us. Maybe there was impetus, but I'll always stick my neck out for you. And the rest," he turned the water off, "there's no easy solution. Catherine is home with her mom and dad. Nick is going to be right as rain. The only concern I have is you."

"I'll be okay." That seemed to be the only fact that I didn't realize until this point. I would be okay. My hand would heal, just like the bruises on my face and hip. I didn't kill Adam, and the men who died gave me no choice. There was no vendetta against them.

"You always are." The slight smile didn't reach his eyes. The bleakness of the situation prevented it. "Which is why you'll push your shit aside and make sure Adalina gets the best outcome, regardless of the rest."

"Well, since you had the answer, why didn't you just start with that?"

"Because I needed to hear you were okay. If not, I would have to stage my own reenactment of the Revolutionary War." Sometimes, Martin's adolescent attitude rivaled that of his romantic side. It often led to pointless clichés and inappropriate jokes. This time, he earned a chuckle and an appreciative kiss.

"Get out of here. One more minute and I'll have to take out a loan to pay your by-the-hour consulting fee."

"Maybe we'll work something out in trade."

* * *

By noon, I separated the documentation into two piles. One would eventually be turned over to the police department; the other would be destroyed. The only remaining question was what Mercer planned to do in the meantime. Not only did the envelope contain information on the kidnapping, but it also provided transcripts of conversations Estobar Santino had with the kidnappers, detailing Rosa and Adalina's plight. Hell, one might even argue the Four Seasons were acting as good Samaritans, at least initially.

Rosa married Miguel a decade earlier. He offered wealth, power, and protection. Or so it seemed until she was treated horrifically. While trying not to judge any of the potential cultural differences, it was hard to find a way to put a positive spin on physical abuse. Miguel Estes was nothing more than a bully. The tabloid stories claiming an impending divorce were real, but after Rosa became pregnant a second time, she changed her tune. For her troubles, she was thrown down the stairs, resulting in a miscarriage. The father of her unborn child was never mentioned, but I'd wager it was Estobar's.

Fearing for her safety and the safety of her daughter, Rosa approached Santino. Estobar Santino intentionally created the cracks in the Estes' security. He allowed the personal security contract to expire, aware it would take a few days to have a new one drawn up. Counting the days, he orchestrated the kidnapping by finding a group willing to abduct Adalina and keep her safe. He modeled their name and tactics after a few cases he read about in the European papers. The Seasons were promised a fifty percent cut of the ransom if they followed orders.

As I continued to read through the communiqués, I realized that Sonia was grabbed by chance. It didn't matter which girl was taken, any one at the school could afford the ransom demands, except for Catherine Cale. Catherine was the secondary target. From the stipulations in Miguel's insurance policy, for a payout to be issued, a law enforcement agency had to verify the actuality of the abduction; although, they were not required to play any part in the recovery or investigation. Since no kidnapper could ever conscionably make the demand to call the police, the only way to ensure they became involved was to kidnap someone with a direct connection, and Catherine Cale was the only child that fit the bill.

The identity of the driver who took the girls from the school was still unknown, but it was someone Adalina was familiar with because there was no other explanation as to why they would have gone willingly with a stranger. Probably Estobar hired one of their relief drivers to make the run. It was likely off the books and didn't seem at all questionable. The girls were delivered to the small hangar bay near the storage units I visited and immediately taken elsewhere. Sonia was released as soon as possible while Miguel and the Cales scrambled to save their children.

The Four Seasons were required to report to Santino twice a day. The girls' favorite foods, games, toys, and activities were provided, courtesy of Estobar's inside knowledge of Adalina. The only way they could have known anything about Catherine's preferences was by asking. Adalina must have known all along what was happening. Her mother probably told her to go with the men, and it would be okay.

Sonia was released without complications, and the Seasons received their cut of the ransom. The two remaining girls were only separated when time ran out on my intended recovery. The original drop-off was a ruse, and the blood on the pier was meant to scare Senor Estes. The only thing I knew for a fact was that it terrified me.

There were two reasons for the delay. First, to make Miguel more desperate. By blinding him with frustration, he would be less likely to point fingers and more likely to give in to any new demands they had. Second, if it was believed one of the kidnapped girls had been killed, it would sell the cruelty of the kidnappers. Unfortunately for the Four Seasons, they underestimated Miguel Estes.

Instead of cowering in fear, the bully of a man who built a gold empire and beat his wife far too often hired a hit squad to take out the men. When the police investigation began focusing on Estobar Santino, so did Miguel. Maybe it was partially my fault Santino had the shit knocked out of him, but staging a kidnapping was not the way to help your lover escape her abusive husband. Then again, I wasn't completely sure how one should go about doing that. The situation continued to go from bad to worse until it culminated in the firefight two nights ago.

Mercer tried to keep the secondary team at bay, but he couldn't do it without jeopardizing Estobar's plan. He knew all along about the kidnappers, and he played me from the start. Everything he said was a lie. The fact he was willing to go so far as to beat a man practically to death, or let me do it, didn't bode well for any of us. It was time we talked because the conclusions I reached made me angry. And although I couldn't grow three sizes and turn dark green, I still didn't think he'd like to see me this irate.

Dialing, he didn't answer. Whatever he was doing now, I wasn't sure I wanted to know. Furthermore, nothing he said could be believed. It was a house of cards built upon a foundation of deceit, and the whole thing just burned to the ground. Locking the files in my safe box, I set out for the hospital. It'd be best to get my hand examined before I had to use it to hit someone else.

After getting x-rayed and having my hand taped, it was suggested I avoid using it in order to prevent further complications. While the threat of surgery served as a great deterrent, particularly since I hate doctors, there was still a good chance I'd have to come back for a follow-up x-ray by the time everything was said and done. It depended on a few factors, like what I would do to Mercer and what he needed help with. If he wanted an excuse to eat all of his meals through a straw, then I was his girl.

Inside my car, I wasn't sure what to do. There were still a lot of questions that needed answers. How long did Mercer know of the actual situation? Who hired him, and what was his mission? Why did he take Adam hostage? Resigning myself to keeping my temper in check, I drove to his apartment.

"Love," Bastian greeted, opening the door, "if you allow me a moment, I'd like to fetch my mouth guard."

"Is Julian here?" I ignored the joke.

"He's in the other room."

Bastian led me down the hallway to the bedrooms. Knocking on one of the doors, Mercer opened. He might have been asleep or devising a plan for world domination. Obviously, I couldn't read him very well.

"Come inside, I don't want to disturb the others," he nodded curtly to Bastian who exited without a word. The bedroom was an appropriate venue for this meeting. It was much more intimate, just like the things we had to discuss. Stepping into the bedroom, I noticed a twin bed in the corner, a table and two chairs were in the opposite corner, and tactical equipment and electronics littered the floor next to the bed. By all accounts, this wasn't the same man. The neat and orderly Julian Mercer had been replaced. "If you're planning on turning me over to the authorities, I'd prefer if you wait until after Rosa and Adalina are no longer within Miguel's grasp."

"What you prefer doesn't matter." I finished scanning the room and sat in one of the two chairs at the table. Closing my eyes, I heard Martin's voice in my head. Keep it together, Parker. "How long have you known about Santino's arrangement with the Four Seasons?"

"I only discovered the connection after the first girl was released."

"You sent O'Connell to get killed." I ground my teeth together, trying to keep the fury at bay.

"He wasn't supposed to have gotten hit. That was a mistake."

"Bullshit." I gripped the edge of the table to keep from knocking it across the room. "They were Teflon coated bullets."

"It was meant to disable his vehicle, not him. These fucking twats lack aim and discipline." The anger in Mercer's voice was almost convincing. Maybe it was convincing, but I was too pissed off to accept it.

"Is that your justification for practically letting me kill one of them?" I snarled.

"As far as I'm concerned, he deserved it. They all bloody well deserved it."

"Then what the hell happened?"

Mercer took a seat and started at the beginning. Originally, the insurance company hired him for Adalina's retrieval. He worked with them before, and they valued his skill set. The day after he arrived on scene, Rosa Estes approached him while her husband was fielding a business call. She begged for his help, but he tried to keep his distance, believing their personal matters were not within his job description. When she showed him photographs and hospital accounts of what Miguel had done to her, Mercer couldn't refuse.

"I'm supposed to believe you're the hero with a heart of gold?" I retorted.

"You'd be sorely mistaken." His eyes burned with self-loathing. "That was when Santino contacted me directly." He pulled out a copy of the same information Bastian delivered. "Their plan relied too heavily on the human element. The Seasons got greedy. I trust you've read through all the communications." I nodded. "Then you see the problem. They wanted a larger cut. Rosa was still willing to give them whatever they wanted, but Santino was afraid this faked kidnapping would turn into the real thing."

"They changed your play." I swallowed. "When?"

"After you threatened to kill them." He tilted his head to the side as if the concept was amusing. "The Seasons didn't know what to make of a private security consultant and former federal agent. I suggested you could be scared off."

"You fucking-son of a bitch." I launched myself at him, but he caught my arm and used my momentum to spin me around so my arms were crossed in front of my chest, and he held me in a firm grip. "You put the blood on the pier." A vague recollection of what appeared to be spilt wine or grape juice from the fridge resurfaced. "You did it yourself." I fought against him, but he didn't release his grip. In all honesty, I wasn't fighting as hard as I could because I didn't want to know what would happen if I was free from his grasp. He kept my back against his chest but remained steady in his speech.

"Santino had supplies taken from a clinic because the girls' locations were moved so often he didn't want to risk the shopping lists alerting the police. The medical items were an afterthought in case of an unexpected emergency, but it was enough to throw you off the scent. Bastian blocked the cameras, and Hans set it up three hours before you arrived."

Crumpling, resigned to the deceit, I was barely aware of my knees buckling and kneeling on the floor with Mercer's arms still keeping me in place. "You did this." My voice sounded foreign to my ears. "Her parents thought she was dead. I thought I killed her." I was shaking with ire, but there was no fight in me. Mercer had psychologically beaten it out of me. His grip on my arms relaxed.

"I apologize for that." He helped me up and let go. "As soon as possible, I made sure Santino sent a proof of life to the Cales. The Four Seasons were becoming more afraid and antagonistic, even to Santino. They needed to be stopped."

"What about Catherine's recovery? Why did you send me through the fucking air vent?"

"At that point, all cooperation ceased. The girls were

separated, and their safety was no longer ensured. You saw the cage they were keeping Catherine in. Santino's plan backfired. The fake kidnapping became an actual kidnapping."

"That's why you took Adam, Autumn, whatever." I was on the edge of the bed, processing his words.

"Yes. He had answers. They needed to believe they were no longer safe from retaliation. They fucked with us, so we were fucking with them." It all made sense. There was no guarantee any of it was true, but it fit. "In the car, on the way to get Adalina, you knew my team was involved with the kidnappers."

I laughed. It wasn't appropriate, but it was all I could do. It was true; I did reach that conclusion, but at the time, it was too late to do anything about it. "Better late than never."

"From your government files and your corporate record, keeping you off balance was the hardest part. Bastian figured emotional manipulation was the easiest way to keep you from thinking straight."

"Because I'm a woman?"

"No. Because you've lost people and your greatest fear is losing more."

FORTY-THREE

Sitting at O'Connell's desk at the precinct, Thompson stood in front of me, asking a question. From the irritated look on his face, he already asked the same thing a couple of times. "Snap out of it, Parker."

"What?" I was preoccupied, replaying my conversation with Mercer on a loop. There was no reason to trust him after all the deception, but someone had to save Rosa and Adalina. He asked for a couple of days to get some fake identities established and make travel arrangements for them. They weren't going back to Peru. He had a network of contacts in the EU, and with the money, they made from the staged kidnapping, they would be able to start their lives over, far from the clutches of Miguel. Until then, I agreed to run interference at the precinct. As of yet, I didn't know if I would turn over the evidence against Mercer and his team, depicting their involvement in the kidnapping, or if it would be destroyed. It depended on how the next two days went.

"Forget it," Thompson huffed. He went down the hallway, leaving me alone in the squad room.

Although I was reviewing interview transcripts and offering some additional insight into the shooting and possible connections between Santino and the Four Seasons, I couldn't provide any hard facts until I received confirmation from Mercer, so I was dragging my heels.

"Are you hanging in there?" Heathcliff asked, sitting on top of the desk and studying me. "Yesterday, you were moving in six different directions at once, and today, you've done nothing."

"I'm just wrapping my head around all of this, and it's given me a headache."

"The Estes family is at home. After what they endured, Moretti thought they could use some time to recover. Adalina's been given a clean bill of health. She had a few minor cuts and scrapes, but it's nothing compared to what could have been." He smiled brightly. "You did a good thing."

"What about Santino?"

"He's in custody. We haven't officially charged him, and we're coming close to deadline to bring him up on charges or cut him loose. Thompson went to take a crack at him."

Licking my lips, I stood up. "Can I get in on the party?"

"Why didn't you just say so when Thompson asked?" Heathcliff shook his head at my irrational behavior and led me through the precinct to the proper room.

Inside, Santino was behind a table while Thompson paced the floor in front of him. With the type of progress being made, it was no wonder it took so long to get Catherine back. Thompson glanced up but didn't say anything.

"Mr. Santino," I began, pulling out a chair and sitting in front of him, "do you know who I am?"

"Yes."

"And you know of my involvement in recovering Adalina from a group of kidnappers known as the Four Seasons."

"Yes," he sounded uncertain, and Thompson's footsteps halted.

"Within the next twelve hours, you will be walking out of this precinct. There will be no uniformed officers for protection or bars to prevent anyone from inflicting further damage upon you." I jerked my chin at his battered visage.

"It's not necessary for you to say what happened." I let my words hang ominously in the air. "The people responsible are still out there, and given your current predicament, it's just a matter of time." He audibly swallowed but fought to maintain his composure. "You should be aware we have nothing on you. But I know the truth."

"Then you know why I can't say anything."

"There are alternatives available. You know enough to help the police detain the person responsible for all of this."

"I don't know what you mean," he insisted.

Getting up, I went around the table and leaned in close. "Estes knows what you've done. Now that his daughter is back, you won't survive."

He shook his head. There was no way he'd sacrifice Rosa after all of this.

"Tell us what you know, man," Thompson interjected. "We can help."

"I promise we'll make sure she's safe. They're both safe," I whispered in his ear. His eyes looked panicked, and it was time to let my words sink in. "Think about it. Maybe you can have a happier ending." Without waiting, I exited the room and went down the hall.

As I slipped into my jacket, Thompson came back. "What the hell do you know?" he asked.

"I don't know anything, but that doesn't mean I can't make shit up. It's called interrogation, Detective. Maybe you need a refresher course." I didn't want Thompson for an enemy, but for the time being, he couldn't know what was happening. "Fifty says before you release him tomorrow morning, he'll ask for a lawyer and negotiate a deal."

"You're on."

"And now, I'm off. Call if you need me to crack any more of your suspects." I winked and grinned, appearing playful in this potentially volatile situation.

*   *   *

My meeting with Mercer left me feeling fragmented. As

the ex-SAS worked out an exit strategy and whatever new scheme they were cooking, I turned my attention back to the more civilized world. Martin dropped off his financial assessment of the countertops, and after reading his report, I knew Francesca's problem wasn't internal.

I pulled my research on Insight International, Craig Robinson, and his team. Conducting a final search, I dialed the precinct where Robinson had been arrested for possession and intoxication and asked to speak to the arresting officer. After the call was shuffled around, I was handed off to a Detective Bell.

"Who are you?" he asked.

"Alexis Parker, security consultant and private investigator." I gave him the pertinent information on my current police consultant status and my private employer, Francesca Pirelli. Although admitting to being employed by Pirelli might have somehow violated my nondisclosure, it seemed permissible to overlook this fact. The records were faxed over, and Bell gave me a name of an officer in an entirely different state and city to contact.

As I began digging, I quickly realized that Craig Robinson had a slew of arrests but nary a conviction. They were all drug-related crimes. It didn't surprise me. Sometimes, it was easier to let an out-of-towner off with a warning than to file the paperwork. Generally, the assumption was he'd get caught elsewhere and be someone else's headache. Unfortunately, he was mine.

After running through a few more contacts, my suspicions were solidified. Robinson was the leak in Pirelli's company. I was on the phone, speaking to a woman in charge of Insight International. This time, I used the tactic of working in the law enforcement community and asked about Robinson's work habits. Only after my credentials were verified at the precinct did the woman explain that Robinson was fired yesterday.

Another company his team assessed experienced a similar information leak. Instead of keeping it quiet, they raised hell for restitution. The name of the company was not divulged, but I was sure there was a lawsuit in the works. The other three members of his team were split up, and each was being carefully scrutinized. If they sneezed wrong, they'd be looking for a new job.

There wasn't anything I could do to fix the situation. I would report my findings and conclusion to Ms. Pirelli, and the corporate attorneys would be salivating over the details. At least it turned out to be much simpler than I thought. Liam Naysley was innocent. A horrible investor but not a thief. If only everything was this easy. Writing a formal letter highlighting my findings, I attached the pertinent arrest records, the highlighted financial information conflicting with Robinson's report, and grabbed my keys. I'd drop it off at her hotel this evening and be free from one of my burdens.

The drive over was pleasant. When I arrived at the hotel, the desk clerk called up to the room, and I was surprised when she answered. I figured she would be out, or maybe that was just wishful thinking. Inside her suite, I handed her the information and gave a brief verbal explanation.

"This is it?" she asked, sounding disappointed.

"You did ask that I identify the leak. It isn't internal, at least not based on similar circumstances happening independently of your business."

"Very well." She put the report down. "Thank you for your time, Alex."

"Glad I could help." Standing, I headed for the door.

"Wait." I turned and looked at her. "Please join me for a drink." Awkwardly, I went back to the couch and sat. She poured two fingers of scotch into two glasses and brought them over. "It's not Macallan, but it was complimentarily provided by the hotel."

"I wouldn't know the difference."

"Jamie would." The reason she didn't want me to leave quickly became apparent. "I owe you an apology. Had I known the two of you were involved, I wouldn't have kissed him at the conference or spoke my mind so bluntly. I hope I didn't cause any waves that evening at his house." This wasn't any of her business, but if I wanted to fit into the normal world, this might be construed as normal conversation.

"No, ma'am, the only one who caused trouble was me. That's usually the case anyway." She narrowed her eyes and glanced at my bandaged hand.

"How does a pretty, young thing like you end up with a job like yours?"

"Martin didn't tell you?"

She chuckled at something she found amusing. "You call him Martin? Does he make you add the Mister when you're in bed?" Wow, she had a set of cojones.

Swallowing the remainder of the scotch in one gulp, I gave her the look I often reserved for criminals in custody before we nailed them to the wall. "I'm just curious, what part of my personality screams out submissive to you?" I stood. "Thanks for the drink."

"Alex, I was only teasing." She laughed as if this was all a friendly joke. "This was meant to be an apology. You've surprised me by being this capable, driven woman, and not at all someone who hides in Jamie's shadow. I can't pretend to know who he is anymore, but there's a chance we'll all be seeing each other a lot more. So I wanted to make sure there was no bad blood between us."

"Of course." Whatever she was prattling on about, I didn't particularly care. I wanted to go home.

"Thanks again. It's been a real pleasure watching you work."

I turned and left her hotel suite. As the elevator doors opened in the lobby, Martin stood in front of me. He smiled, and by the time the doors shut, he had enveloped me in a kiss. Thankfully, no one else was in the elevator.

"How did today go?" he asked, lifting my hand and examining the tape. "Is it settled?"

"Mercer and I spoke. Some things are still up in the air. It will depend on a few factors, but we're trying to work together." I sighed. "Thank you for this morning. I don't know what I would have done without you."

The smile brightened on his face. "When the dust clears and it's all settled, I want a weekend. Fair enough?"

"Absolutely." The elevator dinged, and he hit the close door button automatically. "Can I ask why you're here?"

"Business not pleasure. Well, this was pleasurable. It

could be more so if we pull the emergency stop and block the camera." He waggled an eyebrow at me. "I was on my way to–" He stopped. "This will sound insane. But it's business, and I can't tell you."

"You can't tell me?"

"No." He looked conflicted. "I will tell you later, but I can't tell you now."

"But you're going to see Francesca?" One and one equals two, and I had my suspicions it was business like he said. "Nothing sordid?"

"Only if you want to black out the camera."

"Rain check." He sighed at my response and released the close door button. "I'll see you soon."

"Tonight?" he asked, sounding hopeful, but I couldn't make plans when things were still uncertain with Mercer.

"This weekend."

"Okay."

FORTY-FOUR

Bastian phoned late that night to verify the documentation had been created and delivered. Plans were being devised to get Rosa and Adalina alone and away from Miguel, but after the kidnapping, personal security was on high alert. It was time we created a distraction.

Early the next morning, I arrived at the precinct. There were no familiar faces in the squad room, and I went down to holding to speak with Estobar Santino in private. The officer working the desk was preoccupied with a crossword puzzle, so I went to the holding cell at the end and stared at Estobar.

"Morning," I spoke quietly to avoid being overheard, "whether it's good or not is up to you."

"What do you want from me?"

The question puzzled me. "Nothing. Honestly, I couldn't care less." I found a chair in the corner of the room and dragged it over, sitting down and stretching my legs out. "I understand the reasons for your actions. Although misguided, it'd probably be nice to believe you had the best intentions. Then again, there's really no way of knowing that. Maybe you're not a knight in shining armor. Maybe you're just an asshole, looking to score. Money, a particular woman, maybe both."

"I have no interest in the money besides what it can provide for Rosa," he insisted.

"Sure, whatever pal." Crossing my arms in front of my chest, I continued to stare at him, passing silent judgment. "Despite the fact you're a fucking idiot, you can't be stupid enough to believe your actions wouldn't have consequences."

"It doesn't matter." I opened my mouth to speak and shut it. "What? You have something to add?"

"Quite frankly, your love triangle bores me. This isn't the way to handle a situation like this, but what pisses me off is the fact that you used innocent bystanders as your pawns, which you were more than willing to sacrifice." He blanched. "Y'know, when that slips, I'd say inside a minute, one of two things will happen. Either they'll blame the entire kidnapping on you and you get to spend the rest of your life in prison, or some of my brothers in blue will make you wish you were spending the rest of your life in prison."

"What are you going to do?" This time he actually sounded afraid.

"I don't know yet." Squinting at the lights, I considered my options. "Being in jail, you can't protect them from Miguel. I'd say your plan turned into an epic fail."

"You can't say anything, or he'll know she was involved in the kidnapping. He'll kill her," he pleaded.

"Only you can stop this ticking bomb from exploding." I stood up and put the chair back before approaching the bars. "You're going to ask for a lawyer because you plan to confess. An attorney will be brought in, and you are going to explain the situation, every specific incident you can recall concerning Miguel's treatment of Rosa and Adalina you'll provide a full depiction of to the lawyer. Any other illegal activities you know Miguel has committed, particularly on American soil, need to be divulged."

"It will only anger him. He'll lash out. It'll make everything worse." Estobar was panicking, and I put my hand up and gave him a stern look.

"Listen carefully. This is the only opportunity we'll get

to separate Estes from the girls. Don't be a pussy. It's time you man up, Estobar. The chips will fall where they may, and I can't guarantee what will happen. But this is their only chance. Maybe yours too. Do you believe in redemption?"

He looked uncertain. "Yes."

"Then prove it." Without waiting, I marched upstairs and back to my car to phone Mercer.

"Parker?" he sounded anxious.

"It's done. Santino might crack under the pressure, or he might do as I suggested."

"Okay. We'll maintain eyes on the package until then."

"One more thing," giving him a heads up wasn't something I planned to do, "there's no guarantee who else will be implicated."

"Understood." The line went dead. Gazing through the windshield at the early morning sun, I wondered if by the end of the day Mercer and I would be in adjacent holding cells.

* * *

Thompson placed two crumpled twenties and a five on the desk. I looked at it and then up at him. "I bought your coffee this morning, so we'll count that as even. You won the bet."

"Do we know what he's negotiating?" I asked, feigning confusion.

"Not yet. The ADA's been back and forth, making calls. We're all assuming it's something big, but it's very hush-hush." He propped his leg on the opened bottom drawer and leaned back. "Don't think I believe for a minute you don't know what's going on in there."

"How could I?"

"That's what I thought." He checked the time. It was almost eight p.m. "Why don't we call it a night? Whatever they're working out, I'm sure they'll wait until tomorrow morning to finalize the deal. He's confessing, right? Is there any reason to believe there might be immediate action necessary?"

"Not if he's still negotiating a deal." I considered calling Mercer for an update but decided better of it. If something transpired, he'd phone. "Well, since I suddenly have some extra cash, do you wanna split some takeout? Maybe chill out at my place?" I glanced at Heathcliff's empty desk. He was called away to work a homicide. "Someone still needs to return my spare key."

"Sounds good. I'll meet you there." He rummaged through the top desk drawer and handed me my house key.

Leaving the precinct, I detoured to a pizzeria, called Bastian for an update, and then went home. There were no new developments at the Estes' estate. Unlocking my door, Thompson was twenty feet behind me, coming up the steps. He followed me inside, and as I pulled plates from the cupboard, he went to the fridge and opened two beers.

"Spill," he insisted as we settled down at the table.

"There's a lot I can't tell you at the moment." He looked annoyed. "But what I can tell you is Estobar Santino is responsible for orchestrating the kidnapping. Theoretically, it was with the best intentions." Thompson gaped at my statement. "I know. It's total bullshit. But if Estobar is to be believed, Miguel Estes is evil incarnate. There's a long history of domestic abuse, and I don't know what else. He has a gold mine and practically controls a good portion of a country or enough to make him untouchable, so maybe his business manager will have some incriminating evidence to pass along."

"So what? We revoke Estes' passport and deport him. The only thing I'm interested in is nailing the fucker who is responsible for taking Catherine."

"I know."

"Aren't we on the same page?"

"Yes, but it's complicated."

"Then uncomplicate it," he growled, pushing back from the table and giving me a cold stare.

"Thompson," my voice was soft, almost wounded, "do you trust me to make this right?" We stared at one another for the longest time.

Finally, he let out a sigh and picked up the beer, taking a long swig. "I do. But that doesn't mean I like not knowing what the hell is going on."

"Okay." I heard the vague ticking of the wall clock. "As soon as I can, I'll give you a pile of documents that explains all of this. Until then, I need you to be patient and give me some leeway."

"Who does it incriminate?"

"Besides Santino, I can't tell you."

He shook his head, frustrated and possibly furious. "You've done right by Nick, even if it took him a while to see it." He looked at my taped knuckles. "We have your back. Just make sure none of us regret it."

Throughout the meal, Thompson continuously studied me, wanting to broach the subject but aware I wouldn't budge. The awkwardness continued as the silence lingered. Despite everything we'd been through from my first private sector case until now, a friendship had never been forged. We lacked common ground. Unlike O'Connell and Heathcliff, Thompson rarely opened up about anything, just like me. Maybe we were just too similar.

He just popped the top on a second beer when his phone rang. "Duty calls," he muttered, putting the beer down and answering. It was hard to decipher what was happening by listening to only his half of the conversation. "I'll be there." He hung up and turned to me. "We're sending some officers to pick up Miguel Estes. Santino made numerous allegations against him. Do you think any of them will pan out?"

"I hope so."

"Want to ride along?" he offered, picking up his keys and double-checking that his cuffs and gun were still attached to his belt.

"No, but I might stop by the precinct."

He gave me a skeptical look on his way to the door. As soon as the door shut, I raced to the phone and dialed Mercer. Amazingly, he answered, and I told him what was about to happen. Whatever he was going to do, he needed to do it soon. Hanging up, I loaded my nine millimeter and left my apartment. There was a chance someone might need assistance.

Arriving on scene an hour later, I saw a single police

cruiser with its lights still flashing outside the Estes' house. From the disarray and frenzied security guards, it was apparent Miguel Estes had already been escorted from his estate. Parking my car, I pulled my credentials and headed for the cruiser. A single cop was inside the vehicle, filling out a form. Knocking on his window, I held up my identification, and he rolled down the window.

"Can I help you, Ms. Parker?"

"I'm guessing I arrived late to the party." I glanced at the house. "Are Rosa and Adalina still inside?"

"No, ma'am," he responded, his attention diverted to the form. "I believe Mrs. Estes had her driver take her to the precinct."

"I see. Thanks." Getting back in my car, I looped around, looking for signs of the ex-SAS, but I didn't spot anything out of the ordinary. Maybe Mercer already made his move. If not, Rosa and Adalina were on their way to the precinct. Perhaps there was a third option no one considered, but after the kidnapping, any sympathy for Rosa would be squelched immediately. We were out of options and possibly out of time. In a last ditch effort, I went to the precinct with the hopes of seeing an end in sight.

FORTY-FIVE

Thompson was in Moretti's office with someone whose presence screamed federal agent. They were discussing what to do concerning Estobar Santino and Miguel Estes. From the constant in and out between the two interrogation rooms, I knew Santino must be in one and Estes was in the other. Lawyers, diplomats, and an alphabet soup of law enforcement agencies crowded the halls at the precinct. As I navigated the hallways, hunting for Rosa or Adalina, I heard only snippets. Piecing together different aspects of conversation, it sounded as though Santino had spelled out a laundry list of crimes against Estes. Not only did he give up the identities of the Four Seasons and implicate himself, but he claimed Miguel was involved in drug trafficking, smuggling, and violent behavior. I only knew one of those to be true. Allegedly, payoffs were made to drug cartels, Customs agents, and numerous law enforcement officials because of the constant physical abuse. At least I knew why the DEA, ATF, and ICE agents were standing around, looking bored.

"Parker," I spun at the sound of my name and came face to face with Agent Palmer, "I thought we were dealing with kidnappers, not a shit storm of international crimes."

"You know the saying, go big or go home."

"It's true what they say about you, isn't it?" he asked. "Trouble follows you like a rabid dog." I shrugged. "The AG's office has been on the phone with the consulate. Right now, we're deciding if we want to keep Estes or let his own people deal with him."

"He's too powerful. No one will touch him if he goes home."

"Hence the problem. We need to determine if he's aiding any terrorist organizations, large-scale drug cartels, or if his illegal dealings have impacted American freedom."

"Maybe you should first determine if Santino's claims can even be substantiated. The guy's responsible for a triple kidnapping. He might be crying wolf." Not to mention, I put the idea in his head to paint Estes as the antichrist.

"The FBI and Interpol are checking the allegations, but there's no solid proof yet. We tried to locate his wife to substantiate some of these claims, but no one's seen her since Miguel was picked up." At least that answered one of my questions.

"Well, it looks like your hands are full. No reason anyone needs a P.I. hanging around and taking up space. If anyone needs me, I'll be at home."

* * *

Instead of going home, I went to Mercer's. When I arrived, Bastian was alone. The place was emptied out, and he was doing a final cleaning to remove any and all traces that they were ever here.

"Can I come in?" I asked from the slightly ajar door. "Or do I need to put on a hazmat suit and a hairnet first?"

"Love," he smiled, "glad to see you haven't lost your sense of humor. Although, if you plan to hurt me, let's do it outside because cleaning up blood is a pain in the arse."

"Where is everyone?"

"It's done. Julian picked up the women. By now, they should be in the air. Hans and Donovan are escorting them part of the way, and then they will split off and go home."

"So they left you holding the bag?" I remarked as he wiped off a few light switches. It made me feel good to know I wasn't nearly as paranoid as Mercer's team.

"No. I offered to work cleanup. Jules will be back." He shut the doors to the rooms as he finished cleaning them. "Have you decided what to do with the documents?"

"Not all of them. Not yet." My tone was sobering, and Bastian entered the living room and sat on the sofa.

"We're not running. Julian will take full responsibility if that's what you decide, and I'll go with him. What happened to your friend was a mistake. More importantly, the fact that we knew where his niece was and who had her and did nothing," he met my eyes, "that is unforgivable."

"I'm not asking for an apology."

"Good because you won't get one." He surprised me with that comment, and it must have shone on my face. "There are a lot of things we've done that aren't pretty. Getting our hands dirty happens more than it should. Wet work is sometimes necessary, always costly, and never easy to stomach. Frankly, love, if you don't turn us in, at some point, someone will stop us one way or another."

"Why do you do it?"

"Someone has to." I always said the same thing when confronted with the same question. In all honesty, we weren't that different. "Regardless of what you think, we're not soulless mercenaries. We don't perform contract killings. The business card reads 'Kidnapping and Recovery,' and that is mostly what we do. We've done it dozens of times. Each time is completely different, but this one," he blew out a breath, and his fingers danced as if wanting to flip a lighter, "it was too close for Jules. He didn't want us here. He wanted to save the damsel in distress, and he was willing to sacrifice everything to do it."

"Why?" There was more to Mercer's story than I imagined, and I never expected Bastian to be so forward.

"It's not for me to tell." He let out another breath. "God, I'd kill for a cigarette."

"I thought you didn't contract kill," I joked, and he gave me a small smile and went back to wiping the place.

When he was done, he came into the living room where

I was still sitting on the couch. "Any insight concerning what will happen to us?" He seemed intrigued by the prospect.

"You said Mercer would take full responsibility, so why are you willing to go down with him?"

"We're a team. I owe him everything."

"Okay." That was something I understood, and that sentiment decided what was getting turned over to the cops and what was getting destroyed. "Word of advice," I offered, "find the line and don't cross it."

"Thanks, love."

*　　*　　*

After leaving Bastian, I stopped at home and retrieved the stack of papers before going to the precinct. Detouring briefly at a twenty-four hour diner, I ordered two extra large coffees to go and continued on my way. Placing one in front of Thompson, he looked both annoyed and relieved to see me.

"Don't ask how or where I got this," I passed the papers across the desk, "but that's everything on the kidnapping. It will verify parts of Santino's confession, maybe disprove other aspects, and who knows, maybe there's even some shit in there concerning Miguel Estes."

"My god," Thompson swore, scanning the pages and going into the roll call room, which was now full of most of the alphabet soup agencies I'd seen earlier. I took a sip from my cup and tried to determine what to do now.

"Parker," Mercer called, emerging from the stairwell.

I met him near the double doors. "Why are you here?"

"Did you make a bloody decision?"

"You're off the hook, unless I change my mind." I glowered at him. "How did your rescue attempt go?"

"They're safe and far away. I'm certain Estes will never find or hurt either of them again." His conviction was startling and slightly threatening. "But," he searched my eyes, "I wouldn't mind having a few moments alone with him."

"Too bad." Miguel deserved whatever Mercer planned to

do, but there had been enough bloodshed and innocent people getting caught in the vindictiveness. "I gave you a free pass. Get the hell out of here."

"That's it?" It sounded like a challenge, and with those two words, something inside me snapped.

"Oh sorry, I almost forgot," I stepped back and threw a hard right jab to his face, "that's for Nick." Mercer barely flinched, and I swung again with a right cross. "That's for Catherine." He faltered slightly, only further infuriating me by lacking the decency to go down, so I threw an uppercut, landing on his jaw and knocking him back into the wall. "And that's for me, you goddamn son of a bitch," I shrieked.

Someone grabbed my shoulders and hauled me backward. Cops flooded the area, and I heard questions concerning pressing charges and whether or not Mercer was okay. However, I didn't hear a single response. Thompson had a tight grip and dragged me into another room. "Should I go in there and finish what you started?" he asked, somewhat amused.

"No." Even though my hand was throbbing, it felt good. Cathartic.

"Assaulting someone in the middle of a police station isn't the way to go." He chuckled. "Then again, I didn't see a thing." He winked.

The commotion died down almost immediately, and it became apparent Mercer left without uttering a single word. I hoped it was because his jaw was broken, but I doubted it. No one said a thing about my outburst, and I was sure it was because of the role I played in Catherine's recovery and providing elaboration on Santino's confession.

Moretti insisted I remain at O'Connell's desk for the duration without hitting anyone else. Even though I was an adult, they put me in timeout. Like Mark Jablonsky always said, I didn't play well with others.

By morning, Miguel Estes was released. The only pending charges were for domestic abuse, but without Rosa to press charges, it would continue to remain unfounded. His lawyers flanked him on both sides, and an apology was issued by the police commissioner for the inconvenience. Estes had no idea how inconvenienced he was about to be when he got home, but the asshole deserved it. Men who bullied women were nothing more than cowards, and a part of me wished Mercer had gotten some revenge. But now wasn't the time or place.

Moretti pulled me into his office, asked a few dozen questions, most of which I couldn't answer directly, and then thanked me for a job well done. It was time to go home. Everything was resolved.

"Are you okay to drive yourself home?" Thompson asked. "Or do I have to worry that you might pull over and beat someone senseless just for the hell of it?"

"I'm good. Thanks for asking." It was snarky, and the first normal remark I made in far too long. Life was already getting back to normal.

On my way home, I stopped by the hospital and gave Jen and Nick the good news. Thankfully, he was getting discharged today. He could have gone home much earlier, but Jen insisted, particularly since she didn't want her hardheaded husband to insinuate himself into the investigation when he was on sick leave and still recuperating, but with the investigation complete, the guilty parties dead, apprehended, or being apprehended at this very moment, her concern was no longer valid.

Adam Dowery, Autumn, told the arresting officers everything he knew to save whatever skin he could. Unfortunately, the other three kidnappers were killed in the firefight and couldn't corroborate his story, but the police considered his confession good enough for their purposes. It was up to the FBI and federal government to follow through on filing actual charges since kidnapping was a federal offense. Briefly, I wondered who was responsible for the three dead kidnappers. Maybe it was Mercer's bullets or mine that went through them, but given the firepower Estes' hit squad possessed, I chose to believe they did it. It was easier for me to stomach, regardless of how unlikely it was.

"I thought you were getting x-rays." She turned her nagging on me.

"I did," I insisted. O'Connell looked amused, probably thankful she had someone else to yell at besides him.

"Then why does it look like someone took a meat mallet to your right hand?"

"I was just paying back what I owed," I responded. Nick chuckled, and Jen rolled her eyes.

"Was I mistaken to think this was a male-only thing? Maybe it's a cop thing."

"I've never been a cop," I replied.

"Maybe not, but you're family. We might fight and say things we regret, but at the end of the day, we're still there for one another," O'Connell replied. "And since that goes for Thompson and Heathcliff too, then you might as well consider yourself an honorary cop."

"How many painkillers do they have him on?" I asked Jen, grinning brightly at Nick. Although hokey, truer words were never said. They were my family, along with Martin and Mark. They were all I had and all I needed.

FORTY-SIX

Friday evening, I let myself into Martin's house. I bought a bottle of champagne to celebrate and placed it in an ice bucket on his kitchen counter. Afterward, I changed and went outside to the pool. It was October, and the fall air was crisp and cool. Lighting the fire in the electrical outdoor hearth, I took the remaining stack of documents Bastian dropped off and watched them burn away into nothingness. It would be nice if everything could be this easily eliminated. Stretching out on one of the chaise lounges overlooking the pool, I watched as day turned to dusk and steam from the heated water slowly created a fog.

My phone rang, and I smiled. Glancing at the house, I saw the lights turn on as Martin entered and went from room to room.

"What are you wearing?" he teased.

"A string bikini." Based on the lights, he was in the kitchen now. "Come outside." A moment later, the back door opened, and Martin stood in the doorway. "You're overdressed." I hung up and put the phone on the table as he came over to me.

"Goddamn." He was the only person who could make a single curse sound so sexy and appreciative. "Had I known

you weren't kidding, I would have been home hours ago."
He sat on the edge of the chaise, his eyes traveling the
length of my outstretched body. My right hand was in a
brace, but at least it was removable and not a cast. The
bruises on my face vanished, and my hip was a slightly
yellowish green. "In my mind, a string bikini is more string
and less bikini." His eyes met mine, and I saw the green
irises dance. "But this is still pretty fucking fantastic."

"And just think, we haven't even gotten to the fantastic
part yet."

He laughed. His hand started at my calf and traveled up
my side, coming to rest on the bottom band of my bikini
top. He ran his fingers along the string as I attempted to
untie his tie with my left hand. "How are you?" he asked,
having abandoned the playfulness for a moment.

"Relieved." I glanced at the hearth, and he followed my
gaze as if understanding its significance. Reaching for his
wrist, I manipulated his watch around to see the time,
having abandoned my quest to undo his tie. "Happy to
spend the next sixty hours with you, even if it's not the
beach." I glanced at the pool. "I thought about having some
sand trucked in, but it would make a mess."

"In that case, I'm glad they installed the new solar
heating panels for the pool last week." He stood up. "I'll be
back in a minute. I'm going to change and grab the
champagne."

* * *

When I woke up the next day, Martin wasn't in bed.
Instead, I found him downstairs in his home office, reading
and making notes. Unfortunately, we had bad timing. Just
when my job hit a lull, his was kicked into high gear.
Padding back upstairs, I spent too many sleepless nights in
recent weeks that I would make the most out of my free
weekend.

The mattress shifted, causing me to awaken. "Are you
finished working?" I asked sleepily.

"For now," he replied, wrapping his arms around me. "I
didn't realize you were awake before. I figured after last

night and this morning, you deserved some sleep."

"What time is it?"

"Four."

"You're kidding, right?" I glanced at the clock, amazed half the day was gone. "I'm sorry."

"Don't be. I asked for a weekend, and I'm spending more time with the computer than you."

"They say porn can be an addiction," I teased. A ringing phone broke our banter, and sighing, I wasn't sure which would be worse, mine or his.

"Sorry, that's me." He grabbed the phone off the night table and went back downstairs.

By the time he concluded his call, I had showered and dressed. We were in the midst of determining plans for dinner when my phone rang. "Parker," I answered, hoping it wasn't the precinct deciding they should arrest me for the assault, concealing evidence, or the other assault. Maybe Martin was right, and I needed to stop hitting people.

"Are you standing me up?" Maddock Howell asked.

"Crap," I muttered. "Sorry, I am. Something came up."

"Really? Or you just decided against hearing my pitch?"

"Both." No reason to sugarcoat things. "Although," I paused to make sure Martin was out of earshot, "you might as well be the first to know, I'm done working these corporate gigs."

"You're still at Martin Technologies, aren't you?"

"Yes, but that's it. Mr. Howell, I'm sure you're aware I used to be a federal agent. My heart remains with resolving criminal matters, not corporate ones."

"I see." There was a brief pause. "In the event you ever change your mind, Miss Parker, please give me a call."

"I won't but thanks for the offer."

"Most of the time, I would assume this was a negotiating tactic, but strangely enough, I believe you."

As I disconnected, Martin came back into the room, eyeing me suspiciously. "Who was that?"

"No one important. Just an appointment I missed. Part of the perils of calling in favors when working for Francesca." A look crossed Martin's face, but he didn't say anything. "We have a lot to celebrate, don't we? O'Connell's niece is safe. He's okay. I'm not in jail. You're not in jail for obstructing a police investigation or lying. The leak at Hover Designs was identified." I offered a moment for him to fill in the blank, but he didn't. "And of course, your company is somehow aligning itself with Hover Designs."

"Did she tell you?" he asked, shocked.

"No. Well, not in such explicit terms. Instead, she asked if I referred to you as Mr. Martin when we were in bed."

"What?" The shock might have just turned to anger.

"Hey, she isn't my ex, so what the hell do I know about the things the two of you used to do."

"We were never that formal," he responded, probably out of reflex. "What does that have to do with the merger? I didn't tell you because it's not finalized yet and could be construed as insider trading. No one outside the Board knows."

"You must realize I do this for a living. Supposition, deductive and inductive reasoning, it's kinda my thing." He laughed at his own stupidity. "Don't worry, I'm also great at keeping things quiet." That was the story of my life lately.

"I wanted to tell you," he attempted to apologize, but I stopped him.

"As long as your company is the only thing merging with Francesca, then it's fine." I smiled. "Congratulations, I guess."

"Thanks." He still looked glum. "Of course, that's why I have seventy meetings scheduled for this coming week, and the only thing I wanted was to escape work for one weekend."

"It's okay. We've always agreed to put work first. Last time, it was on me. This time, it's on you. Maybe we'll have better luck next time."

*　　*　　*

Sunday night, I was draped across Martin's chest as our breathing stabilized. He was gently rubbing his thumb across my knuckles as we remained in the quiet bliss.

There were ten hours remaining to our weekend, and although short and interrupted by his work, I was glad to have some time off.

"Y'know, you could never wear a ring," he commented, tracing his thumb along my ring finger, "you'd end up taking half a guy's face off."

"Don't talk about rings," I retorted, not enjoying this uncomfortable conversation topic.

"Alex," he moved his hand to trace random patterns on my back, "if I thought for even a second there was the remote possibility that an engagement was something you wanted, I would have gone to Harry Winston or Cartier and tucked the black velvet jewelry box in my sock drawer, waiting for the perfect opportunity. But," my heart jumped into my throat as I fought the fight or flight response, "I know it's not. You're here because you want to be. It's not because you're driven by a social construct or some misguided and outdated notion of what society expects. Sweetheart, the fact that you choose to be here means more than the promise of a ring or the idea of marriage. I love that about you."

"Jerk." I hit him with my palm for freaking me out with talk of commitment. Yes, we were in a monogamous, committed relationship, but labels didn't sit well. "Is that how it was when you proposed to Francesca? Societal pressure and thoughts of how things were supposed to be?"

"From the moment we started dating, she made a million plans for us. By our fourth date, she had china patterns picked out. There was no choice. No romance. It just seemed that this was what was expected. I was in my mid-twenties, and by the time we graduated from business school, getting engaged seemed the appropriate, mature thing to do so we could be married by thirty and start a family."

"Is that something you even wanted?" We never talked about these things before. As far as I was concerned, the only thing that mattered for either of us was what happened after we met. With his history of sexual exploits and my career issues, we didn't need to talk about the past. It was the past for a reason.

He pondered the question. "No. It's what I thought my mom would have wanted. My dad would have found anything that detracted from work abhorrent, so maybe that added some appeal to the notion." He shrugged. "We would have been divorced within the year. At the time, she wanted nothing more than to be a trophy wife, and I wanted to create an empire."

"Aren't you glad you have a girlfriend who understands putting work first?" I teased, kissing his neck and contemplating using a second round of lovemaking as distraction tactics.

"I'd rather put you first." He was serious, and I leaned back to look him in the eye. "After everything, it's obvious circumstances with us are often life or death. I don't want to regret missed opportunities."

"And on that note," I rolled over, "wake me when you get up in the morning." Serious conversation scared me. The only thing I knew for a fact was emotional attachment was an easily exploited weakness. It wasn't that I didn't feel the same way; I was just afraid to admit I felt the same way.

An hour later, neither of us were asleep. "I'm sorry," I whispered. "The things you say often surprise me. It's hard enough putting up with playful Martin, but serious Martin scares the shit out of me."

"My fault," he murmured, "talking about Francesca after our romp wasn't a well-executed idea. Neither of us do normal relationships well."

"But we're both pretty amazing at this one." Snuggling against him, we fell asleep.

The next morning, I watched as Martin rushed around the house, collecting everything he needed for his numerous meetings. With his briefcase packed with files and notes, he poured a cup of coffee and took a seat at the table.

"I almost forgot, Heathcliff called yesterday while you were in the shower. He wanted to know if you wanted your jacket out of evidence or if you needed," he squinted, trying to remember something, "a copy of the form to file to be reimbursed."

"What did you tell him?"

"That I'd have you call him back." He put the mug in the sink. "All right, I'm going to be late if I don't leave now." I scrutinized his evasiveness, not letting him escape that easily. "For the record, I don't like finding out your clothing got shot. It's preferable to you being shot, but it's still too damn close."

So that's what last night was about. I sighed. "Close doesn't count." I considered the almost bullet to the back of the head. Way too close, but that was neither here nor there.

"Okay," he collected his briefcase, "you're welcome to stay as long as you like." He gave me a quick kiss and headed for the stairs. His driver and bodyguard were in the garage waiting for him.

FORTY-SEVEN

After Martin left, I stopped by the precinct to fill out the reimbursement form and yell at Heathcliff for letting the cat out of the bag. None of that took very long. Everything was quiet at the police station. The frayed nerves were repaired, and everyone who worked overtime had the day off. The officers at work looked ready to deal with whatever new conflicts the city was facing.

Unlocking my apartment, I couldn't help but notice the glaringly obvious signs of a break-in. My apartment remained intact, but on the counter were my dossier that Mercer constructed and his business card. Written on the back were the words "emergency only" and a phone number. Checking the rest of my apartment, the only other thing I found out of place was a bag of potato chips I didn't remember buying. Either I was losing it, or Bastian decided to leave a calling card too. Even though in a twisted way this was supposed to be an apology or comforting, the thought of Mercer in my apartment made me cringe. I had seen enough of their tech toys to wonder if they bugged my place. Yes, you're paranoid, my internal voice commented.

Picking up my house phone, I dialed the OIO, listening for strange clicking noises. There weren't any, but I still called in a favor with one of the tech geeks to sweep my apartment for any type of surveillance or listening devices. He agreed to come by around five and give the place the once-over.

In the meantime, I owed Luc Guillot a huge apology and the level of professionalism he expected from me. I changed into a suit and went to the MT building. The final check had to be run on the protocols, and that would be the end of the security update.

As I entered the building, Jeffrey Myers greeted me. "Ms. Parker, the information you requested concerning your security card is in your office."

"Thanks."

I went upstairs, suddenly dreading what else Mercer stuck his nose into. On top of my desk was a manila envelope and inside was a list of accessed files. Turning on the computer, I conducted a search of each file. My on-file résumé had been opened and a related internal memo outlining my brief stint serving as Martin's personal security. When Mercer said he knew more about me than I imagined, he wasn't lying or embellishing. Hell, he probably knew my bra size too. At least no sensitive corporate material was compromised. The paranoid part of my brain hoped Martin's safety wasn't either.

Phoning Guillot's assistant, she put a meeting on the books for one this afternoon. With some free time to kill, I went down to HR to see how the hiring for the internet security specialist was going. Interviews had been conducted last week, and the new hire was starting Wednesday. At least my involvement in the kidnapping case didn't harm my corporate job any. Frankly, they got along better without me.

At one o'clock, I met with Guillot. We scheduled the protocol review for Thursday so we could include the new hire in the assessment. As I stood to return to my office, he surprised me. "Ms. Parker, I'm glad to see you're much more put together today. Although, the way you worked when," he tried to think of a polite term to use, "you were frazzled was amazing."

"What can I say? I work well under pressure." I took a

deep breath. "Sir, after the protocols are checked and everything is running normally, you should look for someone to replace me. I can't do this job anymore."

He nodded. "Mr. Martin warned me this might happen. May I ask what you plan to do instead?"

"When I left the OIO, I hoped to become more of an investigator than a corporate consultant. It's about time I make use of the office space I've been renting."

"Ah," he smiled, recalling the assistance I provided one of his wife's friends, "you make a fine P.I. I wish you the best of luck. I'll have HR start the search this afternoon. I assume it'll take a month to find a replacement, but whoever we hire won't be nearly as astute."

"Thank you, sir." Smiling, I left his office.

*　*　*

After the tech swept my apartment and found nothing suspicious, I still had an uneasy feeling. Maybe it was my imagination, or the fact Mercer had dug through my federal, corporate, and private background to determine who he was working with that left me feeling naked and exposed. Or more than likely, it might have something to do with the fact Martin was worried about my most recent near miss. Regardless of reasoning, I packed a bag for a week, locked my apartment, and went to his place.

It was after nine when he got home from work, exhausted and shocked to find me still at his house. "I was wondering if it'd be okay if I stayed here for a while." My voice sounded sheepish, even to my own ears.

"Absolutely." He looked puzzled. "Have you reconsidered moving in? That offer is still on the table."

"No," I shook my head, "but since you're so busy, I thought maybe I'd hang around. I'm sure we'll barely see one another with your long hours, but there is something to be said about sleeping next to you."

"Admit it, you're just here because you missed the sofa."

"That too."

"Is everything okay?" he asked as I followed him upstairs while he changed out of his suit.

"I quit my job today."

"Does this mean I can finally tell my friends we're dating?" he teased.

"Wait until Guillot's found my replacement before you start shouting it from rooftops."

"Okay." He assessed me, tilting his head to the side. "I worry about you, and I know you hate that. But it is nice to see that you're in a good place, even after everything that happened with O'Connell and his niece. Sometimes, you get lost in this sea of negativity that surrounds you." I put my finger to his lips to silence him.

"Recently, it's been pointed out that I need to accept who I am and what I do." I thought of Mercer in the back of the van. "It's time I get my life back on track and stop hiding from things I can't change."

* * *

Almost four weeks later, I cleaned out the few personal effects in my MT office. Something about leaving was depressing. Maybe it was the closing of a door, but that notion was ridiculous. My attachment to MT had nothing to do with the job. I loathed the job. But in a way, it was my beginning. The start of a life I never planned to have. Even though I resisted it, somehow things fell into place. I had Martin, a great group of friends, and the freedom that I never had and never realized I wanted.

Knocking on Martin's office door, he buzzed me in. "Ready to go?" he asked.

"I guess so." I looked across the hall at my empty office. "It's strange."

"We could keep you on retainer," he offered, but I shook my head.

"Ms. Parker," Guillot entered through the still open door, "it's been a pleasure working with you. I want to wish you all the best."

"Thank you, sir."

Martin came around and put his arm around me. "Luc," his grin couldn't have been any bigger, "I'd like to introduce you to my girlfriend, Alex." Guillot looked surprised, and I dug my elbow into Martin's ribs. There went one bridge, sacrificed to the burning flames. "It's not new, but it's nice to have it out in the open."

"Congratulations. In that case, you'll both have to come for dinner soon." After making some polite small talk, Guillot left, and Martin and I soon followed suit.

"Are you staying at my place this week?" he asked.

"Just tonight." He took my box and carried it to the parking garage, where we got into his town car. "We have plans with the O'Connell's tomorrow, and then I have to start conducting surveillance on that home invasion thing."

* * *

I was sitting next to Heathcliff's desk, reading through some eyewitness accounts. My private investigator gig coincided with an ongoing police investigation, and although Moretti was avoiding hiring me to consult, he was letting me read through the case files. O'Connell was only two days back and bored to death for being stuck riding a desk. We were bickering back and forth when Thompson and Heathcliff came in.

"It's nice to see mom and pop getting along again," Thompson responded, smirking at the two of us.

"Yeah, us kids were really starting to suffer in the separation," Heathcliff chimed in. "I thought you were supposed to shower us with gifts to buy our love, so it'd be easier to pick a side in the divorce."

"All I got was some takeout that I paid for by losing a bet," Thompson retorted.

"Boys," I glared at both of them, "behave."

O'Connell chuckled. "You do sound like their mom." Of course, that just led to more bickering, but despite it all, this was home.

DON'T MISS THE NEXT ALEXIS PARKER
NOVEL.

CAMELS AND CORPSES
IS NOW AVAILABLE AS AN E-BOOK AND IN
PAPERBACK

ABOUT THE AUTHOR

G.K. Parks is the author of the Alexis Parker series. The first novel, *Likely Suspects,* tells the story of Alexis' first foray into the private sector.

G.K. Parks received a Bachelor of Arts in Political Science and History. After spending some time in law school, G.K. changed paths and earned a Master of Arts in Criminology/Criminal Justice. Now all that education is being put to use creating a fictional world based upon years of study and research.

You can find additional information on G.K. Parks and the Alexis Parker series by visiting our website at
www.alexisparkerseries.com

Made in the USA
Las Vegas, NV
13 September 2021